BREATH AND BURNS

BY

ANDREW SHIELDS

A **BLADES** IN THE **DARK** NOVEL

This work is based on *Blades in the Dark* by John Harper, used with permission. No ownership of the *Blades in the Dark* material is granted or implied. Characters, events, and locations herein are creations of the author and should not be considered canonical.

FOREWORD

About five years ago, I had the opportunity to play in a campaign of the then-new role-playing game, Blades in the Dark. The campaign, named for its central band of miscreants, The Unrecommendables, was ably run by Andrew Shields. I confess, I read very little of John Harper's game. I don't know where Doskvol as written and Doskvol of Andrew's imagining began or ended.

This is what I do know of the place and its people: The old and decaying city is part Victorian London, part Lankhmar. The action is part Scorcese gangster epic, part Hammer Horror. The characters are colorful as anyone in the novels Dumas and often hard-boiled as anyone in the works of Jim Thompson. Andrew brought the basic ingredients of this rich brew to the table and made us, the players, complicit in its manufacture.

Now here we are with one of several novels set in Andrew Shields' rich, grimy, dangerous, sorcerous, and colorful version of Duskvol. Perhaps it's the same as the version you know from the game, or perhaps it has a savor uniquely its own. Either way, whether this Duskvol is new to you or familiar, I expect you'll find much to enjoy by just sitting back and letting Andrew be your guide through its twisting streets and twistier intrigues.

Trey Causey

Hydra Cooperative

You want to study "the humanities"? There is more humanity in electroplasm than there is in any sonnet or painting. Human nature is to expand, extract, and contain. That is our defining core, that is where our imagination soars.

When the Gates of Death broke and flooded the world with ghosts, humanity did not survive by writing a play. We faced the dead as they surged to dangerous levels. We learned to contain them, and we wrested fuel from their threat to power our defenses and ships. Then we expanded our territory. The ephemeral threat now provides raw material to further human enterprise. Look to that ingenuity for inspiration, not to some pretentious fiction.

—From private correspondence, Captain Dell Zahvi
writing to his son

The coach rattled to a halt. Rousing from his reflections, the uniformed man inside frowned through the fogged window as the coach rocked on its leather springs, the driver dismounting from the buckboard.

"What's going on?" the uniformed man demanded as the driver opened the door.

"Well, Captain Nyhus," the driver said with a hunched suggestion of a bow, "we have arrived at your destination."

"This doesn't look like the Sparkhouse Brewery," Nyhus retorted, gesturing at the mostly deserted street to draw the driver's attention as his other hand slipped back to the hilt of his belt knife.

"You aren't going to the brewery anymore, sir," the driver said. "You're going to see the Unseen." His eyes were bright, his smile unsettling.

"Oh," Nyhus said. "Oh. That's different." He leaned forward, ducking out of the narrow coach, and he maneuvered so his back was never towards the driver. The driver barked a laugh and slammed the door, then turned and glanced both ways before crossing the street towards the shadowed face of a wall built across an alleyway. Nyhus followed.

"What do I call you then?" he asked the driver.

"I'm Grull. No harm giving you that; if the Star doesn't like what you have to say, you'll either show up at the brewery after a strange dream, or you won't show up anywhere at all."

Nyhus had nothing to say to that. The two men passed through a sally port built into the wall. Grull took a moment to light a lantern, then they followed the cramped alleyway to a row of doors. Grill produced a ring of keys, consulting half a dozen before letting the rest jangle down as he slotted one into the lock on the third door.

Nyhus looked around the bricked-off courtyard as Grull locked the door behind them. The only feature in the space that drew the eye was the chalk outline of a doorway scratched on a wall next to a rickety bench.

"I'm going to check you for weapons," Grull said conspiratorially. "Arms up."

Raising his arms to the side, palms forward, Nyhus tightened his jaw as the peculiar spicy stink of Grull's personal space enveloped him. The big coachman had a surprisingly light touch. He patted the captain's clothes, removing the belt knife and pistol. He paused as he brushed one of the captain's arms.

"Remove your coat," he said.

Nyhus shrugged out of the coat, folding it over the bench. He tugged off his gloves, then unbuttoned his cuff and pulled up the sleeve. He revealed a gleaming steel hand and forearm, scratched and pitted from years of use.

"It's a prosthetic," he said. "Goes all the way to the shoulder. It's no more or less dangerous than my other arm," he added with a wry smile, a glint in his eye.

"How is it powered?" Grull demanded, brow furrowed.

"It's technical," Nyhus sighed. "Some threads of living Leviathan ink in a closed system, the connecting site was etched on the metal and scarred on my shoulder, with exchange glyphs. I have a very small electroplasmic capsule in case my natural energy lapses too far to feed energy to the metal." He paused. "It doesn't come off," he said.

"Alright, fine," Grull muttered. "You'll do. Any other weapons to declare?"

"No. Let's get on with it," Nyhus said, buttoning his sleeve. He picked up his gloves and started pulling them on.

Grull turned to the chalk outline, and pulled a glittering amulet from his pocket. Holding the amulet in front of the wall, he concentrated, his lips twitching as his eyes glazed over. The coachman focused on the chalk, and it started to hiss and sizzle. A stain swelled in from the borders towards the center, until the wall was somewhat translucent. Wisps of fog drifted out of the half-real doorway.

"After you," Grull said with a sardonic bow.

Nyhus did not hesitate. He walked right through the flickering exception to the real world, and into the murk beyond. Grull followed.

"You'll want to stay behind me," Grull said, raising the lantern. The suggestion of faces and outlines twitched in the fog, which curled around them with peculiar intentionality like shadows echoing in the air. "This place... it's dangerous." His smile was not reassuring.

Grull led nyhus through the mist. He could not see any orienting features his guide might use. Eventually, they approached a throne flanked by pillars and braziers glowing with subdued embers.

Grull called out a phrase in Hadrathi, and Nyhus scowled, glancing around.

A low voice echoed with more Hadrathi, and a robed woman stepped out of the fog to lower herself onto the throne. Regal, she pressed her cowl back, revealing her seamed face and silver hair.

"Captain Nyhus," she said. "Good of you to join us."

"Looking within and without, we shall see," Nyhus said, his Hadrathi clumsy.

The woman's lips pursed around a small smile. "See and be seen," she echoed.

"Though you remain Unseen, of course," Nyhus said, switching to Akorosian.

"That idea is central to why we are meeting," she said. "The Unseen are, as you know, protected by one of the most powerful rituals in the city. It is centuries old, and profoundly influential. All those who learn of our organization, who become aware of any who have accepted the Mark of the Unseen, forget about us shortly after. We are unmemorable. The ability to counter the ritual is vanishingly rare."

"Yet I remember you," Nyhus said.

"There are a handful of people who are born immune, for one reason or another. We recruit them, or kill them," she said with an offhand gesture. "Are you one of those people?"

"I must be," he said, fists on his hips. "I've known about your organization for weeks now."

"So you have a role to play, and the remaining question is what role that will be," the woman said with a somewhat gracious nod. "I am the Star. I supervise the Unseen designs on North Port."

"Does Grull have some kind of code name or title?" News asked with half a grin.

"Titles are earned. So are punishments for impudence," the Star said, unamused. "Our research into you shows you've got some experience working with cults and religious orders. You know better."

"You've looked into me," Nyhus said. "Alright yes, I do have experience. And I am moving into North Port."

"Your Gray Cloaks could be of use to us," the Star said, leaning back on the throne. "Another company of Gray Cloaks once had a clash with a pernicious crew from Silkshore, the River Stallions."

"I heard about that," Nyhus said. "That was, what, about three years ago. Captain Hutch. Shot in the face at close range, from what I understand."

"Their chapter was sufficiently depleted that the Gray Cloaks took no retribution. None that made a mark," the Star said. "I extend to you the opportunity to remedy that. To answer the affront." She cocked her head, looking Nyhus in the eye. "Maybe you can shoot their leader, Saint Suran. In the face. At close range."

"Maybe so," Nyhus agreed. "I hear the River Stallions have been making their move, working out treaties and such. They want to be a big deal in the new territory."

"I don't care about that," the Star said. "They've pressed in on some of our secrets, and there is no forgiveness for that. I am directing the Unseen's efforts in North Port, and I want these upstarts dealt with." She paused. "There are many rewards to serving the Unseen."

"I prefer the terms of partnership," Nyhus said mildly.

"Yes, service didn't end well for your people, did it," the Star said, something cruel in her eyes. "Corrupt Bluecoats, outmaneuvered by even more corrupt aristocrats."

"I suppose that's one way to put it," Nyhus said, his tone quiet as his eyes narrowed.

A low chime resonated through the fog, and the Star exchanged a quick glance with Grull.

"What's that?" Nyhus asked.

"The door to the Shadow Throne has been located, tampered with," the Star said, her brow contracting in a frown.

"Should we, you know, go somewhere else?" Nyhus turned to peer through the fog. "Grull. Return my weapons."

"You don't need them," the Star said. "The mists of this place are lethal to those who are not welcome."

"Do you think it's the River Stallions?" Nyhus speculated, returning his attention to the Star.

"This is none of your concern," she muttered, her frown intensifying.

"I hear the River Stallions have a proper Whisper. So they might be able to cope with your *fog*," Nyhus said.

"Inkletta," the Star said, contemptuous. "She is a savage. Gutter trash with a pidgin mockery of occult tradition." She set her jaw. "But... her raw power has been demonstrated." The Star looked to Grull, exasperated.

"Do you wish to kill them here? Or retreat?" Grull asked, wary.

The Star fluttered a gesture at the question. "The Shadow Throne will destroy them," she said, making up her mind. "Now, back to business. Captain." She settled on the throne. "If your Gray Cloaks hunt down the River Stallions, whatever membership survives this ill-advised intrusion into the affairs of the Unseen, we will support your relocation to Silkshore."

"Sure, that all sounds very nice," Nyhus said as he deliberately ignored the echoes of hissing and cries in the fog behind him. "I'm not interested in Silkshore, I want in on North Port. Competition is difficult to establish there at this point. There's a fresh Bluecoat force, hand-picked for this assignment. Some heavy hitters have invested in the reclamation of the port; people who could take action if they didn't like my people moving in."

"This is of no concern," the Star said brusquely. "The Unseen have suborned all that. Your people will be well paid in what you care about the most. Justice against Strangford for destroying your lives." She raised her eyebrows, gauging his reaction.

Nyhus processed that offer for a moment, eyes wide. "Well that's something," he said quietly. "That's a serious offer."

A flaring ripple patterned the fog.

"My Lady?" Grull said nervously as he peered into the dimness, sweat forming on his forehead.

"Oh very well," the Star snapped. "We will go to the Catacomb Gate for now. Your people will mop up the surviving River Stallions," she said, jabbing her finger towards Nyhus. "Then the Unseen will clear your path to punishing Strangford."

"Deal," Nyhus said.

A snapping crackle commanded their attention as something like lighting or a compound fracture lit up the otherworldly fog, sundering it. A dull shine surrounded several figures an indeterminate distance away as they cleared the area of threats.

"Wow," Grull said, slack jawed.

Too late, the Star saw one of them swivel around with a long rifle. Orienting on the light from the braziers.

"Let's go—" As she hustled off the throne, a report rang out and a streak of light seared through the void, slamming into the Star and driving her back against the throne.

"Star!" Grull shouted, pouncing over to gather her up in his arms.

"We had better fight back, give me my gun," Nyhus gritted out.

"No! We flee!" Grull hefted the Star and led the way into the thinning fog, confident as he placed his feet and chose his direction. Nyhus got a handful of Grull's coat and followed, keeping an eye out over his shoulder.

They closed in on a black pool in the featureless ground, smooth and undisturbed as stone. "Follow me and I will keep you safe," Grull muttered, and he waded into the pool. Nyhus was right behind him.

The heavy water seemed almost plastic, pressing around them. Nyhus resisted panic, but was still glad for the air when he breached the surface into a dark space. Somehow Grull's lantern had made the trip still lit, and its light revealed a rough cave with some chairs, a wardrobe, and an area rug.

Grull laid the Star out on the ground as Nyhus struggled free of the clinging pool.

"Those bastards," Grull choked out, his hands trembling as he fumbled at the clothes around the Star's wound. Her flesh flickered and smoldered from the specialty ammunition of the shot that punctured her. "I will destroy them all."

The shot had been impossibly well placed, crossing flexible distance and pounding right into the Star's center mass. The steaming injury welled dark blood, and as the Star drew a shuddering breath, Nyhus saw the glint of exposed and broken rib bone.

"Confidence aside," Nyhus said, "if they come through that water after us I want a weapon in my hand."

"The wardrobe," Grull snapped. "Oh, Star," he said in a very different tone, "what can I do for you?"

"P-plasmic," she gasped. "And—and twisted. Oh. Twisted. Special—" She cried out in agony. "Grull! Grull. Our re—revenge. You—you must—"

"Anything," he assured her.

Nyhus hauled the wardrobe open and fumbled through the clothes and effects, locating the weapon rack at the back even as he eaves-dropped on the Unseen.

"Sell the secret of Tya and the Heart," the Star hissed in Hadrathi. "Get the best—best price... from Malicoat, and from the Spirit Warden, name of Sysavath. She has a—a long standing—interest."

Grull stared at her. "Star!" he wailed. "No, we must keep our secrets! You can yet use them!"

"Special crafted," the Star said with a snarl. "This bullet—meant—for *me*." She swiveled her piercing gaze to Nyhus. "You. Come."

Nyhus finished slotting two rounds into the breech-loading pistol, and he snapped it shut with a waggle of his wrist. He knelt at her side as she reached up and tightened her fist around his hair, pulling him close. Her flesh sizzled as threads of molten plasmic discharge wormed through her meat and energy.

"Swear to me," she said as steadily as she could, her eyes bright. "You will kill their bitch sniper. *Swear to me*."

"I swear it," he muttered, horrified as he saw the glow that grew in the back of her eyes as a wisp of smoke drifted up from her tear duct.

A single bubble rose to the surface of the black pool.

"Impossible!" Grull shouted. "There is *no way* they could follow us through that!"

"Go—my orders, follow them!" the Star hissed. "I'm—done for. I'll cut them in half," she snarled, struggling to prop herself up against the wall, concentrating on the pool. "Go!"

"Come on," Grull snarled, snatching at Nyhus's arm.

Nyhus stepped back and freed himself.

The confusion only lasted an instant longer. The deception was over.

There was no time to think. Both Grull and the Star realized Nyhus was their enemy, at the same moment, and he had to choose one of them.

Nyhus blasted a round through the Star's head, bursting it. The report was shattering in the confines of the cave. He pivoted away from the plume of smoke to line up on Grull, and fired after where the cultist fled down one of the shadowy exits to the cavern.

Dropping to one knee, Nyhus broke the pistol open, the spent shells twirling up, and he jammed two more in and snapped it shut as he stared through the after-image of the blast into the darkness of the tunnel. Leaning forward, he righted the lantern; Grull dropped it when he fled.

The surface of the pool tore open. The sniper was the first one through, water sluicing off her out-thrust pistols and her long coat. Her rifle was slung across her back. She reflexively knocked a shot through the Star's corpse, her other pistol lined up on Nyhus.

Rising through a flickering aura of corpsebreath, the shaggy and half-naked Whisper followed. Her eyes were wild, and the tattoos covering her face and exposed skin seemed to shiver.

"Where is the other one?" the sniper shouted, ears ringing.

"Ran off," Nyhus said, pointing down the tunnel. "I think this place is a maze. They called it the 'Catacomb Gate.' Which isn't promising."

"Inkletta?" the sniper said.

The Whisper breathed deep, then relaxed, the mist around her dissipating. "We are under the Sanctorium. The Church kills trespassers. So."

"At least we're still in Brightstone," Nyhus said reflectively. "By the way, Red Silver, that was a nice shot," he said with genuine admiration.

"Right?" she agreed, squinting down at the charring corpse at her feet. "Looks like your whammy ritual worked, Inkletta."

The Whisper had turned back to the pool, sloshing in and reaching down through the surface. Leaning back, she hauled at the last member of their entourage, pulling him up. He was broad, heavy, his face almost hidden between low brows and a bushy beard. Though he climbed out of the pool, he was barely damp.

"You okay, big guy?" Nyhus said.

"You should have seen him," Red Silver said as she shook her head. "That fog closed in, and the Hammer just—he just took it. Wiped it out."

The cold radiating from the Hammer began to chill the cave.

Inkletta put her hand on his shoulder, looked him in one eye, then the other. "Alright, he'll be okay. But we should get moving." She looked over to Nyhus. "How about you, Safety? Is the beacon painful?"

"No, I barely feel it," he said. "I think I better keep it in my arm, in case we get separated down here. I do *not* want to make it difficult for you to find me. I knew you'd follow through the first ghost door, but when we relocated from there, especially through a water gate... I was worried," he confessed.

"So glad we didn't keep you in suspense," Red Silver said, arch. "Wouldn't want you to fret."

"By the way," Safety said, turning to her, "the Star here made me swear to kill you."

"Oh, and you swore?" Red Silver said with a fey grin.

"I totally did," he nodded. "Rather, Captain Nyhus did."

"Good luck with that," Red Silver said, and she tossed a playful punch into Safety's metal shoulder. "May the best aim win."

"This is a nice lantern," Inkletta said, examining it. "Think I'll keep it. There's some tracework on there, keeps the water out, keeps the flame going."

"At least it isn't dark," Safety said. "We should probably get going." He looked down at the Star. "Anyone want to check her for, you know, valuables?" he said without enthusiasm.

"The lantern is one thing," Inkletta said, "but anything she had attuned to herself when she died... that's asking for trouble. And we're not hungry enough to go looking for that much mischief." She peered into the shadows of the several corridors exiting the pool chamber. "This is going to be a long night."

"How is this going to work?" Red Silver asked, snapping her pistol open and checking the ammunition.

"The Unseen probably seeded this area with those they slew and buried to guard their secrets. Some of the dead down here would be volunteers, others would be victims. There are likely traps on both sides of the Mirror. Illusions," she said with a loose gesture. "Pits. Spikes. Jump scares. Curses."

"Can we go back through the pool?" Safety asked.

"No, I wouldn't recommend it," Inkletta said. "I was able to follow your beacon, before. Going through blind? The Shadow Throne was heavily masked with layers of generational ritual that was refreshed often with human sacrifice. Aiming for other exits... that's risker than whatever is in the dark down here."

"Then we do it the old fashioned way," Safety said with a decisive nod. "Lanterns, pistols, and a ten foot pole." He looked around the chamber. "This many mystics, somebody has to have a staff somewhere."

The Hammer took a step forward, immediately commanding the attention of everyone in the room. He squared off with the tunnel entrance that Grull had used as an escape. The solid and hairy man set himself, and raised his arm, his hand aimed into the darkness.

Something shifted, squirming against the Mirror surface between the world of the living and the world of the dead.

Halting, yet drawn, a figure emerged from the shadows. With the low grinding screech of chainmail dragging on stone, the glimmering echo of a dead knight took shape before their eyes. A half-real sword wept a pale residue of blood, and murderous eyes gleamed out of the eyeholes in the rusted memory of a bashed-in helm.

Though it reared back as best it could, struggling to escape, it was too close to the Hammer now. Inexorable as gravity, the Hammer stared at the ghost as its outline smeared slightly, hauled towards him by some unseen force. His nostrils flared, and he let out a grunt; something dislodged the ghost's grip, and it flickered into him. He twitched, then breathed out a plume of chilly fog. The ghost was gone.

"We'll be fine," Safety said with a nod. "Few hours tops, we find an exit, back to our own beds by dawn."

"I like your optimism," Red Silver said. "You take point."

The trim man looked up from a table covered in floorplans. "You have the paperwork?" he said brightly.

"Right here, fresh from your guy at the Velveteen Strop," the young woman said, handing him the document pouch. "You have some weird friends, Saint."

"Don't I know it," he agreed, tugging the forms out and smoothing them on the table, eyes flicking across them. "Excellent. One of my many favorite things about you, Niece, is that when I send you to do a thing it gets done."

"As you expected, he wasn't keen to cooperate. I persuaded him," Niece said. "You really think we'll be able to get the Old Custom House?"

"If we can get the Unseen off our backs, I am sure of it," he said. "Now that North Port is all reclaimed and shiny, the bureaucracy is centered in the Dunvil Custom House. New building, much bigger, and secure. The Old Custom House is kind of infested with rats and falling apart from being abandoned for two and a half centuries."

"I still don't really understand why you want it," Niece said, sliding down into a chair across the broad table from Saint.

"We are going to refocus the expectations of all these criminal and legitimate enterprises across the reclaimed district of North Port," Saint said. "Don't underestimate the power of symbol. The Old Custom House used to be where the deals were made and enforced."

"What else though," Niece asked, amused.

"All the basements, of course," Saint grinned. "They had holding cells, impound strongrooms, the treasure vault... No one still living knows what else. If half the legends are true, we will be sitting on top of a thousand secrets—on both sides of the Mirror."

"I never figured you for a home body," Niece chuckled. "Sounds like you'll never want to leave the base."

"Not so," he said. "I'm all about securing those opportunities. Then the people who really care about that sort of thing can buy access and go poking around and stirring up trouble. I'll still handle the wheeling and dealing. That's why I'm the boss," he said sagely. "I delegate."

The door to the meeting chamber rattled and opened, admitting a bleary and disheveled man. He shuffled towards the table, scratching at his ample gut.

"Hark, I see the rising sun," Saint said dramatically.

The rumpled man paused, then unloaded a prodigious belch.

"I can't wait for Inkletta and Red Silver to get back," Niece said reflectively.

"Seriously though, why are you up?" Saint said. "You don't look... ready to be awake."

"I am a man of action. Anyway, it's almost time for my morning nap," he said loftily.

"Come on, Gapjaw," Niece said. "We talked about this. You have a room. A bed."

"And I like napping down here. I know I'm not missing anything. Except some bitterbrew. Be a sweet dearie and mix me up some bitterbrew?" he sort of asked, a hopeful smile stretching the loose skin of his face.

"If you insist, I'll bring you something to drink, because we are comrades. But I can't guarantee it will be entirely bitterbrew," Niece said, arching an eyebrow. "You sure, Gapjaw? You want to risk it?"

"*Still* nicer than Red Silver," Gapjaw said reflectively. "Never you mind. I'll suffer a bit. Keeps me sharp." He slumped down in a chair by the table, glancing over it. "This doesn't look like crime. Nothing circled. No tokens on the map." He snorted, clearing his sinuses, and spat in a cup. "I hope nobody was using that."

"It's all yours now," Saint replied. "You have seen this floorplan a dozen times. Come on."

"Oh, the Old Custom House. You still think we can buy it? The Estate Council of North Port shut us down three times."

"Because the Unseen were icing us out," Saint said. "If our little plan worked last night, they'll back off. We've got to be ready to make a move."

"Our people are awfully overdue," Niece said, crossing to the narrow window and looking down from the meeting room's vantage point halfway up the bridge piling. "I hope they are alright."

"They will be fine," Saint said, confident. "It's our crew up against a hardened ring of criminals and spies that have manipulated the secrets of the city for centuries. Nothing they can't handle."

The door on the other side of the room opened, and a slim child strolled in, his bare feet noiseless on the stone.

"Good morning, Sereen," Niece said. "Did you sleep well?"

"Yes, thank you," he said with automatic politeness. His eyes seemed too large under his bowl cut hair, and his narrow shoulders were poised on the edge of a growth spurt as he approached his teen years. He crossed the room to the sideboard, busying himself pouring a cup of cold water from the pitcher and pulling the cloth off the sporebread.

"Looks like the Hammer's almost back, at least," Saint said in a subdued tone.

Niece opened the door to the stairwell and stepped out to look down. They heard the echo of weary shuffling and clattering gear. Saint took a moment to tidy up his papers, tucking some of them away and straightening the rest. Gapjaw hauled himself to his feet and hustled over to the sideboard, securing his breakfast before the rest of the crew arrived.

"Everyone is back," Niece said as she re-entered the room, downplaying her relief.

Shortly afterwards, Safety trudged in, followed by the Hammer, Red Silver, and Inkletta.

"We killed the Star," Red Silver announced. "So there's that."

"Congratulations!" Saint said with a broad smile. "More importantly, you all made it back. That's some good work, people!"

The Hammer stood off to the side, somewhat dazed, but he focused as Sereen approached. The youngster guided him wordlessly to a chair, where the Hammer sat, and Sereen gave him the cup of water and the plate of breakfast. Even in the muggy warmth, frost clung to the Hammer's moustache and beard, and the beds of his fingernails were blue.

"Many ghosts," Sereen said softly, his hand on the Hammer's shoulder. The Hammer looked him in the eye briefly, then turned his attention to his breakfast.

"Well? I'm giddy with suspense," Saint said with a grin.

"Plan worked out," Red Silver said. "You had Safety posing as a Gray Cloak captain for a month, and finally the Unseen reached out to Captain Nyhus, shortly after we wiped out their third agent in North Port. Just like you predicted. So we were nearby when the little electroplasmic capsule beacon in Safety's arm lit up. Inkletta got us through to the Shadowed Throne, we took on the defenses, and I got a shot off at the Star as she was escaping. We followed Safety again, and killed the Star in the catacombs under the Sanctorium. That was all before nightfall."

"Then we wandered around among the traps, hazards, and ghosts of the catacombs for the rest of the night," Safety said around a mouthful of breakfast bread. "Finally got out through a hidden door to a church basement. And *then* we had to cross the whole city to get home." He put the rest of his breakfast in his mouth.

"So my plan worked," Saint said, looking Red Silver in the eye, expectant.

"Sure did," Red Silver nodded. "So, as agreed, I'll kick in a share towards the Old Custom House."

"Excellent. That's two," Saint said. "We have quite a reserve built up from our various operations, but it's not enough to get the title for the Old Custom House with crew funds alone. We will all have to kick in a share. Half has to be in Coin, the other half can be in currency equivalent. We agreed to pursue this, so we are putting in eight Coin from the River Stallion reserve. We each need to put in two more to get the twenty two we need. So Red Silver and I are in." He looked around the room. "Remember, this title is for possession *and* right of operation in North Port. It's more than a building. Who is in?"

"We killed the Star," Inkletta said. "That doesn't mean the Unseen will back off."

"I'm willing to bet they will," Saint said. "They do their best work out of sight, and even if they do want to take us on, they'd be better served to wait and let us relax first. If they don't back down, we'll go after the Tower himself." He hefted his black lacquer cane, running his thumb along the silver stallion bust serving as its handle.

"Alright then," Inkletta said. "I'm in."

"Conditions," Safety said. "I'm in, as long as I don't have to do any more undercover work as a Gray Cloak." He crossed his arms over his chest.

"Done," Saint nodded. "Gapjaw?"

"What about Niece?" Gapjaw said, somewhat petulant.

"Niece already chipped in," Saint said. "We are all in. How about it?"

"You didn't ask the Hammer," Gapjaw protested.

"You want to be last? Really? You?" Saint said, sardonic. He turned to the Hammer. "How about it then."

The Hammer nodded.

"Congratulations, you're the last one," Saint said with an exaggerated pivot towards Gapjaw.

Gapjaw stared at the floor, shoulders bowed. "No."

"Excuse me, what?" Saint said.

"No," Gapjaw repeated, looking him in the eye. "I don't have it."

"How do you not have it?" Saint demanded. "We've been doing all kinds of work lately—profitable work. What are you spending your money on?"

"None of your business," Gapjaw retorted. "I'm short. That's it. The end."

Saint stared at him for a long moment, then shrugged off the feeling. "Okay then. Gapjaw is out. I'll cover his share." He smiled at the rest of the crew. "It's decided. We're doing it. Moving our operations to North Port. And dragging Gapjaw along."

CHAPTER TWO

The limmer tradition is steeped in corruption, which is why it is now illegal. Even the word 'limmer' is a corruption of 'limber', based on the act of cutting limbs off the trunk of a fallen tree.

Before the lightning walls, before electroplasm, the people needed protection against the clouds of starving ghosts. The strongest thing out there? Leviathans, the immortal god-demons of the Void Sea.

Insane priests figured out they could attract the Leviathans with enough death. They ritualistically slaughtered dozens of people at a time, luring and intoxicating the Leviathans so they would beach. Then the priests would go to work, harvesting limbs, blood, hide, bone; whatever they could get before the Leviathan would wriggle back into the sea.

The priests painted standing stones with undying Leviathan blood and refreshed the patterns with human sacrifice. They made weapons out of the parts they stole from demons and they fought death itself. They ripped power off monsters, and that power changed them. How could it not?

These days we protect ourselves by avoiding contact. We harvest the blood, distill the electroplasm, and burn it for fuel through a series of incorruptible machines.

—From "Progressive Technologies and the Human Spirit"
by Professor Elyis Gutavia

"Hear hear," Safety said. "And to celebrate, I propose a toast. Let's get out some of that nasty cognilease potion."

"We have one batch left, so we'll need some more," Niece said to Inkletta, who nodded.

Red Silver opened the cupboard and pulled the false back out, retrieving an iron box from a hidden compartment. She handed a narrow vial to each of the seven members of the crew.

"What's your toast?" Saint asked Safety.

"Here's to outmaneuvering Unseen danger," Safety said, "and to shedding that damn gray cloak." He raised his vial, as did the others, then he swallowed the foul slurry.

"Oh, that's disgusting," Niece choked.

"Red Silver, please update the book," Saint said.

Red Silver took the book out of the same compartment as the vials, and flicked it open to the page with the silk ribbon. Her handwriting was neat and precise as she began filling in notes from the most recent encounter.

"Just in case," Inkletta murmured, standing at her elbow and reading down the page. "Just in case the potions fail, the ritual takes hold, and we forget all our dealings with the Unseen."

"Better a slim chance than none at all," Red Silver agreed. "Some of us are readers. And I'm seeding the account with inside references, things that only we know about. So if we uncover it, after a period of forgetfulness, we will be more likely to trust the account."

"Let me borrow the recipe from the front," Inkletta said. "I can't seem to memorize it."

Red Silver handed her the blood-stained note listing ingredients and methods in Hadrathi.

"With that out of the way, we do have some complications," Safety said.

"I hate this guy," Gapjaw muttered.

"As the Star lay dying, ravaged by Inkletta's ritual anchored on Red Silver's plasmic ammunition, she gave some final orders to her agent. His name was Grull."

"And he got away," Red Silver pointed out. "Grull did. You let him go."

"Yes," Safety nodded, resisting the bait. "The Star told Grull to sell the secret of Tya, the heart. She told him to go to an aristocrat named Malicoat, I've heard of him. He's a cultist of some kind. She also told him to go to the Spirit Wardens. They were whispering in Hadrathi, and I was rummaging the wardrobe for a gun, so it was hard to make it out. Some specific Spirit Warden, the name started with Sysa-something. Female, I think."

Saint heaved a sigh. "Never a clean getaway, I guess."

"Maybe this Grull fella tripped into some hole or got his blood frozen by ghosts," Gapjaw speculated helpfully.

"We used up all our luck, none left for that," Niece retorted. "We had better check this out."

"Okay, now we're to the delegating part, and that's my thing," Saint said with a sideways glance at Niece. "Inkletta, please go thank your contacts for giving us that journal and the recipe for the cognilease potion. We never would have made it this far without them, so let's keep that relationship friendly. Maybe take a gift."

"I'll do it," Inkletta nodded.

"Red Silver, you figure out Malicoat," Saint continued.

"Safety already heard of him," Red Silver said.

"I like your odds of getting actionable intelligence a lot better," Saint retorted, "so that's your cue to impress me. Niece, see what you can find out about the Spirit Warden."

"You already put me on packing up the base and working out the transfer of possession of the tower to the Gondoliers when we move out." She shook her head. "Adding this is too much."

"That's fair. Safety, you're on figuring out the Spirit Warden."

"Great," Safety said through his teeth. "Any idea how I'm going to do that?"

"You're reasonably bright, figure something out," Saint said.

"Besides, if you could shoot worth a damn none of us would have to do more legwork," Red Silver observed.

"Thanks for that," Safety muttered. "What about Gapjaw? Got any work for him?"

"I guess there's an up side to pretending you can't read," Saint said, rolling his eyes. "We have some other jobs to keep Gapjaw busy and out of trouble."

"Can't do them," Gapjaw said abruptly. "I'm taking a week off." He rose to his feet, and left the room, his steps receding towards his quarters.

"He's taking *another* week off?" Safety said, stunned.

"Don't worry about it," Saint said. "That's our assignments, let's stay focused and keep our boots clean so we don't track old trouble into our new digs." He finished off the potion, and made a face. "Oh, and Safety. The Coursers need some management. Varela has a plan, so... work that out," Saint added with a vague gesture.

"Damn it," Safety said with distinct articulation. He turned and left.

The scoundrels had their assignments, and a safe place to rest after a night of dangerous work. They filtered out of the room, chatting. All but the Hammer, who sat motionless, Sereen patient at his side.

TOWER LAIR, THE EASE. SILKSHORE
11TH ULSIVET, 850. HOUR OF HONOR, 1ST HOUR PAST DUSK

The plasmic lamp buzzed and flickered, bolted in place over the door to the crumbling watchtower. Large winged insects batted off the cage around the lamp, desperate to reach something they would never understand. Safety paused while still across the street, watching the two young women under the plasmic glare. One leaned in the doorway, the other finished tugging her throwing knives out of the cutting board hanging on the wall, retreating to the edge of the light and turning to face the target again.

"Double or nothing," one woman said with a playful jeer.

"I love watching you cry," the other said, flexing to send the knife whizzing at the board. The knife thudded into the wood a hand's breadth from the center, and both women laughed.

"Nice throw, Pilege," Safety said as he emerged from the shadow at the edge of the light.

"Thanks boss!" she chirped, retrieving the blade. "Are you here to talk to Varela about his plan?"

"I sure am," Safety nodded. "Saint told me to come check on you all. Make sure you weren't staying up past your bedtime."

"We don't even have beds, come on," the other woman said as she rolled her eyes. "Beds are for people who don't have boats or wagons to sleep in. Ever tried to make a getaway in a bed?"

"I don't recommend it," Safety said with a grin. "He's inside?"

"Probably," Pilege said thoughtfully. "Sukup?"

"I have no idea, I don't care where that man goes," Sukup retorted. "I just know I'm supposed to show up when he's in an order-barking mood."

"Carry on," Safety said as he passed Sukup, entering the tower and heading down the curve of stairs to the basement.

"There you are," the lanky scoundrel said, turning away from the chalkboard. The board was covered in a precise diagram that was wreathed in scrawled notes. "I was starting to wonder if you forgot how to find our base!" His smile was not sincere.

"I hear you have a plan," Safety said. "Saint says to me, 'Varela has a plan, go check it out.' And here I am."

"Just need you to give the go-ahead and we're set," Varela said. "You don't even have to get involved. Now the Red Sashes have been moving in on the edge of the Ease, around Tilewater. You know the area?"

"Yes, I know the area," Safety said, his patience thinning.

"There's a consultant, a hawker who is checking out the market and considering increasing their trade in chewsticks around Tilewater. The Red Sashes get a foothold there and they will expand, for sure. But, this consultant, Gorenflo, is respected with the Sashes. We get our hands on him, and we can use his well-being as leverage. Back the Red Sashes off. Show them we're not about to share our customers with their perfumed dandies." His grin was wide and savage. "Gorenflo likes cabaret, and we'll know when he is headed to a show because he usually gets a haircut first."

"Okay stop," Safety said, raising his hands. "No."

"What?" Varela demanded, his hands closing to fists. "Why?"

"The River Stallions are about to relocate to North Port," Safety said quietly. "This is not the right time to start a slap fight over Tilewater."

"We aren't *starting* it, the Red Sashes did that already," Varela shouted. "If we let this go unanswered, word gets out, you know? You think the new territory—"

"Stop," Safety said, more forcefully. "You are out of line. You don't have to like my decision, but you don't raise your voice to me. Understand?"

Varela stared at him, quivering with contempt. "Yes," he said carefully, like the word hurt him. "I guess so." He turned away, and kicked the chalkboard over so it clattered down on the floor.

Safety considered him for a moment. "You do this anyway, after I said no, and the River Stallions will leave you here when we go to North Port. Your call." Turning, he mounted the stairs, leaving the fuming gangster in the basement alone.

"Too bold for the old fellas, huh," Sukup said with a knowing grin.

"Maybe if any of you live long enough to get old I might try to explain," Safety shot back with wry amusement. "Stick to your assignments for now. You don't peel shrimp when your nets are out."

"I feel wiser now. Did you get some of that wisdom on you?" Sukup asked Pilege.

"All over my boots," Pilege sassed back, and she hurled her knife. It missed, clattering off stone and glinting into shadow. Both gangsters laughed.

Safety shook his head, and walked away into the darkness. After all, he had some real research to do.

BOCKBAKER WORKER BARRACKS, NAUGHTON PITS. CHARHOLLOW 11TH ULSIVET, 850. HOUR OF SILVER, 3RD HOUR PAST DUSK

Inkletta descended the creaking wooden stairs. Her heavy boots contrasted the light wrap draped over her, and she wore no jewelry to distract from the patterns in her skin. The thick mass of her woven hair was up and back, mostly off her neck and mostly out of the way. She was slick with sweat.

There was hardly a breeze above, but underneath the crushing weight of the workhouse no air moved at all. Even the flies struggled to push through the thickness. The stink of bodies and smoke crawled into the nose and mouth and lay heavy in the lungs so they struggled to move.

Dozens of candles burned in the gut of the building, their light tinged green. As Inkletta moved into the space, word spread fast in a susurration of murmurs, slipping past the cries of babies and children, suffusing the endless coughing and sobbing that was a constant background in the packed worker quarters.

The Lady is here

Our Queen

She's here

As Inkletta left the base of the stairs, striding through the cramped basement, the people pulled back to give her space. Room to move was one of the most valuable resources left in this barracks, packed with exhausted desperation. Inkletta approached a primitive shrine chipped into the wall, heaped with wilting offerings of food as well as carvings of hands, feet, eyes, limbs. The air seemed restless with whispered prayers. Inkletta set her jaw, steadying herself in the wash of sensation.

The wheeled cart squeaked as the shrine's keeper pushed towards Inkletta. The withered woman smiled up at her, showing blackened gums embedded in her face's pouchy mass of wrinkles. With a clack, the woman freed her wrist's hook from the cart's wheel, and the woman hunched over in the best bow she could manage.

"My Queen," she hissed. "Welcome."

"Hello, Rakestraw," Inkletta said dispassionately. "I have not come for sacrifices." Her gaze swept the assembly that was thickening as word of her arrival spread. "No sacrifices. Not this time. Restrain yourselves," she said, stern. The anticipation thrilled through the gathered cultists, and Inkletta resolved to keep the visit short.

"Dey long only to be part of someting," Rakestraw mouthed, her good eye shrewd as she nodded into another awkward bow.

"I understand," Inkletta said. "I have come to thank you. To thank you all. You discovered the book beyond sight, and in giving it to me, you have assisted the River Stallions greatly." She cleared her throat, struggling against the sensations rising in her as she stood among the Shrouded Queen's worshippers. "I have—I have a cart. It is in the courtyard above. It is full of good things. Food, and—and clothing," she said, her voice trembling as the strains of the hymn began. Softly sung, from those who were faithful and disobedient. A hymn of her worship, ancient and joyful and frightening. Irrevocable sacrifice, leading to irrevocable belonging. Their need was a dizzying intoxicant.

WHO ARE YOU

The imperious resonance from within pushed a gasp out of Inkletta. "No," she gritted out.

WHO ARE YOU TO DENY MY WORSHIP

Inkletta felt her jaw tremble, her teeth chattering as the chill rippled through her blood, cooling her skin, unmooring her from senses tied to the flesh of her body.

I HAVE AIDED YOU IN YOUR DESPERATE MOMENTS

STAND ASIDE

Facing a choice, Inkletta knew she could either commit to fight the Shrouded Queen for control right here, right now... or she could acquiesce. Save that battle for a more pressing need. She choked back a sob as the choice was clear. Energies rose from her bones, from the marrow of her life, swelling out of her.

An avatar stood before the cult, majestic in the foul darkness.

GIVE ME YOUR OFFERINGS

I MUST BE WHOLE

Inkletta slithered down into the space left behind as the essence of the Shrouded Queen rose to flow forth from her body. Still, she saw more than she wanted to. The brandishing of the shining scissors, the work blades. The screams of ecstasy. The offerings of digits and limbs. The warmth of accepting those sacrifices, becoming one with the faithful, the Shrouded Queen's energy flowing into the sacrificial sockets and stumps of the fortunate few worshipers.

Surrendering completely, Inkletta settled deeper down, below where she could feel anything but the exultant satisfaction of the Forgotten Goddess that wore her form.

THE CIRCULATORY, THE EASE. SILKSHORE
11TH ULSIVET, 850. HOUR OF THREAD, 4TH HOUR PAST DUSK

Gapjaw pressed his palm along his slicked-back screen of hair, his scalp shining through the stringy mass. Almost wary, he followed the crushed rock path through the oddly rounded chamber, the glowing lamps set along the curved surfaces burning with a steady light. Ranked beds of herbs, vines, and flowers were set in rows, organic in their shapes. He followed the sounds of work, the hiss and chop of spadework stabbing gravelly clay.

Quietly moving through the valve-like opening between chambers, he hesitated as he saw the kneeling matron, working the soil next to a small hand-cart with tools and seedlings. He flexed his hands, unsure of what to do with them, then jammed them in his pockets as deep as he could. He watched the woman's rounded back as she jabbed the clay a few more times, then leaned back with satisfaction.

"I am pleased you came, Colvin," she said without turning. "You know you are welcome anytime."

"Matron Kashindi, I am so pleased to hear that," he said, stepping forward. "I—I don't want to interrupt."

"Then your timing is fit, for you have not interrupted. You're just in time to help an old woman to her feet," she said, holding up a hand. Gapjaw was at her side in a moment, his elbow under hers, and she rose up to turn and face him.

"That's better," she said, something silky in her voice as she looked over her sweat-dewed spectacles, right into his eyes. Her creased and worn face gentled to a smile. "Now, Colvin, you are indeed a refreshing sight."

"You are too," Gapjaw said, awkward. "I forgot when you have your meal break. Are—you are here late, does that mean the night shift?"

"You missed me," she said, a smile warming her features.

"I missed you," he agreed. Then he stopped talking, and nodded. "Yeah."

"Well here I am," she said, matter of fact. She flicked her hand-spade so it dropped to bite into the earth, and she stripped off her gloves. "Time for a break."

"That's great, I'm so lucky," he said with real enthusiasm.

"Because you have fortunate timing?" she asked, wry.

"No, no, because I'm here with somebody who will take a break just because I showed up," he grinned. "That's a lot better than good timing."

"There's wisdom in you, Colvin," Kashindi said.

"That still sounds so weird to me," he replied as he followed her over to the bench. "I've been Gapjaw most of my life. I barely remembered the name they put on me when I came into the world."

"Maybe you should try to get used to it," Kashindi said. "Colvin will always, always be stronger than 'Gapjaw' could ever be. Claiming who you are has rewards that outshine giving your true self up to try and be someone else. A persona who will never really fit you."

"I fit with you," Gapjaw said, earnest.

"That's true. You really do. I have so enjoyed getting to know you better," she smiled.

"I was wondering. If you would mind. If I stayed at the lodgings with you," he said. "For—for a week." His smile was slightly pained.

"Of course you're welcome, I've got a guest space that still has your things from last time," Kashindi said. "I do hope there's no money trouble," she added, brow furrowing. "Are you a fugitive?"

"No trouble, nothing like that. Just... just thinking about what we talked about. About my, you know. Crew."

"Indeed, that's fine news," Kashindi said, raising her eyebrows. "You know a week isn't enough. Freedom takes longer to cultivate."

"I know," he said, looking away, "but they are my people. I'm not ready to leave them. They are my *family.*"

"Anyone who would destroy you for their own purposes is not your family. Not like you mean it. You owe them nothing, Colvin. Regardless of blood or history. You can't see it, but they've extracted valuables from you that outweigh anything they've given in return. Time and sins that can be erased but not recovered." Her voice was firm, certain, and her eyes were direct and fearless.

"You sound like truth feels," Gapjaw said, slightly breathless.

She cocked an eyebrow at him. "And do you like that feeling?"

"I like everything I feel when I'm with you," he said, his voice low.

She was thoughtful, considering him, studying his eyes.

"I have missed you as well," she said. "This work will still be here tomorrow. But this moment will be gone, beyond reach." She placed her hand on his thigh, to assure there was no misunderstanding.

"You could—be available?" Gapjaw said, feeling all the swirling emotions of a teenager.

Her grin was swift. "Let's go," she said.

She tossed her gloves on the cart as she passed it, leading Gapjaw deeper into the Circulatory towards her bed.

ESTATE OFFICES, CLERK STREET. CHARTERHALL
13TH ULSIVET, 850. FIFTH HOUR PAST DAWN

"Congratulations, Madam Selraetas," the angular Estate Manager said as he handed a document pouch and master key ring to Red Silver. "You are now the curator of the Old Custom House, and keeper of its grounds, authorized and empowered by the Ministry." He offered her the polite smile of a professional bureaucrat.

"Darling, you have been amazing," Red Silver said, her tones refined. "I will be certain to send a commendation to your superiors. Having dealt with property in four of Doskvol's neighborhoods, I must confess that the smoothest transaction was this one—even with all its little wrinkles," she confided in him. "I credit you, and I will not forget your service." Her teeth seemed a bit too white. "Is 'Sappenfield' spelled with one 'p' or two?"

"Two," Sappenfield said. "And the pleasure has been all mine. Good fortune with your new property, and please remember to check in with the Dunvil Custom House when you take possession."

"We absolutely will, thanks again," Saint said with a stiff bow.

"Enough out of you," Red Silver said with an exaggerated and playful expression of scandal. "So hard to get servants that understand their place," she said to Sappenfield. "Well, we must be off. Swift blood."

"Swift blood," Sappenfield echoed, and he watched Red Silver leave with Saint at her heels.

"Are you sure you grew up on the mean streets of Doskvol?" Saint teased under his breath as they reached the hallway.

"Silence, peasant," Red Silver said with a dismissive flick of the wrist.

The two scoundrels paused, taking in the sight of the four well-dressed guards flanking the tall aristocrat standing between them and the stairs. The tall man smiled at them, inclining his head ever so slightly.

"Madame Selraetas," he said, his voice smooth. "It is past time we became acquainted with one another."

"Is it?" she said, mild. "I do not believe we have been introduced."

"And yet we have," he pressed on, approaching, his hands behind his back. "We met about a year and a half ago. Though I could see why you might not remember, names can be... so slippery," he said as his smile widened.

"Ah yes," she said graciously as her smile shifted subtly to show teeth between her painted lips. "The Rowan House."

"I believe your assistant was there as well. If I recall, you had to leave early," he said with some sympathy, nodding to Saint.

"Prior engagement," Saint agreed, considering his options if this conversation got hostile.

"You can imagine my delight when I discovered we may have business together," the aristocrat continued, his voice almost hypnotic. "Shared interest, as it were."

"Do tell," Red Silver said.

"Perhaps you could spare me ten minutes now? I know it is irregular, but so is the business we have to discuss." He paused. "But where are my manners. I am Lord Malicoat. Perhaps you have heard of me."

Red Silver attempted a charming and airy little laugh. "Well, sir, *everyone* has heard of *you*."

"But we really must be going," Saint interjected.

"Another prior engagement?" Malicoat said, his lips toying with a smile. "That does seem odd, considering I instructed Sappenfield to approve your application for the Old Custom House without further delay or verification. Surely that saved you a few hours."

Saint blinked, and in the moment of silence, Red Silver took the initiative. "Very kind, and an excellent gesture of goodwill. Something we appreciate in a world where too often motives are inflexible and cruel. Have you a specific meeting location in mind where we could understand one another better?"

"Actually I do," Malicoat said, something dark under the pleasantries shaping his features. "I thought perhaps we could discuss matters in the Barrow Suite."

"Oh, the Barrow—the Barrow Suite," Red Silver said, exchanging a glance with Saint. "How—exclusive."

"Yes," Malicoat said. "I have already seen to it that we will be uninterrupted. Could you see your way clear to joining me?" He smiled, his expensive lip liner accentuating his gleaming and even teeth.

"Fantastic," Red Silver blurted. "Lead the way."

The merged group followed the wide and vaulted hallway to the restricted area at the end, and the guards stood aside and opened the way for Malicoat and his guests, securing the gilded gate behind them. They followed the corridor to double doors.

"Surely we don't all need to go in," Saint said, keeping it light.

"I only need my expert on the subject we'll be discussing. You three stay here. Master Grull, with me."

The guards opened the doors. Malicoat and Grull entered the Barrow Suite, with Red Silver and Saint following. The doors clacked shut behind them with ominous solidity.

"And here we are," Malicoat said with a flourish, like an actor concluding a scene. He gracefully reclined in a leather chair at the head of the mirror-finished solid wood table.

The scoundrels glanced around the room, taking in the mounted trophy heads. The leaded glass on the reinforced span of windows. Two giant fireplaces. Deep and comfortable furniture. Fully stocked bar. Tapestries. Thick carpet.

"Grull, be a good fellow and fetch our guests something to drink," Malicoat said.

"Keen rum, my year is seven seventy seven, no garnish," Red Silver said crisply. Malicoat smiled.

"Brochalla Fields Green, seven eighty two," Saint said. "I like how sweet it is," he clarified to Malicoat.

"See what you can do," Malicoat said to Grull, waving him off. "I am now prepared to satisfy your curiosity, and in turn I want you to satisfy mine."

"Sounds mutually...satisfying," Red Silver said, settling in a chair adjacent to Malicoat as Saint stood nearby. She angled her neck and cleavage to offer a rounded view.

"Please, that's not what I'm after," Malicoat said. "I do hope this is not disappointing; when I heard about your fumbling efforts to research me, I thought perhaps you lot were... overestimated."

"Probably," Saint agreed. "How can we help?"

"I want to make peace between the Unseen and the River Stallions," Malicoat said. "I'm one of the few in this world who were born immune to the ritual that cloaks the Unseen from memory. Unlike you, I need not drink any foul potion to protect my mind. Having discovered the Unseen years ago, I have found them useful collaborators on a variety of projects. It pains me to see them damaged by their clashes with the River Stallions, especially over such low stakes."

"You refer to North Port," Saint clarified.

"North Port," Malicoat echoed, rolling his eyes. "You want to climb to the top of the slick mound of criminal pursuits there. I suppose you must chase your bliss. I don't care about that, and really, the Unseen don't care about it either. The reason you crossed them was because in pursuing criminal dominance you could unwittingly destabilize some things that *do* matter."

Saint eased down into a chair next to Red Silver. "Really."

"The Unseen were playing coy with a mystery over the last year or so, until two days past. Then Grull finally let me in on what the Unseen were about in North Port. I don't appreciate their lack of candor," he said, unreadable, "so I'm looking for new partners in North Port.

When I discovered your role in checking the Unseen's operations, I knew I had found operatives to join me in pursuing my goal."

"You paint a rosy picture," Saint said.

Grill arrived with their refreshments, avoiding eye contact as he placed them before the scoundrels and withdrew.

"I expect I will be working with you, to some degree, but before we delve into the details I want a face-to-face with the entire crew." He paused. "And a one-on-one meeting with Inkletta."

"The first is easy and the second is impossible," Saint said without missing a beat. "I'm with you every time you're in a room with our Whisper. That's non-negotiable."

The barest smile crossed Malicoat's face. "Is it?" he mused. "I suspect that's just your... hunger. Limiting your imagination. Your grasp of the *possibilities*."

"I do have my limits," Saint agreed. He savored his wine.

"We will explore them together," Malicoat said. "Let's meet on my yacht. Tonight. The Hour of Thread. I will join you at the base of the Boldway Canal Street Bridge. We will discuss the future. Even these walls," he said with a gesture, eyes flicking across the opulent room, "are not trustworthy. And... I want you to understand that I am willing to *invest* in you." He reached into his lapel pocket. Unfolding his complex pocketbook, Malicoat lifted a cylindrical bone case, and thumbed the delicate combination catch so it fell open. He ran his fingertip down a dozen of the twenty Coins in the case, and removed them, putting the Coins in a stack on the table, then gently pushing it across to stand in front of Red Silver and Saint Suran.

"Take my Coin," Malicoat said quietly. "Simply that, with no other promise or threat or plan, and the weight of the future shifts." He watched them.

"No promise. Or threat. Or plan," Saint echoed, wary.

"Not yet," Malicoat agreed. For a long and disorienting second, his features seemed too perfect to be human.

"You have our thanks, and our interest," Red Silver said as she swept the dozen Coin into her clutch purse. She rose to her feet. "We will see you tonight."

Malicoat smiled, leaning back in his chair. "Tonight."

Saint took Red Silver's elbow, and the scoundrels left the aristocrat alone with his thoughts.

CHAPTER THREE

The Barrowcleft district has the most spacious lands within the lightning wall, and while its estates may not be the most impressive, they are the least crowded. Privacy was essential for the founders.

Their motto was "Throne to Tomb to Throne." The motto referenced the Barrow Kings, who ruled in life and then were interred in lavish tombs. When the Gates of Death shattered, the Kings rose from their slumber and caused some real problems before the Immortal Emperor destroyed some and drove the rest back. Centuries later, the Immortal King outmaneuvered a coup led by some prominent noble houses in the Capitol.

A number of the survivors relocated as far from the Capitol as they could go, which at the time was the port city of Doskvol. They established themselves at the edge of the city. Even as it grew around them, they invested in radiant fields and eeleries so other development wouldn't nestle too close.

They identified with the Barrow Kings, because they too had seen their futures slain. But they planned to rise again from their shattered barrows, to once again challenge the Immortal Emperor. As many times as necessary, until the Emperor was no longer Immortal.

—From "Treason at Dusk: Sedition in Doskvol"
by Minister Prell Rizajan

"Whose idea was it to have so many people in this crew?" Saint groused. The carriage jolted on a pothole, and he grunted as he was shifted on the bench seat. Across from him, Red Silver was more centered, hardly swayed by the bounce.

"You inherited some of them and curated the rest. After all these years you've got no one else to blame," she said dispassionately. "I've volunteered to shoot most of them at one time or another."

"Except Niece. Everybody loves the baby," Saint sighed. "Anyway, we've got until the Hour of Thread to pull together and make sure we've got the headcount for our meet with Malicoat."

"About ten hours," Red Silver agreed. "And we'll need a contingency plan. In case things don't go our way."

"That's what the Coursers are for," Saint said. "I'll send Safety to get them set up." He frowned. "But Safety's off researching the Spirit Wardens. You can go find him. I think he was headed to the library."

"He hasn't 'headed' anywhere," Red Silver said, dismissive. "He was still gathering the nerve and the focus when we left. Yesterday he didn't follow up on the Spirit Wardens at all. When he finally worked up the motivation to go out, he handled other Silkshore business. Checked on a couple other irons we have in the fire. Not the new work we're managing, or the move."

"You think he's still at the base even though we've been gone for hours?" Saint said with half a smile. "Let's make it interesting."

"I'm not betting with you," Red Silver scoffed. "You covered your share *and* Gapjaw's share of the Old Custom House buy-in. You don't have cash to spare."

"Hey, I'm the leader of a lucrative crime family, we're flush," he grinned. "I've got money to burn."

"Well I'm right, so if you want to do this, then I'll bet you this knife," she said as she palmed a damask stiletto with red enamel and silver trim, "for that pocketwatch." She nodded at his waistcoat.

"My special fancy dress-up pocketwatch?" he said, feigning alarm.

"The very one, in exchange for this namesake blade given to me by the Gondoliers on the occasion of sniping that possessing ghost last year." She twirled the knife in her grip. "It's like I'd be with you always."

"Alright, you put it that way, you're on," Saint said, spitting at his hand and thrusting it out.

"So gross," she said reflectively, and she spat in her hand. They shook on it. She wiped her palm on the seat, and frowned at the upholstery.

"We have to get our own coach," she said.

"You may be too dainty to be a hardened criminal," Saint suggested. "Is there a timeline for when you plan to ease up on Safety?" he wondered aloud.

"There are certain milestones along that road," she replied, unamused. "He is still dawdling along the first leg of a long journey."

"Poor bastard," Saint sighed.

The carriage rolled to a stop, and the draft goat bawled his irritation under the reins. Saint swung out of the coach and offered a gentlemanly support to Red Silver, who graciously accepted. Saint didn't bother paying the cabbie, who deferentially tipped her hat to the criminals before rattling off.

"Rain tonight," Saint said with a wince, leaning on his cane. "I feel it in every broken bone."

"Come along, grandfather, it's time for your soup," Red Silver teased.

"You're pretty, so everyone pretends you're funny," he grumbled as they crossed the street towards the bridge piling entrance to their hidden base.

"You take your time with the stairs, you young and virile grandpa, and I'll get started on our business," she said crisply.

"I don't even have any children!" Saint said plaintively as she unlocked the gate and let herself into the piling door. "That I know of," he added reflectively as he followed her inside and closed the gate behind himself.

Red Silver took the stairs two at a time, up four flights in the square stairwell. Hauling the nondescript door open, she let herself into the River Stallion common room.

"Still here?" she said mildly. A guilty look flashed across Safety's features as he oriented on the doorway, then he smiled broadly to cover.

"How did it go with the permit and deed?" he asked.

Red Silver raised the document pouch with a sardonic grin. "We are ready to take possession," she said. She looked over the empty bottles on the table, and the Hammer seated opposite Safety with Sereen on a stool at his elbow. The Hammer stared into the middle distance, inscrutable and very basically dressed. Safety wore a more professional outfit, to better blend among the well-off. "Having a tea party?" Red Silver asked.

"I figured I'd have lunch here before heading out," Safety said, nettled, "if that's alright with you."

"The clock's hands are sweeping. Leave your work to the last minute and you risk not finishing it." A smile touched at Red Silver's lips. "Hm. It's like I can feel the tick of the seconds," she said, amusing herself.

"I've been buttering up some librarians, asking for this and that, spreading some gratuities around," Safety said, trying not to sound defensive. "I'm weaving my real inquiry into a broader study I made up, so it isn't immediately clear what I'm after. The Spirit Wardens don't like nosy scoundrels, and I would like to avoid questions about why I might be checking into their membership."

"Whatever," Red Silver said, waving that away. "You'll have to postpone your research, and your lunch. We have a mandatory meeting tonight, here, Hour of Silver. Because an hour later we've got a meeting with Malicoat. He's bringing his yacht to us, docking right here, and he wants to meet the whole crew." She cocked her head to the side. "It was *my* job to look into Malicoat. And here we are."

"That sounds like a trap," Safety said, processing fast.

"Of course it sounds like a trap," Red Silver agreed. "So you need to go work out an extraction plan with the Coursers. Make sure they're standing by to cause a distraction, fish us out of the water, spirit us away if we can make it to shore. Got it?"

"Yeah, I can figure that out," Safety said. "I assume Saint agrees we're doing this meet."

"He was with me when I met Malicoat," Red Silver said. "He's just on the stairs still. You know. Infirm leg."

"I think he wants to move to North Port just to get a ground floor entrance," Safety muttered. "There's lots of other places we could headquarter here in Silkshore that don't have four flights of stairs."

Red Silver poured herself a glass of wine, her back to Safety. "For some reason, you're still here," she said aloud in a bemused tone.

Rising with a scowl, Safety snatched his hat off the table, nodded to the Hammer, and stalked out. He met Saint on the stairs.

"Red told me about the meet tonight, Hour of Silver. Said I should prep the Coursers for a possible river extraction," he said.

"Right," Saint nodded, schooling his features to hide the strain of mounting the stairs. "Good."

"Congratulations on the Old Custom House," Safety said. He clapped Saint on the shoulder, then descended the staircase.

Niece was on the way up, her golden hair back in a braid, somehow still fresh even in her work clothes with a coat of grime. "Hey, you're on your way," she said with a grin as she met Safety on the landing.

"Change of plans, I'm headed to the Tower Lair," he said shortly.

"Did they get the deed, though?" Niece asked, earnest. "The Old Custom House? We're still on for the move?"

"Oh. Yes, they got the deed. Saint and Red Silver are up there," he said, glancing up the stairwell. "Big meeting tonight, the whole crew."

"What?" Niece said, surprised.

"Gotta go," Safety said, and he continued down the stairs to bang out the door at the base of the piling.

Niece bounced up the stairs, arriving at the common room at the same time as Saint. "Hey boss."

"Niece, so glad to see you." He opened the door with a chivalrous flourish, then followed her through. "We have a meeting tonight, Hour of Silver. All hands on deck. We may have a breakthrough in setting up shop in North Port. A patron," he said suggestively.

"No problem," Niece said, thinking fast. "I've got the base packed up except the common room and a couple other corners. Do I need to furnish the meet hall?"

"Oh, here but not *here*," Saint clarified. "Lord Malicoat is going to moor his yacht. Down at the quay, just outside. So the barge can't be there tonight. Can you move the schedule so they get done and out before then?"

"The barge was going to arrive an hour before dusk," Niece said, troubled as she thought through the logistics. "We were going to get the barge loaded and on the way by midnight. We're working this in between other contracts."

"Change of plans," Saint said brightly. "Maybe they can do it tomorrow." He paused. "Regardless, I need that quay tonight, and you here and presentable by the Hour of Silver. Okay?"

"You got it, boss," she said, reserved. She nodded to Red Silver and the Hammer, then turned and trotted back down the stairs.

"And that's why you never had to offer to shoot Niece," Saint observed to Red Silver.

"Safety was here," Red Silver said. She patted the back of a chair. "Having a few drinks with the Hammer. He was going to have his lunch, *then* head out," she said, patronizing.

Saint heaved a deep sigh, then dug out his pocketwatch and fiddled with the fob, unhooking it from his vest. Wordless, he held it out. Red Silver delicately lifted it from his palm. She held it to her ear, taking her time, enjoying the busy ticking.

"Still warm with your body heat," she said, luxuriating in the moment.

"It's a good thing you get the job done," Saint muttered, half amused, "because you're an insufferable pain in the ass."

"Hammer, you'll be here and presentable for the meet tonight, right?" Red Silver said as she turned to the hulking shadow at the table. He nodded. "Good. Then we just need Gapjaw and Inkletta." Turning back to Saint, she raised an eyebrow. "Maybe send Niece after Gapjaw, I'll take Inkletta."

"I had best go after Gapjaw, I think I know where he is. We may need some subtlety," Saint said. "I'll send Niece after Inkletta."

"Oh, I'm going after our Whisper," Red Silver said, matter-of-fact. "I need to get Nails some exercise, and I know Inkletta's haunts."

"I was thinking you could keep working on the Malicoat background," Saint said, subdued. "Some leverage would be useful, considering he's showing up on our very doorstop tonight."

"He's old money," Red Silver said, "Imperial roots in the capitol. He has Leviathan hunter investments, so he's deeply involved in the energy economy of Doskvol. He owns about a third of the mills in Coalridge. His family didn't settle in Six Towers, nor do many of them hold rank in the Church, and this is quietly attributed to his family's involvement in the worship of Forgotten Gods and various distasteful occult practices." She raised her eyebrows.

"I was thinking maybe something more personal," Saint clarified.

"Alright. He married four times, and not one bride survived the first year."

"You think he killed them?" Saint asked.

"Each one died in a difficult childbirth," Red Silver continued. "Apparently the only people who want to talk about this are people who don't know anything. Those who do keep their mouths firmly shut."

"Nobles are terrible, but aristocrats are the worst," Saint muttered.

"And yet," Red Silver said reflectively, "before today I never held twelve Coin in my hand before."

Saint nodded, regarding her for a long moment. "There's that," he agreed. He straightened. "We are going to need Inkletta. *After* you put that Coin in the vault downstairs."

"Yes sir." Red Silver finished her wine, set the cup down, and left the room.

Saint shuffled across the room and eased down into a chair opposite the Hammer, who roused to make eye contact.

"Don't *you* go anywhere," Saint sighed.

Red Silver took the steps two at a time for the remaining two flights. The walls closed in so close to the top of the pylon, but there was a small chamber nestled in between the supports. Red Silver opened the door and slid through sideways, smiling as she was enveloped in the musky stink of the bat lair.

"Who is a good boy? Nails is a good boy," Red Silver purred as she stepped over to the sleepy bat hanging upside down on his perch. The massive bat's body was half the size of a human torso, his wingspan doubled her reach. He was tucked into a cocoon of leather and fur, but a beady eye rolled open. He slowly twisted, his claws shifting on the perch as he wiggled under Red Silver's gloved hands ruffling his fur, scratching the ridges of the leather on his wings and face.

Flexing his body, Nails re-oriented, catching at other pegs set in the walls as he shifted to an upright position draped across multiple contact points. He licked Red Silver's forehead as she chuckled. Both his eyelids flicked up, revealing a bright eye and a silver ball set in his other socket.

"I know it's sleepy times," Red Silver soothed. "But we are going on an adventure! We'll go find Inkletta. You like Crow's Foot, don't you. We haven't been there in *a while*," she murmured as she dipped her hand into her pocket, pulling out a dead cave cricket the size of a weedy carrot. Nails eagerly munched the treat as Red Silver gazed out at the view from the pylon.

The shattered embers of the sun were clustered behind the low clouds that seemed to smoulder with trapped rays, suffusing the midday sky with a directionless glow. The river glittered with reflected light like jewelry lit by candles, somehow brighter than the dim vault above.

Red Silver felt the old wound in her leg ache, and she twinged with the remembered sensation—pouncer wolf fangs clamping down, snapping her shin, worrying her right off her feet. Inches from death. Years ago. Yet an echo of pain still rebounded through her, stored in her re-knit bone and old scars. She felt her heart pound. Whether it was from climbing the stairs or from anticipation of an eventful meet, she didn't like the off-balance sense that seeped through her. The pylon shifted slightly in the hot breeze, the flexing motion detectable at the very top. Even the most stable load-bearing pillars of the world had to adjust sometimes.

Having finished the cricket, Nails roughly nuzzled Red Silver for more snacks, letting out a couple clicks that were loud in the confined space.

"Let's not get greedy," she admonished the bat, who blinked at her before cranking his jaw in a prodigious yawn. "We've got a mission, some scouting to do," Red Silver said as she tugged her round mirrored sunglasses out of her jacket. Tilting the frame open, she slid the glasses into place as her eyes half closed. She felt the rapid patter of Nails' heartbeat over her own more sedate pulse. She breathed out and let the world's unnecessary detail flow away until she could center her senses on the bat's breathing. Her eyes slowly drifted open as Nails yipped, and launched out from the tower into the empty air, unfurling his leather membranes to catch the updrafts swirling up from the steel and stone of the bridge.

"Just what I needed," Red Silver mused to herself. Nails slowly wheeled, the sun ruddy behind his wings. Even if the world fell away, even if everything fell down, he could drift above the wreckage. She still felt everything in motion, but there was a fierce luxury in riding the thick air currents, a primal joy that resonated through her connection to Nails. She felt a smile growing on her face.

"Let's hunt."

STARCH CORRIDOR MOORING. SILKSHORE
13TH ULSIVET, 850. SEVENTH HOUR PAST DAWN

Niece stood in the shadow of the piling, a dozen paces from the prow of the wide barge moored to the quay. She took in a deep breath, held it, then let it all out. Setting her jaw, she approached the barge's gangplank, past the name "Lilya" painted on the hull.

"Everyone's favorite niece!" called out the narrow-chested captain of the barge as he spotted her approach. He smiled broadly as he crossed the deck to meet her.

"Caden, we'll need to contact the crew. There's been a change of plan," Niece said.

The edges of the captain's smile faded. "A change of plan, eh. I hope it's not serious. I've paid earnest money on tomorrow's job, I've committed to my people. I suppose we could shift an hour or two."

"We have a guest mooring a yacht under the bridge tonight. We need the berth clear. If we can't go load up the base right now, we'll have to handle the cargo in the morning." Niece was quiet and serious.

"The—now, or come back in the morning?" Caden echoed. "I confirmed the plan with you before dawn today. Before I took steps that cost me money. My crew is already leaving this job early, leaving bonuses on the table. And we are unloading the Invincible tomorrow, I pushed the start time on the contract back by two hours so we could fit your job in. I secured a—a special permit to dock at your quay, and that wasn't cheap!" Color rose in his cheeks as he struggled to remain calm.

"If you don't have time, we'll get someone else," Niece said, stone-faced. "Maybe you should stay on this job, get that bonus."

"Easily said," Caden retorted. "I'm invested in your move. Part of my operation's cash flow. I've already made sacrifices to be available. When you tell people what you need to do the work, then change your mind, it looks like you're gouging," he growled.

"We appreciate your flexibility," Niece said.

"Do you?" Caden shot back. "Enough to cover our extra expenses? I don't mind a little inconvenience as long as the balance sheet comes out right." A smile colored his heated feelings, and Niece caught a glimpse of the shrewdness behind his bluster.

Leaning back, Niece crossed her arms. "Bring the Lilya to our quay in the morning. Before dawn."

"So we cooperate, and there's a bonus?" Caden prompted.

"Cooperate. And we'll see," Niece said. She turned her back on him, treading down the gangplank, and she didn't look back.

Caden watched her go, fuming, his fists tight. A crewman was at his elbow.

"Do we accommodate them, captain?" he asked quietly.

"I guess we do," Caden said. "This time."

TOWER LAIR, THE EASE. SILKSHORE
13TH ULSIVET, 850. SEVENTH HOUR PAST DAWN

The rousing chorus to the Severosian drinking song was somewhat slurred, more of a wander than a charge. Half a dozen Coursers were sitting in the shade of the tower, surrounded by a litter of empty bottles. The song trailed off, and a couple of them hailed Safety as he approached. No one stood up.

"Well, Varela, looks like you've got some day drinking going on," Safety observed, hands stuffed in his light jacket's pockets.

"Indeed I do! We do. Are. Have been," Varela said, slowly groping for a response. "Drink?" He offered a cloudy bottle up towards Safety.

"I'm good," Safety replied. "The River Stallions have a meet tonight, and it could go very wrong. We will need backup. Just in case." He looked them over. "And lucky for us, you've got plenty of time to pull yourselves together."

"Boo!" called out one of the Coursers, and a couple others let out lubricated giggles.

"Huh," Varela said. "Just finished up a thing, right? Thought the Stallions," he took his time with the word, trying to get it shaped right, "would take a break. And it's not like we had to stay sharp to fend off the Red Sashes," he added with a hint of reproach, not looking towards Safety.

"I'll pick up some of the blue flares. Those are still in the pantry, right?" Safety said.

"Still, yep, help yourself," Varela said with a magnanimous gesture. Safety headed into the tower, rifled the pantry, and pocketed a couple handfuls of flares. By the time he returned to the shadow of the tower, the rovers were already shrugging off the worst of their intoxication, preparing for action. The cheap beer fueling their celebration required some cooperation to sway their senses, and it had little staying power.

"Lord Malicoat is going to moor his giant yacht at the base of the bridge, right under our base," Safety said. "We will go aboard to have a little dance and see what he's after. If it gets violent we'll likely try to escape, and there are a lot of us, so at least a few will make it out."

"Goals!" sang out one of the Coursers.

"Split up into three teams," Safety continued. "You need a fishing boat ready to pull people out of the water. A fast coach ready to get to safety. Also a couple snipers." He paused. "The Stallions are meeting for the Hour of Silver, then Malicoat shows up for the Hour of Thread. You need to be in position ahead of time, everything ready by the Hour of Song. Got it? Repeat the plan back to me."

"Right," Varela said, focusing intently. "Couple of us on the water, we'll have a coach ready to go, two snipers. Got it." He snorted. "We'll look after you, no problem."

"Things go wrong, we meet at the Exchange. Signal location with blue lights. Unless one of you gets compromised, in which case you go to the Landing," Safety said.

"Is this about that little adventure you set up a few days back?" Varela asked, bold. "Where you were the Gray Cloak, you had that cover for a while. I guess that's over."

"It's over," Safety agreed.

"What was that about?" Varela said, the question angled so it was almost a demand.

Safety looked him in the eye. "I could tell you," he said, "but you'd forget anyway." He looked to the other members of the gang, nodded, and turned away. His retreating steps were loud in the awkward silence that followed.

Sukup erupted with a belch.

Pilege tossed her bottle in the river, and faced Varela. "You keep pushing him," she said, mild. "Aren't you a little bit worried he'll replace you?"

"No," Varela replied with a smirk, watching Safety vanish around the corner. "Don't you worry about that. My position is secure." He glanced around the gangsters lounging around the tower's shadow. "Alright, let's get moving. We've got some transportation to arrange."

HABITATION CHAMBERS, THE CIRCULATORY, THE EASE. SILKSHORE 13TH ULSIVET, 850. EIGHTH HOUR PAST DAWN

Saint rapped on the polished wood of the doorframe with his silver-headed cane, and glanced both ways in the earthen curve of the corridor.

"It's open," called out a voice inside. Saint shook his head, then unlatched the door, stepping through.

"Well look at you," he said, bemused.

Startled, Gapjaw stared at him. The scoundrel's hair was tied back out of his face, he was shaved, he wore an apron. He stood at the counter, a knife forgotten in his hand, a mound of vegetables cut up and swept to the side.

"How—how—" Gapjaw stammered.

"Really?" Saint said, cocking an eyebrow. "Of *course* I looked into it when you started acting strange a month or so back. I think it's very nice you've made a new friend," he said with what he meant to be a warm smile. "This looks like a very domestic sort of venture."

"You aren't mad?" Gapjaw said cautiously.

"Of course not," Saint replied, waving the idea away. "Are you serious? We rogues need to have that occasional comfort, that reminder of what life looks like for those who do not carry the burdens we bear."

"How did you figure it out? Where I am?" Gapjaw asked.

"Tracked your movements, that was easy enough," Saint said as he crossed to the counter, considering the spread of food. "Asked around. You spent quite a bit of time here at the Circulatory working with Inkletta's contact, when you were getting the components for her fog-binding ritual, for that mess with the Rakes. Around the same time, a fellow matching your description, name of *Colvin*," he said, inclining his head, "started spending time with one of the matrons here." He looked Gapjaw in the eye. "Rumor has it, he's pretty sweet on her. It's getting serious."

Gapjaw stood unmoving, his brow furrowed and his mouth a pouch of discontent. "Let's talk in the garden," he muttered, putting the knife down and wiping his hands on a towel, then leading the way out the patio door to the walled enclosure with waist-high planters. Glass plates were mounted on iron arms over the greenery, magnifying the weak shine of the sun to create a strange texture of light. Two benches faced each other in the center of the garden, and the men sat opposite each other.

"Why are you here?" Gapjaw demanded in a low voice.

"We have an unexpected opportunity," Saint replied quietly. "Lord Malicoat is coming to the bridge, tonight. He wants to meet the whole crew. That includes you." Saint paused. "All you have to do is dress the part and show up. After the meeting, you can return to this, I'm not canceling your vacation. But I do need to borrow you." He looked thoughtful.

"And?" Gapjaw prodded.

"If you don't want to come, I get it," Saint confessed. He considered the plants, breathed in the earthy scent of the garden. "You don't want to go to North Port, or chip in for the Old Custom House. I can take a hint. You're looking to retire, right?" he said as he returned his attention to Gapjaw.

"No!" Gapjaw protested. "What? You think—no!"

"I mean, I remember that conversation we had a few months ago. You were worried I was going to sideline you. And what did I say?" Saint said.

"You said you weren't going to do that," Gapjaw replied.

"Right, I told you I wouldn't push you out. But things change, don't they?" Saint looked down at the snarling horse bust on his cane. "We don't always see the end of things before they arrive. I don't want to make this difficult for you if you've chosen another path." He looked Gapjaw in the eye. "If you're done with all that," he said, something chilly under his tone. "If you're set for life. If you've had enough."

"I'm not done," Gapjaw retorted. His hands trembled slightly, so he clenched them into fists, and rose to his feet. "You know I'm not."

"Well okay," Saint said agreeably, leaning forward and pressing down on his cane as he stood up. "See you at the bridge. Hour of Silver, so you're in place for the Hour of Thread. Presentable." He raised his eyebrows.

"I'll be there," Gapjaw said, chin outthrust.

"Good man." Saint nodded. He turned away, through the doors into the living quarters, and he quietly let himself out.

Gapjaw stood in the garden, brow furrowed, fists clenched. Then he shrugged off the moment.

There was work to do.

CHAPTER FOUR

The single element distinguishing a crew from a gang is the capacity to trade in Coin.

While silver currency ("slugs" or "scales") is now minted by the Empire and distributed to quantify purchasing power, in the early centuries of the age, resource allocation was dominated by nobles. Ultimately, everything belonged to a noble, though it may be made or used by their subjects. To trade goods and services, the nobles used heavy gold coins featuring the Emperor. Coins were, and are, symbolic units representing a noble's commitment of resources, service, and expertise to a cooperative venture.

With the daring rise of criminal syndicates, a measure of their power is their ability to intrude into this quiet and forceful economy of influence. When lawbreakers from outside the noble class gain enough influence to have the use of Coin as currency, then they become a proper crew rather than a gang. An individual or gang who acquires a Coin will not find trading partners who accept it as payment in good faith; without a reputation and history to back the Coin, it's just a piece of metal.

Once a crew trades in Coin, it demonstrates its ability to operate outside the confines of law. Their range of motion is only constrained by the other factions surrounding them.

From "Integral Economics of the Interstinctive Customs Delineating Extralegal Castes"

—by Doctor Cannamount Wallnyver Eggsetunt

Inkletta squinted up into the cloudscape of the mid-afternoon vault above. She saw the wingspan of the bat tilting him in a lazy loop overhead. Just a matter of time now. She returned her attention to the boxy charcoal stove, prodding more twists of dried kelp into the small port in the front and snapping it shut with a stick. She stirred the dented pot of soup sitting on top, and tossed in another pinch of powder.

Red Silver's boots crunched on gravel and debris as she approached, deliberately making noise. Inkletta smiled to herself, and looked up at the approaching scoundrel.

"You're having a good hair day," she said quietly. Red Silver smirked, and swept off her tooled leather hat so its plume waved before her as she dropped into an elegant curtsey. Even in the heat of the afternoon, she wore a long jacket of thin material to cover her expensive pistols and daggers. Her red and russet colors emphasized her pale complexion and dark hair. Her eyes were invisible behind mirrored glasses, and her teeth were sharpened by black makeup on her lips.

"A warmer welcome than I expected," she said.

"You know me well enough to look here, so you get a pass. I suppose," Inkletta mused. She was slouched, comfortable, draped in a single long fabric that was currently over one shoulder and her hips. Much of her coppery skin was exposed, showing off a lifetime of artistic embroidery in her flesh. Patterns wrapped her ribs and trailed down her arms, climbing her neck and reshaping her facial features. Her hair was a dense cloud around her head, unruly in the humidity. Her feet were bare and tough, soiled with the unforgiving urban foulness of the byways.

"I haven't been back here in a while," Red Silver observed. The ruined building at their back overlooked Runwater Corners, a decaying and partially abandoned square tucked away in the buffer between a slum and a struggling business neighborhood. Both areas sent sounds echoing into the space between them; shouts, laughter, cracks and bangs, the clatter and bleats of traffic. "That's fairly new," Red Silver said with a nod to a run-down goat stable across the square.

"It stinks," Inkletta observed. "Owners must be too cheap to keep it cleaned out proper. So they set up here. Where the locals can't make them move. Nobody wants to live next to that," she said with a gesture at the low building, "so it ends up somewhere the neighbors don't have a choice."

Red Silver slid her glasses off, folding the frame with a click. "That's where the tower was," she said. "Where you grew up."

"Yeah, once upon a time." Inkletta stirred the soup once more, then took an experimental sip. "Life moves on."

"Like it or not," Red Silver agreed. "May I join you?"

Inkletta gestured at the paving stone opposite her, across the charcoal oven. Red Silver settled, looking around.

"The tower fell down, what, two years ago?" Red Silver said. "I guess space is too tight to leave a place fallow for long. *Something* was going to go in there." She paused. "And the spirit well under there... is it still, you know, quiet?"

"It's quiet," Inkletta said. "I had to check."

Red Silver nodded to herself, watching the stable. "So the Shrouded Queen, huh. Any changes that I should know about?"

"She likes the worship," Inkletta said, subdued. "Her cult can feel her presence in the world growing. The leaders are recruiting. Maybe the Shrouded Queen is recruiting too, in her way. The more they love her, the stronger she gets."

"Have you found anything out? About other people who played host to some part of a Forgotten God?" Red Silver asked. "Any *better* stories?"

"You mix human meat and spirit with cosmic stuff and it ends up tragic, every time," Inkletta said. "Every story I've heard. Everything I've read. Sometimes the body goes monstrous, or burns away, or gets corrupted into a vampire or a hollow. When the Forgotten Gods get some foothold in this world," she said with a gesture at their surroundings, "they twist. Like when people get trapped behind the Mirror, but up against it. Spirits go mad without their flesh, and when a piece of a god gets stuck in a living vessel they go sour. Every drained and knotted time." She absently drew an abstract pattern in the dust with her fire-poking stick.

An argument in a nearby building escalated to a screaming match, the words indistinct but the frustration clearly audible. Red Silver squinted across the weather-beaten square, letting the silence get comfortable.

"We were barbarians," Inkletta said. "My mom. The Ebon Wings. Violent, crazy, strung out and defiant." She shook her head. "There are still survivors from that time that live around here. Carrying scars older than I am. I learned Hadrathi right over there," she said, gesturing towards a boarded-up well in the center of the square. "That's where the Wings held court. Sure, they were violent, short tempered, they took what they wanted. But people put up with it. Why? Fear only goes so far, you know," she said reflectively, "Nobody was looking out for these people. And if the Bluecoats and the merchants had to think twice about pushing the locals around, because the Wings might take it poorly, well then..." She looked into the glow of the charcoal burner. "That was worth some noise and danger. Nobody would have built a goat stable there when the Wings had the run of the place."

"It is pretty ripe," Red Silver observed.

"They worshiped the Forgotten Gods," Inkletta murmured, barely audible. "So did I. From before I knew words. I grew up drinking from that spirit well. It was my 'normal.' We threw ghosts around and chucked people through windows. I learned my letters and inking skin at the same time." She looked Red Silver in the eye. "I'm twenty six. Never thought I'd live this long. The only old people I knew growing up were cult priests." She returned her attention to the burner. "I wasn't going to go that direction."

"Dying young doesn't seem so bad if you get to strut while you're here. Better than cowering into old age," Red Silver mused.

"Yeah, I decided early on I didn't want to outlast my teeth," Inkletta said with half a grin.

"Have you seen the end of the road?" Red Silver asked seriously.

"No, not yet," Inkletta said, bowing her head, unreadable. "Holy people go strange, you know. The world they see isn't the world other people see. You get tangled up in a god, and your needs change. Your... tolerances." She cleared her throat. "Yeah, I'm scared. But I'm not alone. I don't have long, I don't think." She looked sideways at Red Silver. "If you have to choose, I know you'll choose me over her."

"Every goddamn time," Red Silver agreed.

Inkletta sipped at her soup, but didn't offer Red Silver any. The shadows at the edge of the square thrashed as a hunting stray brought down some bulky vermin. One street over, a furious driver lashed a squalling draft goat.

"You came to bring me back," Inkletta stated. "Something came up."

"We've got time," Red Silver said.

"It's funny," Inkletta said. "Both the Shrouded Queen and I are bound to this world by its needs. We are part of something. Something painful and desperate, something that may not survive without the intangibles we offer." She flicked the pot, scattering the last of the bitter soup. "What's the job."

"Malicoat wants to meet the crew." Red Silver crossed her arms. "And he wants a one-on-one with you. Saint demanded to be there for it."

"Malicoat." Inkletta let the flavor of the word sit on her tongue. "He's deep into the occult. His family is known on both sides of the Mirror. For ambition. And corruption."

"He wants the River Stallions in his pocket."

"If we work with him, we get tangled up in his power," Inkletta said. "His needs. It's more than we are ready to handle."

Red Silver said nothing.

A small, cruel smile curled Inkletta's lip. "So let's strut."

HABITATION CHAMBERS, THE CIRCULATORY, THE EASE. SILKSHORE 13TH ULSIVET, 850. ELEVENTH HOUR PAST DAWN

"You're awfully quiet," Kashindi said, putting her fork down on the plate. "I do hope preparing supper didn't wear you out."

"What? No, it's fine," Gapjaw said absently. He rubbed his forehead. "I've got a headache. Feels like something is chewing on my skull."

"Maybe I could give you a neck rub," Kashindi suggested. "Restore the flow of blood."

"I have to go out tonight," he said abruptly.

Kashindi studied him. "You had a visitor."

"I should be back well before dawn," he said. "Don't wait for me. It's a meeting. Could take a while."

"Just a meeting." Kashindi was skeptical.

"What if it was something else? Or something more?" Gapjaw muttered to himself. "Wouldn't make a difference. I mean, yeah, it's just a meeting tonight. As long as everything goes well. I just stand there, and the boss does all the witty banter. But I need to know what's going on, because we'll have some work to do if we get hired." His scowl pinched off further words.

Kashindi took a deep breath, then let it out. "I see."

"You don't think I should go." Gapjaw stared at her, defiant.

"I think," she said carefully, "tonight only happens once. Of all the nights you've lived through, of all the decisions you've made that have located you squarely here, now, not one can be changed once it moves into the past. You are living through decisions that will continue to adjust what you can do. Who you can be. What you carry. What you leave behind, what you draw into your future path."

Gapjaw blinked. "That's a lot of words."

"Say you do go," Kashindi said. "You make a promise tonight, or lose a friend, or get pulled into some obligation. From there you are pushed into suffering, you are given difficult choices to make, you lose friends and kill people. Then a window in time opens, and you can see back to this moment. Back before any of that happened. And you could make a choice. A choice that would rinse blood off your hands, weights off your mind. Give you a second chance." She slid her hands on the table, palms flat. "Maybe that is what just happened. Maybe this is your second chance."

"Maybe it is," he retorted. "Maybe tonight I stay here with you. Send word to my crew that I'm retired. They go to the meet. Somebody gets killed. Then it's war. My crew gets hunted, or murdered, and some noble gets to be the one who beat the River Stallions." He paused. "Then your magical window opens. And I could be there with them. To live or die by their side. To protect them, to take out our enemies. Give me a second chance. Be there when they need me the most."

Kashindi watched him steadily.

"I've had most of the afternoon to think it over," Gapjaw said. "I'm not ready for make-believe to change my life. I'm just not."

"This make-believe, as you call it, cannot change your life until you are. Ready, that is." Her chin was firm, her eyes glinted with resolve.

"I leave now, and I've done everything I am going to do in that life," Gapjaw said with some heat. "I leave now and there are no more war stories. No more knocking down smug bastards. No more big paydays and big celebrations." He rose to his feet. "I've been building a reputation for years. But if I left right now, would anybody remember me? The Stallions have another cutter. I've been a part of some big things, but I don't think people will tell stories about me when I'm gone. I'll just disappear."

"That doesn't have to be true," Kashindi said evenly. "You could join in the work of the Church. Help the helpless. Feed the hungry. Restore the glory of each body in the city. Those you affect would have your name on their lips with gratitude, not curses. If you want to leave a mark in this world, you can't do better than the Starwalk Wall, with a memorial niche that holds up the entire legacy of the Church in living memory." She focused on him intently. "Money alone cannot secure a place on the Wall. You must work for wholeness, and invest in the less fortunate." She withdrew her hands. "If you earn your place there, then you will know you've made a real difference." She paused. "For the better."

"Just, so many words," Gapjaw observed. "They all sound good. But they don't feel right. If I throw myself into some church job—I don't even know how to do anything but what I'm doing," he protested.

"Yet you made supper tonight, Colvin. You, the man who doesn't cook. You think you're helpless because your 'friends' have promised you that you are. If you can learn and change and grow, maybe the time will come when you realize you don't need them. They cannot abide that idea. They feel entitled to the power to decide what your life means. To you, and to the world." Her even tone was implacable.

"Look. I'm going," Gapjaw said. "So what I need to know from you is, am I welcome back afterwards? Or should I stay away?" His frustration was tightly contained.

"Come back to me. Come back safe. And if you cannot, come back in peril," she said quietly.

Gapjaw frowned. "What I do... it's dangerous, Kashindi. I don't want you to get hurt."

"Pursuing what we want—even *accepting* what we want when it is offered—leads to pain. Discomfort, suffering, heartache. Everything I have ever acquired has cost me. Yet my courage holds. I am no coward," she said. "I want you. So come back."

Gapjaw stared at her. "I love you," he blurted.

"I love you as well, Colvin," she replied. "With my bones, my muscle, my blood, my skin, my breath, and my heart that knits them together. I share them all with you."

"Will—will you pray with me before I go?" Gapjaw asked in a small voice.

"Yes. Of course. Any time." She rose to her feet, smoothing her dress. "Do you want a prayer aloft on my air, shaped by my flesh? Or a silent prayer that travels among ideas?"

"Silent. Just... silent. Too many words," he said, trying to smile.

Kashindi took his scarred and puffy hands and concentrated on his eyes, her breathing steady.

Then she let him go.

BOLDWAY CANAL STREET BRIDGE PILING. SILKSHORE
13TH ULSIVET, 850. HOUR OF THREAD, 3RD HOUR PAST DUSK

"And here it comes," Niece said, tense as she watched out the window. "By the Pump and Slosh, that's a big ship."

Saint stood at her side, looking down from the fourth floor of the bridge pylon. He watched the massive yacht angle over to the side, approaching the quay. Safety and the Hammer moved out of the shadows of the piling, one to the bow and the other to the stern, and they accepted the tossed mooring cables. As they secured the yacht, its crew lowered the gangplank.

"You see the name of the ship?" Saint said, almost sneering. "Kotar's Crown. That's a touch pretentious, don't you think?"

"From what I hear," Niece muttered, "he can be as delusional as he wants. He's got money flowing in from Coalridge to keep him insulated from things like consequences and reality."

Saint looked over at her, serious. "Yes, rich people are all insane," he agreed. "But we work with them anyway. Why is that."

"They have the most money," Niece replied without making eye contact.

"Best behavior," Saint said. He turned, heading for the stairs. Niece gave him a head start as her eyes followed the long smooth lines of the luxury watercraft. Four decks. Tracery enchantments. Radiant garden on the top deck. Electroplasmic lights and a generator aboard. Unstepped masts. Of course it could sail on the sea as well as the river. But not the canals. Too deep a draft.

Flexing her hands to relax them, Niece stepped away from the window and followed Saint.

The crew's leader took his time following the flights of stairs to the base of the pylon where a door admitted access to the quay. He smelled Red Silver and Inkletta long before he saw them, as they were finishing up their cheroot cigars.

"Perhaps someone once told you a cloud of vapors enhanced your effervescent charm," Saint said politely as he limped down the last flight. "Whoever it was, he lied to you."

"There you are," Red Silver said, mild. She took a last drag from the cheroot, and ash tumbled from the tip. She consulted her pocketwatch. "Right on time."

"I don't suppose you've seen Gapjaw," Saint said, ignoring her watch.

"Not yet," Inkletta said. She was regal in a gleaming drape, bangles and jewelry on her wrists and ankles, glitter painted on her facial tattoos. Her hair was a wild cloud, she had not attempted to tame it.

"He's outside, then," Saint nodded. "He wants to make me sweat, but he wouldn't be late. It's important, and he knows it."

"Yeah, sure," Inkletta said. She flicked the stub of her cheroot away to bounce off the wall in a puff of sparks. "Let's go meet this big shot."

"Best behavior," Saint said, stern. "You all remember the briefing, right?"

"Best behavior," Red Silver agreed. "We're on it. Let's go."

The scoundrels traded the cloying heat of the pylon base with the breathless humidity of the quay. They saw the Hammer and Safety standing at the base of the gangplank with Gapjaw. All three were presentable, their tailored clothes long but thinly spun for the city's brief and wet summer.

Grull appeared at the top of the gangplank, a full deck's height above the quay. He stared impassively down at the River Stallions. "Please come aboard," he said formally. "Lord Malicoat has granted you an audience." He paused, focusing on Inkletta. "Looking within and without, we shall see," he said in fluent Hadrathi.

"See and be seen," she echoed, completing the greeting.

The crew mounted the gangplank and joined the thick-necked agent in the shadow of the yacht's bridge.

"Looks like you've found a new employer," Safety said with a smile.

Grull ignored him, eyes shying away from Red Silver. "Follow me," he said, biting the words off, at the very edge of polite. "Please." He led them down an interior ramp to the spacious and compactly decorated lounge just above the waterline. They heard the last strains of harp music fading from the air as Grull opened the way into the luxurious meeting chamber.

Filing in, the scoundrels saw Lord Malicoat seated on the low stage tucked into the bow of the yacht, a harp leaning against his shoulder. Its hinged base was bolted to the stage. He rocked the harp out of the way and rose, smiling towards his guests. "The River Stallions," he said. "So pleased you all could make it this evening."

"The pleasure is ours," Saint said with a stiff little bow. "Your gracious invitation has piqued our interest in the potential of shared future ventures."

"Indeed. Grull, you are dismissed," Lord Malicoat said. Grull bowed, and withdrew. Lord Malicoat approached, steady on the slow swells under the heavy craft. "Please, take a seat."

Concealing their nerves, the scoundrels settled on the fixed furniture positions, all facing the aristocrat as he leaned against the patterned tilework of the fireplace backdrop.

"It appears you have lured Grull away from the Unseen," Saint said. "That could be a problem. I believe he has some strong feelings towards our crew for assassinating his favorite cultist. And taking a shot at him while he scurried off."

"I will handle Grull, thank you," Lord Malicoat said. He rubbed his hands together, his teeth glimmering in the electropolasmic lights as he smiled at his guests. "We will use your war names, yes? Rather than your given names. Since you are here as professionals. Saint Suran, Red Silver, Inkletta, Safety with his metal arm, and you must be Gap-jaw. So that makes you the Hammer," he said as his eyes flitted across the scoundrels. "And of course Niece, perhaps the most famous of all. What happened to your uncle—that fire—so tragic. You have my condolences."

"Thank you," she said, emotionless.

"We are, of course, flattered that you wanted to meet the whole crew," Saint said diplomatically. "Even more flattered that you have committed us to memory. We certainly plan to live up to your investment of attention."

"I am confident you will," Lord Malicoat said. "Every single thing I learned about your dangerous little faction intrigued me further. I had a connection to the Unseen before you clashed with them. The Star, high-ranking operative that you slew, was Marnice Barklage. Few knew that she was a descendent of the Crolaange limmers. I am as well. My mother was Shadiye, who had a tryst with my father and surrendered me to him rather than keeping me as her own. She knew I would have greater opportunities in Barrowcleft than she could offer in Crow's Foot. As you likely know, Shadiye was nobility among her people, afflicted with visions and wisdom. I have striven to extract every ounce of potential from my blood inheritance, her awakened materials flowing within my own veins." He smiled at Inkletta. "But we will discuss that further in closed session."

"Are you still in contact with the Crolaange limmers?" Niece asked, calm.

"Indeed I am, as a patron," Lord Malicoat said as his smile widened. "I heard about you and the Hammer, the dark baptism that you underwent beneath the Gaze of the Fallen Star. To cleanse yourself of the ephemeral tracer of the assassin that was trailing you, back in 48. Such courage! You chose to voluntarily touch on the life force of a Leviathan, however briefly. I am not surprised that the Hammer was so gravely affected," he admitted, "but I am puzzled that you seem to have walked away with your balance intact. That makes you something of a miracle, which only adds to your mystique." He studied her, something hungry in his eyes.

"Indeed," Saint said, "we have braved many dangers." He recaptured Lord Malicoat's attention.

"Those dangers have left you rife with demonic energy," Lord Mali-coat said. "That energy has made you powerful. You are not the first demonslaves I've worked with, of course," he said with an airy waive.

"Perhaps," Saint said delicately, "you could address the substance of our potential collaboration."

"Indeed. Enough chit-chat. We have work to do." Lord Malicoat paused, but no one interrupted or corrected him. He smiled again. "North Port. Your crew is relocating there. You've secured the Old Custom House. And I'm sure you've heard all the propaganda about making the district safe again. But the history is a little blurred, yes?"

"Yes," Saint agreed. "North Port was the earliest settlement in the area. The rest of the city grew around it. But when the lightning walls went up three hundred years ago, North Port was left out."

"The central question, then," Lord Malicoat said, simmering with enthusiasm. "How did North Port fend off the death storm, the clouds of starving spirits, provoked by the warm and flowing blood of the port's citizens, *before* the lightning walls?"

"I don't see how it matters," Safety said. "They used limmer rituals, and those are illegal now. North Port is protected by the Rowan ambient suppression system. The machines drain energy from the Ghost Field, so the ghosts can't take form. Whispers don't have anything to manipulate. With the defense fields in place, attacking ghosts won't manifest. They'll just get pulled into the distillers, and turned into electroplasm."

"Indeed, that was another charming detail I learned about your crew," Lord Malicoat said. "Red Silver was involved in the first live test of the Rowan ambient suppression system in combat conditions, back in 48. I understand you laid a trap in the prototype," he said to Red Silver.

"Sure did," she confirmed.

"Your foe was Razor Wind," Lord Malicoat said. "Apparently he was a talented assassin who blended demonic pact runes into the Whisper ritual forms. Killed your whole family before you brought him down."

"Yes," Red Silver said. "So we have experience with the Rowan system."

"Placement of this new system is critical," Lord Malicoat continued. "You have to have adequate coverage. No pockets where some energy could build up, so a stray pattern of a spirit's consciousness could gather enough plasm to take shape or affect this side of the Mirror with manifestations." He paused for drama. "And that coverage reflects the heritage system that was in place to protect the port before it was abandoned. Before limmers were outlawed."

"Heritage system," Saint repeated.

"The colloquial term was 'the vents.' You've been to North Port, so you've seen them. Posts coming up out of the ground, a few knee high and others almost big enough to crawl into. They look like the vent horns or salvage horns you'd see on a big steam ship's deck. Paint long-since peeled off, purpose unclear. But they have a surprisingly even coverage, along the organizing lines of the city. Where the population is thickest, the vents are the most prominent. And those vents are what I want you to investigate," Lord Malicoat said.

"What, you want them mapped?" Safety said. "You could hire scholars or scouts for that kind of work. They are cheaper than we are."

"I have teams mapping their locations already," Lord Malicoat said with a dismissive wave. "I'm cross-referencing the antique maps that still exist with what I'm discovering now. I need to know more about how they work, and I need to know fast. Digging up a vent horn, you dismantle the street, and find that the vent terminates in a block of stone with glyphs on one side that match glyphs on another block buried nearby. The architects that installed the vent system built in jumps, non-contiguous continuity in an underground network of physically disconnected energy conduits."

"Okay that is unexpected," Red Silver said reflectively.

"But necessary," Lord Malicoat retorted. "I believe these vents drained the energy from the Ghost Field and channeled it to a central point under the settlement. A central point that the founders didn't want anyone to find," he said significantly. "The vents were connected to standing stones that surrounded the port. Those standing stones were removed centuries ago, and destroyed when limmer magic was outlawed." He paused. "I have three. You'll have a chance to study them as well. The Ministry has a few, as do other scholars, and if we need access to those I can arrange it."

"I see," Saint said. "Map the vents, research how they worked, and report to you. We can do that. But you already have teams of experts and laborers on this. You expect violence and trouble with the law or you wouldn't have approached us. More on that, please."

"We are engaged in a race," Lord Malicoat said. "The Spirit Wardens are looking for the same thing I am, and they've got the authority to make my work harder even as they assure their access to anything they want to investigate."

"The Star said something about Spirit Wardens right before she died, a few days ago," Safety said. "A name, Sysa-something."

"Sysavath." Lord Malicoat supplied the title, grimacing at its flavor in his mouth. "The role Sysavath has been assigned for twenty years, and as far as I can tell the same Spirit Warden has borne it the entire span. Sysavath hunts demons, and studies their energy. Her quest is to research ways to thwart and kill them, to close the power gap between the Spirit Wardens and the variety of elemental and Leviathan threats in Doskvol."

"You seem to know her," Saint observed.

"She has pained me at every turn for both decades of her assignment," Lord Malicoat said. "We have similar interests and opposed motives. We are both well equipped and personally formidable. It is a particularly frustrating kind of flirtation," he said, wry. "Our only hope to get ahead of her teams is to exploit her need for subtlety. The Spirit Wardens don't want to admit that they are studying the vents and looking for a central chamber; that would spark controversy and competition and all sorts of headaches. So they're trying to obfuscate their true purpose, just as I am. Neither of us wants to explain to the Ministry or the Church what we hope to accomplish."

"What *do* we hope to accomplish?" Red Silver asked, narrowing her eyes.

"I'll discuss that with Inkletta," Lord Malicoat said.

"And me," Saint added.

"And Saint. Of course," Lord Malicoat said with a thin smile. "If they choose to share that information with you, I will trust their discretion."

"Secrets are part and parcel of our work," Red Silver said, "but privacy is more expensive. What are you offering us for our efforts?" The other scoundrels shifted, uncomfortable and wary as her blunt question squatted unapologetically in the center of the conversation.

"That will be a discussion with Saint," Lord Malicoat said, "but I'll offer standard rates for a week's work, and then we will evaluate the arrangement. That's just the beginning," he said. "I am positioned to assist with down payments, introductions, research, and clearing up legal misunderstandings. I prefer trade in exchanged services rather than currency or Coin." He looked Red Silver in the eye. "Let's try a partnership and adjust our arrangement as needed."

"You seem pretty confident we can figure this out," Red Silver said, keeping her tone neutral.

"Of course!" Lord Malicoat said. His smile was broad and pale, his eyes dark. "The River Stallions have a demon and a god. Spirit Wardens cannot hope to stand against us."

CHAPTER FIVE

The earliest spirit hunters wore masks. They entered a world of different rules, where your name could anchor a curse and the taste of your blood could betray your whole family to a vengeful ghost. For their most famed successors, the Spirit Wardens, the vulnerability extends into the realm of politics and temporal corruption now.

Spirit Wardens erase every trace of their identity. They are scrupulously anonymous. They answer to the Immortal Emperor, not any authority in Doskvol. Titles and roles are assigned, but their disguises, both physical and ritual, make it impossible to know whether the same person is behind the name and the mask when next you meet.

Where we see no vulnerability, we can place no trust. The Spirit Wardens do what they must to protect themselves in their dangerous work—so be it. We must protect ourselves as well, so we will take steps to hinder those who refuse accountability.

—From Lord Dalishar's comments before the City Council in defense of Measure 428: Reinforcement of Manse Privacies (defeated in 712)

"I am intrigued," Lord Malicoat said over his shoulder as he mounted the narrow staircase, Inkletta and Saint following. "I must know more about the Shrouded Queen."

They emerged on the yacht's top deck. Planters boxed in the open air space, with filigree iron lattices containing the boxes of murky water that nourished the roots of the radiant plants. Vines and fronds nodded in the night breeze. Some of them had buds with a steady glow, others had leaves that responded to air currents by brightening and fading. More mundane flowers were nestled between and around the radiant plants, drawing light from them. Four elaborately carved chairs surrounded a low table. The deck lounge corners had globe lamps filled with a milky iridescence designed to compliment the radiant plants, providing a moon-like ambiance.

"Truly breathtaking," Saint said in a properly hushed tone.

"I suppose so," Lord Malicoat agreed. He expertly twirled the framework of a wrought iron globe built into the side planter, revealing a chilled bottle of wine and four glasses. "I was raised in the worship of the Father of the Abyss," he said as he trimmed the wax seal from the neck of the bottle. "I thought the Forgotten Gods were all puppets. Masks, you know, to amuse the Leviathans or lesser demons who crossed time and space to take on whatever aspect human worship wanted to see. It all seemed so dreadfully earnest," he said reflectively as he popped the cork. "What is your experience?" he asked Inkletta directly.

"Leviathans are subtle. I would not claim to understand them," Inkletta said.

"True, but hardly an answer," Lord Malicoat observed. He turned away to pour the wine. "More specifically, what is your experience with the Forgotten Gods? What do you think they are?"

"Incomplete," Inkletta said.

"Incomplete," Lord Malicoat echoed. He turned back to them, offering each a delicate goblet. "What an unexpected response. Please tell me more."

"Have you ever known someone who wanted attention and influence because they were whole?" she asked, her eyes wandering across the radiant plants.

Lord Malicoat's smile was the most genuine version the scoundrels had yet seen. "Marvellous," he said. "I understand completion is the central focus of the Shrouded Queen. She is maimed, fundamentally, yes? Her body, or concept of it, is torn and crippled. So she accepts sacrifices of limbs, digits, and organs from her followers. Over the centuries cults have been banned because they ritually amputated sacrifices from their victims. I understand you, as her avatar, have had contact with a number of cults that cut into themselves. Chop off irrevocable gifts to their Queen." He sipped his wine.

"Both kinds of sacrifice are as old as worship of the Shrouded Queen," Inkletta said, patience thinning.

"Tell me, what becomes of the sacrificed body parts? Do you pocket them? Burn them?" Lord Malicoat asked, eyes bright.

"I'm not here to talk about the Shrouded Queen," Inkletta said evenly. "Are you?"

"I would delight in an evening discussing metaphysics and cult practices with you. But you are right; we are pressed for time, just now. Please join me." He seated himself in one of the chairs, breaking the social convention requiring his guests to lower themselves before him first.

Inkletta sat opposite the aristocrat, and Saint took a seat to the side, somewhat between them. The scoundrels waited as Lord Malicoat steepled his fingers, gathering his thoughts.

"First I must tell you that you are risking your lives to participate in this conversation," Lord Malicoat said. "I wanted to offer you some protection; I weighed the necessity of coordinated action with the risk of carrying the secrets of intensely dangerous and private people. I think Inkletta must understand more completely, but you?" he said to Saint. "I hoped you could trust her and excuse yourself from this hazard."

"I do trust Inkletta," Saint said, mild, "but I would not shirk my role as the leader of my crew. I need to understand the risks we are taking. As clearly as possible."

"Then I will seek to educate," Lord Malicoat said. "So far, there are five known instances of spontaneous hollowing in North Port since it has opened up and increased population. That's a little over a hundred and eighty days. I think there are at least three times that number of victims, but most were not reported or identified properly. I think this hollowing will happen more often."

"I heard about that," Saint said. "People were going about their lives normally, then they were found laying on the ground, or sitting on a bench in a tavern, their bodies breathing and their animating spirit just gone. But why? Normally you make hollows because you want the body or the spirit."

"Why indeed," Lord Malicoat said. "The Bluecoats have not connected the incidents to proximity to vents yet, but they will soon."

Inkletta leaned forward. "What's down there."

"Almost eight hundred and fifty years ago, the Gates of Death were shattered and the Cataclysm followed," Lord Malicoat said, his voice low. "The Immortal Emperor made a trade with the survivors. They surrendered their freedom to him, and he protected them against the death storms. That much is widely known." He paused. "What is *not* widely known is *how* he did it. Have you learned the secret?" he asked Inkletta directly. "You have crossed paths with a few who know the truth."

"I never looked into it," Inkletta said. She could sense her current state; she could feel how she was about to be different under the weight of new knowledge.

"The Immortal Emperor lured a Leviathan from the sea with the ritual sacrifice of hundreds of his subjects," Lord Malicoat murmured, hypnotic. "He pierced it. He cut so deep he removed part of the Leviathan's heart. He knew how to do this," Lord Malicoat continued, barely audible, "because he was the First Limmer. The limmer tradition echoed from what observers could piece together after seeing his work. Each of the settlements the Immortal Emperor ruled in the early days after the Cataclysm was protected by a mass of vital tissue he tore from a Leviathan and ritually embedded under the community."

Saint and Inkletta stared at Lord Malicoat as he gave them a moment for that to sink in.

"An order of demonologists served the Immortal Emperor in those days, and continues to do so today," Lord Malicoat continued. "The Stitchers, they are called. They can sew worlds together. They are the masters of fast travel and ghost doors, of echo realms and dream skating." He leaned back. "The Stitchers created the vents, bound to the undying and flexing heart meat of the Leviathan. Wounded, the demon flesh sought to survive, to reform. So it pulled in loose energy. Energy lodged in bodies was difficult to extract, but the free-floating spirits were drawn into the gravity of the heart's hunger. Sucked through the energy conduits, consumed by an insatiable starvation. The heart used the people of North Port for bait, and the people of North Port relied upon the heart to protect them from clouds of desperate and hateful ghosts."

Inkletta was already assembling the bigger picture. "The Stitchers didn't want anyone to find the heart, so they hid it, the energy conduits not physically connected. The heart could likely subsist after North Port was abandoned, but without flowing blood, the area would not attract the same volume of traffic behind the Mirror." Her eyes widened. "Rowan's ambient suppression system is actively starving the heart. So now the heart is hollowing anyone it can reach."

"I always wondered why the city cut North Port out," Saint said, subdued. "Why leave the original settlement on the other side of your defenses?" He swallowed hard.

"Limmers were outlawed when the lightning wall technology was developed," Lord Malicoat said. "Out with the old. In with the new. The electroplasmic technologies, the spark craft, had no answer to the vents. No way to turn them off. And the Foundation would not allow the system to be dismantled; the spark craft was too untested to rely upon completely. They compromised, leaving North Port intact but empty, outside the wall."

"Why do you want to find this heart?" Inkletta demanded, looking Lord Malicoat right in the eye as she scowled.

Lord Malicoat met her gaze for a long moment, serious. "There is only one true immortality in this world," he said. "Vampires decay over time, their wills are unable to keep a grip through rapid change for more than a few hundred years. Spirits go mad. Only Leviathans drift through the world's foundations unchanged and unchanging, undying, unyielding." He rose to his feet.

"It is possible," he continued, "for the rare few, the truly gifted, to take in Leviathan essence without losing themselves. If they can do so, they become immortal." He paused. "That is how the Immortal Emperor gained his power. How he knew the secret of summoning Leviathans within reach and harvesting essence from them. This is also how the Immortal Emperor's successor was able to depose him to become the Immortal Emperor we now serve."

"What?" Saint said, less shocked and more annoyed. "There has only been one Immortal Emperor."

"How do you know?" Lord Malicoat replied, unmoved. "Because you know his face? Because surely someone would have said something about it? Because there would be a war of succession, or some ripple detectable throughout the empire?"

"It's too big a change to go unnoticed," Saint retorted. "How do you know the Immortal Emperor's throne was usurped?"

"You want the Crown of Isles," Inkletta said, incredulous as she jumped the conversation forward. "You think you can become immortal and seize power."

Lord Malicoat chuckled to himself. "You are very astute," he said with a nod to Inkletta. "That is exactly my plan. The essence of a Leviathan is in all its materials, be they blood, bone, meat, hide, organs... but to extract what is needed to become truly immortal, I would need a *vital* organ to deplete into myself. An eye, or a bucket of blood, or a swatch of hide will not do. I need something woven into the core of the demon."

"This is not wise," Saint said, choosing his words with care. "If any agent of the Immortal Emperor got wind of what you were trying to do—"

"Right," Lord Malicoat agreed. "Agents descend and kill everyone involved, at best. This is a risky move. All known vital organs of Leviathans are inaccessible for several reasons. If the Immortal Emperor realizes what I'm attempting, because we tip our hand, I don't think there is any way to avoid the lethal consequences."

"There are just too many variables here," Saint said, troubled. "There's no way to build a ritual that's going to work to transfer the life essence from a Leviathan's vital tissues to a human, not without experimentation. You won't know what happened with the heart over the centuries; maybe it has withered, but maybe it has grown into some kind of shape capable of self defense—"

Inkletta put her hand on Saint's forearm as she stared at Lord Malicoat. Startled, Saint stopped talking and looked to her.

"Lord Malicoat knows a Stitcher." Inkletta could hardly breathe.

"Excellent," Lord Malicoat said, blinking. "I heard you were intuitive, but you exceed all expectations. You are correct. I know a Stitcher. One who refused to accept the Usurper Emperor, and who was therefore cast out of the Order."

"Cast out and allowed to live?" Saint said skeptically.

"Death was too easy," Lord Malicoat said. "The Stitcher was blasted with one of the mightiest curses available to the profound energies wielded by the Immortal Emperor. He was pierced with a Forgetting. His own mind remains intact, but all who meet him or learn of him are doomed to forget immediately. He was banished to live out his unnaturally long years in suffering and loneliness. He can accomplish whatever short term goal he desires, but he cannot hold power because the workings of the curse are subtle and cruel."

"The Unseen," Inkletta said.

"He became the Tower. The leader of the Unseen," Lord Malicoat agreed. "He wants a new Emperor. One who might break his curse. To that end, he has agreed to assist me, to teach me the secret of how to absorb the Leviathan essence from the sundered heart, to ascend to challenge the Immortal Emperor."

Saint was listening carefully, and he nodded. "But he wants to take his time. String you along. And you want to get on with it."

Only the subtlest tells betrayed Lord Malicoat's surprise as he turned back to Saint. "I'm not immortal yet," he said quietly. "I don't have all the time in the world. The Tower wants to play out his mind games, he wants me to run his errands, prove my slavish devotion to him as an instrument of his will so he might rule through me. I've had a lifetime's worth of placation and manipulation."

"Of course," Saint said. "So you've got a careful course to chart. Make the most of what you can get from the Unseen, the Stitcher—and when you've got it, turn the tables fast. You need to betray the Tower after you adjust the situation to accelerate the timeline of you becoming immortal. But not too much after, or you become the Immortal Emperor and he controls you through whatever nefarious means he has in mind. Right?"

"Something like that," Lord Malicoat murmured.

"And that's where the Star comes in," Inkletta said, thinking fast. "You were trying to recruit her to your cause. Turn one of the Unseen. Through relying on your shared Crolaange heritage," she said. "So when she faced death... she chose your side. Sold you the secret of North Port, the heart. Revealed the Tower's long-term plan for elevating you."

Something like consternation colored Lord Malicoat as he sat speechless, mouth pressed to a tight line.

"You can't trust Grull," Saint said, leaning back in his chair. "Safety overheard the Star's last words to him. She told her agent to sell the secret of Tya and the heart to you—*and* to Sysavath." He sipped his wine.

Lord Malicoat stared at him. "Well. I guess... we are all learning something unsettling," he said.

"Makes sense, in a way" Saint said. "The Star was likely working a bigger picture. What appears to be a betrayal is sometimes more subtle manipulation. Loyalty can be a funny thing. You might be misjudging the Tower. Becoming the Immortal Emperor is a momentous thing, a huge responsibility. Too much power. Maybe anyone who allows manipulation to block their progress shouldn't be helped along to win the crown. There are probably layers of tests, and you might be passing them." He took another sip of his wine.

"Your Crolaange heritage, that may be what altered you enough that you could see through the Forgetting," Inkletta said. "That may be why the Tower thinks you can survive taking in the essence of the Leviathan's heart. You have been primed. Generationally. You may well be part of a very old scheme."

"Astonishing, really," Lord Malicoat said as he leaned forward and placed his goblet on the table. "You know, I am attentive to fate. When I first became aware of the River Stallions, it was because you crossed the Unseen and survived. They assigned the Star to assure you didn't get a foothold in North Port, because some of their divinations warned that you could get involved with the Fallen Star in a devastating way. When you successfully fought back, that was... remarkable. I had you investigated. I found the Crolaange connection, I learned of the dark baptism beneath the Gaze of the Fallen Star... who is Tya, incidentally." He looked up at the rough underside of the bridge overhead. "I can feel the threads pulling together. I believe Hammer especially, and Niece, are fated to pursue the heart and rebalance the whole city. Can it be coincidence that Hammer was touched by the Fallen Star, and now he drinks in ghosts? No. Impossible." His expression subtly shifted. "Given the involvement of fate itself, it's clearly my mistake to underestimate you all."

"Really, we don't mind," Saint said. "Also, it's '*the* Hammer.' A minor point, but still."

"I see," Lord Malicoat said lightly. "I won't forget again." He stroked his chin, and frowned. "Why would the Star tip off the Spirit Wardens?"

"She mentioned Sysavath by name," Saint added mildly.

"Maybe you should ask Grull what else he might know," Inkletta said. "There's further thought to be put into that. For now, I think our attention is best focused on what we're going to do."

"I have my own thoughts, but I want to hear yours," Lord Malicoat said.

"Sounds to me like the Spirit Warden needs to be sorted out," Saint said, casual. "First idea, leak word that information on the heart, or some tantalizing proxy, has been located. Set up a trap. When the Spirit Warden or agents show up, take them out. Repeat as needed. Get Sysavath out of the picture; the Spirit Wardens can assign someone else, ideally someone who needs to catch up on current events, or lacks the experience and passion to be as threatening." He sniffed his goblet. "We've got Red Silver, she's a fine sniper. Some good front line people, and Inkletta knows a ritual that can blow prepared defenses out of place long enough to get some good hits in. We choose our ground, we can deny the Spirit Warden an escape. Sometimes they will kill themselves rather than be captured, so capture may be our clearest path to assassination. They are tough," he said reflectively. "Even if we fail a couple times, the Spirit Wardens get more cautious and suspicious. That slows down their investigation."

"You sure had that plan thought up and ready," Lord Malicoat observed.

"It's basic, sturdy, and generic," Saint replied. "The execution is where the art comes in."

"Then there's the conduit," Inkletta said. "We can feed it some energy, and trace the energy's movement towards the chamber. To do that, we'll need to think up a pretext to dismantle some of the Rowan ambient suppression defenses, and spend some time with relative privacy near one of the more central vents." She scowled. "This will need a ritual. I'll have to check with some specialists to get the right technique prepared."

"There's one more thing," Lord Malicoat said. "I don't think the chamber will be on this side of the Mirror."

"Where do you think it will be? Through a ghost door?" Saint said as Inkletta looked thoughtful.

"The Stitchers use a secret method to secure the chamber space," Lord Malicoat said. "Neither before the Mirror, nor yet behind it. Our only hope to find such a thing is to trace the energy, but even then I don't know that we will find out enough to breach it."

"The Crolaange limmers," Inkletta said. "They might have the answer you need. Their shrine, where they conducted the dark baptism for the Hammer and Niece. It was between also, neither before the Mirror nor yet behind it. They may have the key to getting inside the chamber under North Port. At least they could provide context. Do you think you could find out more about how the shrine is accessed? Anything that could help us locate it?"

"I will look into it," Lord Malicoat said.

"One more thing," Saint said. "You have been sparring with Sysavath for a long time. Why do you think she wants to find this chamber? Surely the Spirit Wardens know what it is."

"They must," Lord Malicoat agreed. "As for what she wants... this could be a path towards ultimate victory, from her point of view."

"Really," Saint said, raising his eyebrows.

"Leviathans are immortal," Lord Malicoat said. "Attempting to destroy them in the ocean is suicide; were they to be sufficiently threatened they have powers and resolve that can come to bear that make the struggles of the Leviathan hunting ships look like slap fights. The Spirit Wardens learned that the hard way when they committed to limmer practices once, using a mass sacrifice to lure a Leviathan up to the beach. There weren't many survivors. Set them back a century of accumulating power, destroyed two generations of their elites. Tore down six Leviathan hunter ships standing offshore to prevent the Leviathan's escape."

"When was this?" Inkletta said, startled. "I never heard of it."

"It wasn't in Doskvol," Lord Malicoat said. "We can discuss it later, perhaps." He smiled. "The point is, the Spirit Wardens have no way to destroy a Leviathan for good. Nor do they have a clear path to develop the capacity to test out weapons, theories, rituals, or poisons. Consider. The sundered heart of the Fallen Star is still interconnected with its life force. Were they to control the heart, significantly inland in a defended location, perhaps they could introduce mortality to a Leviathan. If they could do that, perhaps they could learn to kill one."

"Ambitious," Saint said, sobered.

"Yes. Now. You're going to go back out to your crew," Lord Malicoat said. "They'll be curious." He left the question unasked.

"Not a word about the Stitchers," Saint said. "We don't mention an imperial coup then or now. As for the Unseen, just... they're playing their own game and we don't know what it is. That's true enough. Spirit Wardens, well, they want in on this because they want in on all the secrets of Doskvol and they've got nefarious plans, wheels within wheels."

"Agreed," Inkletta said quietly.

Downstairs

"They sure have been up there a long time," Gapjaw growled, keeping a sharp eye on the two armed guards posted by the door.

"Lots to discuss, I'm sure," Niece said shortly.

"I don't like it," Gapjaw muttered, shifting his weight. "They didn't take our weapons. Didn't even tell us not to bring them. He's pretty damn confident we aren't going to snatch him for a ransom."

"Hey Gapjaw," Niece said.

"What?"

"Shut up." Niece finished her drink, and looked across the lounge to where Red Silver was seated across from Safety. She frowned. "Where is the Hammer?" she said loud enough to get the whole crew's attention.

They were all on their feet at once, but the Hammer was gone.

"He was here when Saint left," Red Silver said quickly. "I know he didn't go with them." They turned to the guards, who also looked alarmed. "Did the Hammer follow them up the stairs?"

"No my lady," the guard replied. He turned to the other guard. "Check the ship. Assure the safety of our guest," he said. The other guard nodded and took off at a trot, calling out.

"Are there secret doors in here?" Niece demanded of the guard. "Some way he could have left without you noticing?"

"We will find him," the guard said reassuringly. "He cannot have gone far."

Red Silver faced the guard. "Send for Lord Malicoat. Now."

The guard hesitated, then his eyes widened. "Lord Malicoat," he said crisply as the aristocrat descended the staircase from the radiant deck, Saint and Inkletta behind him. "Hammer seems to have eluded us."

"It's *the* Hammer," Lord Malicoat said. "You're sweeping the ship?"

"Yes my lord."

Niece stepped over to Lord Malicoat. "Are there any secret doors in here?"

"Of course," Lord Malicoat nodded. He crossed the lounge and pressed up on the molding under a lamp. The wall slid open noiselessly, revealing a shrine.

The Hammer stood in the center of the alcove, dispassionately looking down at Grull, who was curled up at his feet.

"You okay, buddy?" Niece said quietly as she moved to the Hammer. He looked at her, expressionless, and breathed out a narrow plume of chilly air.

Red Silver knelt by Grull and checked his pulse, his eye reflex, his breath. "He's alive," she said, "but if I had to guess, he's been hollowed." She looked to Inkletta.

The others stepped back out of the way as Inkletta approached the shrine. The Whisper knelt, and touched Grull.

"Hollowed," she confirmed.

"You have my apologies," Saint said to Lord Malicoat. "I have no idea what happened, but we meant no harm."

Lord Malicoat raised his hand to still the scoundrel, and he looked at the Hammer. "Anything to say?" he asked.

The Hammer flexed his jaw, but said nothing.

"We'll need Sereen," Saint explained. "That's his assistant. Helps us communicate. We'll find out what we can," he promised.

"Lord Malicoat," Red Silver said. "Is there a secret way into the shrine, from outside the room?"

"Yes," Lord Malicoat said. "One to enter from the corridor, another from the mess hall."

"Did Grull know how to use those doors?" Saint asked, concerned.

"Apparently," Lord Malicoat observed.

"I hope this doesn't come between us," Saint said to the aristocrat.

"The Hammer is a flame," Lord Malicoat said, studying the Hammer's bearded features. "And Grull... a moth." He turned to Saint. "Take your people ashore. We will meet in three days for an update. If you need to communicate with me before then, leave a message at the Nineways Greenkey estate, in North Port." He offered them a distracted smile.

"Thank you, my lord," Saint said with a deep bow. Straightening, he looked over his crew. "Let's go."

Moments later they had passed through the luxurious paneled corridor, up to the deck, and along to the gangplank.

"I thought you were watching the Hammer," Red Silver said in a low voice, aiming a glance at Safety.

"Niece watches the Hammer," Safety protested.

"Niece was on Gapjaw," Red Silver shot back.

"Okay, why weren't *you* watching the Hammer?" Safety demanded.

"Really?" Red Silver snapped as they reached the quay. "Okay, the meet is over. Go tell the Coursers they can go, get some rest, come back at dawn." She looked over at Saint. "Unless we need them for something right now."

"Nothing further tonight," Saint said. "We'll involve them in our plans tomorrow." He exchanged a look with Inkletta.

"So what was the big secret?" Niece asked as the yacht crew unmoored the heavy cables, preparing the yacht to depart.

Saint closed his eyes for a moment. He was pale. Shaken.

"Malicoat was right," Inkletta said in a low voice. "You don't want to know."

"Sounds good to me," Gapjaw said reflectively. "Well, I'm off." He hitched up his pants, and strolled away towards the stairs up to the street level.

CHAPTER SIX

It was always about extracting value from the mud. After the Great Deluge in 223 drowned a pile of miners and filled up the works, the town's future was in question. Best believe when one suckhole fills up, another one yawns open; the torrential flooding washed some sparkly rock fragments into view.

Enterprising rich people checked upstream and realized that the haunted valley was actually an overgrown impact crater. All that murderous water had uncovered fragments from a Celestial Body that crashed down in ancient times. It hit hard enough to crack the Mirror there, and in that clay bog there were treasures. Precious ores, jewels, strange stuff; some of it grew like crystals where the Mirror fractured and the quicksilver behind it seeped into our world.

The site was poisonous and haunted, and pretty soon the Dunslough family couldn't get workers onsite for any wage. Also, enterprising profiteers immediately understood it was easier to get the valuables from the camp rather than from the Mire.

The Dunsloughs solved both problems by dragging together a stone and iron fortress prison they called Ironhook. The courts supplied convict laborers who built the damned place. Then it housed two treasures: the rocks reclaimed from the Mire, and the labor forced to carry out the work.

—From "A Layman's Guide to Curated Recidivism"
by Prof. Canwick Dunslough

"We've got to figure this out," Saint growled. "Niece."

"This way," Niece said to the Hammer, opening the door to the hallway connecting the crew quarters on the piling third floor. The Hammer followed her. Unsurprisingly, Sereen was waiting in the Hammer's room, seated on his narrow cot.

"Sereen," Niece said with a nod as she perched on the stool. The Hammer lowered himself to sit on his bed across from Sereen's cot. "We had an incident on Malicoat's yacht. The Hammer hollowed somebody." She paused. "We need to know why."

Sereen studied the Hammer for a moment. "The fool was bright," he murmured. "He was behind the wall, peeking, and he was so bright with anger. And glee. Dark satisfaction." Sereen looked Niece in the eye. "Malice. It was irresistible. The Hammer was drawn to him. Then the fool was gone."

Niece let that sink in. "Are we in danger?" she asked the Hammer, quiet. "If we are stressed, or enthusiastic? Would we draw you?"

Sereen turned to the Hammer, listening to what he could not say. "Not really," he said. "The fool was... bright," he said again. "Haunted."

Niece raised her eyebrows. "By the Star? His former commander in the Unseen?"

"No," Sereen said. "Litter from many rituals. A lifetime painted and marked by otherworldly influence."

"Some of us are too," Niece said.

"It's different," Sereen said, shaking his head. "The River Stallions are part of him. Of the before." Sereen paused, and Niece slowly looked over at him. Waited.

Sereen looked down at the floor. "The Hammer is hungry," he said in a small voice. "He suffers." Sereen frowned. "Shall I mix the potion so the Hammer can more easily explain himself?" he asked.

"No, not this time," Niece said. She rose, and put her hand on the Hammer's hard-muscled shoulder. Inscrutable, he looked up at her. "Be safe, my friend," she said softly. Then she nodded to Sereen, and left.

Inkletta closed the door, alone with Saint. "Do you need to talk about it?" she asked in a low voice.

"No, I'm fine," Saint said reflexively as he crossed to the narrow window, looking out at the magnificent view. He frowned. "Wait. Maybe." He took a deep breath. "It's a lot," he confessed. He looked sideways at the Whisper. "How about you?"

"Like you say. It is a *lot*. Raises questions." She leaned back against the bookshelf, across the table from Saint. "Big ones and little ones."

"Yeah," Saint said reflectively. "When you're a kid, you have little questions about who you are. Then you get older, and you've got the big questions. Who are *we*, you know? People, families. Then, you get busy. Too busy for that nonsense." He squinted out the window, moonlight draining the color from his face. "Eventually if you get old enough, those big questions come back. Who we are. Humanity. This city. Family. And of course yourself. I figured I had some more years before they would start occuring to me again," he said with a wry smile.

"Are you second guessing our commitment to Malicoat?" Inkletta asked.

"No. No, that's not it," Saint murmured, his eyes following the lights of a boat. Its dim shine was alone on dark waters. "Every human community," he breathed. "Slowly saturating in Leviathan exhalation from below. For centuries." He turned away from the window. "Who were we before the Cataclysm?" he wondered aloud. "Would we recognize what we've become?"

Inkletta considered him, serious. "My my," she said. "Such depth to you. When we get our income sorted out and stabilized, we will enroll you in a course of study at the College of Immortal Studies so you may pursue the cosmic mechanics that flow through all things." She allowed a smile to seep through at the end.

Saint's answering smile was rueful. "You are much kinder in your teasing than Red Silver," he observed. "I suppose that's a good sign you're handling all this more gracefully than I am." He paused. "Do you think there's much truth in it? Malicoat's architecture of conspiracy?"

"I think *he* believes it," Inkletta said. "He may well be right. I don't know of anything that directly contradicts what he said." She thought for a moment. "To be clear, I don't care about the Immortal Emperor. I don't care about secret orders of demon worship, Imperial or otherwise. I grew up in a violent corner of a hostile city. I know that the authority at the top is saturated with evil, and it flows down through the greedy who struggle up towards it." Her small grin was pained. "The great and the good of this city are unbothered by those who starve below them. It doesn't matter to me if demons are to blame or not. I don't care who is at the top of that pyramid. I don't even care about the laws they make," she said. "There is darkness that offers power, and no one pursues control of others without accepting some of that darkness."

"Not even us?" Saint retorted, eyebrows raised.

Inkletta looked him in the eye. "You just shook hands with Lord Malicoat."

Saint blinked, and his smile was genuine. "I really do appreciate my stalwart companions keeping my ego so thoroughly in check," he said. "Here I was offering you a chance to soften this conversation, yay team, but no. You just *went* for it."

Three knocks on the door, and Inkletta stepped over to open it. "Come in," she said to Niece.

"Apologies for interrupting," Niece said as she closed the door behind herself. "I talked to the Hammer. He said Grull was 'bright' and full of enthusiastic malice, so the Hammer was drawn to him. Just like that," she said, snapping her fingers. "He also said we weren't in danger from him—from the Hammer, I mean. Danger of hollowing. I guess he thinks we were part of who he was before the dark baptism, and that's different somehow." She paused. "I don't know," she confessed.

"Enthusiastic malice," Saint echoed. "That doesn't bode well. There is more to this than we can see, we'll have to be careful." He nodded to Niece. "Thank you," he said, dismissive.

"One more thing," she said. "Caden wants a bonus, for changing the plan. Delays, docking fees."

"He does, does he," Saint said, unamused. "You are the Skov folk hero. Sort him out."

"We should pay him," Niece said, serious.

"If we pay him," Saint said, his patience thinning, "then everybody manufactures cost overruns and they milk us dry. It doesn't matter whether he's right or wrong, or what's fair. You pay one beggar, then there's a crowd of beggars. You stop paying them, and they knife you."

"We need friends," Niece said. "We are moving. Angering our allies is poorly timed, Saint. Like you said, I'm in charge of working with the Skovs, and I'm telling you, bad blood here will leak out if we let it."

"Times are tight, we just spent our reserve on the Old Custom House," Saint said.

"Malicoat just gave us a dozen Coin," Niece retorted.

"We're not giving Coin to a barge captain," Saint replied, his tone hardening.

"Give a Coin to me and I'll pay him in currency. I've got some savings." She was steady. "Malicoat caused this problem, let him pay for it."

Saint considered her, thoughtful. She continued.

"We talked about plans," she said. "I had two other locations set up that we could move into if the Old Custom House didn't work out like you expected. What I did *not* plan for was a disruption of the timing. This delay also affects the Fairpole Gondolier Council, who is taking possession of the bridge. We do not yet know which ripples will grow and which will fade. Angering Caden is a stupid risk. He has friends."

Saint cocked his head. "Pay him. That's your recommendation."

She nodded.

"Alright. Do it." Saint lifted a Coin from his waistcoat pocket with two fingers, and considered the heavy disk of metal for a long moment. Then he offered it to Niece. She accepted the Coin, and tucked it in her fist.

"Thank you," she said quietly. "Oh, and I line-jumped Safety."

"Send him in," Saint said with the bare trace of a smile.

Niece stepped out, replaced by Safety.

"The Coursers will be here at dawn," Safety said, weary. "Have you figured out the rest of the plan?"

"We load up the Lilya tomorrow, early, and Caden ships our base to North Port." Saint heaved a sigh. "The Coursers need to protect the shipment, including the *special* box."

"Right. Just the Coursers?" Safety clarified.

"Well, the Coursers, and Niece. I want you to take Red Silver and the Hammer, set out at dawn. At the latest. Go to the Old Custom House and take possession, make sure there aren't... complications."

Safety frowned. "The Hammer? You are putting him back in play already? What about, you know, the thing?"

"I'm not worried about the thing," Saint said. "I don't want to send you in short-handed."

"And Gapjaw?"

"Gapjaw," Saint said deliberately, "is on *vacation*."

"And you two?" Safety said, gesturing at Saint and Inkletta.

"We get to do research," Saint said brightly. "Want to trade?"

"I'll handle the scouting mission. Anything further?"

"Not tonight," Saint said. "Swift blood tomorrow."

"Swift blood to you," Safety said, almost a retort. He closed the door behind himself.

"Research," Inkletta prompted.

"Well don't we?" Saint said mildly. "I've got some background to work up on Rowan's system. And you've got your work cut out for you."

"Indeed." Inkletta crossed her arms. "In some ways, this is foolhardy. I understand that we had to take advantage of this offer from Lord Malicoat, but... we have spent two months working on our transition to North Port. Tomorrow is the day we take possession and put the implementation in motion. We are at capacity just dealing with the move and related schemes. How are we going to do this?"

"We got a pile of resources from Malicoat, and that will paper over the cracks in our plans," Saint replied. "We have a strategy in North Port. Everything is in place. We planned extra to deal with the unforeseen. Our problems bring solutions with them, if we can tilt everything just right." His smile was genuine.

"Time to get some rest, then. Tomorrow is a big day." She paused. "So... our earlier conversation. Is that finished?"

"I have never in my life finished a conversation with you, Inkletta," Saint said. "But it's on hold. If you need to talk, if you *want* to talk, come to me." He fixed his gaze on her, serious. "We are in this together. We've got secrets, and dangerous work. We must stay together."

"Hm." Inkletta grinned, shifting the mood. "What if *I* want a vacation."

"We're done here," Saint said abruptly, but he smiled as he left the room.

CLELLAND HALL, SPARKWRIGHT TOWER. CHARTERHALL
14TH ULSIVET, 850. THIRD HOUR PAST DAWN

Saint limped through the swirling traffic of students, leaning heavily on his cane. As he approached the blocky academic hall, the windows flickered with showers of sparks inside. The flavor of ozone rimed his nose, and a residue of char coated his tongue.

As the heartbeat of the academic schedule pulled and pushed the current of those in its grip, Saint was detached and drifting at his own pace. He took his time with the stairs, eventually closing in on the double doors of the sparkwright workshop at the far end of the building.

Saint left the main hall, following a side corridor to an unmarked door. He let himself in, entering the dim storage room converted to a repair station. The thin woman standing at a workbench swiveled to look at him, her face distorted by goggles and a neck shield.

"Saints alive," she said, sardonic.

"Never gets old," he agreed. "Got a minute?"

"You here for a consult?" she demanded.

"Minimum, sure, we can start there," Saint said. "I have a job for you. A week's work, expenses paid, bonus structure, outside the walls."

"I heard you were sniffing around North Port," she said.

"Would you please take off those goggles?" Saint said with half a smile.

"I strip for no man!" she retorted. "Hang on." Turning away from him, she bent over the work bench, tapping a cabled wand to a plate clamped in place. The wand sizzled, and acrid smoke curled up from her project.

Saint sighed, leaning against the wall and surveying the room. A number of partially constructed prosthetics hung from a row of hooks down the center of the room. The far wall was compartmentalized for stacking plates and rods of metal, and the interior wall was lined with esoteric and mundane tools for metalworking as well as a bits bin and cabinets. An overhead rack bathed the far end of the room in a dim glow from canisters of electroplasm.

"Okay," the woman said. "You here for Professor Flittenback, or Jewel?"

"Jewel," Saint said. "Definitely Jewel."

"Alright then." She tugged off the goggles, hanging them on a stand, and she ducked out of the neck shield. "You know the deal. I'll take currency, but getting my *attention* takes a Coin's worth."

"Pay attention to me. Please," Saint smiled.

"I know your mommy heard that nonstop as soon as you could talk," Jewel muttered, putting up her tools and working her hands out of her protective gloves. She faced him, her green eyes bright in her narrow face. "Go."

"I'm sure you've had a lot of clients looking for your expertise dealing with Rowan ambient suppression defenses."

"Of course," she nodded. "What district are you looking at?"

"North Port," Saint replied.

Jewel made a rude noise. "Good luck."

"You don't know what I want yet," Saint pointed out.

"Don't I? Okay, fill me in," Jewel said.

"We have a Whisper, and we're looking to conduct a ritual. We don't have to breach any heavily defended locations. Instead, we're looking to quietly disable an area of the defense, under the guise of repairing the equipment. We'll need some time. I don't know how much, but, you know, a ritual's worth."

"Better not be human sacrifice," Jewel said, her voice tight, "or I'm out. You still working with Inkletta?"

"Yes," Saint said. "I'll check with her and make sure. I don't know too much about all that; once you get behind the Mirror, I'm lost," he said with a dismissive gesture. "We don't want to draw attention to what we're doing, so we need to avoid destroying equipment or doing a lot of damage, or making a lot of noise. I need a light touch."

"It could work," Jewel mused, "but we'd need more than the technical aspect. There's a grift that would have to go with it. Adepts project their consciousness into the attuned defenses, managing the drain and ambient levels, casting their senses through certain customized equipment. Seeing through mirrors, talking through speech projectors, manipulating door locks and hinges, that kind of thing."

"Right," Saint nodded.

"So in a house defense, they monitor the points of entry and certain vantage points, as well as prestige points to show off to guests. Most of my work has been on manse security, of course. You're looking at public security, and that one... that one is new to me," she said. "I'll have to map out the projectors and collectors, check the thought sleeves, glyph patterns, I'll need to know who the adepts are, that run the segments, and their schedules. Names of the technicians that service the area you're looking at, blueprints, updated uniforms for assigned support. Timetable for your operation, both when you're looking to implement and how long you'll need the system drained."

"Of course," Saint agreed. "You can work with Inkletta directly on some of that. We are, of course, on a clock."

"Who are you racing?" Jewel asked, straightforward.

"Spirit Wardens," Saint replied. "I don't think they know about us yet, but they do know about our patron. They've got some serious resources in North Port. They took over the Hunter's Lodge, fortified it."

"Who is your patron?"

"That's not part of the deal," Saint said. "So give me an estimate."

She considered him for a moment, calculating. "Alright. A week of my time, starting today, will cost you five Coin. Plus expenses, probably three Coin's worth. And our consult, that's one more. Nine, and I'll need five in actual Coin."

Saint slowly nodded, thinking fast. "Done."

"And you brought me a Coin for earnest money, right?" she said. "I'll need the rest deposited with Saltford's Bank. Today. You know the drill, you're a professional," she said with a dismissive wave.

Saint flicked her a Coin, and she caught it, examining it at arm's length with a smile.

"You're on board," Saint said quietly.

"Damn straight," she agreed. "I'll take the day, and maybe tomorrow too, to pull together what I need here and ask around for some background. Quiet like," she said, forestalling any reminders. "Where are you based in North Port?"

"Old Custom House," Saint said. "See you there."

CENTRAL LANDING, THE EASE. SILKSHORE
14TH ULSIVET, 850. FOURTH HOUR PAST DAWN

Inkletta descended the stone steps, below street level but above the canal. The stairs continued down to the water level, where gondolas plied a brisk trade. The triangular end of the block was undercut with a cafe and the offices of the Fairpole Gondolier Council, though there were no signs to identify them.

Inkletta confidently crossed the miniature plaza with open air sides. Her hair was wider than her shoulders, wild, and her facial tattoos simmered pleasantly with the wash of energy flowing from the protective runes painted on the walls. The big Iruvians loitering around the office entry nodded to her, giving way, and she strolled into the offices with a smile.

"Inkletta," called out the trim man standing by the counter inside. He opened his arms, greeting her. "Looking within and without, we shall see," he said in Hadrathi.

"See and be seen," she agreed. "I appreciate your time today, Trajan," she said in Akorosian.

"Well spent, for you," he said with a bow, also in Akorosian. "Any trouble with our plans for tomorrow?"

"No trouble," she replied. "You can take over the Boldway Bridge facility. We have cleared out."

"Exciting times," he said, rubbing his hands together. "Our payment is satisfactory?"

"We will know over the next couple days, it gets a little intricate," Inkletta said. "We trust you. Also, there were two more elements."

"Right," he agreed, reaching behind the counter. "Here is the first." He offered her a narrow case.

She took the box and and tilted the lid open, examining the rune-carved bone knife on a velvet bed. She smiled. "Very good." She glanced out the window. "And I wanted to meet with Griggs."

"I passed on your request," Trajan said. "I also hope he decides to meet with you this morning." He nodded to one of his assistants. "See to it that Inkletta is comfortable, and has anything she desires." He regarded the Whisper. "Just let Tiria know."

Inkletta smiled graciously. "Thank you, Trajan," she said. She turned, exiting the stuffy office and returning to the humidity of the landing. The air was thick with frying garlic, onion, and meat, twined through the body odor and canal murk. She seated herself by the railing over-looking the quay below. Tiria brought her coffee and fried bread. She waited.

Less than an hour later, the sleek craft of the Fairpole Gondolier Council Whisper nosed up to the quay. Adepts hopped to the flag-stones and tied off the craft as Inkletta rose and headed for the stairs.

The gondola was easily double the size of the other watercraft on the canal. Its fabric cabin was colorful and smooth, cunningly worked, and the hull simmered with the enchantments and protections folded into its paint and wood. The adepts bowed to Inkletta, and she nodded to them and boarded the gondola.

"Do come in," the Council Whisper said as her shadow stretched across the wall.

Inkletta ducked to maneuver her cloud of hair through the door, and she slid sideways to rest on a cushion with the grace of one familiar with managing movement aboard small boats.

"Looking within and without, we shall see," Griggs murmured in Hadrathi.

"See and be seen." Inkletta switched to Akorosian. "Thank you for agreeing to meet with me."

"Trajan advised me to do so," Griggs said in Akorosian, almost entirely concealing the distaste in his tone. "How may we assist."

"I need to trace some energy," Inkletta said. "Energy that moves beyond where I can see it. I am mapping a conduit that moves behind the Mirror as well as before it."

Griggs considered her, weighing his response. "I do know a ritual," he said slowly. "We use it to find leaks in pipes, canals. Blood sacrifice, though I'm sure that doesn't phase you."

"It does not," she agreed. "Will I need a human?"

"A rat will do," Griggs said. "The path is burned into the caster's mind. It is not pleasant, nor is it safe. One mistake," he said, shaking his head, "and your molten blood will sear a delta in your consciousness forever."

"I understand," Inkletta said. "That sounds like it might do what I need. I would like to study it."

"You may return with me to the Mistyard. There we can consult other sources as well, develop alternative options, in case this one is beyond you. Or does not fit your requirements," he added as an afterthought.

"I have until sundown tomorrow," Inkletta said in a low voice. "Then I really must be getting to North Port."

"Then let us hope," Griggs replied loftily, "you are a quick study."

FOUNDER'S SQUARE. NORTH PORT
14TH ULSIVET, 850. SIXTH HOUR PAST DAWN

"Smells better than I expected," Safety said philosophically as he looked around the square, simmering in the dim midday warmth. The squat and blocky buildings of centuries past were in various states of disrepair, but massive piles of building supplies were stacked in several locations and a quarter of the buildings were partially sheathed in scaffolding. The shadow of the new Dunvil Custom House was visible rearing up by the waterfront, the new economic center of North Port.

Red Silver spared a moment to consider the cobbles underfoot. "I never thought I'd actually visit North Port," she said. "It gives you pause, considering how long ago people put this street down. How long it's been since people walked on it."

"So many echoes," the Hammer agreed.

Shocked, both Safety and Red Silver looked over at him. He seemed bemused, considering the face of the Old Custom House across the square.

"Feeling okay there?" Safety said, keeping it light.

The Hammer looked over at him. "Yeah, it's fine."

"Movement," Red Silver said, nodding towards the Old Custom House.

One of the heavy doors of the Old Custom House was hanging open. A man staggered out, fumbled with his pants, and started a stream of urine splatting against the wall.

"Classy," Safety sighed. "Let's go introduce ourselves." The scoundrels started across the square.

Dozens of workers were in various stages of engagement spread across the area. Some were resting on benches or piles of stone, others climbing scaffolding or muscling handcarts into position. The square resonated with sawing and hammering, shouting, clattering material.

"You have the gun I gave you, right?" Red Silver said to the Hammer in a low voice as they approached the Old Custom House. He grunted, shifting his jacket to reveal the pistol butt. "Here we go," she breathed, lowering her head so her cowl concealed her features somewhat.

The scoundrels strode right in through the door, bypassing the drunk pissing on the wall. Inside, a big chair had been set up in the middle of the hall, and a man in a greasy Ironhook uniform lounged upon it. The chair was surrounded by goods piled up around its sides and back. Over a dozen stringy toughs with shaved heads sat on benches around the small firepit before the throne or leaned against columns that separated the side gallery from the main chamber. They wore the gray canvas tunics and leggings provided to prison labor gangs.

"There you are," called out the uniformed man on the throne. "I heard something about you lot showing up today. Welcome to North Port," he said with a threatening smile and a magnanimous gesture. "You are now in Meathook territory. You'll find our tribute costs reasonable, for the fine protection you receive in return. Gotta have friends to make it in this world," he explained.

"That's your opening pitch?" Safety said, mild. He looked at Red Silver. "We'll do fine here."

"We could shoot him," she said, considering the leader.

"Not yet. Talk first. We promised," Safety reminded her. She nodded, and squinted upwards.

"I like the skylight," she observed.

"Gives the room an airy feel," he agreed with a circular gesture.

"Oh, we've got wit," the Meathook captain said. He stood up and crossed his arms over his chest. "Bravado. One of my favorite things to crush out of fresh meat." He nodded to one of the biggest brutes, who straightened to his impressive height and picked up the sledge hammer at his side. "Canner, why don't you go recapture their full attention." He grinned, revealing crooked gray teeth.

"Oh, he's big," Red Silver observed.

"No guns," Safety said, both to her and to the Meathooks. "Let's keep this civilized and private. Do the Bluecoats have decent response times yet?" he asked politely.

"Only if we want them to," the Meathook leader retorted. "Weren't you listening? We *run* the Square. Dash, see if they've got bugs in their ears." The long-limbed woman at his side nodded and palmed her stiletto. The crowd of Meathooks fanned out to surround the River Stallions.

"There sure are a lot of them. I think I'm going to kill a few," Red Silver said, dispassionate.

"Like I'm going to tell you not to," Safety said. "Just the ones that use a weapon, yes?"

"Fine," she sighed. "Hammer, start us off."

The big man flexed with startling speed; he had palmed a brick from the loose sleeves of his coat, and he flung it at Dash. The startled woman didn't duck in time, and the brick smashed into her face; she stumbled back, losing her balance.

Red Silver darted towards Canner, who reared back as he lifted his hammer to strike. She shoulder-checked his center mass, and rebounded from his bulk. He slashed down with the hammer, and she pivoted out of the way as she slid a knife free of its sheath. Canner roared as he re-oriented and swung the hammer at her head. She was faster, ducking the swipe and slitting the inside of his knee. He choked on a gasp, stumbling, and Red Silver smashed a rapid fist strike into the face of another Meathook coming up behind her.

The Hammer bodily hurled one of his attackers back to tangle up with two more. Three attackers pounced on the Hammer, trying to drag him down.

An unfortunate Meathook gurgled as Safety whipped a punch into his throat. Stepping to the side, Safety snatched one of his assailants and viciously torqued his wrist, startling the convict and twisting him off balance to flop down on the stone with a painful slap. Safety's footwork was understated but effective, and the Meathooks had to adjust to repeat their attempt to surround him.

"I'm busy," Red Silver grunted, jabbing three quick stabs into her attacker's ribcage; choking, the convict reeled back, and Red Silver sprang to the side, flanking Canner. The big man was cautious now; he spared a glance to the Meathook who was struggling to breathe, making horrible wet gasps as his lung filled with blood.

"Finish them off!" yelled the Meathook leader.

One of the Meathooks that was piled on the Hammer started screaming, his joint in the big man's implacable grip. Furious, the others repeatedly stabbed him, their blades puncturing the armor under his coat.

Red Silver feinted at Canner, drawing his stance to the side, and she pounced. Two vicious strikes with the keen blade chopped into the side of his neck. The impact registered with Canner before the pain did. He stumbled as he clapped his hand to the side of his neck, eyes wide as he began to realize what happened.

The Hammer flung his head back, smashing his attacker in the face, and he twisted his whole body. Another attacker was pulled off balance and down, and the Hammer expertly knelt on his elbow as he drove his head forward into the side of another assailant's skull, smacking him hard enough to knock his grip loose. Desperate, the Meathook pinned under his knee stabbed at him with the knife, and the Hammer snatched a club from the ground where one of his attackers had dropped it. The Hammer slashed a couple strikes across the pinned Meathook, battering his head off the floor, and he rose to square off with a couple of the other Meathooks who had been less enthusiastic to charge in.

Pivoting, Red Silver threw her knife, catching Dash in the chest as the lanky woman tried to surprise her. Dash's momentum was confused, and Red Silver pivoted around and drew another knife; before Dash regained her balance, Red Silver hurled a knife to thud into Dash's gut. Dash dropped to one knee, and Red Silver drew two more knives, raising her eyebrows. With a whimper, Dash dropped her knives, clutching at her wounds, staring at the floor.

Canner roared as he charged Red Silver, bloody and desperate. She ran; he was gushing blood, his cuts were deep. Time was on her side.

"Come on!" the leader yelled at his gangers. He picked up the cleaver with a long handle that leaned against the throne, and deliberately got a good two-handed grip as he scowled at the shifting skirmish.

The Hammer took a wide step to the side, and launched forward. One of the Meathooks didn't re-orient fast enough, and the Hammer slapped his wavering club aside and snatched him by his tunic, slinging him around to smash face-first into the unyielding stone of the column. Howling with rage, one of the convicts led the charge at the Hammer, lashing out with a prybar. The Hammer took the hit on his forearm, and blasted his fist into the convict's chest, completely winding him and disrupting his balance.

One of the Meathooks whacked Safety across the shoulderblades with a staff, and as Safety staggered, another convict risked a big swing with his maul. Safety launched forward, his body crashing into the convict, inside the arc. They both toppled to the floor, and Safety's metal hand jammed a thumb into the side of the man's neck, jolting a choked scream of pain out of his victim.

The Hammer slung a backhand fist across one of the convicts, sending him sprawling. A couple convicts were still nearby, but they had lost their appetite for getting close to him.

Safety squirmed around to get his body weight over his opponent, yanking him up and shoving down hard; the Meathook's head clacked against the paving stones, and he splayed out, stunned.

Canner was stumbling now, his shirt sodden with fresh blood as his eyes glazed. Red Silver rounded a column, snatching up a bucket on a rope, and lashed out. She swung the bucket hard, an arm-span of rope describing its curve, and the heavy bucket bashed Canner's skull. The big man slumped against the column, smearing blood on it, and Red

Silver darted past him. Hopping up, she fired a kick into the back of the staff-bearing convict eagerly poised to strike down at Safety. As the convict staggered forward, tripping over the wrestling match, Red Silver pointed a stare at the Meathook leader.

Then she walked right at him.

CHAPTER SEVEN

Human identity is created by our impulse to meet our needs. You are defined by what you don't have, and how you pursue getting it. Your successes and failures along the way create your story.

This is the essential problem with the aristocracy. Once you provide a human with food, shelter, education, and amusement, that human must need something else. Something unusual. Otherwise they have no identity. When you have a competitive caste who all seek to be defined by needs that the more traditionally desperate human hasn't got resources to think about, those needs become ever more warped and refined.

The wealthy must deviate, and therefore they are deviant. They seek out new hungers, and in so doing, they develop new expertise. Consider, for example, the long road between fermenting fruit to make a disorienting beverage, and a wine tasting festival with critically acclaimed judges.

You will find that nobility are slow to share genuine affection and personal respect, because those are the two most difficult resources to purchase in their highly commodified context.

—From "Formative Concepts for Professional Butlers, Volume V" by Aldar Sifatu

CONTINUED

"This is just foreplay," Red Silver said, her voice clear and sharp as she squared off with the leader. "You wanna go all the way?" She twirled the knife in her grip.

The leader settled into a stance, cleaver extended. "Maybe we can—figure out a discount," he said.

"A discount. What's your name?" Red Silver demanded.

"Hanger," he sneered.

"*Hey,*" Red Silver snapped, tilting her head to the side. "Quiet. The grownups are talking."

The convicts that could still move under their own power hesitated, and stumbled back from the fray, giving the River Stallions some space.

"A discount," Red Silver repeated. "You know, I think most of you will likely survive this little spat, if things end friendly now. But a *discount?* Here's my counter. We pay you *nothing.* Tell your boss we want a meet. And you walk out now. All this," she said, waggling her knife at the goods piled around the room, "is a housewarming gift."

Hanger narrowed his eyes, thinking fast.

"You apparently don't know much about the River Stallions," Red Silver said. "At this point, we are making a decision. Maybe we send you back to relay the message. Or maybe we pin a note on your corpse. With a note, we can really choose our words," she said, mirthless. "Take our time with it. Make sure we're really, really clear."

"This isn't Silkshore," Hanger said, low and savage. "You can't just—"

The pistol report was shocking, booming through the hall. Hanger flew back, smacking off the throne and toppling to the paving. The Meathooks swiveled around to focus on the Hammer, who raised his eyebrows. The gun in his fist had one more shot.

"Take anyone you want to keep," Red Silver said. A far-off bell tolled, echoing behind the Mirror, marking Hanger's death. "This here was friendly. You want to get together a crowd and come back, we *start* with the long guns. Feel free to involve the Bluecoats. Our North Port contacts are better paid than yours." She tugged a folded and sealed paper from her coat, and dropped it on Hanger's corpse. "We wrote a note just in case your boss had trouble enunciating when we were done with our chat," she explained to the wide-eyed toughs.

"Now it's time for you to deliver our message." Red Silver stepped over Hanger's body and seated herself on the throne. She narrowed her eyes. "Get out."

Safety pulled his pistol, and the Hammer continued to stare at the defeated gang. They hesitantly approached the throne and retrieved their fallen leader, and the written part of the message that went with him. Those who could moved on their own, supporting or dragging others. The bell did not toll again; even those who were badly hurt, perhaps mortally injured, would survive their exit from the Old Custom House. There were no further threats or quips. The Meathooks withdrew.

Safety approached the throne. "Ew," he said philosophically, regarding the spray of blood on the throne where Red Silver sat. "Even before all—that—you know this foul man ground his own filth into those... those cushions," he said with a vague gesture.

"I felt it was important to make a symbolic statement," Red Silver said with her best posh accent. She winced slightly. "Are you alright?"

"Oh, this?" Safety said, touching at the trickle of blood on his face. "I'll be fine. Some bruises, some cuts to stitch up." He paused. "I think we probably could have done this without violence," he confessed.

"Oh, agreed," Red Silver said. "But then we couldn't make Gapjaw jealous. He would have enjoyed that little scrap," she said reflectively.

"Vacation," Safety swore, dismissive. He turned to the Hammer. "Maybe we can get Red Silver to post guard so I can stitch you up. Any of those cuts deep?"

"Nothing worrisome," the Hammer growled. "Armor took the worst of it."

"From throne to picket," Red Silver sighed. "Very well. At least we've seen the layout in Saint's plans. I'll head up to the roof."

"We haven't swept the place yet," Safety said, concerned.

"I'll be fine," she said with a wicked grin. She rose from the throne and crossed the chamber, heading for the tower stairwell.

Safety approached the Hammer. "I've heard more from you today than in the last month," he said quietly. "I've missed you. So... why?"

The Hammer squinted around the hall. "Not sure. It's easier here."

"Easier?" Safety prompted.

"Yeah," the Hammer agreed. He closed his eyes, then shrugged at his coat. Safety helped pull it off. He saw the growing blood stains seeping out from cuts in the armor and oozing down at the edges of the tough leather and plating.

"Good thing I brought my stitching kit," Safety said reflectively.

PRIMARY DOCK. NORTH PORT
14TH ULSIVET, 850. SEVENTH HOUR PAST DAWN

Safety took another bite from the bitter apple. He leaned against the stone wall of a warehouse, watching. The incoming barge fought through the low surf under the dim midday sky.

A knot of Bluecoats gathered by the watch tower overlooking the docks. They cast dark looks towards the barge as it closed in. There were jokes, but they were not good-natured, and the tense laughter that followed them was ugly. Safety smiled to himself. He finished the apple and tossed the stem away. Time to move.

The crew of the Lilya secured the casting lines as the Bluecoats marched down the pier. Safety trailed at an unobtrusive distance, approaching earshot as the Bluecoats slowed to challenge the crew.

"We have reason to believe there is contraband aboard your vessel," the gruff Bluecoat snapped at the bemused Skov captain. "We have been granted an exception to your expectation of privacy, and we're going to come aboard to take a look around. Objections?" Without waiting for a reply, he clomped across the gangplank, leading half the Bluecoats to the barge as the rest secured the pier.

Niece stood at the bow of the ship, searching the coastline for a moment before spotting Safety. She did not react, instead turning to watch the Bluecoats as they severed the cables securing the cargo and began carelessly shifting it out of neat stacks to sprawl across the deck. Captain Caden unobtrusively joined her, watching the Bluecoats work.

The Bluecoats were not particularly careful with their sleight of hand. One of them tugged a sealed pouch out of his coat and tossed it among the cargo. "Here, pike," he called out. The leader stalked over and peered down.

"Well, that looks suspicious," the pike agreed. He picked up the envelope and slit it open. One sniff confirmed his suspicions. "This is dream tar!" he shouted, rounding on Caden and Niece. "That's it, then. Smugglers," he said with contempt.

"What? No!" Niece cried out, similarly lacking commitment to the story the scoundrels and Bluecoats were apparently going to play out together. "How could I have been deceived?" She stepped up to the pike of the Bluecoats. "I take full responsibility. I suggest you let the captain and crew go." There was sincerity in her tone this time. "The cargo was sealed when I got it. I could have chosen to break the seals, but in the eyes of the law, the captain and crew are bound not to. They are blameless here," she prompted.

"Right," the pike said slowly as he eyed Caden. The big captain crossed his bulky arms over his chest, and half a dozen barge crew were similarly tense. Three of the Coursers stared down at the deck and tried to lower their profiles.

"You got paid already, I'm sure," the pike said to Caden.

"With a bonus," Caden replied, his tone flat.

The pike glanced at his Bluecoats. "Alright, take this one into custody." He pointed at Niece. "Your name?"

"My name is Asdis," Niece replied. "O misfortune! O ruin!" She extended her wrists to one of the scowling Bluecoats, who roughly clapped her in irons.

A Bluecoat looked right at one of the Coursers, and shoved Niece hard; she smacked into one of the other Bluecoats, who did not yield. Staggered, she was off balance as they dragged at her elbow, forcing her down the gangplank. The Coursers and the barge crew frowned, but made no move. The pike's grin was a petty sneer.

"Now," the pike said, "we commandeer all this," he said with a gesture at the cargo, "to cover court fees. You lot. Unload it all onto the pier."

"We generally charge an unloading fee," Caden said, mild.

"You won't this time, will you," the pike retorted, facing him. "You're grateful we're being so fair-minded and lenient about this flagrant law-breaking." The pike stared him in the eye. "Aren't you, strawhead."

Caden could feel how close he was to pressing the Bluecoat position and forcing them to reveal whether they were bluffing or not. He didn't want to know. He tightened his jaw, and nodded.

"Help out, crew," he said. "Unload all this onto the pier."

They cautiously approached the Bluecoats, and began picking up crates and packages. The Bluecoats strutted back to the pier, and watched.

Niece was pushed from the pier to the cobble street, jostled past where Safety waited. One of the alert Bluecoats caught Safety's eye, and scowled. He peeled off from the group, aggressively approaching.

"You got business here?" he demanded.

"Just resting," Safety replied.

"Rest elsewhere," the Bluecoat growled.

Safety nodded, turned, and walked away.

"Looks like Hanger delivered our message," he murmured to himself.

PORT ROAD. DUNSLOUGH
14TH ULSIVET, 850. TENTH HOUR PAST DAWN

"It's slow, yeah, but that's not all bad," the cabbie continued. "This Port Road is pretty new, and it was built by convict labor, so if you travel it at speed your teeth wanna knock each other out. Get me? Bumpy as hell, especially in the winter."

Saint leaned against the carriage wall, gazing out the open window at the bleak view. The stink of rot wafted over from the eel field, its stone-bounded pools and swampy terraces draining of workers towards the end of the day. Traces of light filtered up through the water from radiant stalks planted at intervals to provide the bare minimum illumination for workers risking life and amputation as they slogged around in the eel-infested bog. Summer haze thickened in the air, obscuring the hulking silhouette of Ironhook that was sometimes visible at this distance.

A drizzle added weight to the heat in the air, but the cabbie prattled on undeterred. "Less haunting than they expected, if you can believe it. Yeah, they've been in North Port over half a year, and only a handful of casualties to ghosts. I can't believe it. Actually I don't believe it," he clarified. "Why would the Ironhook wardens report all the convict 'accidents' if they don't have to? And they don't have to. This little project came right out of the City Council. If they want North Port, they get North Port, yeah? Course. But maybe there's leftover magic, from all the old rituals that used to protect the place, you know. Wouldn't surprise me. Place creeps me out."

The buckboard creaked as the cabbie shifted his weight. "About a dozen more in line before us," he called back to Saint. "We will make it through the gate before the Blind Hour, no problem. Almost always do, only been turned back a couple times when they close up for the night. Lucky you caught me when you did."

"So lucky," Saint muttered to himself. He narrowed his eyes, perking up. Bluecoats, going to each coach. He couldn't make out the words, but the tone was unmistakable. Passengers were handing their travel papers to the Bluecoats for inspection.

"They say the old construction was from 'heritage times' if you can believe it," the cabbie mused aloud. "Heritage. Hah. The easiest nostalgia is for a time you never knew, that's what I hear anyway. But hey, if enough time has passed that we can ignore limmers and pretend all *that* didn't happen, I'm for it. Oh, hey officer," he said as the Bluecoats reached Saint's carriage.

"Papers," the irritable Bluecoat demanded. The cabbie handed down his license, and Saint offered his travel packet through the window.

"Open up," the Bluecoat retorted, rapping at Saint's door. Saint obliged, opening the carriage, and the Bluecoat leaned in and glanced around to make sure no one was hiding. He snatched the travel packet from Saint, and folded it open.

"Michaels Torrent, huh," he said. "Alright, we've got questions. Come with me."

The other Bluecoat with him was on alert, watching for ambush. Saint hauled himself out of the carriage, and the Bluecoat clutched his arm and yanked him down. He stumbled and fell, and the Bluecoat made an impatient noise.

"Get up, you," he snapped.

Saint levered himself to his feet with his cane, and the Bluecoat roughly grabbed it away. "Alright, let's go."

"What about me then?" the cabbie said, plaintive. "I haven't been paid, have I now?"

The Bluecoats ignored him, hustling Saint towards the guard tower a little faster than he could walk on his own.

Stumbling and muddy, Saint was dragged through the doorway, pushed up the tight curve of stairs, and shoved into a holding room the size of a walk-in closet.

"My cane," he demanded, breathless.

The dor snapped shut and a bolt slid into place.

Saint squinted around the narrow room. A bench at the back, a chair with no seat, a pot. A cup was carved into the wall, filled with oil, and a protruding wick burned with a feeble light. Great. He gingerly lowered himself onto the bench, and brushed at the mud smeared on his knees.

The bolt dragged back, and the door opened. A graceful man in leather stepped in, and the Bluecoats closed the door behind him but did not lock it. The newcomer looked Saint over.

"Michaels Torrent. Also known as Saint. I thought you'd likely take the Port Road to join your crew."

"Caught me," Saint agreed with a sardonic grin.

"The boss thinks you're smart, he thinks you'll get the message that North Port is off limits to you scum. But you just don't seem to want to understand," the man continued. His dark hair was pulled back from his face, his eyes were magnetic, his skin had the unhealthy pallor of a prisoner.

"Clearly your boss is wrong," Saint said sympathetically. "Is that why you pulled me in here? To audition, see if you could switch to a smarter crew? I might have a use for you in North Port," he reflected, "but your invitation sure doesn't help your case."

"I heard you were a funny guy," the dark man said, almost to himself.

"Hey, not just funny, also smart *and* good looking," Saint said. "Come on, let's look at how we got here. Dandywine interfered with us, and we took him out. Tracked through the obfuscation and obstacles, all the way back to the Star. You hear how that turned out?" he said, all traces of amusement gone. "We are digging into opposition you don't even know about. The gates that will not open are *broken*. We are coming to North Port," he said quietly, "and you won't stop us. Jace."

"Oh, I'm supposed to be impressed because you know who I am?" Jace scoffed.

"Yeah," Saint replied. "I also know you work for Sir Ousley. You fancy his chances against us? Great, you saw me coming," he said. "I saw you coming too."

Bootfalls were growing louder, coming up the stairs, and Jace cocked his head as they stopped outside the narrow room. A muffled exchange. Saint was composed, patient, gazing at Jace without blinking.

The door opened, revealing a pack of flustered Bluecoats. One with pike markings on his uniform stepped into the room, chin out.

"Hey!" the pike scowled at Jace. "Who the hell are you? Lads!"

Two more Bluecoats pushed into the crowded room.

"I'm Jace, I have a—freelance—" he struggled as the Bluecoats dragged him out.

"That's seriously irregular, I don't know how that guy got into the tower," the pike said to Saint apologetically. "Are you alright?"

"Just fine. I think he's a salesman," Saint said, smooth. "Any trouble with my travel papers?'

"Not at all, Sir Torrent," the pike said respectfully. He handed the papers back to Saint.

"I had a cane," Saint said, mild.

"Right," the pike nodded, and he stepped back out into the hallway and exchanged some strong words with the sheepish Bluecoats standing back against the wall. He returned, smoothing his features to politeness, and offered the stallion-headed cane to Saint.

"Thank you ever so much," Saint said. "Is there anything further?"

"No sir. Enjoy North Port. Everything is in order. Let me walk you back to your carriage."

Saint took his time descending the stairs, favoring his bad leg. He got to overhear a fierce if hushed dressing-down, clearly audible from the office behind the desk. The tower commander reprimanded the red-faced officer that brought him in. Dereliction of duty, compromising of City Watch security, violation of expectations of privacy; apparently the Bluecoat would get some demerits. Jace was nowhere to be seen.

Once out in the muggy swelter of late afternoon, the pike escorting Saint breathed easier. Saint's carriage was third in line now.

"My best to Marn," Saint said to the pike. "You can tell her to expect another big order for her crockery. She does great work."

"Bless you, sir," the pike said under his breath. He helped Saint up into the carriage, and closed the door behind him.

Saint was smiling as he rapped his cane against the roof. "Turns out you were right," he said to the cabbie. "We'll make it through the gate before dark. No problem."

OLD CUSTOM HOUSE, FOUNDER'S SQUARE. NORTH PORT
14TH ULSIVET, TWELFTH HOUR PAST DAWN. THE BLIND HOUR

Saint tilted a handful of currency into the cabbie's proffered hat, and turned away from the cab as the goat grunted and dragged it away. Saint looked over the front of the Old Custom House.

Weary second shift workers were loading debris from the pile in front of the building onto hand carts to remove to burn pits. Light shone out of the upstairs windows of the squat stone fortress. It had no ground floor windows. Still, the double doors were flung open to the fog, suffusing it with light, and the echoing sounds of enthusiastic workers drifted out.

Limping through the doors, Saint took in the scene. A makeshift bar had been constructed between pillars separating the side gallery, and shelving behind it displayed a decent variety of alcohol. A mass of goods was dwindling under efforts to evaluate and sort its contents into smaller piles. Red Silver was unpacking crates behind the bar. The Hammer was carrying ancient battered timbers into the main hall from deeper in the house. Big lamps flooded the room with light, and a central firepit had been uncovered. The remains of a throne had been burning for a while, but the chair was still recognizable in the center of the bonfire. Safety spotted Saint first, and closed in.

"Hey boss," he said. "I thought maybe Niece would get here first."

"Where is she?" Saint asked.

"Still in custody," Safety said. "Far as we know, we are still on track." He looked Saint over, concerned at the mud. "You okay?"

"Jace intercepted me. Our various investments in the South Gate Tower paid off," Saint said with a crooked grin. "How are we doing? Update me."

"The barge was emptied and released, and the Skov crew got away clean," Safety said. "Our cargo was packed into the Dunvil Custom House, and Niece is in there too. We got a nice haul from the Meat-hook leftovers. They didn't want to roll over, so we had a little spat. Killed their leader, sent him with a note to Ousley."

"That was Hanger, right?" Saint said, squinting so he could see his memories better.

"Yeah, that's the one," Safety agreed. "Coursers are split up. Vare-la took a couple of them to pick up the shipment we secured in the warehouse a week ago. If Ousley didn't detect the cargo of alternative furnishings the Gondoliers shipped up here last week, and we pick them up from the warehouse drop, we'll have the Old Custom House operational for tomorrow night. Sukup and Pilege are on site at the Dunvil Custom House. As planned," he said, nodding a little bow.

"Are you alright?" Saint asked, examining Safety's puffy eye and mottled jawline.

"Cuts and bruises, nothing serious," Safety said. "They got the Ham-mer worse than me, and he's over there carrying lumber. Red Silver is fine."

"Good news," Saint said. "I'll feel better when Niece gets here." He patted at his vest, and then remembered.

The click of an opening pocket watch got his attention. He looked over to Red Silver, who consulted it.

"Still early yet," she observed. She snapped the cover shut with a grin.

DUNVIL CUSTOM HOUSE. NORTH PORT
14TH ULSIVET, 850. HOUR OF SONG, 2 HOURS PAST DUSK

Niece breathed deep, her ribs expanding, her guts filling with air. Then out. Thoughts and emotions welled up within her, and she let them rise and drift away.

Her eyes drifted open as she heard a key rattle in the metal door to her cell. She stretched, ready to roll with whatever punches might descend.

The Bluecoat that opened the door had a much more subdued demeanor than she expected. "Please come with me," he said.

"Of course," she replied, polite. She left the cell, and two Bluecoats escorted her down the hallway. No irons this time. No pushing, no harshness.

The Dunvil Custom House was freshly built, its stone cut and shaped within the safety of the lightning wall and shipped out to North Port. Every surface was dusty from the churn of construction, but the smells were still somewhat fresh and the unfinished work had its own charms.

Niece followed the Bluecoats to an inspection room, for sorting out suspect people or goods. A Bluecoat opened the door and gestured for her to enter. Concealing her concern and wariness, Niece boldly entered the room and rounded the table, seating herself facing the door. It closed behind her. She absently rubbed at the raw bruises left on her wrists by the iron manacles.

Her wait was brief. The door opened again, admitting a Bluecoat dressed in a captain's uniform. He was followed by a massive Skov in an expensive tailored suit, his thick wavy hair gelled back and small wire-frame glasses incongruous perched on his brutish features. The Skov's wiry bristle of beard was combed and trimmed, but not tamed. Niece respectfully rose to her feet as the dignitaries entered.

"And here we are," the captain said, formal. "This is the smuggler we apprehended, she gave the name 'Asdis.' But you know how they all use code," he said, disdainful.

"I fear there may have been a serious mistake," the big Skov said, his accent thick. "I have heard of this girl, from friends of friends. She has a reputation," he confided in the captain. "Allow me to introduce myself," he said to Asdis. "I am Cultural Manager Clef, I am with the Ministry of Preservation." The captain flushed with a sudden consternation, realizing etiquette probably required him to introduce the dignitary.

"Manager Clef, it is my honor," Niece said with a bow.

"This is Captain Sillman, he leads the entire company that protects North Port," Clef continued. Sillman shifted further off balance as Clef took over the conversation. "He tells me you are a smuggler."

"I protest," Niece said, earnest. "Times are hard. I accepted responsibility for a shipment to resupply the public houses of North Port, a run that few have the courage to undertake in these early days of the restoration. I did not open the shipment when I took charge of it, and apparently, my trust was misplaced. The Bluecoats examined the shipment and—and they found—" her voice lowered to a shocked whisper. "*Dream tar.*"

"Terrible," Clef said, shaking his head and furrowing his brow. "Did you cooperate with their questions about the true source of the material?"

"I tried," she said in a small voice, her eyes large. "But they had no questions and would not listen. They decided they had chosen the villain to punish for this crime—they chose me!"

"Hm," Clef murmured. He turned to Sillman. "Do you think there might have been a mistake?"

"Of course it's possible," Sillman said, regaining his footing. "However, this individual does in fact have a reputation among the Bluecoats. She is known to be a scoundrel who consorts with dangerous criminals, involved in confidence schemes and theft, among other crimes. She tracks the filth of Silkshore's rackets into North Port, and we won't have it." He set his jaw. "I will, obviously, cooperate to the fullest extent with the Ministry. I appreciate your zeal in pursuing justice. I would remind you that we are specialists in the law, and its enforcement, and we are in a separate administrative line."

"Yes! Oh, I know this, you need not worry about me intervening in your decision about how to handle this matter," Clef said, his voice filling the room. "You will do what is best. I am sure."

"Right," Sillman said, eyeing Clef.

"I am concerned," he said, placing his hand on Sillman's shoulder as he gazed at him intently, brow furrowed. "*Very* concerned. You are likely correct. There has been no mistake. That means there are individuals who are willing to cover for this smuggler. That is serious. *Very* serious! It is possible there is a *much larger* network of corruption here. You may not have the resources to dig it up," he continued, gaining momentum.

"Oh, all indications suggest this is a trial run, a very early—" Sillman interjected.

"That may be!" Clef agreed, "and a thorough investigation will assure it! Doskvol, my adopted home, shall not endure yet another pipeline of outlawed traffic into the safety of its walls. We will bring in an Inspector. Maybe two! We will find *every* infraction, *every* sign of corruption, and make *certain* that those responsible are *punished* and the situation is *righted*. You deserve no less as commander of this garrison!" he boomed.

"And as commander," Sillman said quickly, squaring off with Clef, "I know we must target our resources. Focus our efforts where they will do the most good. We need to handle this in stages—we need to make sure we know what we're looking for. Let me check with the officers once more. Let me make sure we've got the facts straight, and then we can—we can proceed," he said with a nod. "With the bigger resources, and the more rigorous investigation. Yes?"

Clef frowned at the Bluecoat, his hand still on the man's shoulder. "I hesitate," he said. "You already seem to know this girl is a scoundrel. You say she is known to your experts as a troublemaker." He blinked rapidly. "I cannot in good conscience allow you to turn away from such a certain and productive line of inquiry."

"There are other suspects," Sillman insisted. "We're looking at—a Severosian. Part of a hawker crew, testing out a new possible market maybe. Promising initial stages, collecting information on suspects, you know. We don't want to tip our hand when we are looking into various possibilities."

Clef put his other hand on Sillmans' other shoulder, face to face with him. Sillman was a big man, but Clef's sheer size was intimidating. The intense Skov stared him in the eyes.

"You are the expert," Clef said, his voice low. "I trust your command of this district. You know your officers." He allowed a long pause to accumulate. "Do what is right. And if you need Inspectors," he prompted.

"I know you stand ready to assist in pulling together the necessary resources," Sillman assured him. "Thank you so much."

Clef nodded. "It is the least I can do. But now, what of this little one?" he said, releasing Sillman and turning to look at Niece.

"She just arrived in town today," Sillman said quickly, "probably doesn't have a place to stay, so we'll—"

"Oh but I do," Niece said. "I've got a room at the Old Custom House, with some friends. It's a new tavern, a refit."

"Some friends," Sillman repeated, flat.

"Yes, Lady Selraetas, she is taking possession of the Old Custom House. Surely you heard," Niece said, pointing a reproachful look at the captain.

"Your people declined to question this waif, so I can take her off your hands," Clef said to Sillman. He looked to Niece. "You will be staying there, in case they have additional questions?"

"I am eager to cooperate," she said innocently.

"Well then it is settled," Clef said, immensely satisfied. He looked at Sillman. "Yes?"

"Of course," Sillman agreed, doing his best to smile.

"That is good. Swift blood, my friend!" Clef said as he escorted Niece out of the room.

Sillman watched them go, but had nothing to say.

CHAPTER EIGHT

Much ink has been spilled about the legal experiment in North Port. How will the Ministry implement and regulate the Rowan Ambient Suppression Defense systems? The sensational nature of this experiment has been intentionally emphasized to distract from a far more troubling precedent.

As North Port's reclamation began, Lord Kysavant Bowmore was appointed to be Lord Governor of Doskvol while still on the City Council. Of course there was reporting on this event, and a celebration involving a holiday for the citizens as is usual. However, the relentless focus on the new defense technology was a frequent diversion. Those for the system, and against it, described lurid future consequences—sensational speculation to hold the public imagination.

Meanwhile, in the present, the traditional tension between Imperial military and Bluecoats is resolving as both align in the same administrative line. Bowmore is not simply a Council member, he is a foundational authority controlling Bluecoat operations. A flurry of promotions and transfers of establishment officers have unbalanced the incumbent posture in both the military and the watch, weakening tradition and refocusing leadership. We have yet to see the outcome. If Imperial soldiers are no longer isolated from Doskvol's pervasive local corruption, the potential for criminal profit is profound.

—From "The Overview Political Journal" for Kalivet 46, 850, by Evanlina Setter

"You travel in style," Niece observed in Skovic.

"Amazing what you get used to," Clef agreed, looking out the cut and polished glass of the coach window. The coach gently rocked on deep springs as the goats pulled it through central North Port. "You look well. But maybe a bit worn." There was concern in his eyes. "You carry a lot for one so young."

"So do all our people, in these days," Niece agreed. "Thank you for coming. Means a lot to me."

"Happy to help. It has been a good year," he said. "I have learned so much. Life is often so unpredictable."

"Like North Port," Niece agreed. "Submerged for so long neath the Ghost Tide, but now presenting opportunity for new life. We stake our hopes and schemes on a place that was beyond reach just two years ago." She hesitated. "You and Saint. No hard feelings, right?"

"I believe we are past it," Clef said, studying his hands. "All of us hurt people to get what we want. Justice is difficult to see, vengeance is so... subjective. It is childish to hold on to past grudges, when you need your hands free to seize a better future." Clef cleared his throat. "Saint showed me that. A useful lesson for our people, trying to make a life among our oppressors."

"You sound like a politician," Niece teased, hiding a smile.

"Well I *am* a bloodthirsty thug," Clef agreed, grinning. "So, yeah."

The coach rattled to a stop in front of the Old Custom House. One of the four Ministry guards with Clef hopped off the footboard and opened the door. The retractable steps snapped down, and the coach shifted as Clef stepped out. He turned to help Niece out of the coach. Two guards escorted Clef into the Old Custom House.

"There you are!" Saint cried out effusively. "Welcome to the Old Custom House!"

Trestle tables with benches lined the hall, and the fire pit in the center was encircled with comfortable chairs. The air was filled with a mix of smells; basement damp, frying bread, fresh wood, dust. Wall hangings brightened the stone, and workers were laying down thresh straw on the floor. Sounds of construction and talk echoed from deeper in the fortification.

"Good to see you," Clef replied. "And all this. Not what I expected. You just arrived today?"

"Just today," Saint agreed. "But we had a plan." His devilish smirk was somehow endearing. "And thank you so much for being part of it. Did the captain give you any trouble?"

"He played his role and we played ours," Clef said. "He did not want to let our darling Asdis go. But what could he say to keep her?" He grinned, his teeth glinting in the wiry thatch of his beard. "Sometimes I think this is the best armor there could be." He pressed his hand down his black tailored coat.

"Consider this a gesture of our thanks," Saint said, offering a box to Clef with a broad smile.

Clef took the case and tilted it open. "Exquisite," he murmured, lifting the bone knife from its velvet bed and examining the carvings along its length. "Finding this cannot have been easy."

"Of course not," Saint agreed. "Would you like to stay for some frybread?"

"Certainly," Clef said. "Then I will take my people to the Peach Bucket for the night, until the gates open in the morning. I assume you do not have quarters for rent yet."

"Not even close," Saint said. "Speaking of hospitality, we are still on for that shipment of crabs tomorrow, right?"

"All arrangements have been made," Clef nodded. "They will arrive at midday."

"You have our thanks," Saint said. "Nobody gets much sleep until we have our foothold in North Port squared away. Enough of that! Come have a drink with me," Saint said, clapping Clef on the shoulder and leading him towards the fire pit as the Ministry guards watched, expressionless.

Red Silver strolled up to the guards bearing a tray with two mugs. "Something to drink?" she said.

"No, thank you," one of the guards replied. She nodded, and returned to the bar, where Safety was polishing sturdy crockery and setting it behind the counter.

"Hell of a first day," Safety muttered.

Red Silver tossed back a drink. "It's not over yet."

HABITATION CHAMBERS, THE CIRCULATORY, THE EASE. SILKSHORE 14TH ULSIVET, 850. HOUR OF FLAME, 5TH HOUR PAST DUSK

Gapjaw breathed out through his nose, releasing plumes of smoke. He regarded the glowing bowl of his pipe, then looked back up at the rippling curtain of light stretching between towers of the lightning wall.

He heard the scuff and shift of movement behind him, through the open door. He did not turn.

Kashindi joined him in the garden, crossing her arms over her chest, taking in the sight of the lightning barrier. Neither spoke for a while.

"I checked the sheets," Kashindi said. "I didn't find any nettles. Perhaps they stuck in you, and you brought them out here."

"Restless," Gapjaw muttered. "Without rest." He shook his head, then knocked out the bowl of his pipe on the low garden rail. "The nettles are in my mind."

"Tell me about them." Kashindi seated herself on the bench, and Gapjaw lowered himself to sit next to her.

"Today was a big day for my crew," Gapjaw said quietly. "A big day. We planned for it, for a long time. Moving our operations to another district." He flexed his jaw. "Nothing stays the same. Not forever." He looked to Kashindi. "Tell me it will be okay. Tell me everything is alright."

"Oh, Colvin," Kashindi sighed. "Today was a big day for them. So it is a big day for you too. Of course it hurts to step out of your harness. The work that scars you also tells you why you are valuable. It is the same for me," she said, looking down at her knobbled hands. "The soil and the wash are unforgiving to flesh. But I do not think of what happened to my body, until after I think about those I have supported." She looked him in the eye. "Those I supported have made the world better, so the price I paid for them is an honor I carry, written in my flesh so it is always with me. I want that for you."

"That's really not comforting," Gapjaw observed. "I am not so sure my scars made the world better."

"You have more to give," Kashindi said. "Your life is not over. But your flesh will not support all things, for all time. And when it gives out, you must be ready to put down your tools and walk away from your work." She leaned against him. "I want you to be ready to do that, with no nettles. No regrets."

"Are you?" he asked quietly.

"This very moment," she said.

He flexed his jaw. "I'm not sure." He wiped the sweat from his face. "Maybe tomorrow we can visit the Starwalk Wall."

"Yes," she agreed. "That would be nice." She pressed his hair back along his head, smoothing it. "How are your nettles? Do you think you might be able to lie down?"

"Soon," he said. "Maybe. You didn't tell me everything will be alright."

"*Everything* doesn't matter," she replied. "If what's in here is alright," she continued, stroking his hair again, "and here," she touched his chest, "then you can face life and death with equal calm."

"You know, that's what they teach warriors," Gapjaw said with a rueful smile.

"All of us are at war," Kashindi agreed. "Just as much blood spilled, just as many futures ended, on these streets. Just as dangerous and destructive as a battlefield. You *are* a warrior. So am I. Right now, just at this moment, I am on a rescue mission," she said with a private smile. "I have located a good man, trapped, mired in filth and danger and corruption. If we are both very brave," she said with a gentle prod, "I may yet free him."

Gapjaw looked down at his hands and did not respond.

Kashindi gently kissed his cheek, then rose and went inside.

After a few minutes, Gapjaw followed.

REAR DOCK, DUNVIL CUSTOM HOUSE. NORTH PORT
14TH ULSIVET, 850. HOUR OF PEARLS, 6 HOURS PAST DUSK

"This is insane, you know," Safety observed. He leaned back on the roof of the warehouse, with clear sight lines to the rear of the Dunvil Custom House.

Red Silver looked over at him, hugging her knees. "Their security is decent, I guess, but this is pretty low risk. You getting soft?"

"I don't mean *this*," Safety said with a gesture at the fortification. "I mean trying to set up operations in North Port while handling the Malicoat business at the same time."

"Well we can't do what Malicoat needs us to do if we're in Silkshore," Red Silver said, "so we have to get set up here. And we can't wait until after we're set up, not if we're racing Spirit Wardens. So. Insanity it is." Her mirrored glasses seemed out of place in the thick darkness.

"Speaking of insanity," Safety said, "I hope Wringleton is okay in there. She got stuck in a box, what, eighteen hours ago? Twenty?"

"Niece got her packed in a crate on the approach to North Port, so probably about fourteen hours ago. Even so, not a job I'd want," Red Silver mused. "As long as the Bluecoats didn't stack crates on top of hers when they took our cargo into the impound, we should be fine. And if they're burying cargo marked 'fragile' then they are too stupid to run a port." Red Silver looked over at Safety. "She's young and limber. She'll do alright. But if she doesn't meet us at the window, we'll go in after her."

"I don't like our odds if we have to go into the impound," Safety said. "Search for cargo, avoiding notice long enough to get her out, and *then* trying for the strong room seems ambitious for the two of us."

"Well, if we were after something lighter, we'd have let Wringleton handle the whole thing." Red Silver sniffed, and winced, glancing upward from behind her mirrored glasses.

"How is Nails doing up there?" Safety asked.

"Oh, we're learning about the ceiling," Red Silver said through her teeth. "There are more ghosts between the ground and the moon right now than you care to know about. He's got to keep it pretty low."

"I'm surprised that particular problem doesn't come up more in the city," Safety said.

"The lightning walls keep the death storms at a distance, and the ghost clouds don't usually drift high enough to clear the walls, not without being attracted to them or repelled from them or however that works," she said with an offhand gesture. "But here? I guess the ambient suppression defenses feel like a blank spot to the ghosts. It's a whole different...thing." She frowned.

The scoundrels sat quietly for a while. The noises of North Port were far more subdued than the ambient night sounds in the eternally rustling cage of Silkshore.

"I'll feel better if tomorrow goes well," Safety said. "I still think we're really, really exposed. If Saint overestimated or underestimated Ousley, we could get grabbed. Maybe when we're separated, or maybe all together. And this whole thing ends bloody."

"That's why we have contingency plans," Red Silver said. "Saint may be a little bit ridiculous, but he's sharp when it comes to manipulating people. We sunk a fortune into investing in people around North Port, we got a *lot* of background on a *lot* of key players. And we are pretty good at thinking on our feet for the occasional sideways lurch."

"Like Gapjaw taking a vacation right before we go in," Safety grumbled.

"Don't be a child," Red Silver sighed. "Saint thinks in grifts. We'll need a fresh face if we have to pull a con after we're stuck in. Gapjaw doesn't come to North Port, isn't associated with us. So he can arrive late and do what we need to do. It's a backup plan."

"Gapjaw?" Safety said, surprised. "I don't know. He's kind of old. Slow. And a little stupid."

"Yes," Red Silver agreed. "But he's solid when you need someone to get in position and pull you out of the fire. Creaking bones, if you trash Gapjaw like this when he's not around, I can only guess what you say about me."

"You have no idea," Safety said. "Also, you stick up for him when he's not here, but you insult me to my face nonstop."

"Yeah, I wonder how we interpret that," Red Silver mused. She clicked her pocket watch open, and nodded. "Hey. Time to go. Shift change in a few." She tucked her watch away, then rose to her feet and stretched. She crouched down to hang from the edge of the roof and drop into the alley.

Safety heaved a deep sigh, picked up the heavy pack, and followed.

The scoundrels stalked along the edge of the stone wall encircling the Dunvil Custom House compound. A conduit along the top of the wall hummed, energized with electroplasmic charge. They reached the corner, where an interchange was in a cage, the final built-in casing incomplete.

"Do your thing," Red Silver whispered, glancing around the shadows.

Safety was already working, unlimbering the collapsed lightning hook and straightening the pole, tightening the cuff to hold it in place. The pole had a compact electroplasmic charge cell built into one end, and the opposite end had an adjustable cable loop. Safety flicked it on and adjusted the flow. In the glimmering light of the wire, he squinted up at the exchange.

"This ought to do it," he muttered. "These go down all the time." Careful, he extended the lightning hook. Energy arced between the interchange and the hook, and with a burst of sparks, the interchange reset and the hum of the conduit went silent.

Leaning the hook against the wall, Safety hefted a bundle, and let it swing back so he could hurl it up. The bundle was a thick mat, and it unrolled upward, then flopped over the wall. Safety cupped his hands, providing a foothold for Red Silver, and boosted her up to scramble atop the wall. She lowered her hand, braced, and he jumped up to clamber over. She dropped beside him. Leaving the mat over the conduit, the scoundrels stealthed towards the rear dock, slinking into earshot of the guards at the back door.

"You're right, it's out," one guard said with some heat, "but I didn't notice it and neither did you. It's almost shift change. Let shift four deal with it."

"I'm just saying, the regulations—" muttered the sullen guard.

"—state that I get to go drown my troubles in some beer after six hours of your whining," the other guard growled.

The conversation was interrupted by the dull tolling of the bell in the Dunvil Custom House tower. Six strokes, six hours past dusk. The guards ducked inside by the time half the strokes reverberated out. Before the bell was stilled, Safety and Red Silver had climbed the ladder by the door, up to the balcony overlooking the rear dock.

They spotted the pale oval of a face in the center window, and they padded over to it. The window cracked open.

"Good job, Wringleton," Red Silver whispered. "Any trouble?"

The smallest Courser shook her head, almost invisible in her black bodysuit. Safety and Red Silver ducked in through the window, closing it gently. They followed Wringleton down the dimly lit corridor, through a door that was supposed to be secure. The impound strongroom was lined with shelves, and less than a quarter of it was currently loaded up with high-value contraband. They reached the back of the room, and Wringleton brandished a shiny new key. She opened the walk-in iron strongbox at the back of the secure room.

"There they are," Red Silver said with satisfaction. She turned to Wringleton. "Go put the key back. We'll see you outside." She turned back to the open strongbox and hefted a metal-bound box, grunting with the weight. Safety picked up the other one, gently, and glass clinked inside. They managed as best they could, returning to the window and climbing out quietly.

They left the window open, as they were running out of time. Safety quickly snapped a harness around the first box as Red Silver climbed down, and he lowered the box to her. She released the harness, which he pulled up to put on the second box. As he lowered it, footfalls were audible behind the back door. The moment Red Silver had the box, Safety released the rope to flop down, stranding him on the balcony. Red Silver crouched just out of sight of the back door, breathless, as the door opened and two guards stepped out.

"Ugh, it's like an armit out here," one guard said.

"Better than basement duty," the other guard retorted. "I know there aren't supposed to be any ghosts around here, cause of the Rowan system, but damn." He shivered. "This place is creepy."

"Hey, back west corner. Looks like the interchange shorted again," the first guard observed, brow furrowed.

"Sure does," the other guard agreed. "I don't know what they pay third watch for. I'll go get the technician. Stay sharp."

"Yeah, sure," his partner grinned. "I don't think anybody is stupid enough to hit the Dunvil Custom House."

"Never underestimate a drunk idiot horny for cash," the second guard replied, sage. He went inside, leaving one guard at the post.

A stack of tiles shifted and rattled, at the far end of the porch. Frowning, the guard approached, one hand on his pistol. The construction supplies were shadowed, several paces away from the railing.

"Is anyone there?" he demanded as Safety quickly withdrew along the balcony above, and Red Silver strained to quietly move one of the heavy boxes. The guard determined there was no one around the supplies, and returned to the door. By then, Safety was down the ladder and following Red Silver, carrying the second box.

With practiced ease, the scoundrels coordinated their efforts to launch Red Silver up to the top of the wall. Safety tied the boxes together and climbed the wall, then Red Silver helped him drag them up, over, and down. Safety dropped down and stowed the boxes and the lightning hook in a nearby handcart, and covered them with the mat they had tossed over the conduit, while Red Silver perched on the wall.

The interval seemed to stretch on forever, then Red Silver spotted the flitting shadow of Wringleton darting towards the back wall. At the same time, the back door opened, and a technician with a tool kit shuffled out, squinting towards the dark corner of the back wall.

Wringleton sprinted, leaped, and kicked off the wall. Red Silver's outstretched hand caught hers, and the slender thief slung up and over, dropping on the other side, landing with an acrobat's grace. Red Silver slid down, and the scoundrels withdrew into the night, the handcart's clattering progress absorbed into the ambient sounds of North Port.

OLD CUSTOM HOUSE, FOUNDER'S SQUARE. NORTH PORT
14TH ULSIVET, 850. HOUR OF WINE, 8 HOURS PAST DUSK

Some instinct roused Saint. His eyes drifted open where he slumped in the chair, illuminated by the last coals in the firepit, and for a long moment he did not remember where he was. Blinking, he shifted in his seat. He froze, and woke fully.

The Hammer sat upright in the chair across the firepit, looking Saint in the eye.

"Well hello," Saint said cautiously. He cleared his throat. "How are we doing?" Pushing at the arms of the chair, he straightened.

"I think I'm starving," the Hammer muttered.

"I can get you some food," Saint said. "We've got some tins of fish, some bread, some cheese. Sound good?"

"I don't feel the past anymore," the Hammer said, his voice gravelly with disuse. "I don't feel the future. I barely feel the present. All I can reach... all I experience... just the moment. The occasional moment." The directness in his eyes was unnerving. "That starves a soul. When that's all there is. We weren't made to live on so thin a diet."

"I... I don't have any *time* on the menu," Saint said, pushing the vivid image of Grull's convulsed features out of his mind.

"I am becoming something," the Hammer said. "Something I am pretty sure I don't want to be."

"Like a vampire?" Saint said.

The Hammer did not respond, but his stare continued boring into Saint.

"Are you looking for a way out?" Saint asked quietly.

"No," the Hammer growled. "This... isn't forever. Now is forever. But... I will know... a future." His brow clenched with effort, but words wouldn't come.

"When is the last time you ate real food?" Saint said. The hollowness under the Hammer's cheekbones and around his eyes seemed exaggerated by the dying fire. There was still obvious strength in his bandaged body. Saint slowly realized he had not seen the Hammer eat in quite a while, and with blood loss compounding possible breakdown, the Hammer could be in danger. "I'll get you something." Saint rose, sniffing at the residue of sleep in his sinuses, and limped towards the bar.

The front door was propped open, and Saint glanced over towards it to see Sukup leaning in.

"Hey boss," she said. "They're back."

Saint signaled he heard, and continued to the bar. Glancing over the hastily stocked shelves, he saw half a loaf of bread. He picked it up, and turned to see the Hammer slumped in his chair with his chin on his chest. Saint hobbled over to him, and checked for a pulse.

"We're back!" Red Silver called out, almost swaggering as she approached. She saw Saint's hand on the Hammer's neck, and frowned. "Everything alright here?"

"It's the Hammer, he doesn't have a pulse," Saint said, alarmed. Leaning forward, he tugged at the Hammer's shirt, opening it.

"Hang on, relax," Red Silver said. "The Hammer doesn't have much pulse these days. He has, like, one or two heartbeats a day." She reached Saint's side.

Saint stared at her. "Say that again."

"I don't understand it, but it's part of his whole, you know, ghost eating thing," she said with a gesture summing him up. "Niece is worried about him. She said his heart has been slowing down for the last couple months."

"Niece said? To you, but didn't tell me?" Saint demanded.

"You've been working hard, boss," Red Silver said. "Digging into all this. Your head has been full," she said, tapping her temple. "Not a lot of extra room. But you got our North Port plan set up," she said with a wave around the room. "And our next moves, with the Circle of Flame, and the Weeping Lady, and all that."

"Yeah, but I need to know what's going on in my crew," Saint said, sharp.

"Why don't you?" Red Silver retorted. "Who are you blaming for that?"

Saint scowled, so Red Silver continued.

"You aren't upset because the Hammer might be in danger. You are upset because he might not be reliable, he might screw up your plan. So dial it back a notch before you get righteous. You got your schemes, and I'm on board for that. But don't pretend it's something else." She paused. "I'm not here to criticize you. Especially not in the middle of the night. We're back, we got Wringleton out undetected, got the score. Safety is putting it away. We are set for tomorrow. So. We good?"

Saint took a step back. "Yeah. Yeah, we're good. Get some rest."

She nodded. "Big day tomorrow."

"Big day tomorrow," he agreed.

Red Silver passed him, headed deeper into the house.

Saint lowered himself back into his chair, studying the Hammer's senseless form. Eventually, he slid out of the moment, drifting into sleep.

CHAPTER NINE

North Port, as a name, represents a series of moves to push the Skovs out of their own settlement. The district was built around the original Skov port named Doskovol, literally "the Skov's coal." The Skovic king's coal mine motivated construction of a port, to ship the coal home.

The Imperial Navy's cartographers called the settlement North Hook, due to its positioning as a launch point towards Tycheros. The name didn't catch on, because the Akorosian nobles who retreated to Doskovol fleeing tensions in the Capitol refused to be defined by an Imperial naval designation. Under the weight of the confusion and partisan signalling, both Doskovol and North Hook were corrupted in common usage, splitting into "Doskvol" and "North Port."

The Akorosians imported all the resources they needed to take over. They pushed the Skov founders out of all decision making, and almost all profit. The port's new masters kept the local Skovs on to do the work.

—From "Scrying Upon the Future: Ruminations on Post-Unity Skovic Options" by Craliegh Stant

Red Silver snapped her glasses open and ducked into them, schooling her features to blandness. She carefully stretched her aching leg, feeling the pressure shift. Sitting across the firepit, Saint was frowning as he rubbed his leg.

"Trouble, boss?" Niece asked as she approached the firepit.

"Yesterday felt like rain, but today feels like we're going right into winter," Saint winced. He looked to Red Silver. "You feel it too."

"I'll manage," Red Silver said.

"Well you look *extra* dressy today," Niece said to Saint with a smile. "And *you* look like you're headed to the Governor's Promenade," she added, taking in Red Silver's noble costume.

"It's the watch," Red Silver agreed, patting her embroidered dress pocket with her silk-gloved hand. The leather of her tall boots creaked as she flexed her leg.

"If I was a corrupt official, I would find both of you totally convincing," Niece teased.

"Windy!" Safety exclaimed, striding into the hall through the open doors. The lace at his collar and wrists was tousled, his hair wild. "It's like the sky is trying to claw us right off the coast."

"And that's everybody for the morning update," Saint noted, looking over the bleary Coursers standing by the bar drinking their breakfasts. Rising, he rapped his cane against the arm of the chair, getting their attention.

"Big day," Saint said, surveying the hall as his people quieted and faced him. "We have a lot of connections to make, a lot of things that must *absolutely* go right. If we make mistakes today, we scramble, and we likely lose friends. You get to have good days and bad days. But today *cannot* be an off day, got it?" He half smiled to soften, but not erase, the seriousness of the situation.

The scoundrels generally muttered agreement, and he nodded. "Alright, let's review. Red Silver."

"Check in as Lady Selraetas," she said, dropping a curtsy, "at Dunvil Custom House. Then visit Sir Ousley."

"Yes. Safety." Saint turned to the frilly rogue.

"Go with Red Silver, make sure it's all smooth. Then advertise about tonight," Safety said.

"Right. Niece." Saint pointed at her.

"Meet the shipment coming in at the docks, drum up some more staff, and make sure everything is ready for tonight's big opening," she said.

"Good. You've got payment arrangements all set?" Saint clarified.

"You bet, all taken care of," Niece nodded.

"Great. Varela," Saint said, "what are you and the Coursers going to do."

"Spread the word," Varela said with a big smile. "Cover the docks, talk to the day laborers, the Peach Bucket, Heritage Bunker, and the off-duty guards at the Dunvil Custom House barracks."

"And?" Saint prompted.

Varela blinked. "Uh, and Reclamation Point, let them know too."

"And how do you all move today?" Saint said.

"Pairs, nobody is alone," Varela answered.

"Okay good," Saint said. "Keep an eye out for possible recruits. Pocket money and little bribes, on the table, load up on your way out. Questions."

"Yeah, is Inkletta coming back? What about Gapjaw?" Varela asked, daring.

"Inkletta will be back tonight. Gapjaw is still on vacation, but he'll catch up later," Saint said. "Anything else?"

"What about Malicoat's business?" Safety asked.

"We'll handle that tomorrow," Saint said. "Wheels are in motion, and I'm going to set some things up today. We are on it." He paused. "Anything *else*. Okay. Get to it." He nodded decisively, and the scoundrels headed to the table to pick up their currency.

Red Silver moved to intercept Saint. "Are you planning to send the Hammer with us?" she asked in a low voice.

"I want him to do some... self care, or something, today. Stick close to home," Saint said. "I'm concerned."

"So if things go wrong with Ousley. You have a backup plan, in case we get captured or killed. Right?" she pressed.

"If you stick to the plan, you should be fine," Saint assured her. "He won't expect someone to show up on his doorstep before lunch. I mean... if you get captured, then yes, I think we can spring you. I've got some moves there." He put his hand on her shoulder. "Try not to get killed," he said. "I can't fix that for you."

"This is a really bold move," Red Silver pointed out. "Pretty much everything today."

"It is," Saint agreed. "I have a lot of trust in you two." He smiled. "Mainly you. Besides, you heard my speech, right? No mistakes today. You'll be at your best, and you will prevail," he said with confidence.

"That's—just—*so great*," Red Silver gritted out. She turned, spotting Safety. "Alright, let's go."

CENTRAL HALL, DUNVIL CUSTOM HOUSE. NORTH PORT
15TH ULSIVET, 850. FOURTH HOUR PAST DAWN

Red Silver glided into the central hall, Safety as stoic and handsome as he could be at her side. She approached the front desk, an edifice built into the end of the room and looming over the supplicants that approached it. The desk officer smiled at her, eyeing her costume.

"Good morning, my lady," he said, tugging his bright new Bluecoat uniform to attention. "How may I assist you?"

"I need to speak to the manager over the Estate Council," she said. "You may announce Lady Selraetas, of the Old Custom House. I am expected."

"Yes, right this way please," the officer said. He descended from the front desk, exiting the side stairs and leading the way down a back hallway. The ceilings were tall, and a verge of carpet lined the walls with breaks for doors. The trim was real wood, and the arching rafters were carved in repeating patterns, dimly lit by the shaft of light filtering through the stained glass at the end of the hall. A corner office had the door propped open, and the officer half-turned. "Please wait here." He stepped inside and had a quiet conversation, then he returned to the hallway and deferentially waved them in.

Red Silver strolled past him, aiming her most charming smile at the thin woman behind the desk. "A very fine morning to you, Manager," she said. "So good to meet here in North Port."

"*So* good," the manager agreed, trying not to sound sour. "I trust you are here to take possession of your winnings."

"Of the Old Custom House, yes," Red Silver agreed, her tone sweet. "I arrived yesterday, and I want to assure there are no complications with our license before we open this afternoon."

"No complications. Thank you for checking in."

Red Silver produced her license packet from her clutch, unfolding it. "I would also appreciate your signature, just in case there is some silly misunderstanding later on. Thank you ever so much for your time."

The manager selected a pen and scribbled a signature on the document, thrusting it back at Red Silver without making eye contact.

"Lovely, lovely," Red Silver crooned. "Swift blood, my friend."

"Swift blood," the manager replied, wincing a somewhat sarcastic smile.

Red Silver had what she needed. Pivoting, she left the manager's office. Her stride lengthened as she followed the hallway towards the exit.

"It's official," she muttered to Safety. "We have the Old Custom House. Now let's go get the rest."

NINEWAYS GREENKEY ESTATE, SOUTH SKIRT. NORTH PORT
15TH ULSIVET, 850. FOURTH HOUR PAST DAWN

Saint limped up to the stone arch, a bemused smile on his face. "So this is the Nineways Greenkey Estate," he said to himself, eyeing the squat tower. Interior alcoves bumped out the exterior walls, which were built around a central space. The Hadrathi sigils carved into the entry and stamped into the arch identified the site as a shrine for a Forgotten God. The fence that once surrounded the tower had long-since fallen apart, but a new temporary fence was firmly in place, and the compact grounds showed signs of renovation. Scaffolding sheathed a quarter of the building, and a work crew was patching up the masonry along the seaward face.

The front door creaked open as Saint approached, and a weedy young man smiled at him. "You must be Sir Torrent," he said.

"That I am, at your service," Saint said with an elegant little bow. "And you are?"

"Ryland. I work for Lord Malicoat." He tugged his loose sleeve up, revealing his forearm, and he pressed his thumb against the side of his elbow joint. Moments later, a purplish sigil filled out in his forearm's flesh.

"You're with the Cypher," Saint said, eyebrows raised. "Well that's not entirely a surprise."

"Lord Malicoat has a contract with us, to provide messenger service between himself and you," Ryland said, releasing his forearm and dropping his sleeve back down. "*Secure* messenger service. You may speak freely with me."

"How can you be sure I'm the right person, and not an imposter?" Saint asked.

"I checked you out last night, and your associates. And that's really all I'm going to tell you about my particular methods." He was still smiling, but there was something dark in his eyes.

"Excellent. Perhaps we could talk inside," Saint said with a sidelong glance at the work crew.

"Please follow me." Ryland turned, trotting down the steps to the central chamber around a pool sunk in the floor. The air was filmy with residue of long neglect and airless decay. Saint eased himself down the steps, sparing a glance at the fanciful carvings in niches between narrow windows.

"Quite a spot, yes," Ryland agreed with Saint's unspoken reaction, taking in the statuary. "Constructed in a different era." He mounted the short steps to an open alcove shrine, and Saint followed him in. Ryland closed the door and seated himself in one of the two chairs in the stuffy nook. "This is pretty secure," he said, enjoying the understatement.

"Here is my list," Saint said, handing it over. "I need this by tomorrow this time, at the Old Custom House. Malicoat's other cohorts have likely gathered most or all of it already."

Ryland scanned the list. "Map of the projectors and collectors, specs on the thought sleeves, known glyph pattern replicas. Identity of the adepts, their schedules, for Founder's Square." He raised his eyebrows. "Tech uniforms. Blueprints of designs."

"Like I said," Saint said, almost smirking.

"Yeah, we already have most of this," Ryland agreed. "I'll take care of it."

"Tomorrow morning," Saint repeated. "And we're meeting Lord Malicoat tomorrow night. Maybe you can let us know tomorrow where and when."

"Certainly. I communicate with you alone, unless you authorize someone else," Ryland said.

"You can talk to Inkletta and Red Silver." He bobbed a curt nod to Ryland. "See you soon."

"Need me to show you out?"

"I'll find my way," Saint replied graciously. He turned and left, on to the next errand.

THE WORKSHOP, HERITAGE DRYDOCK & CONSTRUCTION BAY. NORTH PORT 15TH ULSIVET, 850. FIFTH HOUR PAST DAWN

"Huh," Safety said, squinting up at the statue that loomed over the gate. A woman, double life size. She was depicted as draped in a thin cloak, cloth over her face, arms extended to the sides. "That seems a little too anatomically specific for a charity."

"Maybe she's the 'Weeping Lady' because she's cold," Red Silver grumbled. "Come on."

Red Silver and Safety entered through the imposing double-wide gate, eyeing the two stoic Bluecoats that stood inside. The Bluecoats were not checking traffic, they were on hand in case they were needed. A grim and severe garden flanked the courtyard, there was a basin in the center, and the paving curved around and back to another walled area. A compact chapel of pale stone was built into the corner of the wall, two storeys tall and embellished with another statue of the Weeping Lady, this one in a swooning pose. A cluster of workers stood off to the side, passing cigars around. A gaggle of unfortunates played dice in front of a lean-to barracks for the indigent along the back wall of the courtyard.

The expensive clothes drew attention to the scoundrels as they approached the chapel office. The presence of the Bluecoats discouraged any onlookers from indulging their growing curiosity about the visitors. Safety opened the door to usher Red Silver inside.

The foyer opened to the chapel, and off to the side there was a door to a waiting room. They stepped into the waiting room, attracting the attention of the jacketed clerk sitting behind a desk. She looked up, arching an eyebrow; the expression tugged at her features, which were twisted by a deep scar that carved her face from forehead to chin, disfiguring her cheek and putting a crook in her nose.

"May I help you?" she said, formal.

"We are here to meet with Sir Ousley," Safety said. "He is expecting us."

"And you are?"

"Oh, this is Lady Selraetas," Safety said.

The clerk rose, and turned to knock on the door behind her desk. She stepped through, closing it behind her. Safety and Red Silver approached the vacated desk, glancing around, wary of ambush.

The door opened, and the clerk stepped out and waved them in. "He will see you," she said, subdued.

Red Silver led the way, and the clerk closed the door behind Safety.

The office had a peculiar bittersweet smell. Reed mat paneling absorbed ambient sound, giving the room a surreal feeling. Several half-full bookshelves were built into the walls. A tidy desk dominated the room, with two chairs before it and a swivel chair behind it. The chair was turned away, its back to the door. The back wall of the office was a window overlooking an unlit chamber.

"Welcome to North Port," said the man in the chair in a hoarse, whispery voice. He pivoted the chair, facing them, his fingers steepled before his face. He was short, his hair slicked to his scalp, a dandy moustache curated on his lip. His pocked face glistened with sweat. His intense eyes locked on Red Silver. "I am Sir Ousley, and I supervise the Weeping Lady charity in this district. Come to make a donation?"

"Indeed, yes," Red Silver replied smoothly. "I have taken possession of the Old Custom House, and as a newcomer to North Port, I want to do my part to care for its unfortunates." She casually tossed a pouch of currency on the desk. It clinked down, and everyone in the room ignored it.

"Oh, you think you'll be around for the gala season?" the short man said, rising to his full height and adjusting his expensive but ill-fitting suit. A blood-red demonbane charm sparkled on his lapel. "Lady Selraetas, you are welcome to dance a few rounds if you think this town suits you. I must inform you that it's mostly laborers, convicts, and sailors. Not many educated patrons of means like yourselves. You may not find it satisfying. At all." His expression darkened.

"So sweet, for you to show concern," Red Silver said.

"That's me," Sir Ousley agreed, picking up the thick leather glove on his desk and thrusting his hand into it. "Real concerned." He held his glove up, hand closed into a fist.

The scoundrels flinched as a shape launched from atop a bookshelf and slapped onto Sir Ousley's leather gauntlet. The shape did not seem to move so much as flicker into different positions. It was a jumping spider, twice as big as Sir Ousley's fist. It perched on the gauntlet, nibbling at the treat he clenched. Its body was a bristled nightmare of legs and humps, and its eyes glittered as they seemed to concentrate the room's light.

"Lovely, isn't it?" Sir Ousley demanded, examining the spider. "This one is just a week old. I like to bring them into my office, tame them just a bit, before returning them to the habitat." His free hand casually gestured at the window into the dim chamber. "Frankly, it doesn't seem to work," he admitted, "since, without fail, any... friendliness they develop to people evaporates as they put on a few pounds. Still. The little ones have venom that's only irritating." He turned his gauntlet, admiring the nightmare gripping it.

"Sounds like they grow out of that too," Red Silver observed, exchanging a glance with Safety.

"Indeed," Sir Ousely nodded. "Not a nice way to die. The agonizing venom feels like ants running through your veins, pulling out pieces of meat and rearranging everything inside you. A hit or three paralyze you, then you might be *days* dying. They don't care to eat humans, see," he said as he warmed to the topic. "They don't bite because they are hunting. They only bite people because they are intensely territorial. Won't put up with intruders. Not at all." He turned his beady eyes back to the scoundrels. "So trespassers end up on the ground, among their castoffs, in agony. Unmoving. It's a slow trip through the Mirror."

"Seems there would be plenty of time to rescue a victim," Red Silver said.

"Accidents happen," Sir Ousley retorted. He flexed his hand, and the spider bounced to a shelf and hunkered down, watching the whole room. "This little habitat only has a half dozen of my favorites. Some time when you're in Six Towers you should drop by my webrift preserve. It is to die for."

"That reminds me. We came to invite you to our big opening night, at the Old Custom House," Red Silver said as her skin prickled at the sight of the unrestrained spider. "We sent an invitation with Hanger, but we couldn't be sure it reached you."

"Oh, I got your *message*," Sir Ousley snarled, quivering on the edge of losing his composure. He tugged a lever by the desk, and the windows behind him cranked open. Light glinted in the jewel-like eyes sprinkling the dimness beyond. "I have one for you. Get out of my district or I'll separate your meat from your bones while I decide whether you live or die. You simple peasants. You are not on my level. Not even close. I am connected, all the way up to the City Council. I have resources you cannot imagine, on both sides of the Mirror. Your every move touches upon the strands of my webs, your plans whispered to me in the darkness. You are outmatched. I will let you leave North Port, if you do so immediately. Otherwise you won't sleep twice more before you cease to wake altogether." His cheeks quivered with rage, and a vein stood out on his forehead.

Red Silver regarded him for a long moment. "I feel we understand each other," she said. Her heart rate accelerated as she spotted stealthy movement in the shadows beyond the open windows. She smelled a trace of sour rot, old carrion leather.

"Excellent, excellent. Get out," Sir Ousley said through his teeth. "Breathe the air. Enjoy the sunshine. Put your affairs in order. Or leave, and keep doing those other things *much* longer."

Safety nodded his farewell as he backed out after Red Silver, and he pulled the door closed. The two scoundrels looked at the clerk, who stood behind her desk. She held a pistol in one hand, pointed at the floor, and she watched them steadily.

"Thanks ever so much," Red Silver said. She turned and strode out of the office antechamber, Safety right behind her.

One of the Bluecoats in the foyer spat off to the side, eyeing them as they passed. They ignored him, heading for the compound exit.

"I sure hope Saint knows what he's doing," Safety muttered.

THE PEACH BUCKET PUBLIC HOUSE, COASTAL VIEW. NORTH PORT 15TH ULSIVET, 850. SIXTH HOUR PAST DAWN

Saint leaned into the gust of wind that unbalanced him. The scrub bushes hissed and whistled as they tossed, anchored against the salty pressure. Almost staggering, Saint reached the brightly painted red door of the public house. He banged against it with his forearm, pushing his way inside.

The common room glowed with clusters of globe lamps, cheerier than the misty bluster of midday outside. Over thirty patrons gave the high-ceilinged room a comfortably bustling feel. Saint limped over to the leather-topped bar, hooking his cane on the rail as he slid onto the stool.

"I'll take a leatherjack special," he said to the pert barmaid as he read the menu neatly lettered on the wall with chalk. Surveying the room, he smiled to himself, and picked up his cane as he lurched off the stool towards a table at the back.

"Well hello sir," he said, beaming with his most charming smile.

Captain Sillman looked up from his bread and stew, unamused. His expression shifted somewhat as he took in Saint's dress suit and fancy cane. He rose to his feet.

"Hello yourself," he said. "Do we know each other?"

"Close enough," Saint said. "Similar interests and a friend in common. May I join you?"

"Of course," Sillman said, his smile thinning. "Please." He resumed his seat as Saint eased down opposite him.

"I am Michaels Torrent," Saint said. "I'm good friends with Captain Rutherford, of Silkshore. He speaks of you in glowing terms. As a professional purchaser, my interests lie with calm and orderly business—same as you. My patron is Lady Selraetas."

"Purchaser, eh," Sillman said, looking Saint over.

"Based at the Old Custom House. Such a distinguished landmark! We won't even need a sign, everyone knows where it is. Grand opening tonight, you are more than welcome to attend. We would be delighted to have you, as our special guest." Saint looked around the room. "I'm checking out the district, getting to know local markets for everything. Saves me a trip, running into you like this," he explained. "I'm in luck!"

"Local markets, well," Sillman said, a scowl brewing behind his blandness. "You will find that in a start-up district like this, some things just aren't for sale. Not at any price."

"Understood, completely," Saint agreed. "If there is something that you want, that doesn't have a market here, let me know. I can keep an eye out for opportunities, I may be able to help." He exuded good natured camaraderie.

"We're done," Sillman said, leaning back, his smile gone.

"Very well. Efficiently handled," Saint congratulated him as the scoundrel took the hint and rose. "I look forward to crossing paths again. Thank you for your time." He bowed, then limped back towards the bar. He intercepted the bar boy with his mug of leatherjack, tossing a handful of currency on the tray.

"Sir, that's too much," the bar boy said quickly.

"That's my drink and the captain's lunch, the rest is for you," Saint smiled back. He turned away, took a deep breath, and headed for the front door.

Grimacing, Saint shoved the door open and braved the fitful winds. The heat of summer had peeled off the land, and the breathy tang of chill swept in from the ink-black waves. Clouds thickened and piled up overhead. Rain was not far away now.

Leaning against the wall of the public house on the lee side, Saint caught his breath, squinting out at the cloaked figures hurrying along on their errands. Across the street, a work crew was dismantling a scaffolding that swayed dangerously in the wind.

Saint felt another presence, and he slowly turned. Across the alleyway, several paces away, a figure armored in stained leather stood at the corner of the opposite building. The figure wore a mask with a jointed air port built into the side and scratched lenses over the eyes, layers of fabric angled to deflect sun and wind.

"Upon my life, we meet," Saint said in accented Hadrathi.

"You know something of the Deathlands?" the masked figure asked.

"Only a little. Enough to seem mysterious," Saint said with a disarming smile. "I imagine this weather seems tame to you."

"All things are strange these days, are they not." The masked figure did not move.

"I don't suppose our meeting is a happy accident," Saint said, eyeing the scavenger.

"No, not an accident. I bring you a message. From Magistrate Drake. She will speak with you soon. Either you can visit her," the scavenger said, "or she'll see to it that you arrive in her chambers for a consultation."

"I see," Saint nodded. "Her chambers annexed to the Dunvil Custom House?"

"Yes." The scavenger glanced back over his shoulder, scanned the rooflines. "There. Message delivered, so that's done. Other business. My name is Mesech. I have a question."

"Let's hear it," Saint said, amiable.

"Apparently the Old Custom House is opening tonight," Mesech said. "Scavengers are not allowed in the other public houses in North Port. Are we invited to the Old Custom House?"

"Absolutely," Saint said. "I am glad you asked. So glad, in fact, that I'll make sure the staff know you are our guest, and you can help yourself to whatever food and drink please you on our first night. How is that."

Mesech did not immediately respond. The scavenger turned, disappearing into the alley.

This time, when Saint ventured into the scouring wind, he bared his teeth in a smile.

Niece leaned against a piling, watching the heavily loaded barge wallow in the surging surf as it angled towards the pier. The deck gun mounts were tied in position with the barrels pointing upward. The smoke from the coal engine chimneys was whipped away and blended with the turbulent mist pouring off the sea.

It took some time, and heavy baffles lowered over the side to keep the hull from battering against the pier so hard both were damaged, but the barge managed to tie up several points along its length. Heaving up and down on the relentless waves, the barge clattered and jostled. Unloading cargo would be a challenge.

The unusually robust crew of the barge was up to the task. About thirty broad-shouldered Skov crew hefted crates and jostled them onto the pier. A delegation headed along the boardwalk to secure a reserved wagon, and Niece stepped out to intercept them.

"Asdis!" the one in the lead said, thrusting out his hand.

"Vicnair, so glad you could make it," Niece grinned as she clasped his forearm in greeting. "You have the kitchen crew, and our shipment of crabs and drinks?"

"All of it and some bonus," Vicnair agreed. "Cooks equipped to feed an army, enough ale and rum to make trouble, and enough muscle to keep order." He glanced around. "And before the barge goes, I must take them news of payment."

"Of course. Go to Trajan, give him the code 'skull on the wall' and he will release the undiluted dream tar we promised you," Niece said. "It is a pleasure doing business with the Knotwork, as always."

Vicnair nodded to one of his Skovs, who trotted back to the ship with the news. Vicnair's smile widened. "We will have a fantastic opening tonight. Do you think the Bluecoats will try to smash it up?" There was a glint of joy in his eye.

"If not sooner, certainly later," Niece assured him. "But we will talk our way out of it. For some reason, a small army seems more eloquent than a handful of scoundrels." Her answering grin was wicked. "We understand that this is a one-day loan of your people," Niece continued, "but I want you to know that we welcome any of your agents who want to stay longer. And we can pay."

"You must be pretty flush already, to offer such things," Vicnair observed. "You know what our time costs."

"Still burning through reserves," Niece said. "Give it a few days. You know how these Akorosians are. Can't do anything in a straight line." She looked back at the pier and the growing stack of crates. "I was concerned you all might not make it, the weather is really picking up," she said.

"It is getting pretty dicey out there," Vicnair agreed. "But we're here now. One less thing can go wrong."

"Good," Niece said. "Tonight is going to have its own turbulence."

CHAPTER TEN

Early Spirit Wardens learned secrets that lured them away from this world into the brightness beyond it. They made secret pacts with the Deathseeker crows.

First they cooperated to locate corpses within civilization's defenses. The Spirit Wardens follow the crows to sear the bodies and prevent the mind's echoes in dead flesh from becoming haunts. The first Spirit Wardens crafted the Bellweather Crematorium bells that toll in the Ghost Field, to amplify the reverberation when a death plucks at the Mirror's surface like a fly struggling in a spider's web.

The Deathseeker crows find the deceased, and the Spirit Wardens follow. But the crows may seek more than the dead, and the Spirit Wardens may follow them to stranger places than you can yet imagine.

—From "The Haunted Recesses" by Professor Eril Funarabat

"I could never get used to the quiet," Gapjaw muttered, glancing warily around.

"This is a peaceful place," Kashindi said reflectively. She wore her best smock and cloak, her cowl pressed against half her face by the hissing wind that swept the courtyard. "Not a place for crowds."

The courtyard was painted with a blended texture of lights. The penetrating beam of the North Hook Lighthouse suffused the courtyard with leftover light as it pivoted overhead, ever so slowly. The clouds were ruddy with late afternoon sun, its light barely pressing through the towering clouds that collected force overhead, promising a storm when they could hold no more. The courtyard was also lit by radiant bushes tossed by the wind, swirling their blooms like a jar of agitated fireflies. In contrast, the wrought iron of the lamp posts held globes with plasmic lamps that shed an unwavering illumination that seemed out of place in the flicker and shift of other lights.

"Before I met you, I hadn't been to Whitecrown in *years*," Gapjaw said to Kashindi. "This is my third time in a month."

"This place reminds me why we strive for better," Kashindi said. "What the world could be. What beauty it can offer the well-focused eye."

Gapjaw swallowed his own thoughts as his eyes followed the top of the stately marble wall that bounded the edge of the Master Warden's Estate, a center of power for the Spirit Wardens. He took some uneasy pleasure in his place on the *outer* side of the wall, rather than inside the hallowed compound.

A Bluecoat approached, wearing an unfamiliar dressy uniform complete with a half-cloak. "Swift blood, my friends," he said formally. "May I assist you?" He eyed Gapjaw.

"Swift blood to you. Matron Kashindi, from the Circulatory in Silkshore," Kashindi replied. She extended her thin wrist, showing the blood-red polished stones in her bracelet, each one an honor or accomplishment. The Bluecoat nodded deferentially.

"Enjoy the peace of this place," he said, and he continued his rounds.

"That still feels like ritual magic," Gapjaw admitted, watching the Bluecoat go.

"Rituals can be taught, Colvin," she replied with amusement. "Yours will fill out."

He looked down at the silver cable around his wrist, and its single black bead. "I guess so," he mused.

They rounded the radiant oak, the glowshine of its canopy swelling and fading like seafoam scattering through a rocky shoreline. A semicircle of pale statues rose on plinths between banks of radiant shrubbery and flowerbeds. Dispassionate and poised, the heroes of the Church were mute testaments to its inspiration. The paving of the path was closely fitted in decorative patterns, flanked by crushed quartz that glittered along the way. Following the path, Gapjaw and Kashindi reached an alabaster arch, its irregular pieces fitted with seams of gold, polished and shaped in a symmetrical triumph of balance.

"I bet that's not what the Gates of Death looked like," Gapjaw muttered.

"Hush," Kashindi said, suppressing a smile. Her chilly hand slipped into his, and together they passed through.

The tall black hedges surrounding the inner courtyard were pressed and shifted by the winds, but the force was blunted. An odd stillness hung in the air as they descended the steps towards the Starwalk Wall.

Polished obsidian formed a lifeless reflecting pool effect, fitted up to the base of the pale wall. A soaring black statue of the Immortal Emperor was centered in the wall, gauntlets fixed around a downward-pointed sword, detailed with breathtaking filigree gold highlights. The translucent alabaster of the wall was riddled with burial niches, the Akorosian name for each drawer of ashes carved beneath a sigil assigned by the Spirit Wardens in tiny print. The wall's reflection on the obsidian glowed with light from deep within the stone.

"I come here to visit my mother, and her mother," Kashindi murmured reverently. "It was my honor to sacrifice independence, and take on their accomplishments." She rubbed at the stones around her wrist. "To add to their legacy." Her bracelet bore more than one lifetime of achievement.

They reached the edge of the stone pool. Gapjaw looked down, unsettled by the wisps and traces of light that drifted beneath the glassy surface of the obsidian.

Kashindi glanced at him sideways. "See it as I see it," she whispered, squeezing his hand. "Let us pray. A silent prayer, to travel among ideas. Today is the day. I feel it. You will see them too."

Gapjaw let his eyes drift half closed, and he listened hard for Kashindi's heart that flexed next to his own. He focused on her as he had been trained to focus on spiritbane charms, aligning with them to repel ghosts. The bright bounce of her shifting blood seemed to open to him, as it did in their most intimate moments. He looked again at the glassy reflection at his feet.

Some of the tracery of light seemed to coalesce around the reflected sigils of the drawers. He was drawn to the reflection of two of the drawers that were near each other. He saw smiling faces, graceful forms; a portrait, an echo in light. Memory reverberating from the wall, through its ashes and sigils.

"I want to join them. Stars we kindle neath the glassy wave," Kashindi breathed, her voice roughened with emotion. She sensed Gapjaw's connection, his reaction.

"You will. You will!" Gapjaw whispered, oddly moved. "I'll make sure."

She smiled at him, eyes bright. "I want you to be there with me. It's not too late. I have opened my life to you. I want to open my legacy to you as well."

All he could do was pull her into a tight embrace as his heart pounded.

COURT ANNEX, DUNVIL CUSTOM HOUSE. NORTH PORT
15TH ULSIVET, 850. EIGHTH HOUR PAST DAWN

Saint shifted in the reed-back chair. The hardness of the seat seemed to be almost aggressive, pressing up into him. He fidgeted with the cane, then pulled out his kerchief and rubbed at some of the grime that found its way into the nooks of the snarling horse face. He glanced over at the clerk, who quickly looked away.

"Did you tell the magistrate I'm here?" he asked, mild.

"Of course, Sir Torrent," the clerk replied, his tone showcasing the same sort of flatness as the chair. "She has many appointments on her docket for this afternoon."

Saint looked around the otherwise empty reception chamber. "Got it." He rose to his feet. "Well, I will try again another time. Maybe I could get an appointment, to make better use of my time."

"She's booked through the next three days," the clerk replied. "If you want to see her before then, you will have to wait in case she has an unexpected opening."

Saint considered that for a moment, effortlessly deflecting the urge to indulge in a sarcastic witticism involving the clerk's 'unexpected opening.'

"I misread the urgency of the situation," he said diplomatically. "I'll be on my way."

He limped down the polished stone of the hall. There was little traffic today, as the clouds tumbled through the sky and the waves lashed the port. Saint nodded to the Bluecoats flanking the door, and he left.

"There you are," Mesech said. He stood in the shadows of the stable. He beckoned Saint, who frowned, and took his time crossing the distance between them.

"Apparently the magistrate doesn't have time for me," Saint said. "You may not realize this, but I've got a lot to do today."

"I was just waiting for you to leave," Mesech said. "You did the right thing, going in the front door. Putting in the time. That sort of thing makes the magistrate happy. She's into games," he muttered, grim. "I'll take you the back way now."

Saint considered him for a long moment, then shrugged. "Sure. Let's just plunge the clot." He shuffled after Mesech, who followed the flank of the Court Annex.

Mesech reached the lean-to equipment shed built against the side of the annex, and he glanced around before stepping inside. Saint followed. Mesech held up a pebble and waved it before the blank wall. The faintest hint of sigils embedded in the wall gleamed to visibility.

"Come," Mesech said, tugging off his glove and holding his hand out to Saint. Saint gripped his surprisingly warm hand. Mesech focused on the wall, and stepped in towards the sigil, pulling Saint along.

Saint felt himself press against a membrane, as though falling from a height and landing on fabric; his weight and momentum were pulled by Mesech, and he stepped through. His boot landed on sand, its slight yield unsteadying him. He stood in a forest of shadows, lined by the ruddy glow of a tall bonfire that was frozen in place unmoving. Looking over his shoulder, he saw a standing stone carved in the old style.

"Welcome to the Echosheath," said a sardonic voice. Saint re-oriented, spotting the severe woman seated on a deadwood throne bound in iron vines and studded with various skulls, including two stag skulls whose horns twined up into stone trees. She wore a fur mantle over her officious magistrate robes, a jarring contrast. Her fingers bore rings fashioned of bone and precious metals. She was shadowed and underlit, her eyes glinting as they reflected the firelight. Her age was difficult to guess, but there were white strands in the crimson hair pulled back to a knot.

"Thank you," Saint said. "I misunderstood your invitation. I thought you meant for me to come to your magistrate chambers."

"I handle my judgements on both sides of the Mirror," she said. She gestured at a low stone bench, its slabs held together by the grip of vines. "I have some decisions to make about you, and I decided you should be here to inform them."

Saint eased himself down, cane across his lap. "Thoughtful."

"As Mesech explained, I am Magistrate Drake. I looked into you, when you started sniffing around the Old Custom House," she said. "Saint. Or, Sir Torrent. An identity purchased four years ago from a Spider in the Ease. Credentials that work if no one takes too close a look. Because the man who originally owned them traveled to the Dusk a decade ago and died in squalor, a hopeless addict, tossed in the fires of the Crematorium with no questions asked."

"You are more thorough than I am," Saint admitted. "I lean more on my charm and strategic distractions than deep dives into background. I didn't know all that about the name."

"What if I told you the Torrent family has been notified of your activities, and they sent an agent to sort you out?" the magistrate inquired, cool.

"I would appreciate the notice, and I'd see what I could do about it," Saint replied evenly. "Is that what is happening?"

"No, but it could be. As I said, I have some decisions to make about you." She studied him intently. "I don't care what you do in Silkshore. But you move to North Port and you could become trouble for me. I don't want trouble. So why don't you tell me what you plan to do here."

"I have expensive tastes and an allergy to smug parasites," Saint said. "So, therefore, I pursue crime." He offered a wry smile. "North Port fits me better than Silkshore. As the reclamation is just getting underway, about a year in, things are relatively simple. There are three main illegal industries here, and I'm only interested in one—and you aren't involved in it. So we should get along fine."

"Explain."

"First, your business. You focus on smuggling. Since you're one of the Seven, with the Circle of Flame, your people are wealthy and connected. You want oddities from the Deathlands, and you don't want them to go through customs. So you work with the Deathland scavengers. They bring you treasure, so some of them can earn your patronage and have their banishment lifted. Then you package the contraband in sealed judicial communications and move it through the Doskvol border. It's low volume, but great for your needs. Of all the Seven, you are assigned to this post since you're a magistrate; an ideal cover. I think it's great," he confessed, "and I'm all for you keeping up the good work."

"Why don't I kill you to keep my secret?" Drake mused.

"Because it doesn't really matter who knows, as long as the Inspectors don't get involved. As long as the Bluecoats don't get greedy and make a move. I'm not motivated to throw a wrench in your operations, neither are my people," Saint said. "Your secondary enterprise is also not one we're planning on getting involved in. You want to dabble in some protection rackets with scavenger muscle, that's your business. Probably just a way to offer them work so they can get patronage faster, right?"

"And you're not interested in offering 'protection' in North Port," Drake clarified.

"Right. I'll have my hands full with the third industry." Saint smiled. "Vice. That's where the real money is, and you've got all the wealth you need already. Just more headaches for you. So we don't need to get in each other's way."

"If you make things noisy with Dunvil's people, that affects me," she said.

"That's why I don't want things to get noisy," Saint agreed. "Right now Dunvil has a tidy lock on the vice in North Port. All those sailors, laborers, the convict crews, not to mention the Bluecoats assigned out here. So much work, so much stress. They all need to relax and have a good time. They all get a little money that jangles around unhelpfully in their pockets. So Captain Sillman looks the other way, and Dunvil's man Ousley has offices in the Weeping Lady charitable setup in the Workshop. He also runs the Heritage Bunker, with the drugs and whoring and such."

"You think you can compete with Ousley's setup," Drake observed. "Right out in the open with the Old Custom House."

"No no," Saint said. "Not compete. Nobody wants competition out here. I'm going to *replace* Ousley."

His audacity surprised a smile out of Drake. "Oh, just like that. Just step into the operation."

"He is one inbred aristocrat with a spider fetish," Saint said. "I bring the River Stallions. We can expand operations. We will have the Workshop for legal contacts. The Bunker for all the really sordid stuff, out of sight. And the Old Custom House, which can handle both legal and illegal contact from its central location in North Port. I will improve a design that's already working," he said. "I have people I can trust, we've been together for years. We can keep the industry locked down, running smooth, and extremely lucrative."

"You are a glib talker," Drake mused. "I trust you less and less."

"That's not ideal, because we could be friends," Saint said. "After all, your operation does have some difficulties."

"This should be good."

"The Silkworms are a problem, just because they're close and they are the other smuggling operation. Reclamation Point is the camp where the military teaches its soldiers Deathlands survival. So military supplies, which are not checked by customs, can come and go to the camp. Smuggle people and more bulky goods. If they took exception to your operations, they could try to push you out and sell you access, knowing your business both ways through the wall," Saint said. His grip on his cane was almost painfully tight as he kept his tone casual.

"How do you assist with that threat?" Drake asked.

"I know the Silkworms, we go way back. Piccolo, the one in charge of the Peach Basket? He used to be a River Stallion. He trusts me, I can help keep the temperature down and keep negotiations open if the situation gets tense. I want them to succeed too, but I like the idea of multiple options for moving goods. It's better for me, in the end," he pointed out.

"You said you didn't want competition in North Port," Drake reminded him.

"Your interests in smuggling are very different than the Silkworms, I think," Saint said. "Besides. All these operations have ties to the Ministry, right?" Saint pointed out. "I mean, you're a Magistrate. The Silkworms have Sanction and all his connections in Silkshore, not to mention Rutherford and the Bluecoats there. If the Lampblacks decided they wanted to push into the market, they would make a lot of noise, throw around a lot of cash and violence, establish themselves. Fight over turf. Considering the current recruits for North Port crime are off-duty Bluecoats and opportunistic convicts under Ironhook's supervision, intruders can escalate to draw attention to corruption in governance out here. Even the scavengers have ties to you, and to the Spirit Wardens. Heightened scrutiny is no good, and hard to avoid if conflict takes a violent turn. We want to avoid heat, same as you." He smiled. "We can all decide, together, what we see and what we don't."

Drake watched him, unreadable, and let the moment stand for a while. "Tell me about the Hive," she said.

"Not much to do with us," Saint replied. "I mean, the Silkworms have dealt with them quite a bit. I guess that's a complicated relationship, I don't know that much about it. The Hive is dug in to Silkshore, and that's one reason we are moving out here. I want to keep it simple," Saint said. "I like to know the lay of the land. Silkshore has a *lot* of layers to work around." He looked Drake in the eye. "Help me keep it simple," he said.

"I will be watching your operations," Drake said quietly. "You speak very sweetly, but your history suggests that doesn't mean much relative to your actual plans and motives. You can go for now." She paused, frowning, as Saint rose. "One more thing."

"Yes?"

"That trash Whisper you've got. Tell the savage to keep her energies tucked in here, we don't need her squatting out her mess on our streets." Drake's voice was cold, inflexible with traditions from centuries of elite occult studies.

"Understood," Saint said with a solemn nod.

"Remember," Drake said, resuming her calm demeanor. "You rock the boat out here, it's not the canals you're used to. There are sharks in these waters. Stay away from my operations, from the scavengers. If you prove you know your place, there is a chance this could work out."

"That is fantastic news," Saint said, and he offered an elegant bow.

Mesech stepped out of the shadows at Saint's side, and Drake waved a dismissive gesture at them. "You may go."

"Swift blood," Saint said, bowing again.

"Indeed," Drake murmured, raising an eyebrow. Saint turned away from her, following Mesech to the echo of the standing stone.

Moments later, Saint was back in the real world, skin tingling and eyes struggling to focus.

"I suppose," Mesech said, "that means we are not invited to the Old Custom House tonight."

"What?" Saint protested with a smile. "We won't talk a single word of improper business. You're fine. Come to the opening."

"But—she just told you to stay away from us," Mesech said.

"I won't go to you. But you can come to me," Saint said, oddly serious. He turned away. "See you tonight."

Thoughtful, the scavenger vanished down a different alleyway.

THE OLD CUSTOM HOUSE, FOUNDER'S SQUARE. NORTH PORT
15TH ULSIVET, 850. HOUR OF HONOR, 1 HOUR PAST DUSK

OPENING NIGHT

The hall was almost crowded in the warm lamplight. The firepit crackled, flavoring the room with woodsmoke that mixed with the smell of seafood, cream, and alcohol. Most of the tables were full, a cluster of workers were singing around the firepit, and servers navigated the crowd with practiced ease. Dozens of Skov enforcers stayed by the walls or moved unobtrusively through the hall. The general atmosphere was festive at the end of a long day. Rain sheeted down outside, rendering the smoky hall relatively bright and cozy by comparison.

A passing server expertly swapped out the low oil lamp on the trestle table with a full one, already glowing, and Saint offered him a smile. Then he refocused on the man leaning on the table next to him.

"You hate to lose more sailors in the port than you do on the sea," Saint sympathized. "You are a captain! Responsible for the ship, the cargo—and the crew."

"Too right," the seamed man grumbled. "It's that damn Bunker. No good telling the crew not to go, that just makes it irresistible. But I've lost seven sailors there, three of them good ones. A couple died, but... the Bunker's got some sharp operations. They mix drugs and gambling, then get my people in deep, and force them to work their debts off in the operation. And while they're stuck, they get addictions, disease. Burn through them, make room for the next crop," he said, sour. He took a long pull of his drink. "Always another ship coming in."

"That's gotta change," Saint objected. "Treating people like that. You know, I'm based here now. I can get your sailors out. Clean them up for you." He glanced around. "But these Skovs are temporary. I'm going to need some people I can trust." He looked at the captain, as though an idea was occurring to him. "Say, Rukia, I'm having a thought. You could ask for volunteers to stay in North Port until you get back. Lend a hand. Some friendly faces to greet the people I pull back out of the Bunker."

Rukia squinted at him, thinking.

"Pay is decent," Saint said, "and we've laid in a supply of hunter's rum."

"Oh, that's nice," Rukia said, and he chuckled. "I could check with my marines. I bet I could find a few who would take it on."

"Exciting," Saint said. He pulled a notepad and pencil stub from his pocket. "Now. Who are you looking to get back from the Bunker?" he asked, earnest.

Across the room, Niece stood behind the bar with her arms crossed over her chest, watchful as she directed the barkeep and servers. She spotted a Skov signalling at her, pointing to the doorway; a trio of scavengers hesitantly entered, looking around, still decked out in survival gear and helmets. Niece waved her enforcer off, and approached the scavengers herself as they worked their way around the edge of the room towards a table.

She had almost reached them when the three stopped abruptly. Their leader knelt, and the other two widened their stance, hands moving in a ritual kind of motion. Niece craned her neck to see what they were facing, and saw the Hammer slumped in a chair, back to the wall. He did not appear to be aware of them as they concluded their strange and brief gestures. Niece caught up as they finished, the leader standing up.

"On lifemeet," she said in terrible Hadrathi. She winced as she switched to Akorosian. "Well, worth a shot. Welcome to the Old Custom House," she said, blushing.

"Good try," the leader said. "I am Mesech, I think we are expected."

"You are, order anything you like," she said. She signaled a server, who headed over. "Hey, Mesech, right?" He nodded, not bothering to correct her pronunciation. "What was that you were doing when I came over?"

"What..." he said, puzzled.

"The, you know," she said, mimicking ritual gestures. "To him." She pointed at the Hammer.

"Oh. Yes. We revere the Hunger any time we meet it."

"The hunger?" Niece said, puzzled.

"It's a force, one of the ways we protect our outposts in the Deathlands. Usually those who are infected with the Hunger die shortly after. But their sacrifice makes it possible to clear out ghosts; I once saw one devour a whole cloud that made it past the defenses. The storm would have destroyed the settlement, drained everyone." He paused, then unstrapped his helmet, pulling it off to reveal pale coppery features and a mat of damp hair. His eyes were an unsettling green. "They die for us," he said quietly. "They embody the space, between the living and the restless dead. They keep that line clear when the dead try to cross it."

Niece was lost in those eyes for a moment, startled, processing. Then she heard her name shouted over the din.

Refocusing, she saw one of the Skovs point over by the firepit. She oriented on the sudden cluster of shouting, and saw a couple big fellows confronting a Skov, then launching at him.

As the brawl erupted, Niece threw hand signals to several enforcers, who started clearing a path from the firepit to the front door with businesslike efficiency. She headed for the fight, and saw the colorful flash of Red Silver arriving on the scene. Niece did not have a clear view of what happened, but she knew how they had prepared to react to this inevitable situation. Moments later, Skovs were bustling down the cleared path, dragging and pushing three big men who hollered threats as they were forced along, the experienced skirmishers gripping them with joint locks. Smiling, Niece hung back in the crowd near the door, letting Red Silver handle it. Her smile dimmed as she recognized one of the agitators as a Bluecoat who arrested her the day before, now dressed like a worker.

Red Silver stood in the doorway, the glowing hall behind her and the braziers flanking the entryway lighting her clearly from the sides. She planted her fists on her hips as the Skovs tossed the agitators out the door, battering down on the flagstones of the square, lashed by rain.

"Good for you!" bawled one of the agitators, clutching his aching shoulder. "All tough when you got these strawheads to heel! If they stay, we'll deal with *that*. And if they go, you're out here with no friends," he sneered. "You won't last!"

"Good talk," Red Silver said. "Oh, and by the way, we don't like threats," she added. "Didn't Hanger tell you?"

The three agitators were on their feet, and they hesitated, looking at the four Skov enforcers standing behind Red Silver. Her fists were still on her hips, but the agitators had a moment to consider the pistol strapped to her leg also.

Passions cooled by the downpour and pain needling through their joints, the agitators had an introspective moment. It concluded with them slinking away.

"You know, one of those guys had a really nice hat," a Skov observed. "Back by the pit."

"It's yours now," Red Silver replied with a grin. "Hey. Look at that stable," she said, pointing across the square.

The ruddy light in the windows revealed a number of Bluecoats peering out through the rain, sheltering and prepared to cross the square and break up a riot that might break out spontaneously.

"What do you want to do," an enforcer growled.

"Take a handcart, deliver a keg of ale," Red Silver said through a smile that showed off all her teeth. "Thank them for their vigilance and their service."

The Skov chuckled as a new round of song roused from the revelers around the firepit.

The bulk of the patrons had drained out of the hall, hours later. One of the servers stirred up the fire and added fuel, and Safety poured another drink for the weary woman still hunched at the bar.

"Just... it's stupid," she said, still remarkably clear after another mug was drained. "They offer danger pay, and that gets the workers to come out. But the hazard bonus, it's totally undercut by the lower wage. They *don't* tell you about *that*," she emphasized. "But hey. If they don't get enough workers, then they get more convict crews from Ironhook." She offered a lewd gesture towards where the fortress probably was, far away in the storm-tossed darkness. "Where you think we should complain? Who'd listen? Since it's all rigged. All through the Ministry. Goes all the way to Dunvil himself, this flood a savings into his coffers." She blearily shook her head.

"It's not like we're greedy," Safety commiserated. "Not like we want their pie. Just a few more crumbs from their table." He slugged back some ale.

"Zakly," she agreed. "Nif you say anything, you have an accident. 'Off duty' Bluecoats," she scoffed, "an Dunvil runs Ironhook, so it's easy to lose track of some convict labor crew for an hour of mischief." She grimaced. "Both sides a th law stitched up." She chewed at the gristle of that idea for a long moment. "Go up against them," she said softly, "get wrecked. Done for."

"Maybe that's changing," Safety said under his breath, glancing around. "You see these Skov? Knotwork. Yeah. And our girl Niece?

Waltzed right out of the Dunvil Custom House the same day she was framed for smuggling."

The work boss considered that.

"And," Safety said with a smile, looking at the doorway, "we have a *real Whisper.*" He nodded towards the door, and the boss turned to look.

Inkletta entered, rain sluicing from her cowled cloak. Sereen was by her side, also cloaked, and two porters followed, relieved as they put her luggage down to the side.

The boss fixed Safety with a shrewd look. "Hm. Alright. How's the pay," she asked, her voice low.

"It's pretty good, Mattalene," Safety said. "Double the day wage for off duty service."

Mattalene nodded to herself, a sour smile twisting her face. "I may know some people," she said significantly.

Safety grinned, and refilled her mug.

CHAPTER ELEVEN

There is a cynically utilitarian aspect to punishing crimes in Doskvol. The goal is clearly not rehabilitation, or even punishment, but instead domination of those who step out of line. If you are sent to Ironhook, you can be used as slave labor or leverage against people who care about you. Once your allies have paid off the right officials (or criminals) you can be released.

For some stubborn cases, or instances where the authorities need to make a point, the transgressor is not imprisoned or executed. Banishment is not common, but it is cruel; the transgressor is sent outside the lightning walls, exiled to attempt survival in the Deathlands among ghost storms and nameless horrors. Banishment markings are ritually inked on the back of both hands to assure they cannot hide their shame.

There is only one way to secure a pardon and return to the city. Pay the penance tax and secure the patronage of a sponsor. The only eligible sponsors are certified noble houses, and the Spirit Wardens. Your sponsor is then responsible for your behavior (and motivated to keep you in line.) The banishment markings are erased.

The flaw in this system is human ingenuity. The Deathlanders reclaimed old limmer traditions to survive, they banded together. The exiles are outnumbered by Deathlanders born outside the walls and volunteer members.

The Ministry created a tough band of disaffected and capable survivors outside the reach of the law. Outside their view. In retrospect, that may not have been utilitarian after all.

—From "A Concise Review of Necessary Legal Reforms"
by Lady Menia Urubask

OPENING NIGHT

CONTINUED

"I thought maybe we wouldn't see you until tomorrow," Saint said as he approached Inkletta. "Since they close the gates at dusk."

"Bribe," Inkletta said, mustering the energy to shrug.

"Are you alright?" Saint demanded as he spotted her eyepatch.

"This?" she said, touching at it. "Yes, my eye is intact. Just part of the preparation for the ritual. You know." She glanced around, lowering her voice. "Tracing the conduit."

"Right, yes," he said. "So, maybe get some sleep?"

"Good, my head is throbbing," she said. "I've got supplies," she added, gesturing back at the pile of luggage.

Saint snapped his fingers and gestured at a server, who recruited a couple enforcers to assist with shifting the gear upstairs. Saint leaned in close to Inkletta.

"Can we do it?" he murmured.

"We will give the task our full attention. Do everything we can," Inkletta replied, her eye steady.

Saint nodded. "Well, that's the most we can ask."

"No it isn't," Inkletta breathed, and she shook the feeling off. "How about you? Outmaneuvering Ousley?"

"He will have a bad day tomorrow," Saint said.

"Well good then," Inkletta said. She turned to see porters hefting the last of her luggage. "Good night," she said over her shoulder. She followed her baggage out of the hall.

Meanwhile, Sereen crossed over to where the Hammer slumped by the wall. Rapid movement caught Saint's eye; he saw the Hammer rouse, snarl, and push Sereen away. The boy stumbled, then stepped back and sat down on a bench out of reach. The Hammer glared at him for a long moment, then slumped back down again.

Saint looked over at Niece, and they made eye contact. Both of them saw the display. Saint approached her, and she met him.

"What was that," Saint demanded quietly.

"No idea," Niece said, disturbed. "I've never seen the Hammer react like that before."

"I've let this drift for a long while," Saint muttered. "Time to get some better answers."

"Well Inkletta's back," Niece suggested.

The scoundrels let that idea soak for a moment, then they headed for the stairs.

Niece and Saint passed the kitchen and headed up the tight spiral staircase, following the dust-fogged corridor to the room spilling lamplight into the hallway.

Saint rapped on the doorframe with his cane, and Inkletta looked up. "I thought we were done," she said, her tone only slightly plaintive. She sat in a padded chair, holding a tumbler half full of wine.

"Something has happened," Niece said. "The Hammer. When Sereen approached him, the Hammer pushed him away." She paused. "Since that creepy kid showed up, we just went along. But I think we need to know what's going on with him."

Inkletta let out a weary sigh, leaning back in the chair.

Saint stepped into her room, followed by Niece, who closed the door.

"So the Hammer is down to a couple heartbeats a *day*, from what I hear," Saint said in a low voice. "I don't really know what happened when the Hammer was beneath the gaze of the Fallen Star, whatever that means, and... I think I need to."

"It's all about demons, right?" Inkletta said, not opening her eyes. "The Hammer touched on a Leviathan. And Sereen, he was a 'gift' from a cult. Showed up unannounced, and he was useful, so after I figured out where he came from I let it drop. We all did."

"Sereen is a demon?" Niece said, cautious.

"No, no, it's... it's saturation. Sereen is from a bloodline that soaked up demonic influence over generations. The limmers found out by accident, that touching on a Leviathan changes you. Humans get twisted. Some of them become mystics. Others become Whispers, or cultists, or... or all of those things. Or worse," she said, opening her eyes. "There are duties that come with the gifts. Demons deal instinctively in an economy of fate, and will, and blood, and... and perception. And knowledge." She winced, and finished her wine.

"Okay so far," Saint said, "but that still doesn't really explain Sereen. How he understands the Hammer. Or their weird relationship."

"I'm not *trying* to explain Sereen," Inkletta said, tetchy. "Look. Sereen doesn't *serve* the Hammer. He's a cultist, yes? Sereen is a cultist. He worships demons, demon energy. The Hammer is not a *person* to him. The Hammer is a *shrine*. A shrine that walks. That demon is intelligible to the boy through the Hammer's life force, because the boy is tuned to the demon. It seems likely to *me*," she continued, "that the boy's whole life purpose has been shaped by the need to connect with the Hammer, and Sereen may turn out to be unable to connect to any other purpose for the rest of his life. So," she said, clacking the tumbler down on the end table, her eye bright, "if the Hammer is now resisting him, it's likely the balance has shifted somehow." She slowly closed her eyes, pinching the bridge of her nose. "The heartbeat was okay at first, but that's... too slow. I'll look at him tomorrow." She took a deep breath, and opened her eye, her hands in her lap. "It wouldn't be safe for me to do it tonight."

"Are you okay?" Niece asked in a small voice. "Your eye?"

"Preparation for the ritual." Inkletta paused, looking down at the floor. "Griggs worked me hard," she said. "Those gondolier mystics, they are snobs. They have their *elegant traditions*," she said with disgust, "so they look down on me. Say I am ignorant." Her expression hardened. "The worst part is they *know* I would kick their asses, every time, and they can't stand it. Makes them feel small. Reminds them there's more out there, more that they don't know. So they have to put me in my place." The words were bitter in her mouth.

"Well, we are just delighted to have you back," Saint said.

"Yeah," Inkletta said without enthusiasm. "I've got some pre-packaged rituals, and a stack of components. All part of the gondolier payment for taking over our bridge base." She looked up at the ceiling. "I should have everything I need to do what I need to do. I've been working on the groundwork for this complex ritual to trace the conduits for

Malicoat." She cleared her throat, and looked at her fellow scoundrels. "So that's my story. How is the rest of the North Port takeover going?"

"You know, dicey," Saint said with a roguish grin. "Pretty much what we expected. Now that you're here, fashionably late, our odds improve." He offered her a genuine smile.

Niece stepped forward and leaned into Inkletta, bending to pull her into a fierce embrace.

"Goodnight," Niece whispered into Inkletta's hair. "I see you. And I love you so much."

Inkletta could not help but smile as she hugged Niece back. "Go to bed," she said, her tone finally warming. "Our troubles will wait."

THE OLD CUSTOM HOUSE, FOUNDER'S SQUARE. NORTH PORT 16TH ULSIVET, 850. FIRST HOUR PAST DAWN

"Hey! Put that down," Safety demanded as he strode out into the hall from the back hallway.

Varela startled, looking over at him, then scowling as he hefted the glowing cylinder of electroplasm in both hands. "Just taking a look. No need to get—"

"I said put it down," Safety snapped. Varela rolled his eyes, and slotted the heavy cell back down in the crate with the others. The crate's interior had a grid of separators, and nine power cells.

"This shouldn't even be *open*," Safety said forcefully, snatching the lid and clapping it back down on the box.

"Well we're moving them again today, so we better make sure it's all here!" Varela retorted, chin up and chest out. "I'm not gonna be blamed if something comes up missing."

The other five Coursers looked away, uncomfortable. They were perched on tables and the bar, a loose circle around the two crates and Varela.

"I checked it yesterday and I'm checking it again before we go," Safety said, lowering his voice but not his intensity. "You want a look at this, you better ask first."

"Okay boss," Varela said, insolent.

Safety looked around. "Where is everybody." He spotted the Hammer, still slumped against the wall, and Sereen drowsing on a trestle table nearby.

"Niece is out front, with the Knotwork," Varela said. "I think Red Silver is back in the kitchen. Saint's getting his beauty sleep, shallow out all those wrinkles." He mugged for the Coursers, but the response was subdued.

Safety headed for the front door, still propped open. Rain was sifting down, occasional silver threads caught in the weak morning light. The Skovs stood in the courtyard, ignoring the rain as they said their goodbyes.

"That was some good work last night," Niece said in Skovic.

"Damn straight," Vicnair agreed, his beard freshly combed and his hair back in a loose braid, rain caught in his lashes. "Let's do this again sometime."

"Any takers on my offer to stay on a while?" Niece asked the group.

"I'm leaving three of my people," Vicnair said, recapturing her attention. "Dayla, Kreb, and Soonthi over there. They are tough. But friendly, like me," he grinned.

"Perfect," Niece smiled. "You can set up in the barracks with the Coursers. Today's job is to protect our house. Lots of locals have bruised feelings and they may come by to complain."

"The rest of us are headed out," Vicnair said. He thrust out his hand, and Niece slapped a grip onto his forearm as he squeezed hers. "Until next time."

"This side or the other," she agreed. She playfully punched his shoulder, and let him go. "At least you can take the road back through the wall."

"We like waves and all, but woof," Vicnair agreed. He turned to his people. "Let's go."

Most of the Knotwork headed out, accompanied by a number of cooks and porters that had come with them for opening night. As Niece watched them go, Safety approached.

"I didn't catch most of that foreign chatter," he said. "I know we're all worn out from getting North Port secured. Tell me you didn't jump that guy's bones last night."

"What?" Niece said, rounding on him with surprise.

"I mean, *awfully* chummy," Safety observed.

"That's really, *completely*, none of your business," Niece retorted. "And if you want to lean in on this one, and you think it's fun to tease me about it, I'll report you to Red Silver," she threatened.

"You know about snitches, right? That the criminal underworld generally disapproves of tattling?" he said, masking his sudden concern as best he could.

"Think it over," she growled. Pivoting, she headed back into the Old Custom House.

Safety squinted up at the clouds. "Huh. Let's hope the rest of the day goes better."

Saint sat on the edge of the narrow cot, fully dressed. He was unfocused, breathing, waiting in the stillness as the turmoil churning within him sought balance.

A light knock rapped on the door. Saint hesitated only a moment.

"Come," he said.

Red Silver opened the door and stepped in. "Breakfast," she said, handing him a warm bundle. He peered at the fresh bread filled with scrambled egg and eelscraps.

"Nice," he observed. "I could get used to living in a place with a staffed kitchen."

"I had them work up something like you'd get at that hand cart down by the Curve," Red Silver said, leaning against the doorframe. She took a bite of her breakfast.

"That's thoughtful," Saint said with a nod towards the bundle. He looked at Red Silver. "You're here to see if there's anything we need to sort out before we reinforce the marching orders and send everyone on their way, I suppose."

"Pretty much."

"We've been planning this for a long while now," Saint said quietly. "Today, we just... we just have to do it. Get it right the first time." He reached for his cane, and levered himself up to his feet. "You all set?"

"Let's get this done," she said. Turning, she led the way down the hall, Saint at her heels.

"Today is the *day*," Saint called out, his grin brilliant as he entered the hall. "Good morning!"

Safety, Niece, and the Coursers oriented on Saint and Red Silver, attentive, and they arranged themselves as an audience as he reached them.

"Three top priorities for today," Saint said. "Protect the Old Custom House and everything going on there. Also, get the score," he said, pointing at the crates taken from the Dunvil Custom House, "into the Workshop. And my part, chatting up Captain Sillman. Red Silver, you work with Niece and the Hammer to make sure we've coordinated our defenses and we don't get hit here. How did recruitment go last night."

"Barracks are about half full," Niece replied. "We got some sailors, some workers, and this morning three of the Knotwork decided to stay for a while. I'm handling payroll and assignments. Total, we've got over a dozen pretty capable recruits."

"Remember they are our diplomats, so let's take good care of them so we have lots of volunteers to choose from going forward," Saint said. "I expect two more people to show up today. First, a leech. Jewel. She's got the expertise we'll need to work on Malicoat's project, and she's been prepping the last couple days. Set her up in the cellar. Second, Ryland. He is bringing information Jewel needs, so make sure she gets it."

"I will," Red Silver nodded.

"Stay sharp. Some of our recruits are certainly paid informants, or will be soon, so let's limit the information and access they get. Also, Inkletta is working on the ritual," Saint continued, "so if she's here you can involve her in defense if needed. But she might need to go out. I don't know. If she does go out, send someone we trust with her. This is a dangerous time."

"Why not just tell her to stay here?" Safety asked. "At least for today."

"I don't know what she has to do to prepare her ritual, and these things often have timing issues that don't make any sense to us. Inkletta is not your problem," he said to Safety, "but getting ready for the break-in absolutely is. You all set?"

"Yeah, I guess," Safety said without enthusiasm.

"Walk me through it," Saint said.

"Okay, so I take the Coursers to the Workshop," Safety said. "The chapel office has a window overlooking one of the smaller drydock facilities, for working on fishing boats or narrow barges. Ousley converted it to be his little spider habitat," he said with a grimace. "We breach the compound from the north, stealth up to the habitat, get to the roof and compromise the big vent as an entry point. We lower the electroplasm cells we got from the Dunvil Custom House into the habitat, and conceal all signs of our involvement."

"Right. Did you figure out the work-around for the spiders?" Saint asked.

"Yeah," Safety said. "The spiders are a Kreptes strain, they get so big because some genius aristocrats, or cultists, or *aristocrat cultists* decided to infuse cute little jumping spiders with demon essence to make them bigger. Adepts generally manage them because the spiders have really specific and unpleasant dietary needs that require a touch of alchemy—and because the spiders back off if confronted with an attuned demonbane charm. So that's part one." He held up a sparkling black charm. "Part two, I got an Iruvian shadow cloak. Part three, nobody likes getting stabbed." He palmed a stiletto, and considered its point.

"You actually saw one yesterday, right?" Saint said. "One of the spiders?"

"Yes. A little one," Safety agreed. "I gotta say, this whole part of the plan is super unpleasant."

"Who are you sending into the habitat?" Saint asked.

"I'm going," Safety said. "I've got the most experience with focusing through the charm, and I can handle the crates if necessary."

Saint put his hand on Safety's shoulder. "I'm counting on you," he said. "You have to pull this off without being detected. It's crucial."

"We will take care of it," Safety promised.

"Good," Saint nodded, withdrawing. "Because my life is in your hands. I'll be talking to Captain Sillman. If my story doesn't match his facts, the situation gets awkward fast."

Saint paused, considering his crew. "Today we crack the bone," he said. "Today we establish ourselves in North Port. It has taken a lot of time and a lot of treasure, but we have made it this far and the end is in sight."

"Let's do it," Red Silver said, decisive.

The crew bustled to pick up gear, preparing to leave. Safety took Saint aside.

"Before I go," Safety said, quiet.

"Yes?"

"Wringleton. Just wanted to let you know. That girl has skills. So much talent. And I like her attitude. Keep an eye on her, I think she could be a lurk for the crew. We haven't had one since we lost Piccolo," Safety murmured, serious. "She's *almost* ready to be the one we trust to go into the habitat instead of me. Just doesn't have the muscle, for the crates," he said with a wry smile.

"This isn't a suicide mission," Saint said. "You have to come back. You know that, right?" he pressed.

"I know, and I will be fine," Safety agreed. "It's dangerous, but I don't choke, and the Coursers are backing me up. We're about to reach a whole new level. I'm going to be there for that."

Saint smiled, and clapped him on the shoulder. "You'll have it done by sixth hour," he said, more conversationally.

"Guaranteed," Safety said.

"Then let's go."

TIME CORNERS, SOUTH SKIRT. NORTH PORT
16TH ULSIVET, 850. THIRD HOUR PAST DAWN

"Sir Torrent!" the Bluecoat said with a wide smile. "Swift blood to you!"

"Swift blood to you as well," Saint nodded as he approached. "Keeping the peace?"

"Pretty quiet," the Bluecoat agreed, looking around the small square. "Storm made a mess, you know?" Scaffolding was battered apart across the streets, workers were pulling together debris from the high winds. The rain was a soaking drizzle, but it didn't stop them from continuing their efforts.

"You didn't get caught up in any of that, did you? Or the little Dreblins at home?" Saint asked.

"No, I was on Dunvil Custom House rotation yesterday. Good day for inside work," Dreblin confided in Saint. "And thanks for asking, the kids are fine. Still quite an adjustment, moving out here away from all their friends."

"I hope the desk doesn't get much action," Saint mused. "I mean, there aren't even that many people out here yet."

"Yeah, the work bosses tend to handle lots of issues of theft or fighting or drunkenness in house, same with the captains, and if we get pulled in to deal with a convict crew issue something went *real* wrong," he grinned. "But there's all kinds of stuff. Things go missing, or somebody wants an investigation, or there's some property damage, or visiting dignitaries, or whatever. You know."

"Always something," Saint agreed. "Now, the captain. You hear about anything worrying him?" Saint asked, watching the workers across the street as they lashed a tarp over roofing tiles. He absently rubbed at a small pouch of currency so the coins inside clinked.

"Oh," Dreblin said, thinking hard. "Uh, no, the captain had a couple meetings, set up a special squad to check out a disturbance in Founder's Square, that's about it. Pretty normal."

"You are the best," Saint smiled, and he shook Dreblin's hand. The Bluecoat smiled, smoothly pocketing the small bag, and Saint limped on his way.

He didn't make it far before he spotted Inkletta following him. Seating himself on a low wall, he waited for her to catch up.

"I specifically told them not to let you wander without someone we trust coming along," Saint observed.

"They were busy," Inkletta said with a dismissive wave. "A bit hypocritical anyway, considering you're out here alone."

"I'm an exception," he said with a winning smile. "Red Silver has standing instructions to rescue me if I get into trouble. If she's in the mood. Otherwise *she* has to run the crew, and ugh," he said, reflective. "Who wants that headache? But see, with you here now I don't feel quite so safe, since she *also* had orders not to let you explore alone."

Saint leaned toward Inkletta. "It's possible Red doesn't pay much attention to my orders."

"So this is how it goes when I'm not around," Inkletta mused. "Loose cannons and mutiny."

"Yes," Saint agreed. "Also when you *are* around." He eyed Inkletta's woolen hose, boots, and sweater under her flowing drape. "I guess summer really is over."

"I guess." Inkletta rubbed her arms. "It's colder here than I expected."

"I've seen you wear a sheet when it was snowing," Saint said, mild.

"Maybe it's the Rowan system, I don't know," Inkletta said. "This seems out of your way. What's going on?"

"Oh, I've been making friends with the Bluecoats based out of this district, and its surroundings," Saint said. "Investing in their families' side projects for extra income. Little gifts. Listening to their stories. Smoothing the way for the next level. I've gotten quite a bit of juicy gossip over the last couple of weeks." He nodded towards the square. "Dreblin there is comfortable taking bribes from me now, and he was on the desk yesterday. At the Dunvil Custom House." Saint paused. "I need to know if the Bluecoats went into the strong room, if they noticed that the two crates of electroplasm are missing. Sounds like they don't know yet." He smiled. "Which is good."

"Do you think they inspected the cargo they confiscated from Niece?" Inkletta asked. "Discovered that you smuggled a Courser in with it?"

"Wringleton covered our tracks on that, put some other stuff in the crate when she sneaked out," Saint said with a dismissive gesture. "We have gone to great lengths to erase all traces of how we got the crates of electroplasm from the strong room, and we'll do the same for moving the crates into the Workshop."

"This all seems a little... elaborate," Inkletta observed.

"Fun, right?" Saint grinned. "Anyway, enough of all that. How goes the ritual preparation?"

"I will be ready." Inkletta paused. "I want to use Founder's Square for the ritual."

"That's fine with me," Saint said. "I mean, that's our base of operations, so any irregularities may point to us. But it's also easier to defend, I guess."

"Good," Inkletta said. She absently scratched at her eyepatch. "I would feel a lot better if you weren't out in the open."

"You can walk me to the Peach Bucket," Saint offered.

"I'd like that," Inkletta said.

"And maybe if the ritual preparation isn't too much, you could take a look at the Hammer today." Saint leaned into his cane, pushing himself to stand.

"I'd rather not do that today," Inkletta said. "I'm... I'm vulnerable right now."

"I trust you," Saint said. "I want *you* to be safe also. Do you feel up to accompanying me to meet with Malicoat tonight?"

"Oh," Inkletta said. "That's tonight." She shivered. "I... I don't know."

"Better not, then," Saint said. "Anyway, like you said, we're out in the open. I would like you to please go back to the Old Custom House."

"I will," Inkletta said. "Once you're settled at the Peach Bucket."

"Then we've got a plan. Right this way, my lady," Saint said with a smile. He offered the crook of his elbow.

"Gross," Inkletta observed. Still, she took his elbow, and together they followed the cramped twist of the street.

THE OLD CUSTOM HOUSE, FOUNDER'S SQUARE. NORTH PORT
16TH ULSIVET, 850. FOURTH HOUR PAST DAWN

The draft goat hollered as he clopped across the flagstones of the square, slowing in front of the Old Custom House. The coach sagged under the weight of its load, and the goat stood panting.

A slender woman batted the coach door open and stepped out, taking in the view. "You there," she said. "Is this the Old Custom House?"

Inkletta opened her eyes. She was seated by the stairs, meditating. She looked over the newcomer, noting her academic tunic and her sharp eyes. "You must be Jewel."

"I'm in the right place, I suppose," Jewel said reflectively. "Is Saint around?"

"No, but I am," Red Silver said as she strode out of the hall. She extended her hand. "I'm Red Silver. We've got space for your workshop in the basement." She snapped her fingers, and several burly porters came out of the hall and started unloading the coach. "Any trouble getting through the gate?"

"Nothing I couldn't handle. I assume we don't have amenities or infrastructure at this point," Jewel said crisply.

"Chamberpots and cookfires," Red Silver agreed. "We'll get some modernizing in place, once there's support for it. Pretty primitive just now."

"Security?"

"Doors are solid but the locks aren't any good," Red Silver replied. "The cellar doesn't have great ventilation, but it also doesn't have windows, so we figured it would be big enough and secure enough for the project."

"Stair width?"

"Wide enough for those," Red Silver said with a nod to the trunks. "They kept tuns of wine down there, so we should have decent space to maneuver."

Inkletta cleared her throat, and Red Silver glanced away from the intense leech to spot another visitor strolling across the square carrying a heavy satchel.

"You must be Red Silver," the young man said as he approached. "I'm Ryland." He extended his hand, and Red Silver shook it. "And you must be Jewel," Ryland said, offering her his hand.

"Charmed," she replied, ignoring the gesture.

"This is for you," Ryland said. He put the satchel down next to Red Silver, and she knelt to open it. Rolled blueprints, concise pages of notes, folded uniforms.

"Thank you, Ryland," said Red Silver. "Do I owe you anything?"

"No," Ryland replied. "Could we have a word in private?"

"This way," Red Silver said, hefting the satchel and returning to the hall as Jewel turned her attention to the porters unloading the coach.

"Is Saint here?" Ryland asked quietly as he followed her across the hall.

"Not right now, but you can talk to me," Red Silver replied. They reached the back corner of the hall, no one in earshot. "Let's have that word."

"Lord Malicoat will be in North Port to meet with Saint and Inkletta at the Hour of Honor, at the Nineways Greenkey estate. They can update each other on their efforts then."

"I will see to it that Saint gets the message," Red Silver nodded. "Anything else?"

"I'm sure there will be," Ryland said.

"Then I'll see you later."

He nodded, turned, and left the hall, effortlessly slipping past the porters as they unloaded Jewel's gear.

THE PEACH BUCKET PUBLIC HOUSE, COASTAL VIEW. NORTH PORT 16TH ULSIVET, 850. SIXTH HOUR PAST DAWN

Captain Sillman settled at his table, adjusting his bowl of filmy chowder and picking up his runcible spoon. He glanced up to see Saint standing opposite him.

"No," Sillman said forcefully, returning his attention to his lunch. "Go away."

"I'm worried," Saint said, watchful.

"I don't want to hear it," Sillman replied, but Saint sensed the hesitation in the response.

Saint sat down opposite the captain. "Please," he said softly.

Sillman slapped the spoon down on the table. "What."

"There are degrees to these things, and where no one is harmed, I see no clear duty to intervene," Saint said under his breath. "It is *not* harmless when refined electroplasm is available outside legal channels. Especially not out here, as the only authorized dealer is the Dunvil Custom House. *Your* house," Saint pressed.

Sillman scowled. "What are you talking about."

Saint slid a scrap of paper across the table. "That's the number on the canister I saw."

Unwillingly interested, the captain looked at the number. "Impossible. We have that batch secured."

Saint raised his eyebrows. "Do you?"

Sillman studied him for a long moment, then rose to his feet. "Get up," he said, his voice flat. "You're coming with me."

CHAPTER TWELVE

*In the 340s, the Immortal Emperor conducted a bloody
"re-alignment" of Doskvol. He arrived with his army and
broke the growing power of the dissenter nobles scheming
against him.*

*His forces gathered and fortified an island off the coast using
his profound sorceries and the seemingly limitless resources
of his empire. Victorious, he commissioned the Sanctorium in
Brightstone, to keep his wayward subjects connected to their
enlightenment. He laid the groundwork for the Master Warden's Estate, with its unique ritual protections. He chose which
bloodlines would survive and ascend as recognized Founding
Families of the city.*

*Influential rebels were executed by the Immortal Emperor
himself, with great ceremony. Crowds gathered to receive
truth, and part of that truth was imparted in blinding light
that burned the flesh from the skulls of his foes.*

*The Imperial bulwark hosting these executions was given the
macabre name "Whitecrown" as an unsubtle reminder. The
traitors who sought the Immortal Emperor's Crown of Isles
received a lethal crown of bone instead. Ever after, the island
has remained the site where the Immortal Emperor's rewarded
servants establish themselves.*

*—From "Considerations and Precedent for Countering
Corruption" by Minister Fygus Crotool*

"And there they go," Safety said under his breath, looking up at Wringleton as she waved a gesture down from the tree. He turned to Varela. "The distraction is in progress. You good with the load?"

"Yeah, I got it," Varela grumbled, the heavy crate strapped to a harness on his back.

"Let's get started," Safety said, and he climbed the ladder leaning against the outer wall of the Workshop compound. He got to the top, and pushed the knotted rope over the wall. It was tied to the ladder, which secured it in place as a counter-weight. Safety swung over the wall as Varela climbed the ladder on the other side. By the time Varela was halfway down the rope, Wringleton peered over the wall, ready to follow.

Cautious, Safety crouched behind an overturned longboat that was weathered past usability. He looked out across the drydock. There was too much cover to be assured of safe passage, but that was better than a wide open space. He led the way, darting from pillar to stack, keeping a low profile, the two Coursers right behind him.

They reached the service ladder at the corner of the boxed-in drydock. Safety shrugged at his load, and nodded to Wringleton, who scampered up the ladder with minimal groans and creaks from the structure. She reached the top, and signaled the all-clear.

By the time Safety clambered onto the roof, he could smell the smoke from the fire. Now that he was higher up, he could see the billowing cloud rolling up from the oil-soaked cart burning in the alley across from the Workshop. Half a dozen guards and workers struggled with buckets, dousing the cart and intensifying the smoke. More guards had been pulled from elsewhere to reinforce the entry. Just in case.

Safety unclipped the bolt cutters from the side of Varela's pack, and handed the cutters to Varela. "Get started," he muttered, nodding at the grating over the roof vent.

Wringleton pulled her sling bag open and tugged loose a cascade of fabric that silently slithered down from her fist. She swung the Iruvian shadow-silk so it billowed over Safety, and she gathered the silken cloth at his neck. He adjusted it over himself, feeling its strange coolness, as though it quieted his skin and blood. He seemed to move into the shade of an object he was not prepared to understand.

Wringleton stepped back as Safety clipped his demonbane charm in place, using it as a brooch. Safety dropped to one knee, focusing. He pressed his finger against the sharpened charm, felt its needle slide through his skin. His blood oozed into the complex metalwork, touching on the ritually infused stones. Safety breathed out as he bled.

He heard Wringleton swiftly knotting the cable, and he released that from his mind. He tuned out the distressing clank of the bolt cutters snapping through one wire after another, like teeth punching through armor. As the chill wind rippled the fabric, the movement somehow invisible, he soothed his mind so that it was as opaque and featureless as the Void Sea. As though drifting downward to rest upon it, he became keenly aware of the angles and bright relentlessness of the demonbane charm. His heart aligned with it, sending pulses out through the gleaming charm.

His perceptions did not form a perfect seal with absolute reality, and the gap pained him for a moment as he concentrated and his features grew slack. He centered himself within the charm, and felt its hard-edged radiance extend from his life force as he donned the charm as armor of a sort. He opened his eyes, a glint of light behind his pupils.

"That was fast," Wringleton said, impressed.

"I used to ride the rails," Safety murmured. "The death storms were just... weather." He turned to Varela, who struggled with the last few snips. The bolt cutters grew slick in his grip, and he swore under his breath.

"Could just—rip—the damned thing—" he grunted.

"Softly, softly. We don't want them to hear us," Safety breathed.

Varela broke through the last wire. He put the cutters aside, laced his fingers through the grating, and hauled back with all his might. The grating peeled up, reluctant.

Safety frowned at the hole. "I thought it would be bigger," he muttered. "Okay." Adjusting, he unclipped the harness holding the crate to his chest, and he lowered it. "I can't carry it down," he said. "So we—"

The door to the roof access clattered open, and a sleepy guard strolled out. He immediately froze, spotting the three scoundrels hunched over the broken roof vent. His eyes widened.

Safety was on his feet, sprinting, and as the guard stumbled back and grabbed at the whistle around his neck, Safety launched at him. Safety's forearm caught the guard in the chest, driving him back so he slammed into the wall, air driven out of him. Safety pivoted, hurling the guard down. The guard smacked on the ground and rolled. Safety pounced, catching the guard up in a sleeper hold, and the unfortunate quickly sagged in his grip, unconscious.

"He saw us," Varela said, his voice flat.

"Yeah, so he's going to have an accident," Safety said. "I'm pretty sure every spider down there is paying *close* attention to this vent," he added, jaw tight. "So I guess we solve two problems with one victim."

Varela took one arm, and Safety took the other. They dragged the guard over to the vent, hoisted him up, and carefully fed him down through the sharp-edged gap. To the side, Wringleton busily lashed the two crates together with the harnesses, clipping the rope in place.

"Bye," Varela said, dispassionate. The scoundrels released the unconscious guard to drop into the thick shadows. Immediately, the scrabble of chitin on wood and stone echoed, and the body thudded as something hit it mid-air on the way down. A chorus of hisses drifted up through the dark opening, along with a new wave of distressing gamy stink.

"This just isn't ideal," Safety said faintly, his skin crawling.

DUNVIL CUSTOM HOUSE. NORTH PORT
16TH ULSIVET, 850. SIXTH HOUR PAST DAWN

"Talk," Captain Sillman demanded as he barged into the inspection room where Saint patiently waited. The door slammed behind Sillman, and the two men were alone.

"As you know, I am introducing myself to various markets in North Port, as a buyer," Saint said. "I met with Sir Ousley, at his offices at the Workshop. Sir Ousley suggested I might be able to fence something for him, as he had acquired it but had no mechanism to exchange it for payment. He didn't have a buyer," Saint clarified. "When he said he had refined electroplasm, I keenly doubted him. He was determined to prove it, so he showed me a canister. He said he was looking for spark crafters, and would be willing to barter in civic grade fuel."

"At his office at the Workshop," Sillman clarified.

"Yes. I was shocked too. And the security there; it didn't seem a very secure location for this kind of contraband. He assured me his *spiders* would guard it," Saint shuddered.

"His *spiders*."

"Yes, that habitat he has connected to the office," Saint said, subdued.

"Well that just tears the cuff," Sillman muttered darkly. "Stay here." Sillman yanked the door open, and tossed it shut behind himself. "Guard him!" he shouted at the Bluecoat outside the door. His boot-falls withdrew.

Saint twirled his cane in his grip once, thoughtful.

HABITAT, THE WORKSHOP, HERITAGE DRYDOCK. NORTH PORT
16TH ULSIVET, 850. FIFTH HOUR PAST DAWN

Sweat trickled down the small of Safety's back, and his muscles burned with strain. His eyes were open, staring. He creaked lower in the dimness, the cable very slowly paying out from above. The crates kept him from swinging, and he felt the demonbane charm getting colder on his chest with some strange otherworldly friction. Eyes seemed to glitter in the deepest shadows all around him, reflecting the red depths of the charm.

Slowly drifting down, Safety looked through the brightly-lit windows, into the office. He saw Ousley's hunched back. Fortunately no one was standing in front of the desk, with a view out the windows, where he may or may not be visible in the center of the open space.

An impossibly long time later, the first crate brushed the ground. Safety dropped, the cloak billowing around him, and hissing echoed all around as the shadows moved with startling violence; lateral jumps through the dark gave Safety the feeling that walls were swapping invisibly as the spiders repositioned. He froze, one hand on the cable and the other gripping his stiletto.

His muscles felt like they were mounting each other, anticipating the hard shock of a spider's pounce, but the cold and invisible radiance of the demonbane charm held.

He could hardly breathe as he slowly lowered himself to one knee and fumbled with the clip connecting the cable and the harness. He managed to undo it, his fingers numb from the strain of holding on for so long. Ignoring the quiet convulsions of the broken guard off to the side, Safety dragged the harnessed crates behind the wreck of a stove-in fishing boat hull that was frosted with webbing.

Careful, Safety let go of the cable to pull a handful of webbing down from the hull, sticking it to the crate netting. A sharp rasp—one of the spiders dropped to the center of the habitat.

Safety stared at it. The spider's body was roughly the size of a human torso, armored and thick with tufts of weird fur. Its two front legs waved in the air, threatening, and a profusion of eyes glittered with reflected light and malice. Its abdomen flexed up and down, stressed and angry, and its dusty legs shifted position too fast for the eye to follow.

With his free hand, Safety clutched his demonbane charm as his heart-rate jumped to skitter hard against the inside of his ribcage. The point of the stiletto wavered as he pointed it at the spider. He sank to one knee, concentrating all his stress into the charm.

The crank wheeled, and the windows to the office opened. Ousley leaned out, crooning some strange phrase in archaic Hadrathi.

The spider flinched back, then recoiled into the darkness. Safety dropped the stiletto and waved his arm around, catching the cable again. He waited, unable to force himself to breathe.

"Silly babies!" Sir Ousley said in Akorosian. "Papa is trying to work! Now, if you settle yourselves, you can play later. I will find you some nice young thing to chase about, hee? Yes I will." He murmured a couple more phrases in an incomprehensible dialect of Hadrathi, and the spiders hissed at him; was it affection? Satisfied, he cranked the window shut, and turned away from the dim habitat.

Saint tugged the cable three times. Relief blended into the blood that still fired through his racing heart as he began the slow ascent out of the pit.

By the time Varela and Wringleton dragged Safety out of the vent, he was nearly too limp to walk. "Oh, by the Sisters," he swore. "Oh."

"Did you hide the body?" Varela demanded eagerly.

"No, no I didn't," Safety managed. "But it's pretty banged up. Saint will have to pretend the idiot stumbled in there somehow. Whatever, it's close enough. Maybe he was hiding the contraband," he slurred.

"Did you get bit?" Wringleton asked.

"No, thank the blood and bones," Safety said, on the edge of hysteria. "That was close."

"Okay. Okay then," Varela said, looking around. "Let's get out of here before anybody gets back."

"You go," Safety said.

"What?"

"You two go, and you can keep an eye on me from the perch. I'm going to stay here. Keep an ear out.." He paused. "If everything went according to plan, then the captain is going to come over here. Maybe I can overhear how it goes."

"But—even with the cloak, you are *clearly visible* on this roof," Wringleton objected.

"I have a plan," Safety said, his eyes squeezed shut. "A terrible, stupid, uncomfortable plan."

"You just got out," Varela said in a hushed voice. "You think you want to go back in?"

"I really don't," Safety confessed. He took a deep, steadying breath. "But we have to know how this plays out. And I can see his office from inside the *habitat*." The word felt too tame in his mouth, as his mind echoed with webs and shadows and eyes.

"I'll do it," Wringleton said. "I'm small. Good at hiding."

"Wringleton," Safety said with a crooked smile, "I can stand by as you get stuffed in a crate and locked in a fortress. But there's no way under the Refractions themselves that I'm going to leave you in a spider pit." He nodded. "This one's mine." He squinted at the wrenched grate cover. "Still. I might give them a minute or two to calm down."

The door to the inspection chamber opened again, and a heavy-set woman with a painfully tight bun came in. "You said you wanted to talk to me," she said. "Asked for me by *name*."

"Yes," Saint said. "Thank you for coming, First Pike Alya. I thought maybe we could understand each other better."

"That's what you thought," she said. "We could... understand each other better." She crossed her arms over her chest.

"It's not that I am causing trouble," Saint said apologetically. "Don't shoot the messenger, as it were. I am a big supporter of Bluecoats."

"Oh, that's what I hear," Alya agreed. "I've been asking around about you since yesterday. Apparently you've made friends with a *number* of our people. Been at it for a while before now."

"I like having friends," Saint confessed. "In fact, one of my good friends operates on both sides of the law; he's a bit of a scoundrel, but he has some admirable qualities."

"Here we go," Alya said through her teeth.

"I have this feeling," Saint said carefully, "that Sir Ousley may no longer support the Bluecoats. His offices might become vacant. And the work of the Weeping Lady is critical to the well-being of the district. It doesn't reflect well on the leadership if there is a vacancy, and we *all* want things to run smoothly."

"This is about the electroplasm," Alya stated.

"Among other things," Saint agreed. "No one thinks Sir Ousley was appointed here because of merit. He is an embarrassment to the Dunvil family, and they wanted him outside the wall. Those spiders," he said with a grimace. "And the sheer arrogance of the man. He didn't make friends here. He didn't even try. He just expected the Bluecoats to cooperate, so he could line his own pockets."

"I'm real busy," Alya said, patience thinning.

"Transitions can be rough," Saint said. "If appointed to managing the Weeping Lady charity out of the Workshop, I may have an advantage in the role, because of my friend. You could ask around about *him*, he's got a bit of a reputation. Saint Suran."

"Saint Suran," Alya repeated dully, her frown intensifying.

"I am sure he would help me out, quiet-like," Saint said. "He's got a demonstrated ability to provide an atmosphere with minimal internal conflict. He's all about repeat customers, not strip-mining the population. Cultivate a real audience. I hear he's worked with the Ministry and the Silkworms, but he's not in bed with the Hive. Doesn't hold grudges. Doesn't want competition. I *hear*," Saint said with emphasis, "he was raised in a fancy den, so he'd have a pretty good idea of how to run the Bunker." Saint leaned back in his chair. "Keep the peace. Keep the currency flowing."

Alya studied him. "Why not pitch all this to the captain?"

"I want him to be able to say he didn't know about my *friend*," Saint replied, "in case he is pressed. I want him to make an informed decision, without having to answer for all his information. And I love your record," he said. "Your time in Charhollow. You knew it was a career-ending move to stand up to Strangford's nephew when he made his power-grab in the Sheets neighborhood. But you did it anyway." He paused. "That's the kind of friend I want on my side."

"You an anarchist?" she growled.

"No," Saint replied. "I'm a noble myself, right? Sir Torrent," he reminded her. "And I'm here with Lady Selraetas. She runs the Old Custom House, which becomes part of our arrangement too."

"You sure are brazen," Alya observed.

"I see an opportunity," Saint replied. "If the captain appoints someone to look after the Workshop, in an interim capacity, then there's every chance that the appointment gets extended if it goes well. And if it goes poorly, another one of Dunvil's stooges gets stuck in and you have to deal with *that*. Removing Sir Ousley isn't an attack on your operations. It's a gift."

Alya slowly nodded. "I'll check into your friend, Saint Suran. See if we could tolerate him as a neighbor."

"Thank you ever so much," Saint said with a warm smile.

Safety was nestled into the crook of the rafter, bundled in the cloak, the demonbane charm a low throb in his consciousness. The cable hanging past the grating was wrapped around his wrist, looping out through the dimness, up to his escape. For now, he was calm. The spiders seemed to have forgotten about him.

He had a clear view into the office from his high perch. Ousley was in the middle of his lunch when there was a commotion outside, and the door to his office banged open.

"Captain Sillman!" Ousely said, outraged as he jumped up out of the chair. "What is the meaning—"

"Quiet," the Bluecoat captain snarled, and Ousely plopped back down in his chair. "I'm not shocked that you *robbed* me. I just figured you could have some subtlety. Some patience," he said. Two Bluecoats he brought with him edged into the room.

"Rob you?" Ousley scoffed. "I have no idea—"

"*Two full crates* of electroplasmic cells?" Sillman snapped. "I figured you'd make off with one, maybe two of the cells. Two crates is too much."

"Stop this at once!" Ousley retorted, jumping to his feet again. "These accusations! I cannot guess how you got these ideas in your head, but I assure you—"

"Interrupt me one more time!" Sillman roared. "See what happens."

Ousley stared at him, quivering.

"You wanted a key to the strong room. You wanted it bad. Made a big stink about our partnership, Bluecoat support of the locals, all that blister and puss. So I gave you a copy. And now the most valuable thing in there is missing. Last week you were going on and on about how you wanted a plasmic wall defense in the Bunker. You were complaining to anyone who would listen. And I'm not supposed to make a connection?"

"I am not *stupid*," Ousley said with his most withering disdain. "Even if I were to fleece you, as you rightly observed, I would not inhibit the ability of the Bluecoats to run their defenses. No one wants intensified scrutiny of North Port! At least, you and I do not. Who else might have done this? And why do you think it was me?"

"We have lots of places to hide things," Sillman growled, "just like you do. But we put the plasmic fuel in the strong room because that's required by regulations. Official business. Tracked and monitored. That's my end. Where do *you* put stuff when you want to show off how untouchable it is?" he demanded.

"Well, my safe, I mean," was as far as Ousley got.

"Take us into your spider hole," the captain interrupted. "Now."

"I do *not* care for your tone!" Ousely shot back, puffing up his chest.

"Are you seriously going to make me ask again?" Sillman said, his voice uncomfortably quiet.

Ousley glared at him for a long moment, then rounded his desk and snatched his key ring from the center of the decorative wreath made of thorny vines and web. He pushed past the Bluecoat at the door, and the captain fell in line behind him, his Bluecoats in tow.

Safety adjusted his position slightly, a smile on his face.

Bars clattered back out of the way on the other side of the heavily secured door opening to the habitat floor. It pushed open, tearing the webbing that was halfheartedly spread across its frame. Ousley strode in, brandishing his demonbane charm, a liquid chatter of archaic Hadrathi spilling out of him. The spiders retreated, a sibilant hissing swelling from wall to wall as they relocated. Bluecoats entered, pistols out, eyes wide. Ousley's clerk followed with a lantern, her scarred face bent with worry.

"Oh dear," Ousley said, spotting the corpse of the guard.

"Look around," Sillman said to his Bluecoats. He aimed his pistol at one of the shadows that gleamed with eyes.

"There's nothing to find," Ousley insisted, "and I resent the implication that there is. There *will* be consequences for this invasion," he promised, seething with indignation.

"Found it," called out one of the Bluecoats. He dragged at the harness around the two crates, pulling them into view, web stretching as it was disrupted.

A moment of shocked silence reverberated.

"So that's why there's a guard in here," Ousley said quickly. "He thought he could frame me, paid by some third party, but he lacked my affinity for the arachnidilia of the habitat! Rouse him, see if he could be questioned."

"He's pretty dead," one of the Bluecoats said, squinting at the broken body.

Sillman pinned Ousley with a glare.

"I am related, *by blood and title*, to Lord Dunvil!" Ousley raged with a dramatic gesture. "You dare not lay a hand on me!"

"You got this posting because you are an *embarrassment*," Sillman snapped. "With your schemes and your appetites and your knot clotted *spiders*. Dunvil wanted you outside city walls for a reason. He knows it's dangerous out here."

"Is that so! Well, I know what you're up to in North Port," Ousley sneered, trying to bury his desperation in bluster. "I know about the corruption, I have seen every facet of your stupid little operation. Enough to get you banished, or tossed into Ironhook yourself! You can't shut—"

Sillman snatched the demonbane charm right out of Ousley's fist, and shoved him. Ousley stumbled over the dead guard and slapped down on the stone floor of the habitat. The spiders hissed.

"You," Sillman said to the clerk. "This jackass came down to play with his spiders, and he tripped. Right? Jumpers can take a body by surprise."

"Oh yes," the clerk replied, not looking at Ousely. "But it could take days to die, even if he got bit a few times. He could be rescued."

"Ah," Sillman nodded. "So we tried to rescue him, shot at the spider on top of him. Missed. Clumsy."

"Looks that way," the clerk agreed.

Sillman turned to Ousley, who let out a squeal as he raised his trembling hands. The pistol thundered, pounding a shot through Ousley's gut.

The sweating Bluecoats kept their pistols trained on the restless shadows.

"Keep this place running," Sillman said to the clerk. "I'll get an appointee in here soon." The clerk bowed.

Sillman left the habitat, followed by the clerk, the Bluecoats warily backing out behind them. Ousley managed a thin scream as the lantern's light was cut off by the slamming door. The bars rasped in place, sealing the habitat once more.

Confident that the spiders were sufficiently distracted, Safety climbed towards daylight.

INSPECTION ROOM, DUNVIL CUSTOM HOUSE. NORTH PORT
16TH ULSIVET, 850. EIGHTH HOUR PAST DAWN

Saint roused as the heavy door swung open. Sillman entered, and closed the door. He turned to regard Saint.

"Hello," Saint said experimentally.

"I went to talk to Sir Ousley," Sillman said. "He was in his habitat. In a moment of distraction, he was attacked by one of his pets. We tried to save him, but in the confusion, we missed the spider and hit him instead. It's a tragedy."

"He was so young," Saint agreed, concerned.

"I got an update from my First Pike," Sillman continued. He sat down opposite Saint at the table. "I always appreciate her perspectives."

Saint smiled and waited.

"I get the feeling you put a lot of thought into your accidental discovery," Sillman said, mild.

"Yet it was convenient for you to play along," Saint murmured. "Ousley may have connections in the city, but he had no friends here."

"You do," Sillman said. "Friends everywhere, apparently. In my experience, people with friends everywhere also have enemies everywhere, shortly afterwards. You're just now moving in. So they'll likely start cropping up."

"That's not why I'm leaving Silkshore," Saint said. "Operating there, you've got intense factional politics. The gondoliers have complicated relationships with the Red Sashes. The Foundation has a stake in a corner store, so you accidentally piss them off when you operate on that street. You've got secret agendas and spy rings working out their rivalries through your business without you even knowing. It's exhausting." He paused. "I did alright there, these last couple years. I got on the gondolier council. Smoothed relations with the Skovs. Corrected a misunderstanding with Rowan House. I am prepared for this."

"I think you mean your friend Saint is prepared for this," Sillman said, bland.

"Right, Saint. Look. The Dunvil House used to run North Port, and now they do again. Lord Dunvil has extra support from Iron Hook because he runs that too. The Clelland House runs the new Bluecoat district," he said with a gesture to Sillman. "The Rowan House is handling the shiny new defensive system. The City Council is *directly* represented in this venture. Anybody operating out here needs to avoid crossing those interests, keep things quiet and profitable. My friends have some experience in staying on their good side."

"Yeah, I hear you," Sillman said. "You coming for my job next?"

"Oh no," Saint said, restraining a laugh. "Oh, captain. No. Nor any of my people. I want Bluecoat *friends*, but no, I don't want your headaches. The hours. It's a little rigorous for my tastes." He paused. "I'm content to manage the Workshop and the Bunker, adding in the Old Custom House. My interests are all on the social side. We can handle problems the Bluecoats and convicts can't. With a softer touch."

Sillman studied him for a long, long moment. "You must have silky blood running through that tongue," he muttered. "This is fun, I guess, but right now you're going to be honest with me."

"Yes," Saint said, leaning forward and looking Sillman in the eye.

"Hive connections."

"None."

"Circle of Flame," Sillman growled.

"Already checked in with Magistrate Drake, told her what I'm telling you," Saint replied.

"How about the Silkworms, the Ministry, the military."

"I've cooperated with them before, and will again," Saint said. "I've got friends among the aristocracy, too."

"Smuggling."

"All I'm interested in is the vice side of things," Saint answered.

"Cults. Forgotten Gods. The Church."

"I've got a cultist friend who will be operating, but not actively recruiting," Saint said. "I have no particular problem with worship. It's a vice like any other," he said with a winning smile. "Just one more way to escape. I myself support the Church's official teachings," he said, "as often as is convenient."

Sillman leaned back, thinking. "The true mark of a gentleman, I am told, is cultivating an interesting conversation," he observed. "You've done that. So." He waited for his instincts to whisper to him. "I am appointing you as interim manager of the Weeping Lady operations out of the Workshop. And all that goes with it," he said, "under your delegatory authority. Let's be clear. I can rescind this appointment at will. I don't have to explain why, or even let you live," he said with a significant look. "This is just an interview. Now you have to convince me you can do it."

"You have my humble thanks," Saint said, rising so he could bow. "When would you like me to assume the duties?"

"Ousley's body should be cool by this evening, and immolated by the Spirit Wardens overnight, so how about you start bright and early," Sillman said.

"I will be ready," Saint grinned.

"One more thing," Sillman said quietly. "I do not like being embarrassed."

Saint let the gravity of the moment sink into both of them.

"Let's work together to make sure that doesn't happen," he said.

Sillman stood, opened the door, and released Saint back into the world.

CHAPTER THIRTEEN

The Weeping Lady is a charitable tradition based on the legend of Lady Devara, the first Lord Governor of Doskvol. She was famed as a champion of the poor. The tradition's public focus is on emulating Devara's compassion and empathy. For the ruling class, there is more practical wisdom.

All noble children are quietly shaped by Lady Devera's sage advice, when they are ready. Devera cautioned her fellow nobles: "Let them see your tears. Charitable pity will blunt their demands for your sweat or your blood."

Heirs are taught that if they appear indifferent or amused by the plight of the governed, smoldering resentment will ignite to rage. They inherit a tradition that fences in their hoard with castoffs, leftovers, and pretty speeches.

Your masters pay for your sacrifices with crumbs and prayer. They know you suffer, and they care for you—one bowl of thin gruel at a time.

—From "An Examination of the Symbolic Figures of the Dusk's Lore"by Captain Niea Wuldar

Inkletta sat upright, her eye half closed. Grull's lantern sat on a stool in front of her. The flame rose and fell with her slow breathing, so the shadows swelled and shrank as she rhythmically fed air to her simmering blood.

A gentle knock sounded through the door, and Inkletta roused. Sighed. Leaning forward, she opened the lantern and blew out the flame. She stood up in the darkness, her limbs fully alive and her joints limber, and she opened the door.

"Supper's ready," Wringleton said. "They wanted me to let you know."

"Thank you, little one," Inkletta said absently. "I will be down shortly." She closed the door.

Again, her skin tightened with chill. She felt a tremor begin, deep in the hinge of her jaw. A coldness like fear, like guilt, like humiliation, shivered in her core. Not quite hunger, or reproach, or lust, or passion; the alien sensation rippled through her muscle, and she felt the subtle clicking as her jaw shivered her teeth together.

She took another deep breath.

Like a shark scenting a distant wound, something within her detected worship rising elsewhere. In the city. More than one location. Offerings to the Shrouded Queen.

Inkletta's foolish meat stood far away from where it was needed. The door through the wall was distant from where the travellers knocked.

"I won't apologize for the limits of the physical world," Inkletta whispered.

The emotion that twisted inside her felt like grief at wronging a childhood friend, abusing a life-long relationship. She steeled herself against it, and reached for the pile of clothes she had borrowed. Pulling them on in the dark, she grimaced as she shoved her feet down into the unfamiliar confines of boots. Bracing herself to deal with the noise and chaos of people, she left her room.

The former store room had been converted to a somewhat cozy informal dining chamber. Two of the trestle tables had been pushed together and surrounded, with Saint at the head. Red Silver was next to

Saint on one side, Inkletta took her seat on his other side. Of the River Stallions, only Gapjaw was missing. The Coursers livened up the far end of the table. Jewel seemed at ease among the scoundrels, swatting Varela's hand away so she could get at the cheese bread and laughing at Sukup's impression of a befuddled Bluecoat.

"I figured we were going to have crab again," Safety was saying. "Like, forever, considering how much the Knotwork brought."

"You obviously don't cook," Niece sniffed. "We burned through almost all of it last night. This is some fresh-caught cod, got it at the market. You know," she said to Red Silver, "it sure would make running this place easier if we had a purchasing agent to handle supplies and such."

"Oh that's right," Red Silver mused. She turned to Saint. "I say, Torrent, Isn't that why I brought you along?" she asked in her most posh accent. "Deary me, for *what* do I pay you."

"You pay me?" Saint said, amused. "Well that's good news."

"On second thought," Red Silver corrected, eyebrows raised and nose in the air, "never mind."

"Now that we're all here," Niece said, "I sure would like an update on how today went."

The atmosphere settled at once, eyes on Saint.

"So far, so good," Saint said. "Safety, how did it go with Ousely."

"Pretty smooth," Safety said. "We were interrupted by a guard, but the spiders got him, so he won't say anything. We placed the crates, Captain Sillman found them, and he wasn't interested in Ousley's explanation. Shot him, left him to the spiders. Saw it with my own eyes," he said.

"Then," Saint said, "the captain appointed me manager of the Workshop and everything under it. Which, between us, includes the Bunker." He smiled. "I take possession in the morning."

There was a general cheer.

"Big progress," Saint agreed, recapturing their attention. "But we aren't done, so no celebrating yet. We have to stay sharp. I also met with Magistrate Drake yesterday. I think it went alright, but she's not on our side at this point. We will have to be careful," he said, draining some of the exuberance from the room. "And I have assignments!"

There was some good natured eye rolling and groans, but the anticipation was palpable.

"Red, track down Jace. I want to keep him on for continuity. I talked to him once, I want you to seal the deal. You are more his type," he said with a wry smile. "The official job offer is spider wrangler, he's got experience with those nasty things. I also want him to consider troubleshooting for us."

"Got it," Red Silver said. "Rates?"

"A little bump up from what Ousely was paying him," Saint said. "Give him a bonus, but don't thin out our margins too much. Also, drop off that present we discussed to thank Sillman." He turned to Safety. "You'll be running the Bunker. Get in there, lay the foundation for the changes we are planning. In the meantime, make sure everything keeps running without a hitch. I will take possession of the Workshop."

"What about us?" Varela said, daring.

Saint turned to Niece. "How are things going here?" he asked. "Kitchen and wait staff, extra hands for security, all that."

"It's early yet, but we already have quite a few people in the hall, and the staff are handling it just fine. I caught one of our new recruits informing and got rid of her. There will be others, but generally we're figuring it all out. I've got a guard schedule, patrols, and security for the hall worked up. We're managing," Niece said.

"Good, then tomorrow the Coursers will work with Safety and make sure things go right at the Bunker," Saint said. "Learn the place."

"I'll make the initial approach on my own," Safety said. "Then bring the Coursers in once I have it in hand."

"That doesn't sound very safe," Varela said, frowning.

Safety raised his eyebrows. "My risk to take," he said. "You'll be in reserve until I call for you."

The moment simmered, then Saint looked to Jewel. "How is the workshop coming along?"

"I'm pretty much set up," she said. "I spent some time with the plans." She glanced sideways at the Coursers. "We can talk about it later," she said.

"Yes, Inkletta and I will meet with you when I get back from my update with our patron," Saint said. "I'm headed over there after supper."

"Anything we need to know about that?" Varela demanded.

"Oh, you don't have enough to do?" Saint retorted, angling toward humor. "Safety, the Coursers are bored. I am beginning to think they feel left out."

"Well, good news," Safety said, playing along, "because we have three rooms full of stuff the Meathooks left behind that we shoved out of the way for opening night, and that's got to be sorted. So we'll handle that tonight," he said to Saint.

"Oh," Niece smiled, "you are the *best*. Sure will be helpful having all that organized and stored."

"Ha ha ha," Varela said sarcastically, trying to ignore the glares from the other Coursers.

"Which reminds me," Saint said to Niece. "Look over the new recruits, pick out some possible leaders. We need to pull together another gang based out of the Old Custom House, so the Coursers can focus on the Bunker and troubleshooting."

"Will do," Niece said with a curt nod.

"You need backup tonight?" Inkletta asked Saint, her voice low.

"I'd rather you start working things out with Jewel," Saint replied. "I'll handle our patron."

She nodded, calm, concealing her relief.

"I'm going to want to know more about the meeting with Drake," Red Silver said to Saint.

"Right, here's the short version," Saint said quietly, leaning in so it was just Red Silver and Inkletta in the conversation. "There's a scavenger, Mesech, he was running errands for Drake. He was here last night, at the opening. Anyway, he opened a ghost door, I think it's old, maybe a heritage placement. Took me somewhere called the 'Echosheath' by the back of the Court Annex. Pretty big flex, she holds court on *both* sides of the Mirror."

"Has she looked into us?" Red Silver asked.

"Yes. Enough to warn me to keep you on a leash," Saint said to Inkletta, "like we thought she would. I kept it charming. Drake is still digging, though, and even if she doesn't move against us she's not going to be an admirer."

"So, pretty much what we expected," Red Silver said.

"So far," Saint nodded, "so good."

NINEWAYS GREENKEY ESTATE, SOUTH SKIRT. NORTH PORT
16TH ULSIVET, 850. HOUR OF HONOR, 1 HOUR PAST DUSK

Saint leaned against the stone arch, taking his time, patient. The fog of the Blind Hour had not cleared away, and there was little breeze. The squat tower behind him was illuminated with lamps built into the exterior, flame twitching and rolling as light diffused into the chilly dark.

The tower opened, and Ryland stepped out. "There you are," he said, amiable. "Come on in."

Saint leaned through the arch gate and followed Ryland inside. The main chamber had two chairs in the shallow pit, the drained pool in the center of the room. Ryland ushered Saint in and closed the door behind him.

"We gather in North Hook," Lord Malicoat observed. He stood across the chamber, lost in contemplation of an elaborately carved frieze.

"Is that what we're doing?" Saint replied, easing down the steps to seat himself in a chair.

"That's the theme of this piece," Lord Malicoat clarified with a gesture towards the frieze. "Dancing along the street, with the believers and the skeptics and the breath from beyond." He turned to smile at Saint. "So let's dance."

"I've established the River Stallions in North Port," Saint said. "Everything isn't settled yet, but we have a foothold. The cover story and resources will be useful to obscure our activities in pursuit of your goals. If you contacted Captain Sillman and expressed your support for Lady Selraetas and Sir Torrent that would be much appreciated," he added.

"Tell me how you are proceeding on locating the chamber," Lord Malicoat said. He seated himself opposite Saint.

"I have secured the services of Jewel, a freelance leech—one of the few who have some familiarity with the workings of Rowan's ambient suppression defense system. She did some quick research on the specifics of our needs, and brought a workshop with her. We have her installed in the cellar of the Old Custom House, she set up today. Inkletta worked with the Fairpole Council Whispers to figure out a custom ritual to trace the conduits to the heart chamber, she's been handling preparation for that and we're ready to go tomorrow. She identified Founder's Square as the place to conduct the ritual. Thank you for getting us the information we needed to aid our preparation," he said with a nod to Lord Malicoat.

"What is your plan to deal with Sysavant?" Lord Malicoat asked.

"The plan is not down to specifics yet, but it has generally taken shape," Saint said. "I think we should involve Magistrate Drake. She is one of the Seven, leading the Circle of Flame. She doesn't like how low class I am, or my operation, so she's deciding whether or not to tolerate us. I think we can create friction and misunderstanding so Sysavath bends her energies to dealing with Drake, who is a sufficiently hard target to give her some trouble. That should be enough of a distraction. If it isn't, we send a provocative invitation to a meet and hit her with our sniper."

Lord Malicoat studied him for a moment. "I expected Inkletta to accompany you," he mused.

Saint nodded, considering his response. "This ritual we are conducting. It's not a casual effort with supplies we had on hand," he said. "The Spirit Wardens have a head start on this. As far as we know, they haven't figured out the location of the heart chamber, not yet. There is nothing trivial about treading along the path left by the Immortal Emperor. There are prices to pay for the sort of energy and expertise we are bringing to bear. We have divided the work, so Inkletta focuses on the ritual and I coordinate with you."

"I see," Lord Malicoat said, something impatient in his tone. "Because your expertise is dealing with me, is that it?"

"My expertise," Saint said calmly, "is looking out for the interests of my crew and motivating them to give their best. I must have a clear picture of what we need. I must understand both the obstacles we must overcome, and the objectives we pursue. Since this work is dangerous," he added, "it's possible that we won't all make it through. I have acted in good faith on your behalf, and the resources we have secured for this task cost more than your initial offering. It is time we agreed upon some compensation that will fall to us even if you do not return from this adventure."

"I do not want to waste time with this," Lord Malicoat said with a dismissive gesture. "My interests in North Port will end when I have succeeded. In the meantime, I acquired operation rights for this tower, and for some neighboring properties in South Skirt to assure my privacy. I will transfer stewardship and right of occupation to you, or one of your associates, and leave the documents with Ryland. Will that suffice?" he demanded.

"That is an excellent arrangement," Saint agreed. "We have also incurred some additional expenses, and we can defray them and prepare against setbacks, for ten Coin."

"Aren't you bold," Lord Malicoat observed.

"Yes."

"Very well," Lord Malicoat said, "and for that princely sum I will have a private discussion with Inkletta, in addition."

"No," Saint said. "For that sum you are welcome to review the ritual preparation and the leech's workshop."

"How much do you think a private conversation with Inkletta is worth?" Lord Malicoat wondered.

"It's not for sale," Saint replied. "Besides. This ten Coin is not paying us for our efforts. That payment is just to cover expenses."

Lord Malicoat scowled, dissatisfaction evident on his face. "I am a skilled adept in my own traditions. I will review the ritual tomorrow morning."

"Very good," Saint nodded. "Did you discover anything that will help us, about the chamber itself?"

"I did indeed," Lord Malicoat said. "For one, we do not have the element of surprise. I discovered an informant in my organization that has been updating the Spirit Wardens on some aspects of my operations. Sysavath knows this tower is mine, and she knows we are working together."

"That's not ideal," Saint said, mild.

"Correct. Still, we continue undeterred. The Crolaange assisted me with context regarding the heart chamber. I am not sure you have the necessary background to understand," Lord Malicoat said, condescending.

"Fill me in all the same, please," Saint said. "You can update Inkletta and Jewel tomorrow morning."

"Very well. I will attempt to make this clear to a layman," Lord Malicoat said. "They have a name for the central location beneath North Port, the location we seek. It is called the Reliquary of the Fallen Star. You may usefully think of our objective as a 'sideways chamber.' That's what limmers call places like the one we seek, or the Shrine of the Fallen Star where the Crolaange worship. You see, the Leviathans can exist solidly on both sides of the Mirror while belonging to neither. Think of a crocodilian drifting along interrupting the surface of the water and present both above and below it by virtue of simply existing, containing air and water but made of something else. With me so far?"

"Yes," Saint nodded.

"Sideways chambers require an anchor point that has profound vitality and does not belong wholly on one side of the Mirror or the other. The Crolaange shrine is anchored in a Leviathan skull; they tore it from the Fallen Star centuries ago, and we can assume the Leviathan has grown a new one by now. The Reliquary of the Fallen Star is anchored by the fragment of Tya's heart. A large and vital mass of tissue provides necessary leverage against the natural order's constant pressure to enforce the rules of displacement."

"I am surprised you have not attempted to absorb the essence of the skull," Saint observed. "It seems you would have easier access to it than this lost chamber."

"Bone will not do for my purposes, it must be tissue. The needs we meet to anchor a sideways chamber differ from the needs for an infusion of immortality," Lord Malicoat said. "Now. For a sideways chamber, we will not be able to break in, nor will we be able to follow the energy conduits to breach the walls." He paused. "There must be a door. A ghost door. The ritual will locate the chamber, outline its shape, and locate the point of entry. Our objective will be breaching the door."

"A door that has been shut for centuries," Saint clarified.

"As you obviously know, ghost doors require keys. Ephemeral 'safe cracking' is a complex business, and there are likely to be curses and haunts and other defenses both in the door and beyond it. It is entirely possible that seven centuries have passed since anyone moved through that door. Finding it is critical, and we must hope that it has not been overbuilt on this side of the Mirror." He looked reflective. "Then again... it is possible the door has been used more recently."

"Oh?"

"My education with the Crolaange added a nuance I previously lacked, regarding the Stitcher," Lord Malicoat said. "Apparently, these... these sideways chambers are bound up in the essence of the Stitcher who creates them. The Crolaange shrine was gifted to them by the Tower, though they no longer remember it. They shared with me some documents, from that time period, and my mind is able to retain some evidence that theirs cannot—the curse, you see. Over and over they have read about how the Tower of the Unseen extracted services from them in exchange for their shrine. Over and over again they have forgotten."

"You think that's why the Tower returned to Doskvol?" Saint said, quiet. "Because the Tower created the sideways chamber under North Port?"

"I think if the Immortal Emperor kills the Tower, then all the sideways chambers the Tower created as a Stitcher might be compromised," Lord Malicoat murmured. "We have no way of knowing what consequences would follow, what secrets and treasures might be lost. It begins to make sense that the Immortal Emperor cursed and banished the Tower instead of executing him."

Saint thought that over. "Could you talk to the Tower, to get clues about where the door might be?" he wondered.

"I cling to the hope," Lord Malicoat said with a trace of bitterness, "that the Tower does not realize my intent. If the Tower knew what I was doing, without his involvement, he would likely be peeved. The entry would certainly be defended, its barriers reinforced, and considering the abilities I suspect a Stitcher has, perhaps relocated." He scowled at Saint. "All the more reason to be swift."

"Let's say we locate the door, and get through its defenses, opening the way. You get in," Saint said. "What happens then?"

"That is beyond the scope of your involvement," Lord Malicoat said.

"But you need Inkletta to do something," Saint prompted.

"Possibly," Lord Malicoat said. "Regarding the Spirit Wardens, I bent my resources to the task of getting a better picture of how they are conducting the hunt. We have not seen overt activity in North Port, and I grew concerned."

"This should be good," Saint said with a wry smile.

"The Spirit Wardens secured the Hunter's Lodge, the heritage training fortification for ghost hunters before the Spirit Wardens assumed their role. They seem to be keeping to themselves there, and the public story for what they are doing in North Port is two fold. One, they are evaluating the Rowan defenses and reporting their findings. Two, and less well known, they are protecting secrets here; building spaces that no Whisper or ritual can breach, under Rowan's new technology."

"And everyone assumes they are digging for secrets that don't belong to them," Saint added, "because that's what they do everywhere."

"They have a sweeping mandate to eradicate traces of the old ways, the 'limmer culture' that lingers in libraries and occult spaces," Lord Malicoat said, a glint in his eye. "North Port is steeped in that lore. The Ministry calls the old sites in North Port 'heritage' locales, and the Church works with the Spirit Wardens to redefine what that heritage contains."

"So that's the public perception," Saint said.

"There is a spirit well beneath the Hunter's Lodge," Lord Malicoat continued. "My sources indicate it was named the Moon Pool in 'heritage times.' From what I could gather, Spirit Wardens are passing through the Moon Pool to move behind the Mirror, exploring the ghost field, and placing beacons. They are trying to locate the reliquary by sifting the layers on the other side."

Saint blinked. "Could that work?"

Lord Malicoat raised his eyebrows. "We had best conduct our ritual sooner rather than later," he replied. "What they are doing is profoundly expensive, and extraordinarily dangerous even for them. Still."

"Sysavath," Saint said. "She's probably been spending more time on the other side of the Mirror."

"Yes," Lord Malicoat nodded.

"So it seems we should distract her, get her attention back on this side," Saint said. "You know her well. What gets under her skin? How would we hold her attention?"

"I do not think it is necessarily wise to distract her at this point," Lord Malicoat said. "If we are on the edge of a breakthrough, we may want to outrun the Spirit Wardens rather than attempt to trip them."

"Fine with me," Saint said. "We focus on the ritual tomorrow. I have some new recruits that we can dress up as technicians, and we can power down a section of Rowan's defenses. Inkletta will inject some electroplasm into the area, and send it down through a conduit while we make sure nothing interrupts her. I will give her some notice on the change in objective tonight, so she knows to look for exterior doors and trace them to where we might pry them open on this side." Saint rose to his feet.

"I will send the Coin to the Old Custom House with Ryland," Lord Malicoat said. "If you were set upon by muggers, losing a fortune would truly be tragic. I am confident he will not be seen if he chooses to move quietly."

"Understood," Saint said. "We are trusting each other here. Aren't we."

"Of course," Lord Malicoat said. "I will richly reward those who serve me well."

"Alright then," Saint said. "See you tomorrow."

Leaning on his cane, he mounted the shallow steps to the exit, and let himself out. The lingering sense of Lord Malicoat's eyes on his back took several blocks to dissipate.

CELLAR, THE OLD CUSTOM HOUSE, FOUNDER'S SQUARE. NORTH PORT 16TH ULSIVET, 850. HOUR OF SILVER, 3 HOURS PAST DUSK

"Here and here," Jewel said, putting lug nuts on the technical map. "These two stations go down, and Founder's Square loses coverage from the ambient suppression defense system."

Lamplight mingled uneasily with the chilly glow of electroplasmic canisters racked up on the workbench, creating a mottled effect on the plans and on the three scoundrels that reviewed them.

"How long will it take for the drainage to stop, and the ghost field to build up some background... juice?" Saint asked with a vague gesture.

"About eighteen hours," Jewel replied, "which we won't have."

"I have a ritual use for refined electroplasm," Inkletta said, eyes on the diagram. "I will release a sacrifice, a *trench rat*," she said with a look to Jewel, who still scowled, "directly into the vent. This will create the necessary traffic through the conduit."

"So the ritual will work, vent travel aside?" Saint asked. "Sounds like it will be pretty dry."

"Don't tell Magistrate Drake, but I have some work-arounds," Inkletta frowned.

"Oh, you know I'm a fan," Saint said quickly. "I just want to make sure you have everything you need."

"Yes, I do," Inkletta said. "How about you?" she asked Jewel.

"I packed for this," Jewel nodded. "I have some power cells for a couple of my tools. To get Inkletta that refined electroplasm, we can use the tanks on the collectors themselves. They distill the background ambience into fuel. If we get unfettered access to the collectors to sabotage them, we also get bonus access to the fuel they've been condensing. That part is easy."

She tapped the diagram. "The harder part will be the misdirect, so the rest of the collectors are working fine and don't trigger an *actual* response where technicians come out and try to fix what we're breaking."

"You prepared for that, right?" Saint said.

"Of course." Jewel tapped her chin. "We can go at this two ways. One is to create a more urgent situation to hold their attention somewhere else while we work this out. The other is to make an arrangement with the adept on duty for our section, so she looks the other way while we do what we have to do."

"Those are both unpleasant options," Saint said, wrinkling his nose. "I've had bad experiences tangling with these system adepts before; their patrons are *really* possessive," he said. "Before they go through the profoundly expensive and time-consuming process of getting keyed to a system, they are *rigorously* reviewed and tested to assure they are difficult to corrupt. But damaging the system is also attracting attention we aren't going to want, during a time when our new neighbors are making up their minds about us." He winced, thinking hard.

"You still with us?" Jewel asked after a moment, concerned.

"Yes. So, we've got an aristocratic ghost that got stranded here and we need to re-form him to take him back to an estate," Saint pitched. "So the adept and techs agree to shut the field down for us."

"That would take time, to get that kind of exception approved, and we'd have to get together paperwork that would hold up under the scrutiny. I don't know," Inkletta said, dubious.

"We could make it urgent somehow," Saint said. "Maybe a dying relative needs the ghost back before he goes."

"This is too complicated to pull off with what we've got," Inkletta retorted. "We'd have to convince Spirit Wardens, if we wanted to deal with legal ghost collection. They'd need a damn good reason."

"Yes!" Saint said, eyes lighting up. "Yes they would! But they wouldn't be required to tell you what that reason was, would they?"

"Oh no," Inkletta said, closing her eyes.

CHAPTER FOURTEEN

The first known worship of the Shrouded Queen was among convicts. In the sixth century, Biter Nell became a priestess of the Shrouded Queen. Her first converts were the guards who secured her solitary cell where she wailed day and night. She went insane, gnawing at her hands and feet, sending joints of her fingers and toes out with her food tray. When she quieted, they thought she died. Maybe she did.

But she still moved and spoke, so she was returned to the general population. She spread a message. Anything you sacrificed to her Shrouded Queen, you did not lose. You created room in yourself by removing flesh. The sockets and scars left behind filled with Her vitality and essence. You anchored yourself in the eternal, and the eternal was anchored in you.

The Shrouded Queen built up enough of a following that the Ministry halted the practice of punishing thieves by removing hands. They stopped cutting feet off of escapees. Too many convicts screamed praises during the punishment.

Biter Nell took Iron Hook over completely in 522 and ruled it for a bloody two year span before the military finally breached the fortress and killed every maniac inside.

—From "Forgotten No More: Tracing the Paths of the Gods"
by Professor Kenton Wastrik

"We are all saddened by the tragic loss of Sir Ousley," Saint declared to the courtyard filled with his new employees. "His memorial is on the twentieth, here, at Third Hour. All of you get the day off, and you are welcome to attend as you feel so moved. Now. I encourage you to return to your tasks. I rely upon your patience during this time of transition. I will continue to rely upon your skill and dedication as we move into the future together. That is all."

Saint stepped down from the podium, turning to the clerk with the scarred face. "Delreese, right?" he said.

"Yes sir."

"Let's take a look at my office. You all can wait here," Saint said to the Bluecoats that accompanied him. The Bluecoats exchanged a glance, and settled in place.

Saint limped after Delreese, pausing to look around the entry area featuring her desk as she unlocked the office. She handed him the key, and he smiled as he pocketed it.

"Everything is just as he left it," Delreese said. "The accident was sudden."

"Thank you," Saint said. "This will do nicely."

"Here is his meeting book. I do not know what the coded entries are," she lied, "but I can assist you with rescheduling any of the others."

"Not much here," Saint said with a small smile as he flicked through the week. "You may go."

Delreese nodded to him, and withdrew. Saint fished around in his pocket for a moment, then removed a basalt statuette. It featured the bust of a horse, rampant. He clapped it down on the desk with a certain satisfaction.

Looking around the office, he spotted the hunched malice of the spiderling atop a shelf. He cranked the window open a couple notches. "Shoo," he growled at the spider, hefting his cane. The spider sidled around sideways, then bounced through a couple springs and crawled out the window. Saint cranked the window shut again, and his smile returned.

"Now, wall hangings mean..." he rapped on the wall with his cane, limping around the room's perimeter, until his knock elicited a hollow thunk. Moving the hanging, he saw the catch, and tugged it. The panel swung open, revealing a small shrine with a smoked mirror and several spider statues, as well as a number of jars. One object caught Saint's eye, and his smile turned into a grin.

The elaborate stand supported a black and silver pocket watch with asymmetrical web etching, elegant and expensive. He hefted it, admiring its platinum and onyx chain and fob. Snapping it open, he was reflected in the crystal over the ivory-etched face. The hands and numbers were studded with tiny gems.

"This will do," he said to himself. The ticking in his hand felt like the heartbeat of new life.

CUTLASS BANK QUARTERS, SOUTH SKIRT. NORTH PORT
17TH ULSIVET, 850. SECOND HOUR PAST DAWN

Red Silver squared off with a handful of workers chuckling at some inside joke, and they sobered as they spotted her.

"I'm here to see Jace," she said calmly.

"Who?" one of them said with some exaggeration.

"Don't embarrass yourselves," she said. "I know he's here." She did not bother to scan the two levels of balconies hemming in the narrow courtyard.

"Bold move for a sniper," echoed a voice from behind her. Taking her time, she pivoted to look up at Jace, who leaned against a table tilted on its side, a pistol loosely held. "Walking right in."

"You know better than to shoot me," she said. "I'm bringing you a job offer. You want to do this out here?' she said with a sweeping gesture that took in a dozen or so interested spectators.

He only hesitated for a moment. "Come on up," he said.

Red Silver rounded the stair post and trotted up to the balcony, strolling over to the wary man. "Good morning," she said. "I trust I am not too early."

"Been up for a while," he replied casually. "Talk."

"Saint wants you to take care of the spiders in the habitat, for an official role," she said. "Keep you on. Smooth the transition. Troubleshooting," she said, examining her glove. "Pay is good; ten percent more than you were making under Ousley."

"You all don't even know me," Jace said, cautious.

"After a change in the leadership, people react," Red Silver replied. "I had to do a little digging to find out where you were. Not a lot, but a little. That's a good recommendation," she explained, "since people aren't keen to be rid of you. Besides. No need to kill you now. If you hire on, and turn out to be terrible, we can kill you later."

"You probably think that is a tempting job offer," he said. He shifted, uncomfortable. "I need some time to think it over."

"This is the end of your time to think it over," Red Silver said. "Saint pitched you the job three days ago."

"A few things have changed since then," Jace said, something flinty in his dark eyes.

"And they'll keep changing. Can you keep up?" Red Silver asked coolly.

Jace stared at her for a long moment. "Okay. I'm in."

"Alright then. Get to work. You're late," Red Silver said. She flashed him a smile, then turned her back and walked away.

HERITAGE BUNKER, GATELAND. NORTH PORT
17TH ULSIVET, 850. SECOND HOUR PAST DAWN

Reflected light off the inky waves was brighter than the dull glow of the sky. The wind sighed through the sawgrass that grew in thick patches flanking the uneven cobble road winding out to the squat fortification overlooking the port. Gusting wind snarled past Safety, flapping his long coat's tails to the side.

"That's close enough," said a rough voice. An old man leaned back against a tree, holding a pistol pointed at the ground. "Give me your knot clotted name or you'll go down that hill a sight faster than you came up it."

"You can call me Safety," he replied. "I work for Sir Torrent, who is also Saint Suran, who is in charge of everything Ousley used to run. I'm here to take over operations at the Bunker."

"You are, are you," the old man growled.

"I came alone," Safety continued. "Keeping it friendly. I've heard about how Ousley ran things. We are going to do better." He braced himself as another gust of wind washed over him. "Now, shoot me if you must, but I'm going inside." He resumed walking towards the Bunker's low profile. The armed man fell in step behind him.

Safety looked over the trash lining the approach to the Bunker. Bottles, food wrappers, clothes, and other debris thickened as he approached the door. Two nervous thugs guarded the entry.

"Stop. We aren't open," one of the guards said, flexing her thick hands on the haft of her mace.

Safety studied her sweaty face for a moment. "I'm not a customer. I'm the new boss. And I'm going in. Step aside."

The guards exchanged a glance. "N-not a chance."

Safety took the guard's measure. "I'm not going to start a fight," he said. "Looks like we have two ways this could go. I can leave, and come back with some friends, and handle this more like a hostile takeover. Or you can go get Bant and see if she wants to talk this over inside."

The guards looked to each other again, their worry deepening.

"I'll wait," Safety said, "for three minutes. Go get Bant. If I try anything tricky, you've got a gun on me," he said, tilting his head back at the man five paces behind him.

One of the guards dragged the door open wide enough to slip through, vanishing into the bunker, as the other one scowled and widened her stance.

When the door opened again, a robed woman emerged. Her hair was silver, her face lined, and her figure was willowy but strong as the wind pressed against her. She pinned her gaze on Safety, her mouth set to a thin line.

"Greetil says you want to be the new boss of the Bunker," she said. "My name is Bant. But you already knew that."

"I'm Safety. Here on behalf of Saint, who is also Sir Torrent, who is now the appointed manager of the Workshop. Let's go inside." His tone was confident, as was his stance.

"Let's," Bant agreed, and she withdrew into the darkness. Safety and the old man followed, and the guards secured the door with a heavy clack.

Lamps burned cheap oil, streaming thin smoke that stained the walls and ceiling. A constant low rattle of coughing echoed in the shadowed background. The stench of indifferently mopped up vomit and waste mingled with the vinegary spills of rough wine, and the lingering stink of unwashed bodies. The Bunker steps led down to a long, broad corridor twenty paces across. It connected to side chambers and hallways with stairs down to its lower reaches. A sullen fire burned kelp in a central fire pit, adding acrid smoke to the air's thickness.

"Saint Suran," Bant prompted, turning to face Saint as they reached the wide corridor. He looked around at the first dozen bystanders, their faces hard to see in the murk but their body language revealing deep worry. He heard the jingle of jewelry, and the rustle of weapons swished behind cloth but ready to use.

"Saint put me in charge of running the Bunker," Safety said. "You can call me Safety, because safety is what I want, and it's what I give. The Bunker is going to change how it operates. Right now, today, your pay doubles," he said.

Immediate surprise and wariness rippled through the bystanders, and Bant cocked an eyebrow. Safety continued.

"We can afford it, because this place is going to double its income. We can do better than this," he said, looking around. "You want to do better, right? Ousley is gone, we got rid of him. You're going to give us your best work if you want to stay."

"Please come to my office," Bant said, glancing around at her startled employees.

Safety followed her to a side chamber with two burly guards posted at the wide entry. She went inside the fabric-draped office lined with expensive furniture, seating herself behind a fortified desk. He stood with his back to the door.

"Aren't you bold," she said under her breath, her eyes sharp.

"The fights will be in the central chamber, twice a week. Orgies will be in the second storeroom annex. Dreamer cots will go in the armory, and our supplier will vastly improve the quality of dream tar you offer here. Nightly performances on the stage at the end of the corridor. The bar will double its length and offerings, and we'll bring in servers who aren't fancy lads and ladies so they don't work two shifts."

"You prepared for this, it seems," she said. She lit a cigar, thoughtful, taking a moment. "What of the Thousand Faces?"

"The cult has already consecrated a shrine here. It can stay. We aren't getting rid of the spider habitat in the Workshop, and if you want to keep offering the baby spider petting events to cultists, we won't put a stop to it," Safety replied. "You can keep the ghost riding too. People will come here and pay for experiences they want, and we're aiming to make that more profitable and attractive. And reduce the body count from all your current...misunderstandings."

"You said you'd double everyone's pay. So you think you know what rates are now," Bant said, examining the glowing tip of her cigar as it wisped its foul incense.

"We've got contacts among your people already," Safety replied, calm.

"Is that why you thought you could come alone, to tell us how you're going to run things?" Bant asked, narrowing her eyes. "If I didn't like your tone, your contacts would out themselves to protect you?"

"I'm bringing good news," Safety said. "You need a layer between you and the Bluecoats if things are going to run without costly inter-ruptions. The Bluecoats have already sided with us. I want to be clear," Safety said, leaning forward, his fists on her desk, looking her in the eye. "The River Stallions will let you run your Thousand Faces cult out of the Bunker. But if you cross me, you are gone. If you go, you take our willingness to trust the cult with you." He cocked his head to the side. "So how about we work together."

Bant took her time, savoring a mouthful of poisonous smoke. "I told Ousley the orgy pit should be downstairs. He thought it was titilating, wanted it 'featured.' Hm." She paused. "You think you can afford to double pay *and* bring on new servers?"

"We'll make money doing it," Safety replied. "There may not be much competition for what you offer here, but the squalor drives people away. Saint was born under the red lamps, raised in a fancy house. He is friends with Madame Tesslyn, she's like a grandmother to him. We are coming out here from the Ease, in Silkshore. We know how to run this place right," he said quietly.

"Well," she said slowly, "Sillman appointed Torrent on a provisional basis. Gave him a chance to prove he can do what he says he can do. Sounds like that's what you and I are deciding to give each other as well."

Safety straightened. "All right. Gillis can stay on the books, I want to talk to him when we're done here. Get a sense of where things stand, how we'll handle the flow. I'll take this office, you can relocate to your shrine."

"Just like that?" she said, eyebrows raised.

"Just like that."

She stood, looking him over.

"So be it. Welcome to the Bunker."

THE OLD CUSTOM HOUSE, FOUNDER'S SQUARE. NORTH PORT
17TH ULSIVET, 850. THIRD HOUR PAST DAWN

The Hammer stumbled towards the bar, snatching at the edge of the table and missing. He dropped to one knee, his face a mask of agony, mouth cranked open in a silent cry as his eyes squeezed shut with the unbearable pressure.

THUD

The heartbeat almost broke bones with its force. He keeled over, not even feeling the flagstones as he flopped down. He was dizzy in a maelstrom of trapped blood, zooming through his flesh, sliding along his bones, carrying energy out of his lungs into the furthest reaches of his extremities. A thin whine escaped him.

Sereen stood over him, watching dispassionately.

The Hammer was dimly aware of one of the servers rushing over to him, trying to prop him up as he was rigid with cramp-like tension. "Buddy! Buddy! You okay!" he heard, a muffled echo.

Then Sereen was talking. "He doesn't eat," the child explained, calm. There were other words.

The Hammer's blurred vision filled with a number of worried faces, coming into focus.

Something about food. Something about a leech.

They were too close.

His blood was on fire.

Thrusting them away, the Hammer managed to regain his feet, and he staggered towards the door. Sereen followed him, out into the blustery morning.

Food. To fill the hole inside.

The Hammer tried to remember a time free of the frostbitten starvation permeating him, slowly re-asserting itself as his blood slowed again.

Time passed, he moved, then a collapse onto a bench. As though at a great distance, he heard Sereen order him food. Sereen could hear his thoughts, even the ones that weren't his, even the ones he had not yet developed. It didn't matter. The hunger didn't matter. The cold.

Then there was a steaming bowl of liquid in front of him. Soup of some kind. He broke the surface of the present, something in him gasping at it.

For a moment he was intensely aware. He felt the wood grain of the table, saw the fleck of dried lamb sauce that wasn't scrubbed off when the table was wiped down. Smelled the frying bacon and eel, the boiling mutton stock, heard the cook's jovial laugh. Saw the server staring at a patron, trying to work up the courage to ask her on a date; he smelled the hair on the back of the woman's neck, his eyes almost rippled with the texture on the woman's embroidered jacket. His hands had a layer of dead skin on the back, the base of the hairs flexing against the extra pressure as he shifted his fingers, his skin pulling and bunching. It would rain in an hour and a half. Sereen bathed overnight, his skin still traced with soap, his nails trimmed. The bowl before him was scored and nicked by use, scrubbing, clumsiness. Pressed fibers from a fungal stalk, laquered for durability. The stew had mutton and cress, onion, thinly cut potato, carrots on the edge of going soft, oval pools of grease sliding against each other pressed up to the surface by the denser liquid below. The bench under him was not quite level, it had been indifferently repaired a year ago and one of the legs was not the same length as the others, it was also made of a different wood. A breeze rippled through as the door opened and closed, and he smelled a hawk drifting above North Port. He felt the wavering elegance of the Mirror, like bubbles trapped under silk, slowly oozing under a plastic surface. Like a post hole, he was an empty gap in the surface. A wound in the Mirror's flesh.

Half consciously, he jammed a spoonful of stew into his mouth. The textures slid into the space, waking his dry teeth, coating his tongue, unfamiliar. The sensations bloomed and twisted somewhere between utterly repellant and profoundly necessary.

A moment later, the stew was gone. Then there were three bowls. He poured it into himself. He felt the wetness of his clothes. More bowls. Worried servers. An angry owner.

He shouted at them. Just a noise.

He was alone in the place, only Sereen there now. He reached the kitchen.

More.

All of it.

He ate and ate.

He felt nothing. The emptiness was untouched, draining his flesh as fast as he filled it.

Sereen watched with fascination. Silent. Useful.

The Hammer gorged until there was no more. Distant, he wondered if this was the last time he would be aware of his body. Perhaps now, at long last, what remained of him would slide down the leathery walls of the endless abyss under his sanity's perch.

Above, the broken sun's embers glowed, as if fanned by the world's gentle breath.

THE OLD CUSTOM HOUSE, FOUNDER'S SQUARE. NORTH PORT
17TH ULSIVET, 850. FIFTH HOUR PAST DAWN

"This is insane," Niece said, tugging at the chestplate. "Insane."

"There there," Red Silver said. "This goes right, you won't have any lines to remember. Just be silent and menacing." She patted down the half cloak on Niece's back, and stepped away to critically consider the effect. "Stunning."

"I'm stunned," Niece agreed. "This is a *terrible* idea."

Half turning, Niece looked down at herself. The black and gold Spirit Warden Initiate uniform was tightly laced, armor secured, gear strapped on. The gambeson was a tight sleeve on her head, only her face free of the fabric. Red Silver lowered the half helmet onto her head, obscuring all of her face but her jawline and lips.

"We are fortunate we can risk so much on this terrible idea because Lord Malicoat actually *had* a Spirit Warden initiate uniform, and further, was willing to lend it to us—on short notice, no less," Red Silver observed. "I guess there's an up side to working with someone who has been clashing with Spirit Wardens for years."

"I guess he'll know if we got it on right," Niece said, glum. "Because he has studied them. Red, this is—"

"Right, I heard you," Red Silver said. "We're doing it anyway."

Niece shook her head, freshly irritated by the weight of the helmet. "Are they still in there going over the ritual?" she asked.

"There's apparently a lot to go over," Red Silver said. "We thought we could get this started half an hour ago. We better get moving soon, before you begin to lose confidence in our scheme."

"Ha ha," Niece said sarcastically. She flexed her jaw. "Why won't Saint let Malicoat meet with Inkletta? Is he worried he'll do something to her, or try to recruit her, or what?"

"That has nothing to do with Inkletta, really," Red Silver said. "Just a basic tactic when you deal with aristocrats. Find something they want from you and don't give it to them. If you cooperate fully, they lose interest in you and assume you are cowed. They stop listening and dispose of you. Saying no is the only way to keep their attention. But you have to pick something to balk on that doesn't sabotage the whole... thing," she said with a vague gesture. She leaned over, confiding in Niece. "He learned that from the fancy house where he grew up. Aristocrats have piles of money, which you need, but they also tend to get you killed. Playing with fire." She half smiled. "Touch it. But don't let it engulf you."

They heard conversation and approaching footsteps outside the makeshift dressing room. Niece assumed a practiced pose; hands clasped out of sight behind her back, head tilted slightly forward, wide stance.

"—twice drowned flesh is a nice touch," Lord Malicoat said to Inkletta as they entered the room. Saint and Jewel followed them in.

Lord Malicoat paused, looking at Niece. "Very good." He tugged the line of her half cloak, and unclipped two of the broaches affixed to the plastron, re-setting them in a different order. "Now, are you ready to grasp the key to getting into a Spirit Warden mindset?" he asked, looking right into the smoked glass lens of the protective helmet's eye slit.

"Yes sir," she said with what she hoped sounded like in-character cool disdain.

"You are making a decision. Right now." Lord Malicoat straightened, looking down at her. "At every moment. You control the situation, you have powers at your disposal. Tactical training, political connections. When you look at someone, you are reflexively weighing how you'll affect their fate. You can kill, you can investigate, you can influence, you can promote. So many options, always sifting through there. Never confused, never at a loss. Always, always, making decisions. You can be surprised, you can be afraid, but those are just winds belling out the sail. You are trained, prepared, equipped, and empowered. You have a mast, cloth, ropes, and a deck beneath your feet. Even in a storm, you steer your course."

"I see," she said, evaluating him.

"Better," he grinned, something malicious shining from his teeth. "Lady Selraetas, you are ready?"

"Sure," Red Silver agreed. "I'm more concerned about the ritual."

"Our 'technicians' are suited up," Jewel said. "If this goes right, we'll be done by the end of the Blind Hour."

Red Silver looked to Inkletta, who nodded mutely.

"Let's hear it for emerging into clarity," Saint said. "Time to go."

ROWAN SENTRY POST, FOUNDER'S SQUARE. NORTH PORT
17TH ULSIVET, 850. SIXTH HOUR PAST DAWN

"You there," Red Silver called out as she strode up to the plate glass window. The stone and metal tower overbuilt a heritage watch station at the corner of the square, a clock face on its upper level. A wary technician looked through the window, and shoved a slot to the side to open a vent so they could hear each other through the barrier.

"We've got an issue, some work to do on the Square," Red Silver said nervously. "We're going to—ah—redirect some of the field. Need to do a ritual," she confided, attempting a smile.

"That's not allowed," the guard said, mild.

"Oh, it's not me, it's just, you know, I'm *assisting*," she said, sweat beading on her face. She turned to the cloaked and cowled figure at her side.

The cowled figure lifted her head, and the technician saw the half-mask of the Spirit Warden initiate. He blinked.

"We're looking for *clues*," Red Silver whispered through the vent. "Something happened. Best you not know about it," she added with a knowing nod.

"Yeah, that's all fine, but you'll need to get the Captain to sign off," the technician said, eyeing the Spirit Warden initiate.

"First, there's no time," Red Silver said, holding up a finger. "Second..." She glanced around. "This could involve a *Bluecoat*." She raised her eyebrows, sobered by the implications.

"We're losing time," Niece said, harsh. "You," she said to the technician. "The readings will fluctuate. Do not call it in. Do nothing. We'll be done by nightfall." She pivoted, stalking off.

Red Silver commiserated with the technician, offering a tight and mirthless smile, then she scurried after the Spirit Warden initiate.

"Do you think it will work?" she muttered to Niece as she caught up.

"Either way, that's as far as we dare push it," Niece replied. "Gotta let his imagination do the rest of the work. Pull this off before the questions catch up."

"I'm known here," Red Silver said as they closed in on the brightly colored sawhorses marking off an access to the machinery built into the corner of the square. "Follow up can touch me. Not as anonymous as we're used to," she grumbled, squinting around the square. "Not when I'm committed to my noble persona."

The metal housing was half the size of a carriage, built into the side of a heritage building. The top hatch was open, and Jewel was bent over adjusting something in the interior, lit by an algae sphere. She straightened, and looked all the way across the square to a similar structure with several nervous technicians standing around it.

"We good?" Jewel demanded of Red Silver.

"We did our part," Red Silver said. "Let's go ahead, and hope for the best."

Jewel nodded. "I got both sides set up, that guy just has to turn the knob I showed him and we're in business." She saluted the technician across the square. He swallowed hard, and bent to reach down into the machine. Jewel leaned into the one under her, and after a couple clicks and clatters, a faint hiss whined out. She straightened.

"So…" Red Silver said.

"The collection is turned off. I'll keep an eye on the readings here. Update Inkletta," Jewel said as she peered into the open hatch.

Leaving Niece with Jewel, Red Silver headed towards the drab tent pavilion pitched by the dry fountain in the center of the square. She ducked through the flap.

Inkletta knelt on a deep cushion, eyes closed, teeth bared. Ritual glyphs were cut into the skin of her arms, the blood trickling down past her grip, onto the skin of the hissing trench rat Inkletta clutched with both hands. The shaved rat's body was as long as her forearm. Its eyes were red with fury. Red Silver saw the cuts on its back where its spine had been carefully snipped to limit its ability to thrash. She felt the tingle that rose in her soft palate, tightening her organs; the swirl of sacrificial ritual energy was already building up friction on the other side of the Mirror.

A brazier glowed before Inkletta, esoteric fuels melting together and releasing peculiar wisps of smoke and mist as the low flame rippled with blue and green hues. An iron pot next to the brazier brimmed with the pale glow of electroplasmic discharge, poured out of its container, its toxins swirling up into the air they breathed. Other implements and supplies were carefully arranged around Inkletta. The grit in her hair and scattered around her was all that remained of the careful ritual gestures she performed with handfuls of bone powder and crystal sand.

"No names," Inkletta whispered without opening her eyes. "Not now. Do not speak. We ready?"

"Yes," Red Silver whispered back.

"The ladle. Just a little at a time. Like I showed you," Inkletta breathed.

Red Silver grimaced as she picked up the ladle, a femur handle lashed to an eel skull dipper with bright copper wire. She dipped the ladle into the electropolasm, and carefully poured it onto the brazier.

Glowing smoke twisted out, coiling and piling against the ceiling, and the rest of the room darkened as mortal eyes were pushed open by the otherworldly light. Boiling up and curdling, the mass drifted to the side, and began to slither towards the vent.

One corner of the pavilion was anchored around a chest-high vent post with a flared horn at the top, opening like the mouth of a trumpet. Red Silver dipped the ladle and draped another thin coat of electroplasm on the brazier, fueling more rising poison to funnel into the vent.

Inkletta focused on the movement, her eyes snapping open; Red Silver frowned with dismay as she saw the luminous infection that glowed through Inkletta's prepared eye now that the eyepatch was gone. In the strange light of the ritual, she thought she saw three or four pupils flexing inside the glowing jelly in Inkletta's socket.

Hissing a brutal Hadrathi command, Inkletta twisted. The weakened rat in her grip squealed and broke. Sucking in a gut full of air, Inkletta inhaled the dying creature's essence, holding it in the taut bellows of her chest for a few seconds before gusting it out into the vent.

Subdued, Red Silver knelt and waited, watching her friend with concern.

Inkletta felt her blood twitch this way and that, her sight locking into the burning glyph carved into the rat's life force. Helpless, the spirit was slurped into the vent. Hissing and twisting, she felt the energy slide down, around, pulsing through ephemeral conduits under the earth and somehow also beyond it. She heard the vague echo of her body screaming as her plunge into the conduit seared a blistering path through her consciousness, reverberating out, tracing a path across multiple dimensions in a spatial awareness she did not previously know she possessed.

She was dimly aware of other conduits, dry and faint, converging with her. A barrier loomed up. Far away, her hand spasmed again, and she broke free of the rat's life force, splitting out of the conduit as the slick of energy flowed into the bottomless dark that radiated out from both sides of the Mirror.

Gazing at the unfathomable emptiness, she was aware of the craft that deftly leveraged it into creating another way of being, another space beyond the known world. The dim memory of ritual and death surged.

This was the Reliquary of the Fallen Star.

CHAPTER FIFTEEN

The district was named Charhollow, trying to attract investment by promising inexpensive fuel and an inexhaustible workforce. The industrialists tamed the bogs, channeling the water for the mills; it seemed reasonable to tame the workers next.

Occultists tried tearing the spirits out of the condemned, or volunteers who were hollowed in exchange for clearing their debts. Competitive ghosts inhabited the hollows, working the flesh to death in an effort to outdo each others' productivity.

In the end, the masters gave up on their dream of a hollow industry. Turns out it is cheaper, easier, and safer to make sure your working population is so desperate they will accept your terms no matter how predatory.

The masters control the price and availability of fuel, food, water, and shelter. Then they match the wages they offer to be the thinnest margin more, curating the illusion you can prosper in those conditions. I suggest greed is more effective than rituals, when it comes to swapping out a living spirit for a merciless ghost in flesh.

—From "Occult Experiments in Industry" by Sir Oren Dyluria

Like a swimmer with lungs full of air, deeper than light could penetrate, she maintained a kind of stasis for a few seconds as she acclimatized to the depth. She felt the slight tremor of the conduits, reverberating with the Reliquary's meal. But there must also be a door.

Drifting, she pressed through the earth, the memory of soil and stone that soaked into the back of the Mirror.

The faintest curve, a hint of a shape, caught her attention. The simmer of her blood approached a boil as she propelled herself over to it. Stairs, of a kind. Reaching out, she touched the echo. She felt the Reliquary, locked and frozen solid with desperate starvation, at the bottom. On the other end—

A pinpoint of light locked on her, piercing across distance. Her heart leaped in her chest.

Time to go.

She instinctively felt her body, fighting hard to suspend her consciousness across such strange distance without collapsing. Kicking off of the muted echoes of the back of the Mirror, she soared towards it—but something was following her now. She had been detected. Something faster than she was closed in as she hurled towards her flesh.

Inkletta tucked her consciousness into a tight package and crashed into her body, rocking back and flopping on the cushions. A wild moment of panic ricocheted through her blood as she spotted the Spirit Warden initiate looming over her, gripping her arm—Niece.

"Run," Inkletta gasped.

Niece hauled Inkletta up to a standing position. The Whisper's deadened limbs were clumsy and unresponsive, and she found herself struggling to force her lungs to breathe. Red Silver drew a pistol, glancing around for the threat. Jewel stepped forward, flicking a light into Inkletta's eyes, professionally checking her for damage.

Too late, too late—

The pluming brazier emission rippled, and light gleamed in its depth. Like fabric pulled taut on a frame, the smoke twisted into a shape—the top half of a humanoid form. An eye-searing glyph shone out of the chest.

Explosive discharge rocked the pavilion as Red Silver fired a plasmic round into the cloud, warping its shape. A streamer of smoke blown out of the mass whipped around, lashing across her, sending her toppling into the tent wall and tugging the whole pavilion so its supports torqued and shifted.

Inkletta struggled to refocus, but she was in disarray; her ability to attune was badly skewed as her spirit pressed back into the flesh shape on this side of the Mirror. Before she could challenge the ghost, she collapsed back on the ground as Jewel and Niece spasmed in the apparition's grip.

You will pay for this, impostor snarled a sensation, crawling through Niece's shuddering nerves. She tried to scream as the flesh of her neck peeled and split, as though clawed open from within.

Red Silver was back on her feet. She tucked her fist back by her ribs, her stance wide. Her eyes flickered with an ethereal reflection as she matched energies with the apparition. She fired her fist forward, and it shocked into the semi-corporeal manifestation, blurring its edges. Screaming, Red Silver clawed at the smoky shape, her raking strikes leaving bright streaks in the form, tearing it. Whipping her whole body forward, Red Silver smashed her forehead into the center of its mass, and the shape burst. The impact flung everyone in the tent towards the walls. The overstressed tent pole snapped, the guy-ropes dislodged, and a mass of canvas buried the scoundrels.

Moments later, flame licked up from the center of the fabric, where it landed on the brazier. By now the "technicians" reached the scene of the battle. They pulled at the collapsed tent, locating those inside and dragging them out as the fire caught some of the strange components of the ritual, triumphantly spreading.

Red Silver dropped to her knees beside Niece as the young Skov gasped, staring, clutching at her bloody throat. "Get Jewel over here!" Red Silver shouted.

"She's dead," one of the gangsters said, eyes wide.

"Inkletta?" Red Silver demanded, biting back her frustration.

"I think she'll be okay," another one of the gangsters said, supporting Inkletta as she struggled to sit up.

Of course the fire attracted Bluecoat attention.

"Get the Coursers. We have to get to the Nineways Greenkey estate," Red Silver said through her teeth. "Now."

"That could have gone better," Saint muttered to Inkletta as he looked over the room.

Niece was dressed in more familiar clothes, propped up on cushions. Her throat was tightly bandaged, her neck in a support splint restricting her head's range of motion. Her eyes were closed, her face twisted with distracted pain. Red Silver sat next to her, hands sheathed in bandages like pale mittens. Jewel's corpse was wound in a sheet, motionless. Varela stood guard over the room, arms crossed.

Inkletta cleared her throat, hoarse. "I found the ghost door," she rasped. Her eyepatch was back, her arms wrapped in bandages.

"That's great," Saint scowled. "What hit my people?"

"I can answer that," Lord Malicoat said as he stepped through a doorway across the room. "I can smell her on you." He descended the shallow steps to the center of the room, looking down at Niece and Red Silver. "A better question; how did so many of you survive?" he wondered. "You had a run-in with Sysavath."

"She was on the other side of the Mirror," Inkletta said, her voice rough. "Projected force through a cloud of plasmic discharge. Still did all this."

"She must have been close to where you were," Lord Malicoat said with suppressed excitement. "Tell me what you discovered."

Inkletta exchanged a glance with Saint, who almost imperceptibly nodded. "Well," Inkletta said, "the ghost door doesn't connect here. It connects to another shadow realm, on the back of the Mirror. So you have to go front to back, then sideways."

"Did you get a sense of where?" Lord Malicoat demanded.

"Oh, yes," Inkletta said. "The ghost door connects to the Echosheath."

"I think we have more pressing issues," Red Silver said, brittle.

"We don't," Lord Malicoat disagreed. "Sysavath crossed your path, so as soon as she returns through the Moon Pool she'll make a move on all of us. Our only hope at this point is to get to the destination before she does."

"I slowed her down," Red Silver said, eyes narrow.

"Red Silver is an exorfist," Saint explained to Lord Malicoat. "Hit her with plasmic shot, discorporated her borrowed form."

"The only reason we've got any time at all," Lord Malicoat said as patiently as he could, "is because Sysavath was operating with a level of discretion. She did not deploy all the Spirit Warden resources, because that attracts attention. Even within the order there are... competitions. Struggles. The Wardens are cagy with matters internally as well as externally. Make no mistake, she will come for you now."

"That's why we are here," Red Silver said, focused. "Figured you could fend her off. It's like your hobby."

"If she straight-up slew people, *through the Mirror*, she's in a mood," Lord Malicoat said. "I will deflect the Bluecoats, but if she wants in she'll get in." He turned to Inkletta. "So. The Echosheath."

"I've been there," Saint said. "A scavenger, Mesech, got me into it. Had a little rock he waved at the back wall of the Court Annex, the Dunvil Custom House. Magistrate Drake was holding court there." He frowned. "It seemed... roomy in there. That's a step closer, but it's not the door itself."

"I touched the door," Inkletta said, a hiss behind her voice. "I'll be able to feel it." The seared path of the conduit still burned, like an ember resting lightly in her mind, a chip of bright pain.

"Let's go finish this," Lord Malicoat said, feverish.

Saint turned to Inkletta, who steadily looked him in the eye. He shook his head.

"Inkletta needs to rest," he said. "We get one shot at this. She's the only one who knows where it is. You'll need all your strength," he said to Lord Malicoat. "We dare not burn up our Whisper just getting in. So we'll need cover."

"Cover," Lord Malicoat echoed.

Saint thought fast. "Some cultists crashed Founder's Square. Grabbed Niece, pulled back to Charhollow. We pursued. We will rescue her and return triumphant. There may be casualties along the way." He turned to Lord Malicoat. "Can you sell that to the Bluecoats, and if pressed, the Spirit Wardens?"

Lord Malicoat's nostrils creased with distaste. "I suppose," he muttered.

"Oh," Red Silver interjected, "and point out the cultists were pulling a fast one on the Rowan system in Founder's Square, that's how they crossed us. Impersonating Spirit Wardens, had Lady Selraetas at gunpoint," she prompted.

Lord Malicoat ignored her. "When will you be ready," he demanded of Saint.

"Midnight. We don't need an airtight story. Just give the Bluecoats permission to ignore all this. Nobody wants to get tangled up in Spirit Warden business. As for the Spirit Wardens, we'll do what we have to do on the other side of all this."

"Very well. I will involve Ryland. Spread some cover, deflect attention into the city, and find this Mesech fellow," Lord Malicoat said.

"Wait, the Coursers can find Mesech and bring him here," Saint said.

"Even better," Lord Malicoat said with a dismissive gesture. He turned, and left the room.

"But what about you all?" Varela protested to Saint.

"Go," Saint replied evenly. "Find Mesech. Bring him here. Don't antagonize him," Saint said. "We need him in a cooperative mood."

"What if the Spirit Wardens come at you here?" Varela scowled.

Saint leveled a look at the rover, and waited.

"Okay, right," Varela growled. He pivoted, stamping out.

"Thanks," Inkletta whispered to Saint.

"Now all you have to do is get some power-rest in," Saint replied, eyes elsewhere, "so you can sprint after you spent all day at the obstacle course." His voice was surprisingly gentle.

"Nothing relaxes the mind so much as desperation to prepare for a feat that's likely beyond your capacity," Inkletta grated out, droll.

Niece cracked an eye open, and reached for Red Silver's sleeve. Red Silver focused on her, unreadable. "Hey, kid."

"What is this smell," Niece said, her voice small.

"Some unguents, pretty standard stuff," Red Silver said.

"No it isn't," Niece said wearily. "Been patched up lots. Never smelled this."

"Malicoat had some custom gel, I don't know," Red Silver said. "Plus, it's this place. Kind of funky."

Niece let her eyes drift shut. "I know this smell," she said. "I have smelled it before." She swallowed hard. "Beneath the Gaze of the Fallen Star. When I saw my death."

"You are *not* going to die," Red Silver said, chilled.

"A great wind," Niece said, dreamy. "Leaves swirling past. A great... crashing noise." A smile traced her young features. "The moon, whole."

"Then you've got nothing to worry about," Red Silver said over the lump in her throat. "The moon is casting two Dimmer Sisters tonight. Nowhere near whole."

Niece patted her sleeve, and drowsed.

Red Silver set her jaw. Rising, she approached Saint. "A word."

He leaned to the side, open to her.

"Where is the Hammer," Red Silver asked, her voice low.

"Resting, under the Old Custom House," Saint said. "He had some kind of attack this morning, went out and trashed a local eatery. Some of our new recruits found him, brought him back." He paused. "Why?"

Red Silver looked over at Niece. "I'm worried," she said simply.

Saint considered what she said, and what she didn't. He looked down at her hands. "How are your burns? Can you still shoot?"

"Something comes for my girl," Red Silver said through her teeth, watching Niece, "and you'll see what I can do."

THE CIRCULATORY, THE EASE. SILKSHORE
17TH ULSIVET, 850. TENTH HOUR PAST DAWN

Gapjaw opened the door and stepped in, light on his feet, glancing around. "Kashindi?" he said, his voice low.

"Here," she called out from the garden. Relief smoothed his forehead, and he closed the door behind himself, turning to the garden.

"They said you wanted to talk to me," he said, brushing his dirty hands against each other. "Is everything—"

Kashindi sat on the bench, her hands folded in her lap. A Spirit Warden stood behind her. Not an initiate. One of the masters. The full face mask covered the woman's features, her armor was ornate and custom-fitted, and her flowing cloak absorbed light and sound, giving nothing back.

"You've got... company," Gapjaw said weakly.

"I've been given an opportunity," Kashindi said, her eyes alight. "A martyrdom."

"What."

"This is Sysavath," Kashindi said, gesturing to the Spirit Warden. "She has a task for you. I will help you do it," she said, oddly animated. "I drink this poison—"

"What!"

"Colvin," Kashindi said, her tone sharp. "You must let me finish." She relaxed again. "Sysavath has a task for you. If you complete your task, then I get the antidote. I rise up from the bed, my body carrying me onward. If you try to complete your task, even if you fail, I receive the antidote and rise again. The only way I die is if you refuse to aid Sysavath in the work." Her smile faltered. "You wouldn't do that, would you?"

"Ooh, the guts squeeze towards the end," Gapjaw murmured, the obscure curse steadying him. "Here we go. How about it, Sysavath. What do you want."

Sysavath handed Kashindi a small glass vial. Kashindi smiled.

"Don't," Gapjaw groaned.

"A *martyrdom*," Kashindi said. "A legacy that—that alone, independent of my life's service, opens the way for me to join my kin, to rest in the Starwalk Wall. And you can join me. One task. Such an opportunity—few people recieve it." She raised her eyebrows. "You swore."

Gapjaw stared at Sysavath, mute.

Kashindi raised the vial and drained it in a single smooth gesture. She tossed it aside, her chin raised, defiant. "There. My trust in the Immortal Emperor, and his appointed guardians the Spirit Wardens, is complete." She looked to Sysavath. "And demonstrated."

Gapjaw rushed forward, pulling Kashindi to his chest, his lungs frozen and unable to pull or push air. "No," he whispered.

In Sysavath's implacable shadow, he felt the life slide out of Kashindi. His throat closed.

"If you fail," Sysavath said, her silken voice seeming to resonate from every direction, "my people will still revive Kashindi. She lives her life, and upon dying, goes in the Starwalk Wall. But if you defy me, if you refuse to attempt your task, she goes in the fires under Bellweather. I will personally scatter her on the sea."

Gapjaw cleared his throat, and rose to his feet, adjusting Kashindi to lay glassy-eyed on the bench. A thin trickle of blood seeped from her nose. Gapjaw took a couple steps back, mastered himself, then aimed a vicious squint at Sysavath. "What do you want me to do."

"The task is simple enough. Even you can understand it," Sysavath said. "Go to North Port and kill Inkletta."

Gapjaw stared at the Spirit Warden.

"I don't care how you do it," Sysavath said, her voice seeping into Gapjaw's skin. "I want her dead by the Hour of Silk. You have a little over eight hours to manage it."

Gapjaw did not move.

Sysavath cocked her head to the side. "Here we are," she purred. "The Circulatory. You know, the poison I gave her was grown here. Excellent security, some of the best minds in the city curating the garden, along with some of the Church's most faithful servants. Here we have knowledge, protected from extinguishment or abuse. Rare treasures. Esoteric harvests for the trusted elite of the city." Gapjaw could hear her smile. "Supporting every part of the name. The church. The ecstasy. The flesh."

"How... did you find me here," Gapjaw managed.

"Your little outfit came to my attention today," Sysavath said, an edge to her voice that carried more menace than a berserk scream could. "Took less than an hour for me to get up to speed on all of you. My first thought was that you were here working a longer game, like your man Safety did as a Gray Cloak. Since your boss is a confidence artist, that would make sense. But no. By all accounts, you seek redemption," she said, the coy inflection devastating. "Here you stand. Dirt under your nails. Filthy knees." Her amusement was intolerable. "And I offer you redemption. So you really could find it here," she mused.

"Do... do you know where... they are?" Gapjaw ground out.

"There are sixteen locations in North Port that Malicoat warded against scrying," Sysavath said. "We are working through them, and should be prepared to strike by dusk. I can hold off a little longer if you are getting into position."

Gapjaw's shoulders sagged with defeat. His eyes fixed on Kashindi. He sniffled, and wiped his nose with the back of his hand, skin rough on his bristly beard. "Damn," he said softly.

Then he snatched up a chair and smashed it on Sysavath.

Startled, the Spirit Warden rebalanced—but Gapjaw roared as he clutched her cloak and tugged her into his lashing fist. She parried, jamming a thin blade into his ribcage. He flexed and pivoted, tearing the blade from her grip and driving an elbow strike across her mask. She snatched his wrist and twisted, locking him up to swing around into the wall. Somehow he yanked the blade out of his chest and shoved it through her elbow, grinding the hilt against her joint.

Her fist battered the side of his head, rupturing his ear and bouncing him off the wall. He rebounded into a body check, his greater mass unbalancing her, and he followed up with a two handed shove. She rolled easily across the floor, bouncing up, but he was right there. She banged a kick into the side of his knee, folding it, and as he dropped he snagged a handful of her tunic and pulled. She twisted to blunt the force, getting behind him as he whacked into the floor, looping a wire over his neck. He launched up off the ground, back towards her, crashing into the wall; she squirmed out of the press, jabbing a few cuts into his shoulder joint and ribs.

Bleeding freely, he grunted as he whipped a candle stand at her. She caught it on her forearm, thrusting a blade into his chest twice; he locked her forearm up, and she pivoted to get momentum to break free, but his grip was implacable. He choked on his rage as he bent his entire body and will into a sharp torque. She gasped as bone snapped.

"Enough," she hissed. She was half his size, and injured, but Gapjaw no longer had surprise. Sysavath let him reach for her again, and she drove her stiletto through the back of his hand, pinning it to the wall. She sprang back out of reach, pulling her pistol, and shot him in the gut. The blow tore him off the wall, and this time he hit the ground. The gun jumped out of her hand, and she trembled with pain from the recoil, the shock passed through her broken wrist.

"You *idiot*," Sysavath seethed. "Your friends won't even know you died for them."

All he managed was a strangled chuckle.

"What," she demanded. "What's so funny."

"Obvsly," he slurred, "you don hav frens."

Sysavath stared at him as the pool of blood grew around his body.

"Take your time," she sneered. "Make your peace. I'll see to it you aren't disturbed."

Then she was gone.

Gapjaw struggled to breathe as one of his lungs filled with blood.

NINEWAYS GREENKEY ESTATE, SOUTH SKIRT. NORTH PORT
17TH ULSIVET, 850. ELEVENTH HOUR PAST DAWN

"Just like that, the fog rolls in," Saint said. He stood in the narrow rotunda on the top floor, above the central chamber. He turned to regard Safety. "Quite a day."

"It was," Safety agreed. "I was thinking about the Bunker."

"You should rest while you can," Saint said, returning his attention to the soft waves of silence and oblivion layering through the streets below.

"Yeah, I'm done," Safety said. "Calm before a battle. So. I was thinking we need a physiker for the Bunker. It's a big enough operation to support one. Be on hand for overdoses, check the spread of disease, maybe even help the cult with their potions and drugs."

Saint smiled to himself. "That's a good idea, Safety," he agreed. "Check with Blue Gleena. Her daughters are finishing up their apprenticeship. One of them would jump at the chance to get established out here." He paused. "I don't remember. What is the Bunker doing for a healer now?"

"Oh, it's pretty great," Safety said with a rueful grin. "This old drunk woman. Tries to cure everything with various bat parts."

"We are saving lives," Saint observed, eyebrows raised.

"Hey." Safety frowned, staring intently into the fog. "The Hammer."

Saint looked down, and spotted the unmistakable bulk of the Hammer parting the fog as he strode towards the tower, Sereen in his wake. "Better go meet him," Saint said. "I'll catch up."

Safety navigated the tight spiral staircase as quickly as he could, darting out of the confined space and crossing to the door. He hauled it open as the Hammer arrived.

"You made it," Safety said, feeling suddenly foolish.

The Hammer nodded, and passed him, entering the tower. Sereen followed. Safety pushed the door closed again, following the Hammer into the central chamber.

"Spirit Wardens have set spies outside," the Hammer said, his voice hoarse.

"That's not ideal," Red Silver observed, checking her pistol. "And you? How are you feeling?"

The Hammer looked down at his hands. "I'm here," he said. "I think this... is it."

The River Stallions watched him, struggling with that idea.

Saint limped out of the stairwell. "Then I am honored to be here," he said, and he pulled the Hammer into a hug. Pushing him out to arm's length, he nodded. "I'm grateful for all you've done for us."

"I'll drop a neat coil before I accept that," Red Silver said. "I have had it with fate."

The Hammer almost smiled. "Nobody expects you to accept reality, Red."

"Good," she said, scowling. "Reality is disappointing. We can do better."

The Hammer looked over at Inkletta. She was meditating, oblivious. He scanned the room. "Gapjaw?"

"Back in Silkshore," Saint said.

"I... feel like he's missing," the Hammer faltered.

"Inkletta is going into danger tonight," Saint said.

The Hammer nodded, and it was decided.

Saint shuffled towards a chair, moving like an old man. The Hammer stood next to Niece, looking down at her. She smiled at him, wan, dark circles under her eyes.

"Hey there," she said. "How you doin."

"I'm a rock," he rumbled.

Her chin creased as she tried to smile, tears welling up in her eyes. He knelt beside her, gripping her hand.

Together, they waited.

Red Silver and Safety joined Saint.

"Spirit Wardens. Watching the place," Red Silver said significantly.

"I know," Saint said. "But we can't do this without Malicoat." He looked to Safety. "Tell her about the rear exit."

"I scouted the place," Safety said to Red Silver. "The fountain room, there's a stud by the eel's gill. Pops a secret door, a tunnel to get out. In case we get trapped."

"Come on," Red Silver breathed. "Let's get this over with." She checked her watch.

Smiling, Saint opened his watch too. Red Silver was distracted, raising an eyebrow and looking it over.

"Nice," she said.

Together, they tucked their watches back into their pockets.

Less than an hour later, the front door groaned open, and Varela led Wringleton and Mesech into the central chamber as Safety pushed the door closed behind them, briefly glancing around outside first.

"Good work," Saint said. "Mesech, welcome. We need you to open the way to the Echosheath for us. Tonight."

The scavenger looked around the room, noting all the injuries and the fugitive cast of the crew. "I see."

"Will you aid us?" Saint asked.

"The Circle wouldn't like it," Mesech mused.

"Are you looking for a pardon?" Saint guessed.

"This task, it is for Inkletta, yes?" Mesech said. Saint nodded. "I have asked around. Found out who she is." He paused. "I'll do it. If she inks me. She's a master, she knows the Old Forms. Not many like her left."

"You'll do it for a tattoo," Saint clarified.

"That's it."

Saint considered, then limped over to Inkletta. He put his hand on her shoulder. Slowly, she drew in a breath, rousing. Her eyes opened. "Seems early," she breathed.

"It is," Saint agreed. "Mesech says he'll open the way to the Echosheath if you'll ink him. I won't speak for you."

Inkletta considered the scavenger, her eyes direct. "I will do it," she said. "If I survive."

"That's all I ask," Mesech said. "When do we go?"

A loud clack reverberated from a back room, and the scoundrels turned with hands on weapons.

Lord Malicoat ducked into the room, out of breath and wide-eyed. "They're onto us. Sysavant is incoming. Let's move." He withdrew quickly.

"Alright, just like we planned," Saint said as he tried to smile. He helped Inkletta to her feet, and made eye contact with Red Silver.

"You taking the brat?" Red Silver asked the Hammer casually.

The Hammer shrugged. He followed Lord Malicoat. Inkletta fell in behind him, as did Sereen. Red Silver tugged her gunbelt to adjust it, and followed. Mesech brought up the rear.

They were gone.

"We should relocate too," Safety said quietly. He bent down and pulled Niece into his arms, lifting her. "Should we leave through the front door or the back door?"

"It's not us they want," Saint said, bemused. He shook off the mood. "Come on."

Reaching the front door, he braced himself for a moment, then opened it. He deliberately relaxed, his torso tense and ready to flinch with impact. None came. So he limped out into the slowly tumbling fog. Safety followed, Niece's face burrowed into his shirt.

"We aren't outrunning anyone like this," Safety muttered darkly. "I miss the canals."

"Really?" Saint groused, pale as he coaxed more speed out of his aching leg.

The scoundrels cut through a heritage garden, not yet reclaimed by the new residents. The withered sticks of old trees and bushes jutted from calcified soil, only a few of them still alive. Saint paused.

"I don't like this," he said. His grip tightened on his cane. He felt his skin shiver.

Safety grunted, knocked forward off his feet; he desperately pivoted so he didn't land on Niece. She cried out, her stitches jarred as she smacked down.

Saint whirled, yanking out his pistol. A wheel kick bashed it out of his hand, but it fired. The plasmic round hissed through the garden, detonating in a bent tree. The energy of the shot didn't have much physical punch, but it raced through the starved wood so a low and eerie flame consumed it. An almost casual throat punch robbed Saint of his air, his plans, and his strength; he dropped to one knee, choking.

"Now," Sysavath hissed. "Where are the others."

CHAPTER SIXTEEN

How are we bound together? Our first names are often ties to those our parents admire, our last names identify our people. We bond with those who live near us, from a neighborhood to a district to a city to an empire. We study faces, looking for features like our own. We have the same kind of relationships and experiences, giving us common ground to find connection.

Spirit Wardens are stripped of all these bonds. They are masked, their senses honed to wallow in the unnatural. Only foreign-born are recruited. They give up their names and local allegiances. They are anonymous, only forming relationships within their ranks—or not at all. The Immortal Emperor created elite monster hunters that are untethered from those they ostensibly serve.

What sort of social experience shapes these elites who wield practically unrestricted authority as agents of the empire? I do believe they have bonds we do not know about, connections that are indeed powerful enough to form them in community. Otherwise the Spirit Wardens would constantly go mad, layering regrettable precedents until public acceptance collapsed under the weight of tragedy. I suspect there are very good reasons the answers to these questions remain secret.

—From "Deviations in Social Contracts: The Living and the Dead" by Lord Castor Filk

Safety rolled to his feet and drew his pistol, but Sysavath was too fast. She snapped a kick into the gun before he could raise it, and it blasted at the ground. A precise thrust with her heel knocked the gun out of his hand. She scattered flash powder in front of his face, and as he staggered, she jump-kicked him in the chest. He flew back, battering his shoulder blades against an iron planter.

"Stay down," she said, her cold voice too placid over an almost inaudible growl. She looked over the three scoundrels, her cloak settling in place so she appeared a monolithic force.

Winded, Safety struggled to his feet, wheezing. Sysavath raised her arm towards him, and one of the inlaid gems on her forearm greave flashed. Choking, he clutched at his throat, dropping to his knees.

Sysavath oriented on Saint. "You can talk before or after your bones begin to smoulder inside your body," she said, adjusting the gauntlet on her other hand.

"Okay," Saint said. "We cooperate, and you, what, let us go?"

"Care to find out what happens if you *don't* cooperate?" she asked.

"Right. Look, we don't want any trouble with you. Malicoat is insane. Do you know what he's trying to do?" Saint demanded.

"Where did they go," Sysavath repeated.

"I don't fully understand," Saint admitted. He cleared his throat, and again, struggling to recover from the throat punch. "Somewhere—a secret place," he said.

"You don't need an ankle to tell me what I want to know," Sysavath said, and she freed a collapsable crossbow from her cloak. It snapped open, the quarrel pre-loaded.

"The Echosheath," Saint said. "Some place called the Echosheath."

"That wasn't so hard, was it," Sysavath purred. "Looks like you're the winner. I only want one of you for leverage." She aimed the crossbow at Safety, and pulled the trigger.

That same moment, plasmic ammunition burned into her, driving her back as the discharge crackled across her amulets and ritual defenses. The second shot blared into her torso like a punch, another energy wave ripping through her gear. Shuddering with the feedback,

Sysavath barely deflected the incoming knife strike. She leaped back to perch on a low stone wall.

Niece tossed the empty pistol aside, and twirled the blade in her grip, resetting. "You won't make it to the Reliquary," she said quietly, certain. Blood trickled down from the bandage around her neck. "The Fallen Star will not allow it."

"Oh no?" Sysavath said, rising to her full height, taking a moment to catch her breath. "Say, you're the imposter. Looks like you survived." Sysavath's hand tightened to a fist. "I'll remedy that."

Niece held the knife pointed at the Spirit Warden, and she waited. The perfect moment was coming. Inevitable. Exquisite. Her blood and sweat mixed with the unguent smeared under the bandage, that scent layering atop the acrid stink of burning wood.

That was the smell.

She felt a stirring in her blood. She was not alone. As though she stood, a wave, and within her something deeper moved to the shallows.

Above, she sensed the shining of the Maiden Star. The way home.

Sysavath cried out in Hadrathi, flinging a handful of pebbles at the ground. They snapped upon impact, and a shockwave thundered out. Safety and Saint were tossed away, sailing through the air, but a Leviathan breath anchored Niece in place. She was unmoved as the wave rolled by, stripping all the trees and bushes of their leaves; trapped in the stone courtyard, the leaves whirled and streamed through the air. In the flickering distortion, the moon and her Dimmer Sisters rippled, merging into a single pale disc.

Sysavath leaped at Niece.

Niece drove the knife forward. It punctured the Spirit Warden's breastplate, slid between her ribs, plunged into her pounding heart.

Niece and Sysavath fell back and landed hard.

The moon flexed apart once more, refracted by the broken sky.

"No no no no no," Saint babbled, scrambling to his feet as best he could, staggered. Blood slid down the side of his face, and he dropped to his knees to crawl over to where Niece and Sysavath sprawled, neither moving. "No!" he shouted, shoving at the Spirit Warden. The corpse rolled aside.

Niece was gone. Her glassy eyes reflected the moons. The hilt of Sysavath's stiletto protruded from her chest. A dry wracking sob wrenched Saint as he pressed a trembling hand over Niece's face, closing her eyes.

The twin tolling of Bellweather bells reverberated behind the Mirror.

Pain jolted through him; someone pulling at him, talking. "Now, we have to go *now*," Safety was saying. Saint stared at him stupidly.

"They are coming!" Safety shouted. As he pointed at the gate, Saint saw the crossbow bolt lodged in his metal forearm.

"Bring her!" Saint demanded, his eyes staring and his face twisted. He pointed at Niece. "Pick her up!"

There was no time to argue, so Safety struggled to heft the dead weight. He staggered after Saint, who barely had the presence of mind to stoop and collect his cane.

They left the garden.

OUTSIDE THE COURT ANNEX, DUNVIL CUSTOM HOUSE. NORTH PORT 17TH ULSIVET, 850. HOUR OF HONOR, 1ST HOUR PAST DUSK

"Don't wait for me," the Hammer breathed. He closed his eyes, letting the tolling bell's resonance fade away.

"What was that?" Red Silver said, turning to him.

The Hammer lowered his head, and said nothing. Red Silver looked to Sereen, who returned her look with the guileless and unhelpful gaze of a cat. Flaring her nostrils, Red Silver turned back to Mesech, who led the way along the flank of the new custom house.

When Mesech opened the door to the lean-to equipment shed built against the wall, the adrenaline flowing through the scoundrels intensified. They crowded inside. At last, they stood on the threshold of lethal secrets and irrevocable loss of ignorance.

"Link hands," Mesech said, tugging off his gloves.

Malicoat also removed his gloves, tucking them into his baldric. He wore a long black coat, tailored to accommodate his lean form and also his matching pearl-handled pistols and daggers. Red Silver took his hand, and the Hammer's. Sereen and Inkletta completed the chain.

Mesech nodded to Inkletta, then waved a pebble before the wall. The wall flickered, then shone with a deep red sigil that smoldered in the mind. Mesech stared.

"It—it's never done that before."

"Go," Malicoat said grimly.

Mesech nodded, stepping forward, pulling the others into a doorway that crossed a peculiar distance. They passed through the surface of the Mirror.

Stepping into the yielding sand, they were together in the Echosheath. This time, there was no bonfire. Still, they did not feel like they were alone in the misty forest.

"It's you," Mesech said, turning to the Hammer.

As the Hammer looked into the forest, a tree sifted off ancient ash and dust, a red glyph glowing dully under its bark. The Hammer walked toward the tree, and another began to glow deeper in the glade. The others exchanged a glance, then followed the Hammer.

Inkletta put her hand on Mesech's forearm. "You should turn back," she said quietly.

Mesech looked after the Hammer, and nodded to himself. "Yes, my lady." He bowed to her, then returned through the Mirror, leaving the Echosheath.

"This is your last chance," Inkletta said to Sereen, looking him in the eye.

"I go with the Hammer."

"So be it." Inkletta and Sereen followed the dim red glow through the trees, rejoining the other scoundrels.

"Are we going the right way?" Red Silver muttered to Inkletta.

"Yes."

They weren't sure quite how to feel about that. But they continued through the chilly darkness, dusted with ashes.

"That corner of the Dunvil Custom House," Malicoat said. "That's where one of the engraved plinths once stood. The Elders could use them to step between worlds." He looked at Red Silver. "Did your betters choose to burden you with their secrets, fill you in on what we are attempting?"

"They did not," Red Silver said, not looking at Inkletta.

"Yet you risk death to join us."

"Yeah."

"We are going to enter a space that is neither before nor behind the Mirror," Malicoat said as he followed the Hammer's deliberate pace. "We are sure to encounter ancient defenses, because we seek the heart chamber. A prison. For a piece of a Leviathan's heart."

"The Reliquary of the Fallen Star," Inkletta said.

Malicoat paused, looking back at her. He nodded. "Indeed." He resumed. "Once we reach it, I will conduct... a ritual. And then we can return to the world of the living." His teeth reflected the ruddy red glow of the tree sigils as he smiled.

"No wonder the Spirit Wardens keep an eye on you," Red Silver said reflectively.

"Any objections to this plan?" Lord Malicoat pressed.

"It's your funeral," she said, mild. "I guess this guy isn't enough of a cautionary tale." She gestured towards the Hammer. "Do what you gotta do." She glanced at Inkletta. "Limmer stuff *always* ends well."

Cinders crunched underfoot, and the temperature was dropping. Their breath plumed out in the cold. The Hammer stopped walking, facing a tunnel. A ragged emptied abscess. A wound in the flesh of this place. Two massive trees flanking the entry hissed, then flared with the red glyph, burning deep within. Elaborations on the sigil became visible as the design filled out, deepening and expanding, becoming more specific. The bark of the trees crisped and blackened with the force.

"We have arrived at the door," Sereen said.

"Thank you for the update," Red Silver muttered, glancing around uneasily.

Malicoat considered the tunnel. "Well, we should test for defenses."

"We are welcome," the Hammer said abruptly. He looked at the others. "I am welcome, anyway. And you're with me." He looked Red Silver in the eye.

She knew it was almost over.

Malicoat frowned at Inkletta. "Are you alright?" he said, concerned.

Her jaw shivered, her teeth jittering together as she trembled. A pale and sickly light glowed through her eyepatch, and the edges of her tattoos glittered, constellations on her flesh. She sniffed at the back of her hand, rubbing away blood, and she swallowed hard.

"I'm—here at the edge of things. I'm not alone," she said. "I can handle it."

"We haven't been alone for a while," the Hammer agreed, oddly gentle.

"I've about had it with gods interfering with my people," Red Silver muttered through her clenched teeth. She swallowed hard, and tugged her gunbelt.

"You are an unexpected treasure," Malicoat said, eyeing the Hammer.

"All my life," the Hammer agreed, almost smiling. He turned, and led the way down the ash-coated scar tissue of the tunnel.

Perhaps other travellers would experience a maze, entering that filthy abyss. The scoundrels followed Hammer along a clear path, glyphs glowing in the traumatized fleshy passage ahead of them as they walked, and fading behind them. The symbols seemed to be passing thoughts, surfacing and sinking in a drowsing mind, roused by the shifting of a nearby loved one.

Inkletta felt her gums begin to bleed as she recognized this as the internal shape of the architecture connecting the ghost door between the Echosheath and the Reliquary of the Fallen Star. Its appearance was so different, inside, than it was from the outside.

"Red," the Hammer said, his voice more normal than it had been in months. "I, uh... You know what, just go easy on Safety. Yeah?" he said with a distracted smile.

"Sorry, can't do it. I mean I literally cannot do it," she said apologetically as her heart sank. "No last words, man."

"Do your best," the Hammer said. He sniffed. "I can almost feel myself again," he mused. "After the war... See, during the war, I did things," he said, squinting at her. "Personally. And I commanded people... made decisions." He flexed his jaw. "They haunted me, Red. I don't know if guilt is the right word. Maybe regret. I had to carry the consequences of hurting a lot of people. A *lot* of people." He gathered his thoughts, his pace steady. "Then I came Beneath the Gaze of the Fallen Star," he said. "It was all... wiped away." He looked sideways at her. "I didn't feel it anymore. I didn't feel my dad's pride, or shame. I didn't feel my past... relationships. Any of them. You know how things *matter*?" he said, gesturing towards his chest. "They didn't. That was the first thing to go. Before the dreams, before the... all of it. It was the mattering that went first."

"But they do now?" Red Silver prompted. "They matter again?"

He aimed a look at her; she knew better. "This next heartbeat," he said. "It will be my last, I think." He swallowed hard, as it was already building through him.

"Why are you telling me this?" Red Silver asked, steady.

"Don't give up," the Hammer said. "I felt myself slipping away. I thought about ending it. You know? Death isn't too hard to find. But I didn't. I didn't even try. Partly because the Fallen Star wouldn't allow it," he said.

A new alertness settled in Red Silver.

"What was the other part?" she asked in a low voice.

"This... all this? I'm not sure... it's forever." He sniffed again. "I have always... felt. There might be a way out." His bristled features took on a reflective cast. "Outside of time."

"We'll find it," Red Silver said, something demanding in her tone.

Malicoat lagged to draw level with Inkletta. "We never did have our evening of discussing metaphysics," he said pleasantly.

"Yet here we are," she gritted out.

"I don't think Sysavath could follow our path," Malicoat said, looking back over his shoulder at the darkness, the glyphs faded out. He returned his attention to her. "If she did, I am confident she would be *intrigued* by your manifestations," he said with a gesture. "This doesn't seem to be demonic energy."

"Seem." Inkletta scoffed. "They have a deeper tool chest than our poor senses can imagine." She looked Lord Malicoat in the eye. "I don't know what the Forgotten Gods are. I never will. Neither will you."

"I suppose time will tell," he replied with a secret smile.

Eventually, they reached the gate.

"That's not okay," Red Silver breathed.

The surface pulsed and squirmed. Shiny and black, it printed with echoes of pain and starvation. It coated the wall like a ragged swatch of tar.

"This is going to be tricky," Lord Malicoat frowned. "Inkletta, your thoughts?"

She said nothing, but she watched the Hammer.

He stepped forward, and the Leviathan blood flinched, quivering.

"This, uh. This isn't blocking the way," the Hammer said.

"It *is* the way," Lord Malicoat said, eyes alight with realization. "Can you get us through it?" he asked.

"Yes," he said slowly. "But... it's a dark baptism. You'll touch the Leviathan blood," he said. He looked at Inkletta and Red Silver. "You two... haven't done that before. Maybe go back."

"Wait, *they* have?" Red Silver said, gesturing at Sereen and Lord Malicoat.

"Yes," the Hammer nodded.

Red Silver rolled her eyes. "I don't know why that surprised me," she muttered.

"I will need your help," Lord Malicoat said, intense as he looked into Inkletta's eye. "You came here to support my ritual."

"That's not the reason I'm going through," Inkletta said coolly. "But I *am* going through." Another shiver rippled through her.

Red Silver looked the Hammer in the eye. "Niece told me a story," she said quietly. "She was on the run, an assassin marked her with a tracer so she couldn't escape. She ran to the limmers, and you were with her. The only way she could clear that mark was one of these dark baptisms. But she was... she was terrified," Red Silver said. "And she didn't have to do it alone. Because you were there. You went into that water too. For her. To give her courage. So she wasn't alone."

"It was a mistake that destroyed my life," the Hammer observed.

"Yeah, but... it was a hell of a move," Red Silver said. She looked to Inkletta as a secret smile grew on her face. "We all go out. But that's what makes us who we are." She looked back at the Hammer. "We *strut* first." Flicking her wrist, she opened the frames of her round mirrored glasses. She ducked into them, and set her jaw.

He nodded. Stepping away, he turned to the writhing slick, and offered his hand back to the other scoundrels. Red Silver took his hand, then Inkletta took hers, then Lord Malicoat, then Sereen. Together, they leaned forward, touching the undying gore from the Leviathan's heart.

Inkletta felt the core of light within her flare outward, swelling past her skin as she touched on the membrane of the blood.

SHE IS MINE

Inkletta gasped, suspended in a strange glow.

YOU ARE CLAIMED

What felt like a rough shake followed, and she was tossed out to slap down on a smooth stone floor. She passed through the blood slick, but it did not coat her.

Lord Malicoat dragged himself free behind her, stumbling, then standing straight and dusting off his sleeves.

"I belong to the Crown of Night," he said through his teeth, "and you cannot have me." He snarled a grin, and turned to see the Hammer emerge, dragging Sereen.

The boy collapsed, sobbing, convulsing. The Hammer turned away and left him on the floor.

"Red?" Inkletta breathed.

The Hammer frowned, then thrust his arm back into the blood, up to the shoulder. A moment later, he leaned back, hauling at a weight. The surface breached to disgorge Red Silver. She slid out, dazed and limp.

Malicoat stepped forward, marveling. "At last," he breathed. "I wondered how it would appear. Whether it would fill the room, or fit in my palm. Yet still, I am amazed."

Beyond the chamber, tributaries of vents fed into four conduits that breached the walls. They were long since calcified, and buried in strange worls of dried-out alien meat. At their center, dominating the room, a twisted and spiny shape like a stem stripped of a dozen grapes arced across the space.

"You have been so deprived," Lord Malicoat said. "I will see to it you are fed."

"Will you?" said a sardonic voice.

Startled, Lord Malicoat focused on the dimness beyond the arch. He saw a seat of rulership worked into the wall, and upon it, a black-clad figure with a helm. His gauntleted hands rested on the arms of the throne.

"The Tower," Lord Malicoat said. "I—you—"

"You think you can go around me," the Tower said. "Just like that." He snapped his fingers, the metal clacking. "How very bold."

"What did you expect?" Lord Malicoat demanded. "How many years would you want me to run errands for you, sit at your knee awaiting crumbs of wisdom? I suspect you engineered this series of events to bring me here. This is not a failure, it is a graduation," he said, jutting his chin out defiantly. "Since you are here, you can conduct the final ritual. To bind the Leviathan essence within me." His eyes burned. "Make me immortal. Fit to ascend."

"Fit to ascend," the Tower echoed with a trace of mockery. "Indeed, I think you may well be." He looked past Lord Malicoat at the other scoundrels, in various states of recovery. "Don't you lot worry. I'll get to you." He returned his attention to Lord Malicoat. "Where were we. Ah yes. Petulant demands." He leaned back. "And it surprises you that I could sense your approach to this place, and reach it before you did. As though I am not bound to this place, and aware of all that happens here. You are still so very, very easy to surprise. Yet you may have a use. The Crown of Isles, after all."

"I would shatter your curse," Lord Malicoat swore. "I pay my debts."

The Tower rose to his feet, and Lord Malicoat took an involuntary step back. He firmed up, bracing himself as the Tower approached, passing under the withered twist of vital Leviathan flesh. The Tower ignored Lord Malicoat. He considered the Hammer.

"Ah, my boy," he said in breathtakingly expressive and precise Hadrathi. "The Hunger entered you. My adventuresome pet still swims, after all. Still shares with the limmers."

"I have reached the final beat," the Hammer heard himself say, speaking words he did not know.

"Perhaps some part of you will live here," the Tower mused in Hadrathi. "This flesh that carries you could be connected to the conduits. You could remain useful in this place, even though it is not vital flesh. You'd last maybe a year, while this place slid towards the back of the Mirror."

"No," the Hammer shuddered, brows clenching.

Woozy, Inkletta felt the Shrouded Queen withdraw, racing out away from her consciousness. For a disorienting moment, she wondered if the inky blood had exhausted the essence of the Forgotten God, driven her away. Then she blinked as she realized what was happening.

A smile tugged at her face, and blood spilled out one corner of her mouth.

The Tower looked her over. "A Whisper. Of the Old Forms. I like it," he said. "Train many apprentices!" He turned away from her, glancing at Red Silver. "Hm." Stepping past her where she curled up on the floor, he stood over Sereen.

"Little one," he said in Hadrathi. "You stared into the sun." He let out a barely audible sigh. "So, Lord Cydney Malicoat, you once wondered what I used for a needle. Since I am the Stitcher, welding together what is and what is not, what has been and what could be."

"Yes, sire," Lord Malicoat said, trying to sound reverent.

The Tower's hand flexed, then twitched upward. Sereen abruptly silenced, his blood flicking up in a razored thread, animated by his repurposed life force. The Tower stepped around Lord Malicoat, the gorethread trailing through the air after him, weightless and bright.

"Cultists," the Tower said knowingly, as though sharing an inside joke. "Now. Let's stitch up your *ascension*," he said, enjoying the flavor of what might be sarcasm. "This might sting a little." A subtle gesture, and the gorethread swirled up and settled into a many-dimensional glyph, then another, and its color shifted to white as it began to glow.

The Hammer swayed, and widened his stance. He felt it rising; the pressure, the beat. The last one. He felt his teeth loosen, his joints flex.

Inkletta stepped in front of him. She saw a faint puzzlement in his eyes.

"You are one with the R—Riven Heart—t," she said. "Your Hunger. You are connect—ted. It is y—yours," she insisted. Her eyepatch hissed, and sizzled off her face, the weird shine in her eye socket intensifying. Her teeth chattered uncontrollably.

Behind her, the white-hot gorethread darted forward and punched through Lord Malicoat's neck. Writhing up, it hissed towards the rind of the heart, skimming the iron-hard surface and closing the loop to zip through Lord Malicoat's chest. Around again, it tightened as the Stitcher gestured, pulling them together. Lord Malicoat was in agony, unable to scream as he was tugged through the intervening space and impaled on one of the withered stubs of the heart.

Inkletta smiled at the Hammer, then the light within her roiled out as she became an avatar of the Shrouded Queen.

The Hammer understood.

"What? No!" shouted the Tower, pivoting as his shadow lengthened—

"Take it," the Hammer breathed, opening the heartbeat, attuning his consent to the cosmic welter of the Shrouded Queen.

The last beat landed.

YOU HAVE FOUND RIVEN FLESH

ALL IS FORGIVEN

The Shrouded Queen swept up her arms, accepting the Riven Heart as the Hammer gave it up. She tore it from him. The freed connection pivoted her to face the rind between conduits, and the gurgling figure struggling on one of its spines.

The Tower cried out in Hadrathi, and a dozen more gorethreads dart-ed out of his robes and aimed at the Shrouded Queen—

Red Silver snapped off a pair of shots, plowing into the Tower, knocking him back. She fired a couple more, battering the startled Stitcher and fracturing his concentration.

The Shrouded Queen swelled over the Riven Heart, stretching her tether to Inkletta. Closing on the shape like fingers closing around a handle, the Forgotten God twisted the whole world as she wrenched at her sacrifice.

Red Silver ignored the struggle between the gods that played out behind her. She squared off with the Tower, a knife in each hand.

"No you don't," she said through her teeth, her glasses pale with reflected light.

The Tower straightened imperiously, and raised his gauntlet to pluck the life from her. But something was wrong.

The Riven Heart was stitched to him too.

Refocusing as he felt the relentless drag kick in, he fired his gorethreads to the walls, giving him leverage to resist. The walls were also bound to the Riven Heart. An echoing crack reverberated.

Red Silver leaped over to the Hammer and Inkletta. She snatched them, launching towards the curdling and steaming slick of blood on the back wall. Screaming her desperation, she hauled on them, dragging the half-conscious scoundrels along the buckling flagstones.

A horrible swallowing sensation tugged at them as they hit the filmy and undying blood.

Smoke poured off of them as the three tumbled out, sliding into the cinders of the Echosheath. Red Silver awkwardly scrambled, checking Inkletta for a breathless moment. She slid over to the Hammer. Then she collapsed back, staring up at the interlaced rafters of the canopy, her heart pounding.

"Oh," she said. "Thank you."

Inkletta struggled to sit up, her cheek hissing as her empty eye socket leaked hot bile. "Red?' she slurred.

"We made it," Red Silver said. "We made it."

Inkletta rolled over to prop an elbow on the Hammer's chest, peering into him. "He's breathing," she said, hardly daring to hope.

"Off—my chest," the Hammer managed. Inkletta pushed herself up to kneel over him, and he shifted, wincing.

"Are you—you know?" Red Silver asked breathlessly.

The Hammer laughed.

CHAPTER SEVENTEEN

Fabrication teaches us an essential lesson about the nature of materials. Some can be melted together, some can be tied, and others can be such a cunning fit that they mesh naturally. Still, most objects must be pierced that they might be bound. Knock a nail to connect two pieces of wood, thrust a needle through cloth to stitch it tight, bang a rivet through sheets of metal.

People are the same. While the rare exceptions may bond through commitment, or compatibility, most relations that hold us together are strongest where our wounds connect. I sense how your pain shaped you, and you sense how my pain shaped me. Sharing that moment, that understanding, brings us together. You will find that war creates bonds that cannot be rivaled by study, politics, and romance together.

We want to seal our wounds. I challenge you instead to use them as windows, to see outside yourself. If you want to learn empathy, suffering is your finest instructor.

—From "Within and Without: The Search for Truth"
by Carter Uribes

Rain breathed against the window, tapping like a gentle inquiry. Saint stood with his hands clasped behind his back, staring out into the night. All he could see was the darkness between the lights.

The tower room was half full of crates, bales, and furniture, not yet unpacked or organized. The scent of canal water and fried food permeated, soaked into the piles of material the gondoliers put in the space.

Safety sat on the floor, his back to the wall, leaning over his arm. He rubbed a scrap of sandpaper over the hole where the crossbow bolt punched into his prosthetic. Over and over, he smoothed the metal so the puncture wouldn't have a metal burr.

Neither one could bear to look at the body tied into a sheet, silent and motionless.

The door opened, and both of them turned to see who came in. Trajan stood framed in the doorway, somber.

"We just got word from the Circulatory," Trajan said. "They found Gapjaw. Someone murdered him, and poisoned his girlfriend."

"Murdered?" Saint said, raising his eyebrows. "Like, completely dead?"

"I'm afraid so," Trajan said. "I've got my people checking into it, see if we can find out more."

"Any news from North Port?" Safety asked.

"None yet." Trajan paused, then closed the door. His steps receded down the stairs.

"Kind of him to let us stay here," Safety said.

"I'm so glad you made it," Saint murmured as though he had not heard. "We might be the only survivors." He swallowed hard.

"The Hammer didn't expect to make it much further," Safety said. "Even if he makes it through this. And we've been worried about Inkletta for a while." He paused. "If Red tries to pull some stunt to save them..."

"Yeah," Saint said, bitter. "There isn't much hope. And if Malicoat doesn't make it," he added, "our position in North Port becomes a question."

Safety looked back down at his arm, sanding the hole.

"I—I feel like I can't breathe," Saint said. He tried for a deep breath, around the lump in his throat, his mind racing.

"I had a boss once," Safety said reflectively, "told me we had to watch the gauges on the steam engines. You know, on the rails. Said that we needed water and air to live." He smiled faintly. "But the heat is the thing. Cool water and air give you breath. Heat them up enough, and you get burns." He paused. "Maybe we did overreach."

Saint realized it was possible that neither Gapjaw nor Red Silver would ever say something insulting to Safety again. Grief sat in his chest like a stone.

Time passed.

A commotion in the stairwell got their attention. Safety climbed to his feet, pistol out, and Saint gripped his cane and waited.

The door banged open, and Red Silver strode in with the Hammer and Inkletta right behind, gondoliers following in the stairwell.

"You made it!" Saint said, and Red Silver pulled him into a tight hug. She pushed him away, and nodded to Safety, looking around for more of the crew. Her eyes stopped on the still form in the sheet.

"Dammit," she hissed.

"Gapjaw's dead too," Saint said, and he frowned as he peered at Inkletta. "Your cheek." The burns from her melted eye ruined the edges of a section of her face tattoo.

"A small price to pay," Inkletta said. "We got out. Malicoat didn't."

"But I did," the Hammer said. "Left the Hunger behind."

"What?" Safety exclaimed. "That's awesome!"

"*That's* your takeaway from all the news?" Red Silver snapped at him.

Saint's smile was bittersweet.

"Feel the feelings you have to deal with in this moment," Saint said. The scoundrels turned to him, and he set his jaw. "Then we have a lot to do."

EMBANKMENT, SOUTH STAINS. SILKSHORE
18TH ULSIVET, 850. SIXTH HOUR PAST DAWN

"Pretty good turnout," Red Silver observed, standing at Inkletta's elbow.

Inkletta surveyed the embankment. Over three hundred Skovs came out, even on short notice. She returned her attention to the priest as he finished the Skovic funeary poem, and nodded to the Hammer.

The Hammer stepped forward, and lowered his smoking torch. The fuel on the longboat caught, racing over the pyre neatly stacked in the middle. Flickering across the winding sheet.

Niece drifted out on the Dusk River, a brighter star than the obscured glow of the sun overhead. A hymn rose from the assembly, twining with the rising smoke.

"The Hammer was like a big brother to Niece," Inkletta murmured. The two women stood on a balcony, several storeys above the throng. "He went into that dark baptism with her, and ever after, I think they... understood each other. Better than most." She turned to Red Silver. "I won't forget that you went into that dark baptism yesterday, for me. For the Hammer. I don't think we would have escaped were it not for you. Do you want to talk about it? What you experienced in there?"

"I can't," Red Silver said, still watching the flaming longboat. "Not yet." She turned to Inkletta. "But I haven't forgotten that the only reason you carried the Shrouded Queen was because you were all in. You said you'd help me break that curse. And you did. We broke it. Still. It cost you." She returned her attention to the river. "You never brought it up again. What I owe you."

"You don't owe me anything," Inkletta said softly.

"And you don't owe me anything either," Red Silver replied, an arch smile nudging her features.

"You are impossible," Inkletta said, rolling her eyes.

"Until the day I die," Red Silver agreed. She snapped her glasses open, and slipped them on.

Overhead, Nails tilted his wings, angling around the column of smoke from the burning boat. Together, they let Niece go.

THE OLD CUSTOM HOUSE, FOUNDER'S SQUARE. NORTH PORT
19TH ULSIVET, 850. THIRD HOUR PAST DAWN

"I'm in pain, and Gapjaw would like that," Safety said in a muffled voice, his head down on the table.

"That was a hell of a party last night," Saint agreed. He looked down at his hands.

"You okay?" Safety asked, squinting at him through his hung-over haze.

"I will be," Saint sighed.

Red Silver approached the table, crisply dressed. "Shoo," she said to Safety. He only thought about it for a moment. Then he rose, and stumbled away to another table. Red Silver sat opposite Saint, studying him.

"What," Saint said, wary.

"You talked to the gondoliers. Found out more about how Gapjaw died."

Saint grimaced. "You don't want to know."

"Right," she agreed, "but you have to tell someone. So tell me."

"Sysavath. I think she tracked him down. Killed him. Signs of... a struggle. His woman was poisoned. He died with his head in her lap." Saint swallowed at the lump in his throat. "He died alone. Then they fed him straight into Bellweather's fires." Saint covered his eyes with his hand.

"Well Sysavath is gone," Red Silver said, cool. "And as for the fires." She managed a crooked grin. "You know Gapjaw. He said he didn't care what happened to his meat when he was done with it."

"We all say things," Saint agreed, hedging the bitterness out of his voice. He took a deep breath, looking around the room. "What's done is done. Have you seen Inkletta this morning?"

"She's supposed to check in before she goes to take possession of the Nineways Greenkey Estate," Red Silver replied. "It's a damn good thing we got those deeds worked out through Ryland before Malicoat failed to return."

"Yeah," Saint agreed.

"What are you two talking about?" Inkletta asked, startling them. They turned to see her standing in a partial shadow, arms crossed, smiling.

"I'm so glad you're feeling better," Saint said, wry. "We were just discussing Malicoat."

"Malicoat," Inkletta echoed. "That first night. He was determined to find out what the Shrouded Queen did with the sacrificed flesh." Her smile widened. "Now he knows."

"Speaking of the Shrouded Queen," Red Silver prompted. "Is she still, you know?" She gestured.

"We needed different things," Inkletta said, once again serious. "But we were never... enemies. We were familiar to each other." She thought for a moment. "I'm not her avatar anymore, not really. She got more than she could easily manage, taking on the Leviathan's Riven Heart. If I wanted her back, I think... I *think* I could restore our connection." Inkletta tossed her wild mane, and sniffed. "But I've got a life to live. And I think now she'll let me live it."

"Ooh, that's a good line, I'll have to remember it," Red Silver said. She turned back to Saint. "I need a vacation."

"No more vacations!" Saint protested, surprised by a smile. "Besides, m'*lady*, you have to run this place."

"It's in good hands," she said. "The Hammer is in charge of the bar and managing the staff, as well as the gang. What do you think of the 'Customers' as a name? Like 'Old Custom House,' I guess?"

"Ugh," Saint said, and Inkletta wrinkled her nose.

"We can do better," Red Silver agreed. "So how is it going with the Bluecoats and the Spirit Wardens?" she asked Saint. "You get all that cleaned up?"

"It was expensive," Saint admitted. "Sillman knew there would be some growing pains, and I think we have our misunderstandings ironed out. As for the Spirit Wardens, I asked Mesech to point out to his contacts that the Reliquary of the Fallen Star is *destroyed*. So the vents aren't a problem anymore, and nobody else will go for that prize. Asked if we could maybe call it a draw. I didn't hear back, and I think that's the best we can hope for."

"Did he carry that pitch to the Circle of Flame as well?" Inkletta asked, cool.

"Maybe," Saint said. "Whether he did or not, I'm not going to put much effort into placating Drake. She may not like you, she may not like what we did with rituals in North Port, but if she wants to do something about it we'll sort her out. Right?"

"Hell yeah," Red Silver said, putting on her mirrored glasses.

"Sounds good," Inkletta smiled. "I'm meeting with Mesech this afternoon at my tower. I think we may yet sway the scavengers away from the Wardens and the Circle of Flame. They don't like being sneered at any more than I do. Anyway. I'm off."

"Wearing that?" Red Silver said, looking over the long wrap that provided basic modesty and some shelter, but revealed plenty of tattoos.

"They'll just have to get used to it," Inkletta replied, regal.

"Swift blood," Saint teased.

Inkletta rolled her eyes, and headed for the exit.

"On that note," Red Silver said, "I have work to do."

"Don't forget Ousley's funeral tomorrow, I want you there," Saint said. "You're respectable. Gotta show solidarity for a fellow noble."

"You wouldn't care if I went to these things or not, if you had a date on your arm," Red Silver groused.

"You think I'd willingly surrender all your charm? Your wit? Our sparkling conversation?"

"*Just* the thing for a *funeral*," Red Silver grinned. "Swift blood to you!" she called back over her shoulder as she headed into the back hallway.

"No, swift blood to *you!*" Saint yelled after her. Smiling, he pulled himself to his feet, hefted his cane, and limped to the bar, leaning against it.

"Trouble with Red?" the Hammer asked conspiratorially, polishing a mug.

"Not really," Saint said. "Just games." He looked the Hammer in the eye. "So you're back."

"I'm not better," the Hammer said. "But I guess the Hunger is gone. I left it in the Reliquary." The moment settled between them, unsatisfactory. "It's not killing me anymore," the Hammer clarified. "So I will be... okay."

"That's all I really want from you lot," Saint said. "I don't want you too happy, or you'll retire or something. I don't like it when you're miserable, makes you unreliable. I just want you to be, you know, functional. Pliable. So it's a great outcome," he said brightly. "I also invite you to see me as a patriarch figure whose approval you require, so I can withhold it to manipulate you."

"Oh, all of us do that," the Hammer agreed. "Please love us."

"I'll think about it," Saint said loftily. He paused. "Good to have you back."

A smile took years off the Hammer's face.

NINEWAYS GREENKEY ESTATE, SOUTH SKIRT. NORTH PORT
19TH ULSIVET, 850. NINTH HOUR PAST DAWN

"Hello?" echoed the call from the open doorway. Mesech leaned in, and banged on the open door a couple times.

"Come in," Inkletta called from the central chamber, her voice echoing.

Mesech cautiously stepped into the entry corridor, passing into the central chamber. Smoke hung in the air, and a small fire burned in the center of the pit. The space between the flame and the rim of the pit was just right for squatting or sitting in a circle. Inkletta hunched opposite the doorway, rippling in the heat distortion from the crackling fire, comfortably settled with her feet flat and her shoulders almost touching her knees. She held a poker with a curl of meat impaled on it, cooking it over the flame.

"Smells good," Mesech said. He switched to Hadrathi. "Looking within and without, we shall see."

"See and be seen," she replied. She continued in Hadrathi. "You brought a friend."

The Deathlands scavengers exchanged a glance, then pulled off their protective face masks.

"This is Richter," said Mesech. "He's our leader, around North Port. I wanted you to meet him."

"I brought you a gift," Richter said. Inkletta beckoned to him, and he circled the firepit as she rose. He offered her a leather wrap, inset with beads in peculiar patterns. She took the wrap and opened it, admiring the chipped obsidian knife within.

"This is old," she said quietly. "Simple. And it has drunk so deep." Her finger traced it, and she twitched. "So many deaths." Her eyes drifted closed. "Several summonings." She felt the reverberation of more than one Leviathan, drawn to the ritual sacrifices of hundreds of humans, their blood staining the beaches over centuries. She opened her eyes. "A worthy gift," she said.

"You are a Whisper. Of the Old Forms," Richter said. "You know the rituals we once used out here. You know how we survive," he said with a gesture to Mesech. "I wanted to see if you had the Sinking Sun."

Inkletta shrugged, and her drape slipped down to reveal her upper arm and the stylized pattern on her skin.

"You know secrets that we have forgotten," Richter said, serious.

"I do," Inkletta said. "I studied at the feet of Granny Threadknife and the Hog of Trostle. I learned the needle brush of the desert forts, and I practiced the Six Deep of the Six Codes. Four years ago I became a Confessor."

Richter's eyes were wide, his posture reverent. "We would be honored to have you as our ally," he said.

She regarded the lean warrior. "I owe Mesech ink," she said. "You would like ink as well."

"Yes," Richter replied. "Would you consider me? As a canvas?"

"Do you want to take that ink into the city?" Inkletta asked coolly. "Serve the Spirit Wardens and the Circle of Flame, get your pardon, retreat from the Deathlands?"

"Maybe not," Richter said.

Inkletta smiled.

Red Silver whacked the peg with her mallet one last time, gripping it and testing its firmness. Stepping back, she looked around the narrow tower room, ignoring the soreness in her bandaged hands.

"You like it, boy?" she asked Nails.

The perch was braced, pegs jutting from the wall here and there around the room. Her massive bat swung towards her, nuzzling into her coat.

"Greedyguts," she teased, and she pulled a fish from a paper sleeve in her pocket. "No crickets out here, not yet."

Nails sniffed the fish, then snipped at it, sucking it down in a single slither.

"Good work," Red Silver said, ruffling his fur.

The Blind Hour was upon the settlement, the sun's afterglow staining the sky as fog rolled in off the sea. Red Silver looked out over the view. Scaffolding was scattered around the upper levels of ruins and buildings. The Dunvil Custom House was the only new building visible as the fog filled the streets. The fog's fabric was stained by lights now, where two years ago all would have been dark.

"This is my house," Red Silver said as she absently scratched her bat's head. "So it's our home. Keep watch." She felt the wiry alertness rousing in him as the sun sank, and she stepped to the side of the tower's view port. "Do your thing."

Nails gripped a peg with his wing claw, swinging around and over, slipping through the narrow port. His wings snapped out, and he hopped, gliding down to coast through the air as it belled his membranes up. He wheeled across the darkening sky.

"We're going to be okay," Red Silver said quietly. Then she turned back to the stairs, descending towards the light.

"A man of faith," the preacher said, "and of convictions. He celebrated this temple of flesh we pilot, using it as a conduit to add discipline to the world, and bolster the work that undergirds our blessed order."

The generic eulogy droned on, but the preacher's grieved expression was clearly more inspired by lying about the dead man than it was by grief at his loss.

"This does end at some point, right?" Red Silver murmured, leaning slightly towards Saint.

"One way or another," he whispered back. "I brought a gun. And the place is already decorated for a memorial."

The Workshop's main tool shop was draped in a wild excess of cloth and silk flowers, purple and red and white. Almost a hundred congregants were stuffed into the space, most of them lured with an offer of lunch to follow. A magnificent larger-than-life painting of Ousely was hardly recognizable, as the features were smoothed and dignified and his pet spider was almost cute. The body had vanished into the city days ago, presumably headed for disintegrating flame.

There was music, from a cello and understated throaty vocalists. A fire eater calmly doused symbolic life in his mouth. Nothing unusual. The scoundrels did rouse to attention as Ousley's uncle rose to say a few words.

"North Port is a triumph of the human intellect," growled the industrialist. "The old limmer foundation of this settlement has been expunged, its traces fading day to day. Replacing that superstition and fearful sacrifice to the darkness, we bring Rowan's ambient suppression defense system. We bring the steel hulls of our Leviathan hunters. We bring the lighting walls that fence off our valuables and assure our safety. The time for cults is past! Now is the time to replace rituals with procedure. Now is the time to replace alchemy with chemistry. Now is the time to bring the masses meaning through sweat and productivity, not slavish worship. We have replaced prophecy with strategy. We sacrifice for our future, yes—but not with stone knives and alien words filling our mouths. Now we sacrifice our comforts and pleasures to secure a strong foundation for a future with untold promise."

The forcefulness of his presentation was purpling his face, and his wild gestures added rhetorical flourish. The crowd enjoyed his continuing speechifying, but Saint shifted uneasily.

Best not to think of the uncanny insight that shaped the conclusion of this clash over the Reliquary. Gods and demons, still directing action through their corrupted agents. Vital tides of undying blood, driving the city in unpredictable directions as the constellations wheeled beneath the Void Sea.

"What a relief," whispered Red Silver, rousing Saint from his reflections. "I thought maybe there *were* such things as monsters."

"Not in this enlightened age," Saint replied under his breath, suppressing a smile. "Not anymore. Obviously."

"Obviously."

The memorial was running long, and the delicious scent of lunch was filtering into the hall.

MOWBRAY HOUSE, SOUTH SKIRT. NORTH PORT
21ST ULSIVET, 850. FOURTH HOUR PAST DAWN

Safety heaved the box up onto the table, then brushed the dust off his coat. "There. I think that's the whole cart," he said. "Tiana?"

"Yes, Tykia," she called out, and she bustled into the house. "Thank you, dear brother," she said, kissing him on the cheek. "I can't believe you got me a house in North Port!"

"Way better than that little apartment in the Ease, right?" Safety said. "I think getting out of all that smoke will do your cough good." He smiled fondly at his sister.

"Maybe we can start a family," Tykia sighed. She stepped over to the window. "Oh, an ocean view. I always dreamed of an ocean view."

Varela grunted as he squeezed through the door, carrying cases in both hands. "Remember that," he called out. "When the storms blow off the water and freeze us where we sit, remember how you like seeing the ocean." He offered Tykia a wolfish grin, and put the cases down. "Now we get to start the *unpacking*."

"Right, you all figure that out," Safety said. "My work here is done."

"As soon as we have the kitchen set up we'll have you over for dinner," Tiana said. "Vee Vee and I can take it from here."

"That's right," Varela agreed. "Bring it in here." He opened his arms, and she hugged him tight.

"You take such good care of me," Tiana said into Varela's chest.

"And I always will," Varela said, his chin on Tiana's head as he looked Safety in the eye.

"Be good," Safety said. Stepping out into the mid-day chill, he closed the door behind himself and took a deep breath. Then he vaulted up on the empty wagon's buckboard, flicked the reins, and rolled away.

THE PEACH BUCKET PUBLIC HOUSE, COASTAL VIEW. NORTH PORT 22ND ULSIVET, 850. FIFTH HOUR PAST DAWN

Saint held the door for Wringleton. Her eyes were almost comically large in her waifish face as she looked around the grand yet cozy public house common.

"This is way fancier than the Old Custom House," Wringleton observed.

"True," Saint agreed, "but we have *heritage*."

They perched on stools at the leather-topped bar, and Saint hooked his cane on the rail. "Two leatherjacks, my good man," he called to the barkeep, who nodded.

"So what's the occasion, boss?" Wringleton asked, trying to play it cool.

"It's time you and I had a talk about your performance," Saint said quietly. "I thought it best we meet offsite."

Wringleton swallowed hard, and waited.

"Well well well," said the man strolling up from the side. "They'll let *anyone* in here." He grinned. He was tall, slender, and pale, a certain grace marking every movement. He wore a tailored suit deliberately rendered casual, the tie missing and the collar unbuttoned.

"Wringleton, let me introduce you to Styles. He's the owner and operator of this fine establishment. A visionary! We are within the walls of his dream, built to serve the workers returning to reclaim North Port," Saint said effusively.

"Pleased to meet you, sir," Wringleton said in a small voice, offering Styles her hand.

"Charmed," Styles said. "So this is the one."

"Indeed. Brought her here to explain the situation," Saint said conspiratorially.

Wringleton still didn't rise to the bait, patient in her discomfort.

"I already like her," Styles admitted. "She's got the skills?"

"And my complete confidence," Saint said. "Wringleton, this is also Piccolo. He was the River Stallions' lurk, a few years back. Got into and out of a really impossible number of scrapes."

"You're Piccolo?" Wringleton said, eyes wide.

"Man, the new ones get younger every year," Piccolo said, imitating the bluster of the previous generation. "Yeah, I'm also not retired yet. It can be surprisingly involved running this branch of the Silkworms; North Port has some complicated little wrinkles," he said. "I guess you all figured that out already. Congratulations on making your move, it's great to have you all as neighbors." He paused. "Sorry to hear about Niece and Gapjaw."

"Thank you," Saint nodded, and they moved on. "So I was thinking maybe she could get a few pointers from you, now and then. If she needs them."

"Sure," Piccolo agreed. "The River Stallions gotta have top notch talent."

"What are you saying?" Wringleton asked, breathless.

"Put simply," Saint replied, "I'm offering you a share. River Stallion ink," he said, patting his arm where the crew tattoo marked his skin under the cloth. "Join our crew. We could use a lurk."

"Okay, wow," Wringleton said. "Varela, though; he won't be happy about this."

"That's the thing," Saint said with a crooked grin. "You get to be one of us by doing things other people won't like. From time to time."

"I get that," Wringleton said. "I'm in."

Saint and Piccolo exchanged a look, and Saint nodded to himself.

"You're gonna need a shadow cloak," Piccolo said.

"Got it," Wringleton retorted. "I could use some dark-sight goggles."

"Get two pair," Piccolo said. "Accidents happen."

Their drinks arrived, along with one for Piccolo. He raised his glass. "A toast!" he said. "To what we see coming."

"And to what they don't!" Saint and Wringleton chorused. Their mugs clacked together, and they drank deeply.

Wringleton's leatherjack lowered first. "I hear you all run a hagfish fighting ring downstairs," she said. "How much setup does it take to get in on that action?"

"She'll do fine," Piccolo grinned.

DOSKVOL

ALSO KNOWN AS DUSKWALL, NORTH HOOK
Imperial Province Of Akoros
Circa 847 AC

THE LOST
DISTRICT

WHITECROWN

Governor's
Stronghold

NORTH HOOK CHANNEL

THE DOCKS

BRIGHTSTONE

SIX TOWERS

CHARTERHALL

CROW'S
FOOT

SILKSHORE

CHARHOLLOW

NIGHTMARKET

COALRIDGE

BARROWCLEFT

Ironhook
Prison

Gaddoc Rail
Station

DEATH LANDS

RADIANT
ENERGY FARMS
& EELERIES

DUNSLOUGH

DUSK RIVER

OLD
NORTH
PORT

TIME	HOUR	
1 AM	SILK	
2	WINE	
3	ASH	
4	COAL	
5	CHAINS	
6	SMOKE	
7	1	DAWN
8	2	
9	3	
10	4	
11	5	
12	6	NOON
1 PM	7	
2	8	
3	9	
4	10	
5	11	
6	12	
7	HONOR	DUSK
8	SONG	
9	SILVER	
10	THREAD	
11	FLAME	
12	PEARLS	MIDNIGHT

THE IMPERIAL CALENDAR HAS SIX MONTHS, SIXTY DAYS EACH.

A MONTH IS TEN WEEKS WITH SIX DAYS EACH.

MENDAR	
KALIVET	WINTER
SURAN	
ULSIVET	SPRING
VOLNIVET	
ELISAR	FALL

PATREON SPONSORS

PATREON

Image courtesy of NaNoWriMo.

www.ingramcontent.com/pod-product-compliance
Lightning Source LLC
Chambersburg PA
CBHW052027020726
47501CB00004B/1283